BY G. GORDON LIDDY

Nonfiction

WILL: THE AUTOBIOGRAPHY OF G. GORDON LIDDY

Fiction

OUT OF CONTROL
THE MONKEY HANDLERS

THE MONKEY HANDLERS

G. GORDON LIDDY

ST. MARTIN'S PAPERBACKS

This is a work of fiction. All of the events, characters, names, and places depicted in this novel are entirely fictitious or are used fictitiously. No representation that any statement made in this novel is true or that any incident depicted in this novel actually occurred is intended or should be inferred by the reader.

THE MONKEY HANDLERS

Copyright © 1990 by G. Gordon Liddy.

Library of Congress Catalog Card Number: 90-37247

ISBN: 0-312-92613-8

Printed in the United States of America

St. Martin's Press hardcover edition/October 1990
St. Martin's Paperbacks edition/September 1991

10 9 8 7 6 5 4 3

To First Lieutenant Raymond J. Liddy, USMCR,
injured severely in the course of explosive
ordnance disposal, Panamanian jungle, 1989,
this book is dedicated by a proud father.

ACKNOWLEDGMENTS

The author wishes to acknowledge with thanks the contributions to this work of the following: Diana Louise Coe, for lending her expertise on the divers factions of the animal welfare movement and their motivations, as well as introducing me to the works of Hans Reuesh, whose research into animal experimentation is acknowledged with appreciation; Captain Larry Bailey, USN, for his information on SEAL training at BUD/S and many courtesies; Commander Scott Lyon, USN (retired), and Command Master Chief Petty Officer Gary Gallagher, USN, for sharing their knowledge of U.S. Naval Special Warfare tactics and lore; Michael Parker, Esquire, foremost American technical expert on small arms, for, among other contributions, demonstrating that one can insert a CHICOM AK-47 through a six-inch hole with one hand; Roger Campbell, Chief Clerk, and Jack Gamby, Rip Track boss, Burlington & Northern Railroad, Tacoma, Washington, for technical information and advice on modern railroading; Kenneth Oliver and Tom Fitzgibbon, Bridge Operations, The Port Authority of New York and New Jersey, for helping me research the structure of the George Washington Bridge and live to write about it; Captain Stephen Davis, NYPD, for helping out a former FBI agent; Robert Dellinger, for his information on the inside workings of the Mossad and for getting me started in creative writing; several former members of Her Majesty's Special Air and Special Boat Services who must remain nameless, for sharing information on antiterrorist techniques and mechanics; Steve Dunleavy, international journalist and friend, for sharing his whiskey and his contacts, both of which he possesses in seemingly inexhaustible supply; and my friend and editor, Michael Denneny, for his unerring instincts and help in bringing three books to publication.

THE MONKEY HANDLERS

1

● THE JARRING RING OF THE TELEPHONE SNAPPED
Michael Stone awake, adrenaline pumping. Before he moved a muscle,
he forced himself to be sure of exactly where he was: at home, in bed,
no apparent danger.

The phone rang again, and he brought it to his ear. Stone moved
no other portion of his body, nor did he switch on the lamp. From
long habit, he sought to preserve his night vision.

"Yes?" he said into the speaker. His voice was low, strong, controlled. There was not a hint that he had been sound asleep a moment
before.

"Michael Stone?" It was a woman's voice—youthful, anxious.

"Speaking."

"The lawyer?"

Stone cocked his left wrist. A black rubberized watertight digital
watch was on it. All Stone could see were the numbers glowing softly
out of the dark: 0423:12.

"Yes. But I don't usually practice at four A.M. The office is open
at eight-thirty. Call then for an appointment. Good night."

"Please! Please don't hang up! I'm sorry to wake you, but I don't know what else to do. I can't come to see you because I'm in *jail*. They've got me charged with *burglary!* I wasn't trying to steal any—"

"Wait," Stone commanded. "Hold it right there. I don't know who gave you my name, but you've got bad information. I don't practice criminal law. I specialize in real estate. If you've been busted for burglary, I'm the last person you want. Get a hold of the public defender. He'll give you the names of some heavy hitters in the criminal bar. I'm sorry I—"

"No! I can't trust them. I can't trust anyone in this town. Except you."

"You don't even know me."

"My brother said I could."

"Who's your brother?"

"Barry Rosen."

Stone paused to search his memory. "I don't think I . . ."

"He changed his name to—"

"Saul," Stone supplied. "Saul Rosen."

"Yes."

"All right. Where are you, Mohawk County Jail?"

"Yes."

"Have you been before a magistrate? Any bail set, anything like that?"

"No. I'm supposed to go to city court at seven-thirty tomorrow morning. I mean *this* morning."

"All right, tell anyone who asks that I'm representing you. At least for now. Has anyone tried to question you?"

"No. Down the Riegar plant, when I was arrested? They read me my rights. I said I wanted to call a lawyer."

"Good girl. Don't—"

"I'm a woman."

"Right. Good woman. Don't discuss this with anyone. Not just the police, *anyone*—other prisoners, chaplains, I don't care who. Keep it to yourself. Anyone tries to talk to you, just keep telling them you want to see your lawyer."

"I thought you said you weren't a criminal lawyer?"

"I'm not. I watch a lot of television. Good ni . . . Hey! What's your name?"

"Sara—without the *h*—Rosen."

Stone felt for the cradle and hung up the phone. You never told me you had a sister, Saul, he mused. But, then, Saul never really told anybody much of anything.

Stone checked his watch again: almost 4:30 A.M. No chance of going back to sleep now. For too many years, his day had begun at zero-dark-early. Only within the past year had life afforded him the luxury of sleeping in until six, and he still felt guilty about it.

Michael Stone felt guilty about a lot of things. Now he could add to the list this Rosen girl. Either way he decided about representing her, he would have felt guilt. Viewed objectively, he had no business representing Sara Rosen. It had been years since he had passed the bar exam and had even that tenuous claim to expertise in criminal law. While it was quite legal for Stone to represent her, he couldn't help feeling that it was hardly moral. On the other hand, the woman had invoked a powerful emotional claim upon him from his former life, the military. Saul Rosen had cross-trained with Stone's outfit and once, in combat, taken a wound in order to warn Stone and his men of an ambush. How could anyone with a shred of honor walk away from a debt like that?

"Shit," Stone said quietly, into the night. He raised both legs simultaneously and kicked back the covers, then swung up to sit on the side of his bed. What was done was done. He was due in city court in three hours.

Part of Michael Stone's clinging to the past was his voluntary continuation of a formerly mandatory program of two hours of "killer PT" every morning, six days a week. He wasn't all that much under forty, and he was fighting it every inch of the way. Today was running. He left the light off. There was enough fog-filtered street light coming through the window for him to find his running gear laid out on the chair the night before. He went to the bathroom down the hall, took a towel and wrapped it around his neck, stuffing the loose ends into the front of his T-shirt, then slipped quietly downstairs to the vestibule, where he stretched.

Feeling sufficiently warmed up and loose, Stone slipped out the door and began running easily down the darkened streets of the city of Rhinekill, seat of the government of Mohawk County, New York.

Rhinekill sat on the east bank of the Hudson River, about midway between New York City and the state capital at Albany. Even at 4:45 A.M., the streets, though in immediate pre-dawn darkness, were not deserted. The midnight-to-eight shift of the city of Rhinekill police department, the Mohawk County Sheriff's office, and the nearby barracks of the New York State Police had patrol cars out. Early-morning delivery trucks moved. An ambulance took an emergency patient to St. Martin's Hospital.

At a corner, Stone elected to run through a puddle rather than break his stride to avoid it. The cool splash of water against his shins refreshed him. Another puddle, this one of light from an ancient street lamp, loomed ahead. As he ran through the yellow glow, Stone checked the timer function on his digital watch. He was moving much faster than usual, without the slightest labor to his breathing. Then it dawned on him why; he had been running almost entirely downhill. "Down the Riegar plant . . ." Sara Rosen had given as the site of her arrest. Unconsciously, Stone had been heading for it. Rhinekill and its suburbs ran steeply uphill from the valley through which the Hudson flowed. The Riegar plant, once the century-old Hudson Drug Company, was located at the lowest and oldest point in the city, on the bank of the river. Now by default the city's main employer, it had been taken over by West Germany's giant Riegar Farmakologie, GmbH.

At a decrepit, potholed street overlooking the railroad tracks that ran north and south along the river's edge, Stone turned left toward the plant. He wasn't far from it now, but the dark and the fog rolling off the river obscured it from his view. Stone knew what it would look like. A citizen's group, seeking to save the plant "from being gobbled up by foreigners" had successfully petitioned to have the hideous nineteenth-century red-brick building declared an architectural landmark for historical preservation. It did them little good. The practical Germans, noting that the building was only slightly less solid than the pyramids, simply gutted it, left the facade, and added an eighteen-story tower. Then they filled the inside with the Medusa-like monster-scale nest of pipes and retorts that make up a modern drug research and manufacturing plant.

Stone heard and smelled the place before he could see it. The strange odors rose out of the fog and spread down the dirty old streets. Great machines rumbled and hissed in the night. The first thing he could see was the glow of lights, diffused through the smelly mist. Then the outlines of the building could be made out: huge, looming out of the dark. Catwalks, twelve stories high, dully lit. So oppressive was the place that Stone, without thinking about it, slowed his pace to a jog in instinctive caution lest he play the fool, rushing in where a prudent angel would pause.

A sudden noise, like a combination of the sound of escaping steam or a released air brake and a high-speed electric motor, drew Stone's attention down and to his right. There, railroad tracks glistened dully and bifurcated to form a series of sidings between the plant and a shipping dock that disappeared into the blackness of the river. One of the sidings appeared to run right up against the near wall of the plant, which formed part of the foundation of the tower. The wall seemed to split open, and the crack, straight up and down, glowed with light as it grew.

A small switch-engine diesel barked to life, then moved slowly toward the lighted opening. As the two great steel doors completed their electrically driven run and the opening was complete, the light coming from within the bowels of the building glowed so intensely it reminded Stone of the door to a furnace. The small diesel murmured forward into the maw of the furnace and out of sight. There was a clanking and hissing. Moments later, the switch engine emerged pulling a black tanker car. Even as it did so, the huge hangarlike doors started to close. The timing was perfect. The doors whined shut just after the rear of the tanker cleared them. It was as if the diesel and its load had just barely escaped great jaws trying to snap shut upon them.

Stone cut left again to run along the front of the plant. At the building side of the sidewalk, a six-foot wrought-iron picket fence guarded a thirty-foot perimeter lawn that ran up to the side of the building. Whether from the foggy light or the chemicals in the air attacking it, the grass looked to be dying. He gazed up at the tower, which disappeared into the night and fog. What in God's name would Sara Rosen be doing down here? he thought, then leaned forward to start the long running climb back to his home.

* * *

Not long before Michael Stone asked himself the question about Sara Rosen, an inquiry into that very question had begun in an expansive office at the top of the tower he had just passed. Inside it, behind a broad Danish Modern desk, sat a thickset middle-aged man with eyebrows so dark and dense, one didn't notice he was nearly bald. His shirt and tie looked as if he had worn them yesterday and hastily thrown them back on. His name was Georg Kramer, and he was trying to control his anger long enough to get all the information he could from the frightened young uniformed security guard who stood before him.

"Let me see if I have this correctly," Kramer said, leaning forward and glaring at the guard. "At two o'clock in the morning—"

"One fifty-eight, sir," the guard interrupted, taking refuge in useless precision.

Kramer rolled his eyes heavenward. "One fifty-eight," he repeated in exasperation, "you detected a person having no employee identification of any kind lock a bicycle to the perimeter fence, use it to climb up and go over the fence onto company grounds, then run to the lobby downstairs, where you were posted, *and from which you have seen all this,* and who then sends you on a wild-goose chase . . ."

"It was a cat, sir. She said it was a cat . . ."

"All right, then! A wild-*cat* chase! The point is, you were distracted long enough for her to disappear for more than twenty minutes before you found her again, in a most sensitive area, *with a camera.* Am I correct so far?"

"Yes, sir," replied the hapless guard.

"Whereupon you detain her, ask her nothing about what she was doing here, just called the police and promptly delivered her, *and her camera and bicycle,* to them, and then, then and only then, *do you call me!*"

"Sir"—the guard tried to defend himself—"I figured she was one of them outside agitators. I mean she was young an' all, and like on a bicycle an' all, you know? And she kept yellin' about how the scientists are torturin' all the animals in the labs downstairs doin' all them experiments, an' she goes, 'You're not gonna do that to my cat!'

An' with all the trouble we been havin' with the agitators and all, I just figured—"

"But you didn't figure, did you," Kramer replied icily, "that if she *was* an agitator and she took pictures in the labs, we'd be seeing the pictures, poster-size, in the hands of the pickets tomorrow? And you didn't figure that it might be a good idea to retain that film? Or that she might be using all this antivivisection nonsense as a ruse to cover that she was really from a competitor seeking proprietary secrets? That *that's* what she might have been filming? And that there was plenty of time to turn her over to the police, and *I might want to question her first?"*

"But, sir, it was a Polaroid camera. An' ya have to give suspects in custody their Miranda warnings—"

Kramer exploded. *"You're not the police!"* The futility of further discussion overwhelmed Kramer. He sank bank in his chair and waved his hand at the guard. "Get back to your post. Go on!"

The guard gone, Kramer glanced at his wall clock and made a quick time-zone calculation, then picked up a telephone. He punched in two digits, then spoke: "Overseas operator, please."

"What country, sir?"

"West Germany."

"You can dial that country directly, sir."

Kramer wasn't used to placing his own calls, but with no secretary available at this early hour, he had no choice. Irritably, he asked, "Can't I give you the number and be connected?"

"Yes, sir, but you can save—"

"Just connect me," Kramer snapped, and read off the number.

Moments later, a secretary answered the phone in German. Kramer spoke to her in English, which she understood perfectly, and asked to speak to Walter Hoess, chairman of Riegar. Hoess recognized that it was the middle of the night in the eastern United States and his top man there wouldn't be calling at this hour if something wasn't wrong. He was sharply attentive.

"Yes, Kramer. What is it?"

"There has been a penetration, sir. Middle of the night. Person with a camera."

"The explanation?"

"Unknown at this point, sir. Unfortunately, the guard made an assumption it was connected to the animal-rights protesters and delivered the person, a woman, to local police. They have the camera and, presumably, the film. In any event, we were fortunate in that there were no subjects in the apparatus at the time. The last series of tests had been concluded, and the new series not yet begun, awaiting new subjects—"

"But a knowledgeable person, seeing the apparatus, might . . ."

"Yes, sir. I am sure we can regain any photographs from the police on a claim of proprietary intellectual property. The city government is cooperative. It will be handled."

"It had better be. What of the product?"

"Still unsatisfactory. The latest batch and the contaminated test subjects had been disposed of in the usual way prior to the entry. Security will be increased substantially before the new tests begin."

"I want this matter resolved promptly. We have a deadline for development of the new product. It is urgent, you understand? Now, I want to know who was responsible for this incident, what they were after, what was photographed and why. And I want them discouraged permanently from any repetition of such conduct."

"Yes, sir. But it may well be just those animal fanatics. They can be embarrassing, but I doubt that they're intelligent enough to be dangerous—"

"Now you're thinking like your guard! The stakes are too high to make any assumptions but the worst. I'll send Metz over on the next plane. You are to cooperate with him fully. Keep me advised until he arrives; after that, Metz will communicate with me directly. Good day, Kramer."

Hoess hung up. Kramer noticed that his hand holding the now-dead telephone was wet with sweat. The last thing he wanted was Metz. Chief of security for Riegar worldwide, Metz would have felt right at home in his native land fifty years ago.

As Stone was running and Kramer was on the phone with Hoess, Sara Rosen was yawning. Out of habit, she tried to stifle it by putting a hand over her mouth. She was prevented from doing so by the hand-cuff chain looped inside a belly chain around her waist. She was yawning because she had not slept all night. As she had been led back to the women's detention pen from the matron's office at the conclusion of her telephone call to Stone, the female deputy sheriff guarding her said, "Don't get too comfy, sweetie. Chow for court cases is five o'clock."

"What happens then?" Sara asked.

"R&D. Where you processed in at. Receivin' an' Discharge. You gets your own clothes back to wear to court. Then, when ever'body ready, you takes the van to court."

"How about a bath first?"

"Bath?" The deputy laughed. "This the jailhouse, sweetie. Ain' got no bath here. Shower, maybe. But you only been here one night. You gets to shower ever' third day like ever'body else."

Swell, Sara thought. When I meet my lawyer for the first time, not only do I look like *drek,* I get to smell like it, too. Well, why not. The closer she got to the holding tank for women, the more she realized that the whole place stank of it. And urine. And sweat. And floating over it all was a powerful disinfectant odor, intended to mask the others, but that only added to the general stink. The combination smelled to Sara like . . . hopelessness.

When she entered the tank itself and the barred door clanged shut behind her, her sense of smell was assaulted anew. The drunk in the corner on the tile floor had vomited all over herself and everything else in range. But before Sara had a chance to react, a different female deputy called to her through the bars. "Rosen."

Sara turned. "Yes."

The guard opened the door. "C'mon."

"Where are we going?"

"R&D to get yer shit. You going for a ride."

"But court's not until seven-thirty. And I'm hungry."

"I only work here, lady. Let's go."

The city court of the city of Rhinekill was located upstairs on the second floor of the two-story building at the corner of First Avenue and Main Street. The first floor housed Klein's Retail Wine & Liquor. Apart from affording drunks given suspended sentences a convenient place to resupply themselves downstairs—thus guaranteeing another appearance upstairs—the location was convenient to the lawyers and the police. The county courthouse was on the opposite street corner; the police station across the street.

Michael Stone skipped breakfast to arrive early at 7:15. He climbed the stairs and slipped into a seat at the rear. The place looked as much like a storefront church as it did a court. A high but crude wooden bench held the center of the front of the room. To the left and right of the bench, at a slightly lower elevation, were two matching boxed-in enclosures. One served as a witness box, the other as a workplace for the stenographer. In front of all was a fencelike low wooden railing. Everything was stained a deep brown by a combination of varnish and years of accumulated dirt.

Six feet back from the railing, pews taken from an old church ran to the rear of the room. An aisle separated the rows of pews. Once upon a time, the floor had been stained. Years of footsteps of people who had rejected society, or been rejected by it, had long since worn the flooring into raw wood.

Along the right wall, prisoners sat on benches under the watchful eye of a police sergeant. Lawyers sat in the front pews, but Stone didn't know that. The police sergeant noticed Stone and recognized him as a lawyer—it was his business to know who was who in his small city. The sergeant spoke to the court clerk. "We got a newcomer, sittin' in the back, observin'." The sergeant chuckled. "Maybe he's gonna run for your job."

The clerk, also a lawyer, glanced back at Stone. The lawyer sitting next to the clerk caught the motion and glanced back. He was an assistant district attorney: very young; the lowest in seniority or he would not have been there. Next to him were another young lawyer, an old-timer who had never made it, and at the far end, keeping her distance from the DA's representative, a woman in her early thirties from the public defender's office. Together, they composed the bar of the city court.

The whispers started.

"Who is he?"

"Don't know."

"Yes you do. He was at the bar association dinner in September. Stone. Old Harry's nephew. Took over his real estate practice, such as it was. All he does."

"Must have some kind of service pension or something. Can't be earning much."

"He's some kind of aging, frustrated jock. Always exercising down at the athletic center."

The old-timer broke in, "Watch who you call aging, kid. That guy doesn't look forty. Dry behind the ears means aging to you?"

"All rise," interrupted the bailiff.

Stone searched the prisoner bench. There was only one woman. She was black. He waited as the court processed the prisoners, one after another. Mostly they were Discon—disorderly conduct; D&D—drunk and disorderly; Possession—of misdemeanor amounts of a controlled substance. Then there were the arraignments on serious charges that could not be heard by a court of such lowly jurisdiction: Assault Two—assault in the second degree; Burglary One—burglary in the first degree.

For these defendants, the proceedings consisted of advising them of the charges against them, seeing to it that they were represented by counsel, and, when on occasion they were, scheduling a hearing for the judge to determine whether there was enough evidence in the hands of the state to bind the defendant over for the grand jury.

Defendants represented by counsel usually demanded the hearing at the earliest possible date so they could learn something of the prosecution's case. The assistant district attorney always tried to have the hearing put off as far as possible. It was the official start of a race. If the grand jury, whose proceedings were secret, could hand down an indictment before the date set for the preliminary hearing in city court, the hearing was rendered moot and the defendant effectively precluded from learning anything about the state's case against him. The result was known among criminal lawyers as "trial by ambush."

As Sara Rosen failed to appear, Stone grew more and more uneasy. By the time the court started to try petty civil disputes, it was clear to him that something was wrong. He made his way up the center aisle to meet the assistant public defender. She was on her way to the stairs to leave. Stone stuck out his right hand. He knew the woman's name from listening to her being addressed during the proceedings.

"Miss Hannigan, Mike Stone. Could I take a few minutes of your time?"

"Ms.," she corrected, automatically. "Sure, counselor. What brings you to the awesome chambers of city court?" Stephanie Hannigan was a short, shapely honey blonde whose fashionable horn-rimmed glasses emphasized eyes that reflected an elfin wit.

"Good question," said Stone. "I've never been here before, and I'm not eager to come back, but I'm trying to do a favor for an old service buddy whose sister got picked up last night, apparently trespassing on the grounds of the Riegar plant. She told me she was due in city court at seven-thirty this morning, but she never showed."

Hannigan frowned. "If she was out on her own recognizance and didn't show when she was supposed to, they'll issue an warrant for her arrest and—"

"She wasn't out. She was in custody. This was to be her first appearance before a magistrate."

Hannigan combed her fingers through her shoulder-length hair, "Hmmmm. Come to think of it, they would have called her name. They didn't. It could be one thing, but I doubt it."

"What?"

"Well, as you probably read in the paper, some animal-rights group has targeted Riegar—picketing, blocking the gate, and so on, just generally making a pain in the ass of themselves because Riegar, like every other drug manufacturer, tests out new stuff on animals. It's the law, you know. FDA. They have to, before they can get permission to try it out on humans. The cops busted a bunch of them last week, but they were all let out on their own recog because most were from the area, and we're talking like a twenty-five-dollar fine here. They'll probably not even have to pay that. They *want* a trial so they can try out a screwball application of the necessity defense. They want the publicity. But the city fathers aren't going to give it to them. Riegar's about the only real tax base left in this town. The major employer.

The council's not about to blow it for a bunch of guinea pigs. Is your client their leader?"

Stone moved aside to let some people pass them. "I don't know, but I don't think so. Why?"

"Well," said Hannigan, "if she was, they might be pulling something the cops and the DAs do from time to time to harass a defendant they're pissed at and to try to get information. They 'put 'em on the bus.' A police car, actually. Take them from the sheriff's to the city PD to the state police barracks, et cetera, on the pretext that each of those jurisdictions needs to question the defendant about uncleared crimes, so they can get all the charges together and present them to the grand jury in one fell swoop. For efficiency. It's bullshit, of course." Hannigan looked directly at Stone. "A good defense lawyer wouldn't let them get away with that."

Stone looked back at Hannigan with eyes that went suddenly hard. "I do real estate. Searches and closings, mostly. But I don't like being fucked around. I *really* don't like it when someone I'm supposed to be taking care of is being fucked around. Where should I start? The sheriff's office?"

"No. You don't play that sucker's game. No matter how fast you drive from one place to another, they've got radios. She'll be long gone before you get there."

"So what do I do?"

"Look," said Hannigan, "if it gets known you're helping these wackos, you're gonna get some heat. If it gets known that I'm helping you, *I*'m gonna get some heat. But what they're doing is wrong. So I tell you what. Go to that park down the street there, and read the paper for a bit. I've gotta hit the office or they're gonna wonder where I am. I'll see you in a few minutes."

Stephanie Hannigan turned and loped across the street to the public defender's office. Stone, eager to find his client and chafing at the delay, reluctantly put thirty-five cents into a street-corner vending machine for a paper and pulled up on the handle. It jammed. "Consistent with my day so far," he mumbled to himself, then struck the side of the machine a sharp blow. That freed the handle, and he retrieved the paper, tucked it under his arm, and walked to the park. He was about to sit when he noticed that the benches were all covered by pigeon droppings. Standing, he checked out the news.

The front page was full of the latest from the Mideast. Libyan leader Muammar Qaddafi was once again beside himself with rage. Months ago, Israeli bombers had taken out the Libyan chemical-warfare manufacturing facility at Rabta. Claiming that it could not have been done without the aid of photo intelligence from a U.S. KH spy satellite, Colonel Qaddafi had hurled threats of vengeance against the United States as well as Israel at the time, but, so far as was known, had not followed through. Now the Libyan colonel had suffered another blow, and the U.S. role was not a matter of conjecture.

The Soviet Union had provided Qaddafi with a dozen new Sukhoi Su-24 swing-wing fighter bombers, each capable of carrying up to 24,250 pounds of bombs. Even stationed at the air base at Bumbah, on the eastern seacoast of Libya, their 805-mile operational radius was insufficient to reach Israel. The Soviets, however, had mischievously provided Quaddafi with two Ilyushin I1-76 air-to-air refueling tankers. Using them, the Su-24s could reach London, let alone Israel.

Qaddafi had apparently tried for Israel. A flight of six Su-24 "Fencers" had intruded on Israeli airspace. Three had been shot down immediately by Israeli fighters. The other three had jettisoned their bombs and fled west to link up with the two Ilyushin tankers, Israelis hot on their tails. The Ilyushin pilots, hearing all this going on over their radios and knowing the Israeli fighters had over twice the speed of their 500-mph tankers, panicked, made a 180-degree turn, and tried to escape.

The Israelis ignored the tankers and went after the "Fencers," who ran out of fuel and ditched at sea. The frightened Ilyushins ignored several warnings from a U.S. guided-missile frigate protecting the carrier U.S.S. *John F. Kennedy* that they should change course. The four-engine Ilyushins had the same radar signature as bombers. The U.S. frigate launched missiles and shot them down. Qaddafi had now lost half his Su-24 fleet and, more importantly, any long-range capability. He was certain the United States had done it purposely and promised a strike against the United States that would "change history and avenge the honor of the Libyan people." The Department of State discounted the threat as rhetoric for internal consumption but noted that U.S. antiterrorist forces had been placed on "heightened alert."

Stone looked further through the paper, all the way to the back page. Nothing about the arrest of his client. Nothing about any protests at the Riegar plant. He was just folding up the newspaper when Stephanie Hannigan walked up.

"Lemme see your paper," she said.

Stone handed it over. Inartfully, Stone noted, Hannigan slipped some papers into the newspaper, pretended to look at it for a few moments, then handed it back to Stone.

"What you do," said Hannigan, "is you go storming noisily into county court with a writ of habeas corpus laying out the facts and demanding access to your client immediately, followed by a hearing before a magistrate. Threaten to go to supreme court if the county court doesn't order it done yesterday. What you have in the paper is a Xerox of our petition the last time they tried to pull that shit on the public defender. The court built the DA a new ass. Good luck."

Hannigan paused. "Is she pretty?"

"I don't know," Stone said, "I haven't met her yet."

Hannigan looked up at Stone. Her eyes sparkled.

"Congratulations, counselor," she said, "you've got the makings of a real criminal lawyer."

2

THE SLENDER HISPANIC MALE IN HIS LATE TWEN-
ties sat on a bench just inside the international terminal at John F.
Kennedy airport in New York looking carefully over the top of an
opened copy of *The Wall Street Journal*. His clothes were elegant.
Everything, including the gleaming black leather shoes, was of Italian
cut and manufacture. The man's wristwatch was the epitome of taste,
a Patek Philippe with a leather strap. No knowledgeable person would
have questioned his presence in the lobby of the most exclusive hotel—
except, perhaps, hotel security, to whom, unfortunately, he had recently become a bit too well known. The Patek had come from the
wrist of a Swiss businessman checking into the Waldorf Towers.

Angel Garcia was a master pickpocket. A gypsy, he had been studying his craft since the age of six. He was a "cannon." He took but did
not "hold," passing off almost instantly to an accomplice anything he
had lifted with his extraordinarily skilled right hand.

This morning, his accomplice was an attractive gypsy woman of
nineteen, her hair colored blond at one of Manhattan's finest salons so
as to look gloriously natural. A seductively cut dress that would
distract the eye of any male not in a coma enabled her to do more than

merely receive a handoff from her partner. The two of them knew a number of short routines, like plays out of a football coach's playbook, to distract, decoy, or upset someone for just a moment—and a moment was all it took for Angel Garcia to work his magic.

Garcia checked the Patek. He had in his head the arrival schedule and had already clocked how long it took the first-class passengers, the first off the plane, to emerge from customs, immigration, and out the door into the general-population area of the terminal. Next up was British Airways' Concorde supersonic transport direct from London.

Garcia preened. As effective as his partner, Magdalena, was at distracting men, Angel Garcia prided himself as being equally effective with women. He wasn't, but he'd never have believed that, even from his mother, who was a gypsy princess.

Right on time, the doors from immigration burst open and the Concorde passengers headed for the street, to waiting limousines and taxicabs. Garcia scanned them. A thickset man in his early forties with thinning sandy hair and a hard jaw strode rapidly ahead of the others, clearly determined to get the first cab. He was wearing an expensive black capeskin leather trench coat. In his left hand, he carried with ease a well-crafted two-suiter.

It was what was in the blond man's right hand that attracted Angel Garcia's attention, however. It was briefcase-sized, but not a briefcase. A computer, Garcia concluded, one of those five-thousand-dollar 386-chip portables. Garcia nodded to his partner across the room and fell in behind his mark at a discreet distance.

The man in the black greatcoat paused before the first taxicab in line and nodded affirmatively in response to the inquiry "Cab, mister?"

At that, the driver started to get out to put his fare's bags in the trunk, but the big man shook his head. "I keep them with me."

The driver closed his door and reached around to unlock the passenger door. His fare, feeling the warmth of the May New York sun being rapidly absorbed by the black leather across his back, put down his luggage and shrugged off his coat.

It was the moment for which Angel Garcia had been waiting. He nodded to Magdalena. Immediately, she rushed up to the cab shouting "Taxi!"

"Lady," said the cabbie, "I already got . . ."

The sandy-haired man cocked his head slightly toward the woman and slid his right arm free of his coat, then shot it down toward his briefcase, snapping his thick-fingered hand around the delicate fingers of the would-be thief, already encircling the grip of his intended loot. Garcia gasped at the strength of his mark's hand.

The big man reached his left arm through the cab's driver-side window and pressed the horn. As he did so, he increased the pressure of his grip on Garcia's hand like a hydraulic press. Caught between the terrible crushing of the big man's grip and the rock-hard handle, the gypsy's hand started to break; finger bones, knuckles, and then, one after the other, the long bones leading to his wrist. Garcia screamed in agony but was drowned out by the taxi's horn. He would never use his right hand to steal again.

Magdalena, seeing the excruciating pain registered on her partner's face, whipped a straight razor from the sash around her waist and brought it up toward her partner's tormentor. Without letting go of Garcia, Magdalena's target released the horn and snapped his left fist into a powerful backhand karate blow directly into her left breast. Magdalena's mouth opened but no sound came out. As she sank to her knees, vomiting, her assailant released Garcia's now-crippled hand from his right, then used it to deliver another backhand punch, this time to the gypsy's temple, felling him on top of the vomiting woman.

The cabdriver was filled with apprehension as his fare quickly put his coat and bags into the rear of the cab and entered.

"Mister . . ." he started. Then he saw his passenger's face in the rearview mirror and thought better of it.

"Drive," said Helmar Metz.

County court for the county of Mohawk, state of New York, convened every weekday morning at ten o'clock. The three county-court judges rotated the taking of motions and hearing of trials. The Honorable William B. Martin, senior of the three judges, was winding down his service on the county court by having assigned himself out of turn to hear motions for the month of May. The aging Manny Weiss, justice of the supreme court of the state of New York assigned to sit at Rhinekill, had finally been persuaded to retire a year before elections to solve two problems. First, Old Manny was getting a bit forgetful and had become something of an embarrassment to the bench. Second, his early retirement enabled the party to appoint its own selection and give this person a year to become fixed in that position in the mind of the public before running for election.

William B. Martin was the de facto head of the party in Mohawk County. Nevertheless, skillful politician that he was, he had waited until it was "his turn" before engineering his elevation to the supreme court bench. Things were, as usual, going his way, and he was in an affable mood on this warm May morning. Only forty-nine years old, he could see himself on the court of appeals before he was sixty.

Judge Martin got where he was by being able to handle difficult problems in their infancy. So it was with confidence that he picked up Michael Stone, Esquire's petition for a writ of habeas corpus in the matter of one Sara Rosen. Martin pressed a button on the desk in his chambers. His clerk put his head through the door to the chamber's outer office cum reception room and said, "Yes, boss?"

"I think," said Martin, jerking his thumb toward the door at the opposite end of his chambers that led into his courtroom, "you'll find a lawyer named Michael Stone sitting outside waiting for court to convene. Bring him in here, will you?"

"On my way, boss."

The Mohawk County courthouse had been built in 1903. It was five stories tall, of red-brick construction with brownstone trim. Inside, the floors were of white marble, never a problem to keep clean in 1903 when the city was full of Irish and Italian immigrants only too thankful for the opportunity to swing a heavy wet mop all day. Now that the Irish and Italians were the judges and lawyers, and others deemed such labor beneath them, the floors remained dirty.

Stefano Seri was short, dark, and overweight, but he moved with surprising alacrity when on a mission in his role as clerk to Judge Martin. He ushered Stone into the judge's chambers through the courtroom entrance behind the bench, introduced the two men, and kept right on walking to the other side of the room and out to his little office. Martin was on his feet, left hand gripping an ever-present massive cigar, right hand reaching across his desk to take Stone's and shake it as only a politician can.

As he did any time he entered a location for the first time, Stone scanned it quickly and thoroughly. Martin's chambers were second only to those of Justice Weiss over on the supreme court and surrogate side of the building. On the fifth floor, they overlooked the heart of the city at First and Main. The decor was turn-of-the-century legal; that is to say, wood—dark and everywhere.

The big old mahogany desk, behind which Judge Martin stood offering Stone a cigar, dominated the room. Stone declined the big corona politely; he was already feeling green from the cloud of tobacco smoke that hung like ground fog around the judge. There was a small chair to the right of the desk where a stenographer sat when taking dictation. To the left was an overstuffed armchair whose maroon leather had been buffed to a fine patina by years of lawyers' serge. "Sit down, sit down," Martin said, gesturing to the armchair.

Stone did as he was bidden, and the judge settled back down into his spring-loaded leather swivel chair. Its back, Stone noted, was so high that no matter how far back Martin leaned in it, he was protected from that injury most beloved of the legal profession—whiplash.

"See from the papers congratulations are in order," Stone ventured.

"Oh, well"—Martin waved it off with his cigar—"the committee had no choice. Don't get me wrong, Manny Weiss is a wonderful man and been a credit to the profession. He just got a little too old." Martin's eyelid dropped in a sly look. "Know how you can tell when a guy's gettin' too old?" He went on without waiting for Stone's answer. "In the first stage, he forgets to zip up. Poor Manny was in stage two—he'd forgotten to zip down."

Martin laughed appreciatively at his own joke, then swiveled to face Stone directly.

"So how's the practice goin'? You makin' a living?"

"A living's about it, Your Honor, but it's enough. I'm alone, and my Aunt May, my Uncle Harry's widow, won't let me pay her any rent. Give her a hundred a month for food and utilities—and I know that doesn't cover it—and had to threaten to leave to make her accept that. She's a neat lady."

"Yeah," agreed Martin, "and your uncle was a good man, too. Good lawyer. Well liked in this county. Nice little real estate practice, got along with everybody. Took it kinda hard when right outta law school you joined the navy. . . ."

"I believed in the war," Stone said, his voice cold.

"Right, right," Martin said defensively, "I was in Korea. I know what you're saying. Anyway," he said, trying to recover, "your uncle was really tickled when you retired outta the navy and joined him. Shame about his ticker. His practice and your navy pension . . ."

"I didn't retire from the navy," Stone said, anger tinging his voice. "Not in long enough. I was forced out on a bullshit disability. Minor hearing loss. I get something from that."

Although Martin couldn't know it, the anger in Stone's voice was directed at himself because he knew in his heart that what he was saying wasn't true.

"Well," said Martin, emitting yet another cloud of noxious smoke, "every little bit helps." His face brightened. "Meanwhile, you been getting Harry's share, right? Some guardianships, few estate appraisals for the surrogate, stuff like that?"

"Yes, I have, Your Honor, and I do appreciate it. . . ."

"Well, as I said, your uncle was well liked around here. Besides, you're doing your duty as a member of the bar. Somebody has to do it, and some of the guys around here have such a successful practice that little stuff would be a burden. You know," Martin said with obvious emphasis, "a smart man like you, well liked, links to the community through your uncle, navy vet, no reason some day not too long from now you couldn't run for something or build a pretty lucrative practice. You just need to be around long enough to get the lay of the land."

"Uh-huh," said Stone, trying his best to be agreeably noncommittal.

Martin kept right on talking. He scooped up Stone's writ and said, "No need to waste your valuable time out there arguing this writ in the courtroom. I'm gonna grant it right here. The order's already prepared. You're right on the merits. They should know better than to still be pulling this shit. We used to do it all the time, years ago when I was DA. But times change. People"—Martin looked at Stone knowingly—"have to learn how to change with the times."

The judge rose and walked to one of the floor-to-ceiling windows overlooking Main Street, five floors below. "Look out there," he invited Stone. "You know what you see out there? A city on its ass. You know why? Stupidity. Sheer stupidity."

He turned back to Stone. "Twenty-five years ago, the biggest manufacturer of electronics in the country wanted to build a plant in this city. The dumb WASPs who'd been running this town since New York was New Amsterdam turned up their patrician noses. The good times were gonna go on forever. Screw growth. Who needs it? You know what happened?"

Stone shook his head. "Before my time."

"That company built a plant just outside the city limits. Then four more. The suburbs became where it was at for employment. Then housing. Then the downtown department stores went—all the shopping action was in the suburban malls."

Martin sat back down. "You know what this city's tax base consists of now?" Martin answered himself: "Just one plant. And it was dying, too, before Riegar bought it and kept us alive."

Judge Martin handed the signed writ to Stone. "The little lady should be waiting with a deputy downstairs outside the Family Courtroom. Give him the bottom copy of my order."

Stone rose and took the sheaf of papers. "Thank you, Your Honor, I really—" The judge came around his desk and cut him off in mid-sentence as he clapped an avuncular hand on the younger man's shoulder. "And, counselor," he said, squeezing Stone for emphasis, "you have done your duty for your client. Stick to real estate."

Judge Martin opened the door to his reception room, eased Stone through it, then paused as he was closing the door. "You know," he said, speaking around the clenched stub of his cigar, "the members of the criminal bar in this county aren't such bad guys. Quit breakin' their rice bowls." Like the Cheshire cat, he receded into a cloud of cigar smoke and was gone.

There was such a knot of people in front of the fifth-floor elevator door that it was clear to Stone he wouldn't make the next trip, so he opted for the stairs, the springy muscles in his legs taking them like a dancer. He spotted the two women he was looking for from the landing midway between the first and second floors. The women could not have been more different.

The female deputy sheriff was large to begin with, but three years of helping herself to free meals and snacks from a jailhouse kitchen that put out more starch than the laundry had so stressed her uniform that a sneeze would have produced casualties from flying buttons. To her beefy wrist was attached a handcuff, linked by a short chain to another locked around the wrist of a woman almost as tall as she. Just as the utter boredom of the life of the deputy was reflected in her bovine inertia and expression, intellect and the intensity of the deeply committed glowed from the sloe eyes her prisoner had inherited from a Mediterranean Sephardic mother, their near-purple blackness in startling contrast to the light skin bequeathed her by her northern German Ashkenazi father.

Sara Rosen's hair was jet black, dense, thick, and with a natural curl that made her a virtual stranger to beauty salons, going in only on special occasions for a professional cut. Her black eyebrows had a high arch, were a bit thicker than was fashionable, and guided the eye to a thin, Semitic nose that divided feline cheekbones and pointed directly to full lips over a strong but pointed chin. She was twenty-six, and when she was dressed and entered a room, women hated her for the way their men's heads snapped around and their gazes held overly long on a body that combined thinness with just that last trace of baby fat that bans wrinkles and is the unmistakable stamp of youth.

Michael Stone took the last steps slowly to observe Sara Rosen for as long as he could before he was himself observed and his scrutiny proved offensive. Even in her present state—sleepless, curls in disarray, dressed in jeans that set off her long legs and tight behind and a hooded workout sweatshirt that rendered her shapeless from the waist up, fidgeting on the bench in angry impatience—she changed Stone's attitude toward her in an instant. What had been approached as a chore had metamorphosized into anticipation from one side of him, clashing with apprehension from another. He remembered another woman whose eyes had burned with commitment-driven intensity. So, for that matter, he supposed, had his own once. Unfortunately, the objects of those two commitments had been 180 degrees apart.

Stone stepped up to the two women and held his right hand out toward Sara Rosen. "Michael Stone," he said. "We meet at last."

"Stay away from the prisoner," snapped the deputy.

Stone shook Sara's hand anyway, then peeled off a copy of the writ signed by Judge Martin, handed it to the deputy, and said, "She's your prisoner but my client. You'll note that according to the writ I've just handed you, Miss—Ms.," he corrected himself, "Rosen is to be brought before Judge Martin upstairs forthwith."

"Uh," grunted the deputy as she hauled herself to her feet and headed toward the elevator. Sara Rosen sprang up lithely, saying, "I have been all over this county since last night. Where have you—"

Stone held up his hand. "Wait," he said, "anything you say to me in the presence of a third party is not covered by the attorney-client privilege. I have every reason to believe you'll be released shortly after we get upstairs. Then we can confer privately."

"Then," said Sara as the old elevator's doors squeaked shut and the crowded car began to groan upward, "I take a bath. Then I eat. *Then* we have a conference."

Because of the crowd, Stone was standing unwillingly against Sara, trying to keep any intimate part of his body away from her by holding in his muscles. Her unwashed body's odor, loaded with pheromones, was advertising her sex to any nearby upper-Paleolithic males whose subconscious receptors had not been numbed by the recent advent of modern civilization. There was nothing wrong with Stone's receptors and her closeness disturbed him.

When the three of them entered Judge Martin's courtroom, the clerk had just called another case. The judge spotted Stone and announced, "Ladies and gentlemen, the sheriff's office has just responded to a writ of habeas corpus issued by this court. Will Mr. Stone and Mr. Sibley"—Martin beckoned to the assistant district attorney— "please approach the bench."

Stone and Sibley walked up to stand before Judge Martin's elevated bench as the deputy seated Sara Rosen and herself behind the defendant's table inside the bar.

"Your Honor," began Sibley, "I'm afraid I'm not prepared to make a recommendation for the setting of bail in this case. I don't have the file—"

"The file," snapped Stone, "was supposed to be in city court at seven-thirty this morning. I was there. The district attorney was there, but my client wasn't."

"Gentlemen," admonished Martin, "I'll have no bickering here."

Turning to Sibley, he said, "The file should be downstairs in the office, right? That's where we always kept it when I was DA. If you want a few minutes to run down and get it, I'll give them to you. But what's the point? This is one of those agitator trespass cases down the Riegar plant, right? The defendant has a local address?" The judge looked at Stone, who nodded affirmatively. "So we're talking recognizance here, not money bail, right?" Martin looked at Sibley.

"Your Honor," protested Sibley, "from what I understand, this is a Burglary Two charge. The defendant was caught inside the plant at night by a security guard."

"*Alleged* to have been caught inside by the guard," argued Stone.

"She was inside when picked up by the local police," countered Sibley.

"Of course," said Stone. "If the guard caught her on the grounds, he'd have to take her inside to *call* the police. The point is that this is all at the accusation level now, my client has a local address, and, as the court has noted, this is a simple trespass case. We're not dealing with the Star of India here."

"*Alleged* simple trespass," Sibley retorted, "and as I'm sure the court will also note, the formula for a new drug breakthrough can be worth a lot more than the Star of India."

"All right, *all right*," said an exasperated Martin. "You want a hearing, right?" he said to Stone.

"Correct, Your Honor. The sooner the better. Like this afternoon. We—"

"Okay," Martin cut him off, "and the district attorney obviously needs to find his file and prepare." He looked out over the courtroom toward Sara Rosen. "Will the defendant, Sara—" He looked at the writ before him for help.

"Rosen," Stone and Sibley said simultaneously. "Rosen," repeated the judge. "Will you come forward, please."

Sara, by this time unshackled from the deputy, stepped forward, and Stone guided her to his side.

"Does the defendant," said Martin, looking at Stone and, to her annoyance, ignoring Sara, "understand that she is charged with burglary in the second degree and waive further reading?"

"Yes, Your Honor, through counsel; for the record, Michael Stone.

S-t-o-n-e," he said, looking over at the court stenographer and enun-
ciating clearly.

"How does the defendant plead?" Martin asked, still looking at Stone.

"Not guilty."

"That's ridiculous!" blurted Sara Rosen, her patience at an end. "I—"

"A simple 'not guilty' will suffice, Miss," said the judge. "The court
is mindful that you had a rough night. But please, you have counsel.
Unless you are dissatisfied with his performance and want to dismiss
him, let him do his job."

Sara Rosen bit her lower lip to contain herself. She was not impressed with the way her attorney had let her be dragged all over the
place by the police, but she had no alternative in mind at the moment.

"All right," said the court, "this is set for preliminary hearing before
the city court of the city of Rhinekill no later than two P.M. today.
Defendant is released on her own recognizance until that time so that
she can consult with counsel or obtain new counsel, whatever her
preference."

"But . . ." protested Sibley.

"I believe," said Martin, ignoring him, "the clerk had already called
another case, and the court wishes to thank both counsel for their
patience. Proceed."

Stone pushed aside the swinging gate in the wooden bar that gave
the legal profession its name and led Sara Rosen back down the center
aisle of the spectator seats. A handful of people were scattered about
the benches in ones and twos. Most were old. While their contempo-
raries were closeted at home watching ersatz courtroom drama on
television, these people had opted for the real thing. It was far more
interesting and, to the relief of some of their long-suffering married
children with whom they lived, it got them out of the house. Stone
and his client interested them. Stone was new to these precincts. They
hadn't seen him in action before. Whispering together, several of them
decided to go over to city court at two.

From the front row, the row where the press sat during trials in
which there was public interest, a young woman in a business suit rose
and followed Stone and Rosen down the aisle, turning left after them
toward the exit. Once outside the courtroom, she approached them.

"Ms. Rosen? I'm Terry Caulfield with *The Wall Street Journal*. We're planning a feature on the impact of the animal-rights movement on affected industries—fur, agriculture, and so forth. This ruckus at Riegar interests us because there's been no organized protests, until yours, directed at the pharmaceutical industry. Is this just a local problem your people have with something going on at this particular plant, or have you targeted the pharmaceutical industry as a whole?"

Stone frowned. Someone else had followed them out the door. He was a tired-looking middle-aged man who was color-blind. He had to be, Stone thought, to have voluntarily purchased the sports coat and slacks combination he was wearing. Now he was pausing a bit too long for a drink at a fountain just a few paces away, where he could overhear the conversation.

"Excuse me," Stone said as Sara, with a look of eagerness on her face, opened her mouth to reply, "but I have not yet had the chance to confer with my client." Noting the frown of annoyance with which Sara Rosen reacted to his interruption, he said, "I'm not saying that my client will or will not give you an interview. It's just that *I* want to be the first one to interview her. Then I'll advise her as to what I believe is in her best interests, and then she can decide what she wants to do. She can hold a press conference if she feels like it. Fair?"

Before the reporter could answer, Sara Rosen responded with a resounding "No! I'm tired of you answering every time someone asks me a question. I can speak for myself."

"Speaking for others is what lawyers do, Ms. Rosen. Especially when those others have been accused of a crime and anything they say can and will be used against them."

"I've already been told that Miranda stuff!"

"Then you were told about your right to counsel. I'm your counsel. Not, in the immortal words of Brendan Sullivan, a 'potted plant'!" Stone turned to the tailored woman. "Do you have a card, Ms. Caulfield?"

Caulfield nodded and produced one from her pocketbook. She scribbled on the back of it and said, "Here's the number where I'm staying locally. When you're ready, give me a call."

"Deal," said Sara, and fell in behind Stone as he headed for the stairs.

Ahead of them, the sports jacket, having consumed two gallons of water, moved rapidly down the stairs, perhaps in urgent search of a men's room.

Stone moved fast out the courthouse doors, down the broad steps, then headed right toward the public parking lot. Sara Rosen stayed with him as he came up to a metered space, some two-thirds of which was filled by a low convertible. The fabric top was white. The paint job was "Up yours, Officer" red, except for a stretch leading out from the windshield across the hood. That, like the similar space in front of the pilot's canopy on a fighter plane, was a nonreflective flat black. There was no chromium trim; it, too, was black. The wheels were alloy, the tires big, wide, and of a soft rubber compound with a unidirectional tread.

Sara Rosen studied the car as her lawyer unlocked the passenger-side door for her and opened it, disclosing individually articulated bucket seats and a stubby center-mounted gearshift.

"What is it?" she asked.

"Mustang GT," Stone said as he let himself in. "It's an 'eighty-five."

The way he said it, Sara could tell she was expected to appreciate the significance of the model year. She didn't. "An 'eighty-five?" she said, inviting his explanation.

"Best one made since the sixties. Five liter V-Eight. Overhead valves. All the new ones are fuel-injected. This one's got the last of the big Holley four-barrel carbs on it. Low-tech, low price, and high power. Three hundred pounds feet of torque out of the box. But with a four-barrel, a good ol' boy mechanic can do his stuff on the engine. Could and did."

Stone gestured toward the dash and doors. "No air conditioning. Manual window winders. Factory-installed SVO steering wheel. No excess weight." He started the engine. It burbled from two exhaust pipes as big around as Sara's wrist.

"So how powerful is it now?" asked Sara.

"That's classified." Stone grinned as he pulled out of the parking slot and headed toward Main Street. "The safety Nazi's would have a fit if they knew."

Sara's voice registered disapproval. "Polluting the environment is not a funny matter."

"Who's polluting? I'm talking about the goddamn do-gooders want to make us all wear helmets in the shower in case we slip and fall. I'm serious. Next they'll want a federal statute that all males over puberty have to wear a condom twenty-four hours a day in case of impure thoughts."

Sara giggled. "What about women?"

"Don't ask. They'll think of something."

The confines of the small car were soon filled with the aroma of Sara's body, and Stone became uncomfortable again. He rolled down his window, gestured toward rows of bushes along the street in full pink bloom, and said, "Smell that rose of Sharon. I love spring."

"I stink, don't I?" replied Sara.

"What!"

"Rose of Sharon doesn't have any odor." She rolled down the window on her side. "Turn left up here and take me home. I'll take a bath."

Stone turned. "Will you settle for a shower?"

"No. I want a *bath*."

"I was afraid of that."

"What do you mean?"

"Time. We don't have time for you to take a bath. The woman wasn't born who can take a bath in under an hour."

"And the man hasn't been born who understands that for a woman, a bath is to cleanse the spirit as much as the body. And that takes a good long soak in a nice hot tub. After where and how I spent last night"—she looked at him accusingly—"that's what I need and that's what I'm going to have."

Stone reacted to the note of accusation. "Look, who called whom at four o'clock this morning? Am I confused? I don't recall thrusting myself upon you as your counsel. I don't recall holding myself out to you as an ace criminal lawyer. I'd never heard of the stunt they pulled on you. And I had to ask advice to find out what was going on and how to get you out when I did. And I don't like owing favors in this town, 'cause they're too ready to call 'em in in ways that are outta line. Where along here do you live?"

"Second from the end of the street. On the right."

As Stone headed up the street of old brownstones, he continued sounding off. The more annoyed he got, Sara noted, the more quiet and controlled his voice sounded. She wished he would yell at her, though. His voice was taking on a hard edge that made her uneasy.

"I'm here because you invoked the name of your brother. Him, I *owe*." Stone saw that there was only one parking space open in the block and pulled into it. It was well down the street from the old apartment house Sara had indicated was hers.

"Tell you what," he said, "you hop out here, go up and wash any way you want. I'm going to pick up an evening paper and see how they're playing this thing—what the press has been able to get out of the cops and Riegar. Every bit of information helps. I'll be in front of your place, double-parked if I have to, in exactly thirty minutes. You want me to continue to represent you, be there. Then. Not five minutes later. You're not there? I withdraw."

"What do you think you are, a husband?" Sara snapped, pulling the door latch and getting out of the car. She leaned into the open passenger window and said, "I don't appreciate ultimatums!"

"Ultimata," replied Stone.

"What?"

"The plural of *ultimatum* is *ultimata,* not *ultimatums.*"

"Impossible!" Sara Rosen shouted at him as she stalked off.

"Thirty minutes!" Stone shouted back as he drove off.

There were plenty of street-corner vending machines in the downtown area, but, Stone discovered, he didn't have the necessary thirty-five-cent coin combination to get a paper. He headed for the only remaining old-fashioned newsstand, located around the corner from the courthouse. One could find any major eastern newspaper there and, if so inclined, get a bet down on any horse race, prizefight, football game, or other major sporting event anywhere in the country.

The proprietor was an old buddy of Stone's late uncle. His name was Ira Levin, and it was rumored he was connected. There were a lot of rumors about Levin. Stone's favorite was that as a teenager, Ira Levin had been an apprentice of "Lepke" Buchalter, founder of "Murder, Incorporated" in Brooklyn. True or false, the rumor had served Levin well. Everyone went out of his way to be respectful to him, let alone not to bother him or, God forbid, do something *really* stupid like try to stick him up.

Levin was short, stout, and irrepressibly cheerful as he handed Stone his paper. "Hello, counselor, how are ya? How's everybody's favorite candidate for the next opening on the supreme court?"

Stone grinned. Everybody enjoyed Levin's brand of bullshit.

"Supreme court of the state of New York? I thought Judge Martin had that all sewed up."

"State of New York?" Levin responded, eyebrows up and palms waving. "That's nothing! A waste of your talent. We're talkin' the whole United States of America here!"

"I love you, too, Ira. Listen, could I come by later sometime and we could go in the back and talk? I'd like to get your take on something. Uncle Harry always said you knew more about what's going on around here than the FBI and the CIA combined."

"Rumors, rumors! I'm just an old Jew tryin' to make a living. What do I know? But sure, c'mon back later. It's always a pleasure to talk to good people."

"Thanks, Ira."

"My pleasure, my pleasure. Here, take one of these cigars with you."

Stone backed away from the cigar as if it were a gun pointed at him. "Those things will kill you, Ira. I'll see you later."

"Who's gonna die?" Ira Levin called after him, "I've canceled my reservations!"

Stone sat in his car to check out the newspaper. More ranting by Qaddafi. Then, on an inside page, he found the article:

INDUSTRIAL ESPIONAGE SUSPECTED IN RIEGAR PLANT BURGLARY TRY

By Alice Burns
Staff Reporter
Rhinekill, May 20th

Security guards at the Rhinekill plant of Riegar Pharmaceuticals last night turned over to Rhinekill police officers Sara Rosen, 26, of 1337 Clifton Avenue, Rhinekill, whom security officers said they had apprehended inside the plant, armed

with a camera. Ms. Rosen was said
to have gained entrance to the plant
by a ruse. "We think it's pretty clear
she was trying to photograph secret
proprietary technology, probably for
sale to our competitors," said Georg
Kramer, local Riegar chief. Ms.
Rosen was taken to the Mohawk
County Jail pending an appearance
before city court this morning on a
charge of second-degree burglary.
No bail has yet been set.

Stone folded the paper and checked his watch. Time to head back
to Sara's place and learn her decision. He slid the five-speed into first
and eased out into traffic.

3

THE STREET WHERE SARA ROSEN LIVED WAS ONE of unrelieved sameness. Both sides were taken up by identical eighty-year-old brownstone-faced apartment houses in sets of two, side by side, the sets separated by narrow alleys. The wrought-iron street lamps were equally old. They reached upward, then curved out over the street like a shepherd's crook embellished with what once had been recognizable as stylized leaves but now were so many lumps under eighty coats of thick dark green paint. Every so often, a surviving plane tree rose from the sidewalk, still surrounded by a fencelike circular iron guard meant to protect the young saplings from chewing horses. The streets were dirty, the alleys dirtier, and the whole place gloomy. At least it was to Stone as he guided the muttering Mustang toward Sara Rosen's dwelling.

She was there, and Stone didn't know whether he was relieved or not. Then he noticed something that alarmed him. Sara was sitting on the bottom step of the front stoop, elbows propped on her knees, face in her hands, in exactly the same clothing she was wearing when he had left her thirty minutes before. Two parking spaces were open in front of the stoop, and he glided in easily, shut off the engine, got out, and walked over to her. If she had noticed his arrival, she was pretending not to have.

"I have never," said Stone to the forlorn figure, "seen anyone so eager for a date with me in my entire life."

Sara Rosen raised her head and looked at him. She wasn't laughing.

"My apartment," she said, "it's been totally trashed."

Stone sighed in resignation. "Let's take a look."

Sara got up wearily and started up the stairs. Stone fell in behind, scanning the area as he did: quiet, nothing unusual.

Sara's apartment was on the fifth and highest floor of the ancient walk-up. The hallways were dark and smelled old. The ceilings were of pattern-embossed galvanized tin, covered by many layers of dirty paint. It would be depressing to live there, Stone thought, even without having your place vandalized.

The door to the apartment was closed, and Sara let them in with her key. The place was a shambles. Books were tossed out of orange-crate containers onto the floor. The cheap old sofa's cushions were slashed and the stuffing partly ripped out. The bureau drawers were on the floor, too, at odd angles where they had been thrown after their contents had been emptied out. Clothing was strewn everywhere—jeans, a few dresses, cheap cotton panties, and a couple of expensive athletic bras. Sara Rosen didn't have much, but what she did was out there for everyone to see. "I feel violated," Sara said tonelessly.

Stone picked his way through the mess, trying not to do any more damage, and looked into the bedroom. Same story. Mattress hurled off and ripped, more intimate clothing, bedclothes on the floor and over the radiator, shoes strewn about. There was no closet. A hanging hamper lay on its side, empty. It was easy to guess where the dresses had come from.

The bedroom had one window. It was open, the bottom sash raised all the way up. Outside was the landing of a fire escape leading down into the alley.

"That's how he came in," Sara said.

"He?"

"Look in there."

Sara nodded to an open door into a small bathroom off the bedroom. Stone crossed over to it, Sara close behind him. To the right was a frosted window with a paint-encrusted steam radiator beneath it. Opposite the door was a cracked porcelain sink with the brass showing through its worn fixtures. Left of the sink was an old-fashioned large-tank toilet with a wooden seat, and left of that a white enamel cast-iron bathtub sat against the left wall on ball-claw feet. A torn plastic shower curtain hung from a ring above the tub. Stone looked at the shower head. It looked as if it belonged on a watering can.

"Pull the door back," Sara said.

A small wicker clothes hamper lay over on its side. On the back of the door, hanging from a hook, was a translucent yellow rubber bag. It had been slashed open. A white rubber hose dangled from the bottom of the bag. Whether it had been used as an enema or a douche could no longer be determined; the tubing had been sliced off below the clamp, and the nozzle was nowhere to be found.

"The sick bastard," Sara said. "Look." She pointed to the empty hamper. "He even took my dirty underwear!" Tears rolled from the corners of her eyes. "It's just so humiliating."

Embarrassed, Stone left the bathroom and made his way to the alcove, which housed an efficiency kitchen. The gas stove's pilot light must have been loaded with soot, he surmised from the odor of gas. "You leave this open?" he asked, indicating the refrigerator door.

"Yes. I wanted you to see everything the way I found it."

Stone studied the little kitchen. There were plastic food-preserving containers on the floor, their contents spilled out in a moist mess. A milk carton was open and lying in the sink, where it was clear the carton had been emptied out. The salt and pepper shakers had been emptied and discarded. Dishes, silverware, pots, and pans had all been swept from their proper place and ended on the floor with food from the refrigerator. A plastic kitty-litter box had been taken apart and the litter spilled out. Clumps of cat feces were in it.

Something caught Stone's eye. He reached down and picked up a large canned Polish ham from among canned vegetables, soups, and cat food. "Ham?" he asked quizzically.

Sara stared at the floor, looking sheepish. "I'm not religious."

Stone dropped the subject and went back into the living room. He opened the front door, then squatted down and intently studied the face of the cylinder lock beneath the doorknob. Then he got up and went to the open window. He raised the shade a few inches to examine the window latch. "You leave the window to your apartment un-locked when you go out?"

"No. I could have sworn I locked it before I left last night. But so much has happened . . . I just don't know. I guess I did."

"No, you didn't. There's no indication of it being forced at all, but there are tool marks on the keyway of your front-door lock."

"So," said Sara, "instead of a sadistic pervert, we have a *skilled* sadistic pervert."

"Not sure we have a pervert at all," said Stone. He sat on what was left of the arm of the ruined sofa. "Why would a nut out to sniff your panties pick your front-door lock, then try to make you think he got in through an open window? What would he care?"

Sara closed the refrigerator door and turned to him. "So what do you think?"

"I don't think we've got a pervert. I don't think we've necessarily got a sadist. Or even a man. It could be a woman. Or more than one man. But whoever they were, they're smart. What we have here is the result of a very thorough professional search."

Stone got up and gestured toward the kitchen. "All the opened food containers were dumped. They didn't do that to make a mess and piss you off. Those are the favorite hiding places of clever people. They gave you credit for brains—and having something to hide." Stone paused. "So, you have something to hide, Sara?"

"Oh God," said Sara. "You, too?"

Stone checked his watch. "We're running behind, kid. We can talk while we eat. C'mon, let's get outta here."

"Okay. But don't call me 'kid.' "

If anything, the experience Sara Rosen had gone through had caused her to sweat even more. Once again in the close confines of the Mustang, Stone felt himself responding to her natural chemical attractant and made a conscious effort to dismiss it.

"I'm really not hungry anymore," said Sara.

"Yeah, I can understand that. We don't have all that much time, anyway. Tell me about it. Start at the beginning. Don't leave anything out. Lying to your lawyer is as stupid as lying to your doctor. When you die or get convicted, they're embarrassed, but *you* do the dying or the time."

"Okay," said Sara, "it's not that long a story. Barry . . . Saul and I have dual citizenship. We were both born here, in Brooklyn. He's six years older than I am. Anyway, right after his bar mitzvah when I was seven, my father and mother, in a fit of religious fervor, gave up everything and moved to Israel under the law of the return. That's how we got dual citizenship."

Stone negotiated a curve that led to a park down at the riverbank. "I didn't know Saul had U.S. citizenship," he said.

"Well, he does," said Sara. "Anyway," she continued, "we did the whole thing, including the kibbutz. Barry ate it up. I hated it. I bitched, pissed and moaned, and generally made life miserable for my parents until they sent me back to my grandparents in Brooklyn when I was thirteen. They're well-off and were delighted to get me, because they'd been feeling robbed of their grandchildren and now at least they had *one* back that they could fuss over. I guess they spoiled the hell out of me, because I ended up doing pretty much what I wanted. Which was kind of cruel, because what it turned out I wanted was to go to college at U. Cal., Santa Cruz, which, as far as they were concerned, was as far away as Israel."

"Santa Cruz?" Stone said as he parked the Mustang at the seawall. This conversation was important, and he wanted to be able to look Sara in the eye during it.

"Yeah, yeah, I know." Sara grimaced. "Okay, the *town* is a living museum of that goofy hippie stuff that went on thirty years ago, but the *school* is good. One of the best Shakespeare departments in the country."

"You studied Shakespeare?"

"Undergraduate. English Lit. major. Shakespeare concentration. But I minored in bio. That's biology, not biography. I got good grades. Never fell into the 'do dope and fuck off' trap. So I got into Berkeley for a master's program in bio, made it, and decided to try for a Ph.D. Never made it."

"Why?" asked Stone.

"I met some people at Berkeley. Sort of 'Save the fill in the blanks' types, and I guess I decided my life needed some direction, something other than myself, finally, to devote my energies to. Anyway, I met this guy, he was into raptors—"

"Raptors?"

"Birds of prey. Really bright guy. Got me interested in the whole animal-testing thing, and, with one thing and another, I never did get the Ph.D."

"So what are you doing here?"

"About four months ago, Eddie—the raptor guy—and I broke up. We're still friends, and I have tremendous respect for what he's doing, but I needed to get away—change of scene. Our thing had been pretty intense. Some of the movement people told me about the campaign that was going to start here, against Riegar, and it's only eighty miles away from my grandparents, so I packed my cat and rode the dog back here."

"Rode the dog?"

Sara laughed. "Greyhound bus." It was the first time since he'd met her, Stone thought, that Sara Rosen had laughed. He liked it.

"So who's running this protest group," Stone asked, "you?"

"Oh, no. The movement's not that structured. In fact, that's one of the main things wrong with it. Why it doesn't get very far. Too many factions. It's just from time to time they jell on a target—like Riegar. In fact, I think I'm the only real representative of what I guess you'd call my faction. Naturally, I think it's the only one that makes sense and has any chance of getting anywhere. I mean, I understand and can even sympathize with where the others are coming from, but their actions are, for the most part, counterproductive."

Stone glanced at his watch. "Tell you what. We're getting a little short of time here. We'll hold the philosophical exposition until after the hearing, if you don't mind—I'm not blowing you off; I'm interested—but that's not going to be the subject matter of the hearing. Don't worry, I'm not going to put you on the stand. . . ."

"But I *want* to testify. This story has got to get out! People just don't understand; they think our position is based on emotion and bleeding-heart-fuzzy-good-for-animals shit! The whole point—"

"The whole point," Stone interrupted her, "has nothing to do with what we've just been talking about. I need to know everything you can tell me about last night. Not because I'm going to have you testify about it at the preliminary hearing—we're doing this to *get* information, not give it. I need to be able to cross-examine any of the people's witnesses intelligently, and I can't do that if I don't know what happened. Why'd you go down to the plant in the middle of the night with a camera? You on some kind of photo-recon mission for your group?"

"No! It's like I told them. I was looking for my cat!"

"Sure."

"Goddamn it, Stone! I've got this cat—Romeo—a big old tom. Tiger markings. Head and ears all notched up from getting laid in alleys from here to California. I tried to keep him in, but no, he's gotta go find himself some pussy—no pun intended. So he shot out of the apartment between my feet the minute I opened the damn door. And I mean he's *gone!*

"Usually, he does his thing and comes back. This time, he didn't. Well, have you noticed there're no stray cats running around Rhinekill?"

"Can't say I have," said Stone, "but then, now you mention it, I *haven't* seen any. Not lately, at any rate."

"Right!" said Sara, warming to her subject. "Now, the protest people have three theories—about the cats I mean. One, the Chinese restaurant, if you check the records, got convicted a year or so ago for serving cat meat. They promised never to do it again, but who knows? Two, there's a rumor that some sick city cops on the late-night shift amuse themselves by shooting stray cats with silenced twenty-twos—but if that's true, where're the bodies? Three, we *know* Riegar's using animal experimentation to develop new drugs. They admit it! So, I took my Polaroid, got on my bike, and cruised the streets from here to Riegar. One, to find my cat. Two, on the off chance I spot someone grabbing him, I nail him in the act with the Polaroid—it has auto focus and auto flash—I.D. the bastard, and I've got my cat *and* Riegar!"

"How does that scheme," asked Stone, "get you ending up inside the plant?"

"Look," Sara shot back, "I saw nothing until I got down to the plant. Then I saw *a* cat—wasn't sure it was mine—inside the fence on the Riegar grounds. I locked my bike to the fence, took my camera out of the saddlebag, used the bike seat as a ladder, and went over the fence after the cat. I guess the guard saw me. Anyway, he came running out, yelling, and the cat zips right past him into the place. I pointed at the cat and ran past him. No cat. Guards coming. I ran around the corner, hit the elevator, went up—I dunno, ten or so floors—got out, hit the fire stairs, and found myself on one of the floors where they do the animal testing."

"See any animals?"

"No."

"So how do you know that's where they do the testing?"

"I saw the *equipment*. It's horrible. They had Ziegler chairs, Blaylock presses, Collison cannulas, even some Noble-Collip drums. God, it was awful. You know what they use that press for?"

"You can tell me later. Wha'd you do then?"

"I photographed everything in the room as best I could. There're only ten pictures in a pack of Polaroid film. I got off eight before I heard the guard coming. I think what happened is he heard me first. Or the camera, rather. It makes this buzzing sound when it ejects the film? Anyway, I hadn't stopped to close the door to the hall behind me, and I think that's what happened."

"Okay, so he nails you. What happened to the pictures? He grab them, too?"

"No," said Sara, irritated, "he *didn't* 'nail' me, not then, at any rate."

"But you just said—"

"Damn it, Stone, if you would just stop interrupting me and *listen* for a minute, I *might* be able to—"

"Okay, okay." Stone lifted his hands, palms outward in a placating gesture. The sleepless night and the shock of her vandalized apartment had clearly taken its toll on his client, and he had a hearing to face. "Just tell me in your own way."

"Thank you," said Sara. "Anyway, I heard him coming, stopped shooting, looked around, saw this inner door. Thought maybe it was a closet. Ducked in to hide. Turns out to be like a monitoring room for the lab—bank of TVs on the wall, PCs on desks. All off. Secretary's section partitioned off to the right, L-shaped desk, word processor, In-Out trays, postage meter, phone, phonebooks, stuff like that. I hid behind it."

Stone started the Mustang's engine and let out the clutch a bit too fast. The red convertible bolted forward, snapping Sara Rosen's head back against the headrest. "Sorry," he apologized, suppressing the impulse to ask her what had happened next.

Sara reproached him with a look, then said, "Minute after I got down behind the partition, I could hear the door open. I kept waiting for his head to pop over the partition and get me, but I guess he just looked around, then closed the door behind him. I waited a bit till I thought it was safe, then sneaked back out to the lab and headed for the hall. *That*'s when he got me. Bastard outsmarted me. He was waiting behind the door to the monitoring room."

Gingerly, Stone ventured another question, "That's when he got the pictures, too?"

Sara had been waiting for him to ask that. "No," she said with an air of triumph, "because *I* outsmarted *him.* With any luck, I'll be able to show them to you, although I didn't wait to see what I had. No time to watch them develop."

Stone passed a slow truck on the right. "What happened then?"

"They caught me, yelled at me, called the police, and turned me over to them."

"Were you read your rights?"

*"Every*one read me my rights: the guard, the cop, the sheriff's deputy . . ."

"Did you tell them anything?"

"Just that I was trying to find my cat, which was true. But when they wanted me to give a statement, I remembered what they said when they read me my rights and said I wanted to talk to a lawyer. When I was down at my grandparents' in the city, I talked to my brother on the phone for the first time in quite a while and mentioned I would be up here doing movement work. Well, you know how big brothers are. Right away, he assumed I'd get in trouble and made me promise to call you if I did. He's really high on you, you know. Says you're real good at what you do."

"Did," said Stone.

"Did? Past tense?"

Stone's smile bordered on the sardonic. "Your brother and I fought together in Nam, where we used weapons, not law books. He's never seen me in a courtroom in his life."

"He said you were honest, and I could trust you with my life. Is that past tense, too?"

"No. So I have to tell you. I'm a lot better at keeping people alive than I am at keeping them out of jail. One thing's for sure, though."

"What's that?"

"I can't do either for someone who won't follow orders."

They were back in the parking lot now, where they had started from after Stone had effected Sara's release. They got out of the car and walked toward the city court entrance.

"Okay," said Stone to his client, "as I said, I'm no criminal lawyer. But I know a hell of a lot more about what's going on here than you do. I want your promise that there'll be no outbursts, or anything else. We're here to find out what the other side has—or as much as we can. On the other hand, we want to give them nothing. You understand?"

Sara nodded.

"Does that mean you agree?"

"I'll do my best."

"Bullshit!" Stone barked. "There are times in life when your best isn't good enough. You're not out to do your best; you're out to do what is required. There's a hell of a difference. Do you understand?"

"Yes."

"Do you agree?"

"Yes."

"Okay, then," said Stone, "let's go in there and play guts football."

As Stone and his client walked into city court, they found it virtually deserted. A young man of about Sara's age, wearing too much hair and a three-piece suit, sat before the bar in the front row, the place usually reserved for lawyers. An aged bailiff, seeing the couple enter, rose stiffly, walked over to the door to the judge's chambers, and tapped on it gently.

Almost immediately, the door opened and a man of sixty with a full head of naturally wavy white hair and kindly blue eyes behind rimless glasses entered. His black robe marked him as a judge. As he crossed to his seat behind the bench, the bailiff chanted his mantra: "All-rise-the-city-court-of-the-city-of-Rhinekill-is-now-in-session-the-Honorable-Judge-Abraham-Gershen-presiding-draw-nigh-and-ye-shall-be-heard."

A stenographer, late, scurried into place and looked up expectantly from her machine. "Call the case," said Judge Gershen, and the stenographer's fingers played the keys.

"*People* v. *Rosen*," said the bailiff.

"Mark Cole, assistant district attorney, Mohawk County, ready for the People," the young man said. Still standing, Stone followed suit.

"Michael Stone, ready for the defense."

"Proceed," said the judge, settling back in his chair.

"Your Honor," Mark Cole began, his expression that of a bridge player who is in the process of trumping his opponent's ace, "it is my duty to inform the court that within the hour the grand jury of the county of Mohawk handed down a true bill indicting the defendant for one count of burglary in the second degree in connection with the incident that is the subject of this scheduled preliminary hearing, thereby rendering these proceedings moot."

"To no one's great surprise, I'm sure," said the judge. His voice weary, he continued, "Very well, ladies and gentlemen, I assume whatever bail arrangements made previously are to continue?"

Stone spoke up: "Defendant was released on her own recognizance by Judge Martin after a habeas corpus proceeding in county court earlier today, Your Honor."

The judge looked over to the assistant district attorney.

"Counselor?"

"If the court please, People at this time advise defendant that arraignment is set for ten A.M. tomorrow morning before Judge Carlini in county court. At that time, the People intend to move for setting of bail. People therefore request, in view of the short time before arraignment, that defendant be remanded until ten A.M. tomorrow."

Stone looked as if he was about to rip up the bar, but Judge Gershen cut him off before he could begin to object.

"No, I won't do that, counselor. If recognizance is good enough for Judge Martin, it's good enough for this court."

"But, Your Honor," Cole expostulated, "in the intervening time, the grand jury has spoken and—"

"The ruling stands, counselor." Judge Gershen's eyes were no longer kindly. "There has been reference to a habeas corpus hearing, and the court notes that this defendant was originally scheduled to appear before it at seven-thirty this morning and was not produced here by those who had her in custody. You have your indictment. Quit while you're ahead, counselor."

With that, the judge banged his gavel sharply and said, with obvious irritation, "Adjourned."

"All rise," said the bailiff as Judge Gershen left the bench for his chambers. As the door shut behind him, Stone took Sara Rosen's arm, wheeled her around, and said, "C'mon, let's get out of here."

On the now-familiar walk back to the parking lot, Sara asked, "What do we do now, coach? Punt?"

Stone, who wasn't sure, gave no hint of it to his client. "Leave the legal stuff to me. More important right now is your lawyer is about to die of starvation. How about an overdue meal."

"Still don't feel like eating. I'm the one who just got indicted, remember? I've *got* to get a bath and change of clothes or *I*'ll die. Only I can't face that apartment right now. How about lending a client a few bucks for some new underwear, jeans, and shirt and use of your credit card for a night in a hotel? It won't screw up your card; I'll get some money tomorrow and pay cash when I check out."

"It won't screw up my card, just my reputation. This is a small town, Sara. All I need is to have everyone buzzing about how I spring my very first criminal law client on a writ of habeas corpus, only to check her into the nearest hotel at the first opportunity. You know what *habeas corpus* means?"

"No."

" 'You have the body.' I can hear the lawyers now: 'Stone goes into court and says "you have the body." Then he goes to the desk clerk and says, "I have the body." ' " Stone grunted. "That's the literate ones; the rest'll just think you're paying my fee in a manner that, unfortunately, is not all that unusual in this town."

"Nice people," said Sara.

"Human beings," Stone replied, "only too ready to think the worst in any given situation."

"Okay," Sara said, throwing up her hands as they reached the Mustang, "what's the solution? What do we do now?"

Stone reached into his hip pocket and produced his wallet.

"Here's a hundred. That should get you dressed if you stay away from designer jeans. Then I take you home to my Aunt May. You'll love her; she's a real character. She'll like you in spite of the fact you're associating with the likes of me. Wait'll you see where I live. Big old Victorian mansion. Belonged to my uncle. He and May lived there. His law offices were on the first floor. They're mine now. You want a bath? May's got a bathtub just this side of a swimming pool. They made 'em big in the nineteenth century; nobody dieted then. Stay there till you feel up to facing your apartment again. But don't stay too long. May's food will blow you up like a balloon."

"Wait a minute," Sara protested. "How come it's going to ruin your reputation to check me into a hotel, and it's okay to move me into your house?"

Stone smiled. "Because I'm using the credit card to check *me* into the hotel. If you think my Aunt May would let me use the home she spent forty-seven God-fearing years of monogamy in to make moves, forget it. Wait'll you meet her. You'll see what I mean."

"That may be," Sara said, still protesting, "but there's no way I'm putting you out of your room—"

"You're not," Stone interrupted. "That old place has as many rooms as Versailles. May'll probably have you in the room farthest away from mine anyway, just for propriety's sake."

Sara smiled as she stuffed the hundred-dollar bill into her pocket. "You must have some love life. Or are most of the charges on that credit card the local hotel?"

Stone grimaced. "Very funny."

"Oh. So . . . what do you . . . I mean, are you . . . ?"

"I'm straight, if that's what you mean." Stone headed the Mustang up a highway entrance ramp and betrayed his annoyance at the conversation's subject by rocketing out onto the highway directly in front of an oncoming eighteen-wheeler. Only the blistering acceleration of the V-8 sucking fuel through all four barrels of the big Holley kept them from being run down. It was a dumb move, and Stone knew it. He eased into the slow lane, then turned to Sara and said, "Look, it's none of your business, but let me explain something to you. When I was in the navy, I lived by the navy's rules, written and unwritten. The unwritten rule was that for a single officer, any woman was fair game except enlisted, a military wife, or a single sister or daughter without the ranking male's blessing. That was the culture. That left a big field, and I played it. Here," said Stone, gesturing toward the surrounding town, "everyone marries young, then spends the rest of their lives in bed with their neighbors! Some culture."

Sara held on. Stone was starting to go fast again.

"So," he said, "after I'm here a couple of months, I broke down and dated this eighteen-year-old stunner. Took her to dinner across the river. Great restaurant. Great date. The conversation ran out when we finished with the menu. She had a frame of reference began last Friday. Didn't know Ho Chi Minh from Jefferson Davis."

A shopping mall appeared on the right, and Stone entered the lot and headed toward a discount chain store. He pulled into a slot and said, "There you go, the polyester palace. The finest Taiwan, Singapore, and Korea have to offer. I'll wait for you." As Sara got out, he tilted his head back against the headrest and closed his eyes. It seemed only moments later that he was awakened by Sara returning and opening the passenger door.

"How'd you make out?"

"Fine," said Sara, holding out some small bills and change to him. "Here's your change, and thanks."

Stone started up the car and waved the proffered money away as he drove back out to the road. "Hang on to it. You might need it. And besides, I can keep a hundred in my head a lot easier than some odd number."

"Okay. Thanks." Sara turned to put her packages into the backseat.

The rest of the short ride over to Garden Street was in silence save for the raspy exhaust note of the Mustang. Stone brightened as he turned into the driveway of number 182. The house was outsized for the neighborhood. Others like it from the nineteenth century had long since been dismantled and their lots subdivided. Number 182 reigned in its original size and gingerbread splendor. Only the lack of a fresh coat of paint kept it from looking new.

Stone drove on past the porch that started at the front of the house and continued round the corner, becoming integrated into an equally beknobbed and spindle-trimmed porte cochere. He parked in the shelter of its enclosure. Sara looked out at the vines—so old they were two and three inches thick around—that had grown to nearly enclose the open side across from the steps leading to the double-doored entrance to the old mansion. The vines had started to green.

The two of them got out of the car and walked up the steps. To the left of the doorway was a discreet sign that read:

STONE & STONE
COUNSELORS-AT-LAW

A black hard-rubber button projected from an ornate brass doorbell. Stone pressed it. From inside came the clear tones of a chime, much like those of a grandfather's clock.

"Sounds like a grandfather's clock," said Sara.

"Yeah," said Stone, "and the grandfather's clock sounds like the goddamn doorbell. Drives me nuts. Every time I hear the doorbell, I have to check my watch to be sure it's not the clock. Thank God May answers the door. After forty-seven years of practice, she can tell the difference."

The latch clicked, and the right-hand side of the double doors opened, to reveal a diminutive woman of about sixty-five. Her hair was pure white and worn in a half-undercurl short bob of a "flapper" from the 1920s. She looked like a platinum blonde whose face had aged but whose hair had not. One look at Sara and Aunt May's expression turned from one of expectant greeting to accusation.

"What," she asked Stone, "have you done to this poor girl?"

"I look that good, huh?" said Sara.

"Aunt May," Stone said, ignoring both remarks, "I'd like to present my client, Sara Rosen. Sara, Aunt May."

"Oh, my. Please do come in, Miss Rosen."

Sara didn't try to correct Aunt May to "Ms." She accepted the invitation and entered a large vestibule, then continued into a much larger front hall. A living room with a great stone fireplace was to the right. It was so vast, the concert grand looked insignificant. Directly ahead was a stairway that could have come from San Simeon. The first landing was illuminated by a magnificent stained-glass window of a design that made it appear of Moorish rather than Western origin. To Sara's left was a law library dominated by a long conference table at its center. Farther to the left was a closed door with a brass plaque that stated simply OFFICE. The woodwork was heavily milled, the gingerbread removed for a cleaner look. The original darkness had been lightened by stripping the finish and restaining it a honey-golden hue. To the left of the stairway was the grandfather's clock. It belonged in a museum. Sara found it all impressive and beautiful.

"Sara's had a bit of trouble, Mazie," Stone said. "Some thieves have vandalized her apartment. She has nowhere to stay and is, understandably, upset. Knowing your generous nature, I felt it would be all right to offer her one of the guest rooms." As his aunt frowned, Stone hastened to add, "Knowing how you feel about sailors bringing girls home, I'll be packing a bag and staying at a hotel."

Aunt May brightened. "It's for your own good, dear," she said to Sara. "God made men, but the devil motivates them."

Sara made a face at Stone. "Amen to that!" she said. Then, to Aunt May: "I have some fresh clothes out in the car. I'll just be a minute."

"I'll have a hot tub ready in no time," said Aunt May.

"God, that sounds wonderful!" Sara exclaimed. "The condition I'm in, I'm surprised you didn't want to hose me down first out in the yard."

Stone chuckled. "I'll volunteer for that."

Aunt May smiled at Sara. "Considering what you've been through, my dear, your condition is just fine. Of course," she continued, the smile vanishing as she looked at Stone, "the company you're keeping is something else again."

4

● "COUNSELOR!" IRA LEVIN GREETED STONE WITH typical effusiveness. "Come on in! You came at a good time. Business is slow. Tell me everything. What can I do for ya?"

Stone smiled. He had to; Levin's greeting had that effect on people. "Oh," he said, "just trying to get a little scoop on what's going on from Rhinekill's greatest source of intelligence."

"Intelligence? I dunno about intelligence," said Levin. "Information, maybe. If I had intelligence, I wouldn't be runnin' a cigar store. I'd be rich with beautiful damsels hangin' all over me." Ira Levin's face glowed at the thought. "Anyway," he continued, "who ya wanna know about? Just name 'em. I'll give ya sex life and finances on anybody but me. On accounts, I ain't got any 'a either of 'em."

They were both laughing as Stone said, "Nothing that interesting, Ira. It's not a person, it's a company—Riegar."

Levin's face clouded instantly. "Yeah," he said. "Riegar." He paused, brow furrowed, collecting his thoughts. "Well," he said, "I don't *know* anything, but, you know, I hear things. Some of what I hear I don't like."

"Such as?"

"Well, it's almost like someone was stirring up the Indians, ya know? There's a lot of bad feeling going around about the animal people and what they're trying to do. *I* know they're just tryin' to stop testing stuff out on animals—and I ain't sayin' they're right or wrong—but there's rumors going around that they want to shut the plant down. Now *I* know the research is just a small part of the operation down there, an' if ya stopped all the animal testin', probably the only jobs would be lost would be the monkey handlers, and they're not from here, anyway. But a lot of people don't know any better an' think all the production and shipping workers from town here are gonna be thrown outta work. There's a lot of resentment building up."

As he listened to Levin's recitation, Stone's look grew troubled, a fact that did not escape the shrewd eye of the stout little storekeeper. Ira Levin was a good source of intelligence because he was equally good at collecting it. "What's a matter?" he asked. "Harry leave ya a lotta Riegar stock?"

"No. It's just I'm representing a woman picked up down there last night. One of the animal-rights people."

Levin looked up at Stone quizzically. "You doin' criminal work now, counselor? That's a first for you, ain't it?"

The troubled look on Stone's face turned pained. "A first and last, I hope. It's kind of a long story. Seems she's a relative of an old friend. I said yes in a weak moment, and I'll probably regret it. What bothers me more is, the way things are going, *she*'ll probably regret it."

Levin reverted to form. "Nah, counselor, you're gonna do fine. She's better off with you than Clarence Darrow. You're gonna be another Perry Mason. Watch, you'll see! . . . Hey, is your client that nice Jewish girl I seen her name inna paper, Sara Rosen?"

"You got it."

"Ya know," said Levin, "it's kinda too bad they did that."

"Did what?"

"Put her name inna paper an' all. She's the first one of them animal people to get named in the paper. When they busted all the others for protestin', they just gave the number an' said they were all from outta town."

"Figures," answered Stone. "The others were just arrested for disturbing the peace or some such. My client was charged with a felony . . . burglary."

"Yeah," said Levin, "still an' all, it could be a problem."

"Why?"

"Well, like I said, there's resentment. Before now, it was just at the animal people as a whole. An' unless one of them's carrying a sign, who's to know? Try to keep her picture outta the paper. Bad enough now the yahoos got a name to focus on, know what I mean?"

"Good point," said Stone. "Fat chance of pulling it off, though."

"I dunno," Levin protested. "You could . . ."

"Ira, it's gonna be all I can do to keep her from giving a press conference!" Stone frowned. "You think someone might want to physically hurt Sara Rosen? I mean anyone in particular or just she'd be a natural target of bozos at the local gin mills?"

Levin ran his hand over his hair and hesitated. "The bozos, sure. They're bullies and would go after anybody unpopular at the moment. But that's not what I mean. I'd say you got two problems. One is the monkey handlers."

"The monkey handlers," Stone repeated, "that's the second time you mentioned them. Who are they?"

Levin looked Stone in the eye. "Look, I'm an old Jew. Old enough to remember things, right? So maybe I'm making too much of something." Levin paused. "The 'monkey handlers' is what the other workers, the ones from around here, call the guys who handle the animals for the experiments in the research labs. Nobody from here works there. No local people. No one really knows what goes on in there. The monkey handlers are all from the old country. They're all Germans. They work three shifts a day, like cops, when the animals are there."

"How often is that?" Stone asked. "Sara said there were no animals in the lab she saw the other night."

"I don't know. But there's more than one lab. A number of them, I think. So one could be empty and another full at any one time. Now the word the company put out is that this is all secret research, and they can't let anyone know what's going on until they get a patent. So the Germans keep that all to themselves."

"Sounds reasonable," said Stone.

"Yeah," Levin replied, "but these guys are supposed to be some tough cookies. They don't mix with the Americans. Stay strictly to themselves. But they look like you don't wanna fuck with them, know what I mean? Anyway, you're probably right. It's reasonable. It's just I get the creeps still when I put Germans and laboratories and experiments together in my old Jewish head."

"That's reasonable, too," said Stone. "Anything else?"

"Yeah. There's a rumor, just a rumor, that the company's bringing in some strike-bustin' headbreakers."

"Strikebreakers?" Stone looked puzzled. "There's no strike!"

"Yeah," said Levin, lighting up a huge cigar that prompted Stone to take a step backward, "but there's demonstrations. Word is they paid off some skinhead biker gang from across the river to beat the shit out of the demonstrators."

"You know the name of the group?"

Levin gave a mirthless smile. "The Heads from Hell. They wear embroidered signs on the back of vests—"

"Colors," Stone interjected.

"Whatever," said Levin. "You'll be able to tell them by it. It's got two connected *H*'s tilted over to the side. The connected parts of the *H*'s are red and woven thicker than the rest, which is black. Looks somethin' like a red lightning bolt through a swastika."

"Wonderful." Stone grimaced. "Anything else?"

"Well, I dunno," Levin said, exhaling a deadly cloud of cigar smoke, "but when I saw your client's name in the paper? Something clicked. But it's probably nothing," Levin concluded, dismissively.

"Let's hear it, anyway."

"Those monkey handler guys? Would your client know any of them? Or would they know her? Crossed paths before or somethin' like that?"

Stone was attentive. "Not that's she's given me any indication of. Why d'you say that?"

Levin scratched the back of his head with his cigar-holding hand, spilling ashes on his collar. "The Germans. They talk German among themselves all the time. Only speak English when they have to, to talk to the locals. Probably figure none of the Americans can speak German, so they can talk in private. And they're right, I guess. But our guys hear them goin' at it, and it's like in a World War II movie, you know? Where every other German word is *jawohl* or *oberst*. And after a while, you notice it. From what I hear, *these* guys talk a lot about someone named Sara."

"What?" Stone's voice was suddenly intense, probing. "What did they say? How do you know?"

"I *don't* know," Levin protested. "This is all second and third hand, remember. It's just that the Germans say Sara a lot. Enough for some people around them who don't speak German to notice it as a familiar word they say."

Stone drew a long, slow breath. "Well, I'll certainly have to have a talk with my client about that one. Boy, you're full of good news, Ira." He put his hand to his face and pulled his nose in thought. Then his expression changed. "I didn't mean that the way it sounded, Ira. I really appreciate the information, believe me. I can use all the help I can get on this one. I'm beginning to feel I'm in over my head. I'm a real estate lawyer, for Christ's sake!"

A customer entered the store. Instantly, Ira Levin was the storekeeper everyone knew. "Counselor, you're gonna do great. You're gonna do better than Tom Dewey. Dewey hell, Oliver Wendell Holmes!"

They reached the door. As he patted Stone on the back when they walked through it, Levin muttered: "Watch your back, counselor, yours is not a popular cause."

"Thanks," Stone whispered back. Then, loudly: "See you, Ira!"

"This will do very well," said Helmar Metz, the small eyes in his heavy-boned face sweeping over the private bathroom off Georg Kramer's office suite. "The facilities are sufficient. I sleep on the sofa. The food will be brought up from your employee dining room."

Kramer, standing so close to Metz that when the burly German turned to move away from the bathroom door they nearly collided, was unhappy at the prospective intrusion. "But," he protested as he backpedaled, "wouldn't you be much more comfortable at a hotel? We could . . ."

Metz stared at Kramer for a moment, then spoke slowly and deliberately for emphasis: "I . . . am . . . not . . . here. Can't you understand that!"

Kramer looked miserable. He stood motionless, not knowing what to do or say next. Metz had no such problem. He picked up the briefcase that had been the subject of attempted theft at the airport and put it on Kramer's desk, then sat himself in Kramer's desk chair and opened the briefcase. He looked up for a moment at Kramer, said, "Sit, sit," then turned his attention to the telephone on Kramer's desk.

By those two words, and by planting himself firmly behind Kramer's desk, Metz assumed de facto command of the Riegar facility at Rhinekill, and Kramer, by sitting gingerly in a leather wing chair to the side of his own desk, confirmed it in the minds of the four vice presidents he had assembled in his office to meet Metz.

Metz busied himself removing the thin wire that led into Kramer's telephone and plugging it into a receptacle in the portable secure telephone inside the briefcase. Kramer sought to recover some of the face he had just lost before his vice presidents. "You won't need that," Kramer said. "All plants are equipped with scrambler phones to protect proprietary information in conversations with Germany. Mine is inside the long cabinet behind you."

"The scrambler system is obsolete," said Metz. "On my recommendation, it is being replaced by units like this. It uses advanced techniques for voice digitization, an enhanced LPC-10, and sophisticated digital encryption algorithm. Voice signals are transformed into a stream of digits, then encrypted by a randomly generated three-level key system that produces different combinations up to ten to the fiftieth power. Far superior to anything used in the past. Any questions?"

The vice presidents, to a man and woman, looked nearly as uncomfortable as Kramer. The three men sat on the sofa that Metz had selected as his sleeping place. The woman was seated in an armchair diagonally across from the wing chair occupied by Kramer.

The room reeked of wealth derived from science. A century-old thirty-by-forty-foot Kirman covered the floor. On the paneled wood walls hung framed and matted originals of patents issued by governments around the globe granting Riegar a long-term monopoly on drugs the world believed it could not live without. Interspersed were autographed photographs of famed inventors from Edison on up to Dr. Riegar himself, an unloved tyrant during his lifetime, now venerated as the company founder.

Kramer made the introductions. He started with the woman: "Marilyn Winter, Sales and Marketing; Steve Brikell, Production; Bob Hunt, Administration, and I believe you know Dr. Letzger, Research."

Each of those introduced mumbled in turn a polite response, except Dr. Letzger, who merely nodded. Metz gave only the barest recognition of the introductions by eyeing each in turn, adding a slight nod. He sat hunched over, elbows on the desk, hands clasped, massive shoulders straining at the seams of his suit coat.

"You are all aware of why I am here?" Metz asked the group.

"Dr. Letzger, of course, as well as myself," Kramer replied for them all, "and I thought that in view of their positions, you might want to fill in Steve, Bob, and Marilyn on a need-to-know basis."

"If I might just interject, at this point," said Marilyn Winter, "I think if we just keep cool and low-key and avoid overreacting, this whole animal-rights protest thing will have no effect on sales. I mean, our products carry no visible sign of connection to animals. It's not as if we're talking fur coats here."

"There's been no effect to date on production," chimed in Steven Brikell. "Our workers are loyal to the company, and, if anything, resent these people. I'm inclined to go along with Marilyn."

"And you, Bob?" asked Kramer, trying to reassert himself.

"Administratively, we've had no problems, and I don't foresee any. If there's any wish to change guard companies because of the incident last night, it won't be a problem. Easy to do. Rent-a-cops are all pretty much the same, though—under *their* company discipline, not ours. I want to point out," he added defensively, "that none of them report to Administration. The only analogous situation is the monkey handle . . . er, Dr. Letzger's personnel, and," he added quickly, "there has been no problem with them. I have no problem with them reporting directly to Dr. Letzger. . . ."

"What did you call Dr. Letzger's people?" asked Metz, fixing a squirming Hunt with a baleful stare and leaning even farther forward.

"I'm sorry," Hunt apologized. "It's a slang term, a nickname used by the other workers to refer to Dr. Letzger's assistants."

"All of whom were personally selected by me," said Metz.

"Yes, sir," said Hunt, flushing at his blunder.

"Thank you all for your views," Metz said. It was a dismissal. He moved back to an upright position in his chair. Then, to Letzger, he said, "Doctor, if you will stay with us please."

Letzger remained seated as the other three rose and left the room.

"Your assessment of the damage?" Metz queried.

"I don't know. The woman saw, so far as we know, only one laboratory, and it was empty of test subjects. You are familiar with the equipment that is in there. We don't know how long she was there—not long from the report. Everything was there to be photographed, but we don't know if she photographed anything at all. None were found, then or later."

"Later? What do you mean, later?" Metz leaned forward again.

Dr. Letzger read the anger in his superior's eyes and the forward lean. Letzger was good at body language.

"I believe that question would more properly be directed to Herr Kramer." Letzger and Metz were speaking English for Kramer's benefit. The lapse into the German *Herr* betrayed an anxiety otherwise masked completely.

"So?" Metz looked to Kramer.

"On my order," Kramer said, trying to be mindful about it, "two of Dr. Letzger's men searched the girl's apartment for the photographs, on the theory that she might have had an undiscovered accomplice or corrupted the guard to get them out. They found none."

"On *your* orders! You knew I would be here today. You know I am responsible for resolving this matter. And yet you use two of *my* men for something that even now must be reported to the police and can only call *more* attention . . . ach!" Metz's disgust was enough to propel him to a standing position. He started to pace.

"What else?" Metz bellowed.

"What?" said Kramer.

"What else has been done without my knowledge or approval?"

"Nothing . . . only . . ."

"Only what?"

"Some motorcycle people . . . thugs, really . . . have been recruited to make life difficult for the demonstrators."

"A further escalation! More attention called! Cancel it!"

Kramer was wilting under Metz's anger. "I'm afraid that might be hard to do. They were rather enthusiastic about the idea. I think they might have been willing to do it even without the money."

"Pay them more. 'Money talks' is an American saying, not so?"

"And bullshit walks," Kramer muttered under his breath.

"What?"

"I said I'll take care of it," Kramer said, a bit too loudly.

Metz let it go. "Good," he said, then turned from Kramer back to Letzger.

"So. Everything in the laboratory was exposed to the intruding woman, who had a camera, but no film was found. We must assume she could have seen the scale."

"Yes," Letzger agreed.

"And that at least one or more of the photographs, if any, might show it."

"Yes."

Kramer brightened as a thought occurred to him.

"She's promised a press interview. It might even develop into a conference. Her lawyer opposes it, but she wants to do it. The point is, the scale is of such importance that she could not fail to stress it if she saw it. It will be her whole story."

"She would need proof," Letzger opined. "A photograph could give her that."

"No," said Kramer, "it would be circumstantial evidence but not proof. Her lawyer would know that and certainly tell her. And without proof, the charge would be viewed as the hysterical and incredible imaginings of a woman given to extremes, such as burglary to find a pet cat—if we are to believe her—or a calculated smear by someone in the employ of competitors seeking to distract attention from her attempt at industrial espionage—our position. Either way, I think the situation can be contained."

Metz pounced. "How do you know she promised a press interview, and her lawyer opposed it?"

Kramer's expression was that of a man who's stepped into the same trap twice. "I had our security company assign one of its investigators to follow the girl and her lawyer. He overheard the conversation in a hall in the courthouse."

"I ask you again. What more have you put in motion without my authority!"

"Nothing," the hapless Kramer replied. "That's it."

"Call him off. I will handle everything from now on with the people I placed under Dr. Letzger." Metz stopped pacing and looked from Letzger to Kramer. "The other three who were just in here. They know nothing of the special laboratory work, or the object of the research?"

"Nothing," Kramer said. Letzger nodded in assent.

"I brought them up here for two reasons," Kramer continued. "One, so that they would not question your being in charge managing this particular crisis; two, because to exclude them would have caused them to wonder why."

Metz understood Kramer's first reason to be a lie. Kramer had hoped to be in control himself and impress the others with that for future reference. The tactic had backfired on him. Metz let it pass. He was content to win the engagement. Kramer wasn't fooling Letzger and certainly not himself.

"All right," said Metz, seating himself again, "the heart of our vulnerability is that we cannot suspend operations. The experiments must proceed. We are already behind schedule, and the deadline must be met. When do the next subjects arrive?"

"Tomorrow," said Letzger. "As usual. By rail to our siding."

"That's not how you ship the product when ready?"

"No. We have a dock, and the Hudson River is navigable by oceangoing vessels. The product will go by sea." Letzger rose and went to the windows overlooking the river eighteen stories below. "You can see it from here."

Mertz got up, walked over to the window, and looked down where Letzger was pointing. Between the side of the building and a heavy shipping pier was a single track siding and a traveling crane to serve either railroad flatcars or the cargo holds of a freighter. Between the large pier jutting into the river, a breakwater several hundred yards to the north, and a floating gate between them was created a huge water-filled enclosure.

Metz looked at the enclosure appreciatively. "Is it tidal?"

"Yes."

"There will be underwater machinery for the gate—piles, muck, and debris. The tide and the dredged cavity will make for powerful currents. The water will be dark, dirty, and cold."

Kramer had joined them. "I suspect you're right. How do you know?"

"I was *Kampfschwimmer* for the *Bundeskriegsmarine,*" Metz replied. "I spent much time in such places. And worse."

"Kampfschwimmer?" asked Kramer.

"Frogman for the West German navy," Letzger translated.

That, thought Kramer, accounted for the massive thickness of Metz's upper body and, perhaps, for the aggressiveness of his personality.

Metz turned away from the window, dismissing his reminiscences. "What do we know about the girl?"

"Virtually nothing," said Kramer. "She's not from around here. Came here about the time the demonstrations started. Does not appear to have much money. Lives in a very modest apartment."

"And her lawyer? He is good?"

"Him we know more about. I checked him out through our local law firm. Nothing very special. About your age—also ex-navy, I might add. Modest real estate law practice. The odd thing about him—about his being the lawyer for this girl—is that so far as anyone can remember, this is his first criminal-law case. It's something of a mystery why she chose him. Other than that he's probably quite cheap compared to an established criminal lawyer."

"So?" Metz raised his eyebrows. "Some romantic attachment, perhaps?"

"Not unless it developed in the last twenty-four hours. Maybe she was looking for a bodyguard as much as a lawyer. He's a big guy, ex-athlete, who's said to spend as much time keeping in shape as practicing law. But a loner. Nobody close to him."

Metz digested Kramer's information. Then he said, "Those ruffians with the motorcycles. Have them test him. I want to know what we're up against in him. And have that security company try to find out anything on the girl's background. I want it quickly. Double the security guards; that would be normal in a situation like this. And, Dr. Letzger, I want to speak privately with all your men as soon as they can be assembled."

Progress came slowly, if at all, to Rhinekill. So it was that the telephone booth into which Michael Stone had stuffed his broad shoulders was the old-fashioned, total-enclosure kind. The fan didn't work, so to keep from being stifled, Stone propped the door open as he spoke to Aunt May.

"But she's my client, and there's a number of things I need to talk to her about as soon as possible. . . ."

"Now you listen to me, young man! That girl is exhausted. She fell asleep in the bathtub. Didn't wake up till the water got cold. I put her to bed, and that's where she's staying till she wakes up again. Then I'm going to feed her a good hot meal and send her back to bed. There's nothing you have to talk about that's so important it can't wait until morning."

"Okay, okay, morning. But is it all right if I come over and pick up a few more things? I need some athletic stuff and underwear."

"You may so long as you don't try to bother Sara."

"Promise. Any mail?"

"Just the latest case supplement from West Publishing and a navy-reunion final reminder for you—"

Stone felt a pang at the mention of the navy reunion and cut off Aunt May. "File the case supplement for me, will you, Mazie? And stick the reunion notice in the letter holder on my desk."

"All right." Aunt May continued as if uninterrupted, "—some bills for me and a package for Sara."

"A package for Sara! Addressed to 182 Garden?"

"Yes."

Stone's mind raced. "Has she seen it yet?"

"I told you, she's asleep. I'm not going to wake her up for some mail."

"Where is it now?"

"On the table in the law library, where I always leave the mail."

"Mazie. Listen to me carefully. Wake up Sara. Throw a robe on her and get her and yourself out of the house. Do it now! I'm on my way."

"I'll do no such thing! I'll not have that young girl running around outside in her bathrobe! What's all this about, for heaven's sake?"

Stone invoked his command voice from his navy days: "Mazie, do as I told you! Immediately! Take her in the backyard if you're worried about how she looks. And don't tell her about the package. She'll be curious and want to open it. Don't *touch* it. I'll explain when I get there, which'll be as fast as I can."

5

MICHAEL STONE'S MIND WAS RACING FASTER THAN the Mustang as he turned it onto Garden Street. The nearest bomb squad was in New York City, eighty miles south. Handling the package that was lying on the conference-room table would be up to him. He searched his memory for what he had learned in Explosive Ordnance Disposal class years ago and grimaced at the first thing that popped into his mind, Master Chief Swenson smiling at the class and announcing, "Just in case there's any swingin' dick here ain't motivated to pay attention, remember rule number one." The smile widened to a grin. "You fuck up, you blow up. Any questions?"

As he swerved into his driveway, Stone had plenty of questions—and few answers. The problem with the EOD course was that it was named correctly, explosive *ordnance* disposal. All sorts of mines, from pressure to magnetic, but no letter bombs. He'd have to rely on general principles.

Aunt May and Sara Rosen were waiting under the porte cochere as Stone drove up to it. Before he could get out of the car, Sara was at the driver's side window. She looked ridiculous, swallowed up as she was in his terry-cloth robe, but any inclination he had to laugh was suppressed by the look on her face and the tone of exasperation in her voice as she said, "Now, what!"

Stone decided that he could deal at that moment with a bomb or Sara Rosen, but not with a bomb *and* Sara Rosen. He got out of the car and pretended she wasn't there, waving to Aunt May as he disappeared behind the house. He emerged a moment later carrying a garden spade in one hand and a garbage-can lid in the other, then walked swiftly to the front door. Aunt May let him in, then held up her hand as Sara attempted to follow.

"When they get like that," Aunt May said to Sara, "it's best to just let them finish whatever they've got their mind set on. It's some 'man' thing. No matter how silly it may seem to us, there's no point in even trying to discuss it with them. They won't listen. Not to do whatever it is would strike directly at their masculine identity and self-esteem. Just let it go."

Sara looked hard at Aunt May but made no further attempt to follow Stone.

"That's pretty perceptive stuff," Sara said, her voice respectful. "Did you major in psych?"

Aunt May smiled. "I lived with one of those creatures for forty-seven years. I suppose you could say so!"

Before Aunt May could continue, Stone's voice came from behind the door.

"Mazie! Open the door please. Then you two get back away from it."

Aunt May did as he asked, shepherding Sara back with her behind the Mustang. A moment later, Michael Stone emerged, holding the spade at arm's length in front of him with his right hand, his left holding the garbage-can lid in front of him like a shield. Most of his face was covered by a skin diver's face mask. Lying on the end of the spade was an eight-by-ten-inch manila envelope bearing a postage-meter stamp and hand-printed address. Sara stared at it, then at Stone, then put her left hand over her mouth and pressed her right hand tightly into her midriff. Aunt May watched her with concern as her body began to shake, then bend forward from the waist. Tears streamed from Sara's eyes. She gasped for breath, then slumped against the Mustang and started to slap the cloth roof.

Alarmed, Aunt May was at her side in a moment. The movement caught the attention of Stone. He saw the look of concern on his aunt's face. Quickly, he walked into the backyard, lay the spade and its contents down on the grass, dropped the garbage-can lid, and removed the face mask as he ran back to where Aunt May was now holding a gasping and protesting Sara Rosen.

As Michael Stone reached the two women, the look of concern on his face turned to chagrin, then anger. Sara was still holding her midriff, but now her left hand was stretched out before her, pointing directly at Stone. She was trying to speak, but couldn't. She was laughing too hard. Seeing the dark look on Stone's face, Sara tried to control herself. It was a losing battle. She'd just about stop, then start to giggle again, convulsively.

"What," Stone demanded, "is so goddamn funny!"

Sara looked at him, then turned away to laugh again.

"Listen," said Stone, "I've got what may well be a bomb over there, okay? And I suppose 'better laugh than cry' and all that, but this is no time for hysterics. So control yourself, all right?" Stone switched his attention to Aunt May. His voice exasperated, he asked, "How do you get the water supply to that old horse trough out back to work, Mazie?"

Sara gulped air, then shook her head and said, "No."

"What?" said Stone.

"It's not . . ." Sara struggled to keep control. "It's not . . . a . . . bomb."

"Look," said Stone, "your apartment's trashed in a professional search. Now you get a large letter addressed to you here, where no one could know you are unless we've been followed. So what do *you* think it is, the Welcome Wagon?"

Sara Rosen composed herself. "*I* sent that package. It's the photographs I took at Riegar. Remember, I told you with any luck I'd be able to show them to you? Well, thanks to Riegar and the post office, I can!"

"You mean you—"

"Right!" Sara interrupted. "When I was hiding in that steno area, it was easy to just use their stuff. I looked up your address in the Yellow Pages, put the pictures in between some of their stationery to keep them from rattling around in their envelope—look at the return address—"

"I did," said Stone. "It made me even more suspicious."

Sara ignored the interruption and kept on speaking. "—and counted on the universal spirit of bureaucracy to carry on. I just threw it in their Outgoing."

Aunt May walked to the door, saying, "Well, I think I'll go back inside." She opened the door, paused, and said, "Michael, please don't forget to put back my spade and garbage-can lid." Then she closed the door behind her. The door was no sooner closed than Sara lost control again.

"Do . . . you . . . have . . . any . . . idea what you l . . . looked like in that m . . . mask holding that shovel out in fr . . . front of you and . . . and . . . with that *garbage-can lid!*"

"Shit," said Michael Stone.

Helmar Metz ushered out the door of Kramer's office the last of the contingent of men he had assigned to assist Dr. Letzger, then glanced at his watch as he crossed the room to resume his seat behind the desk. The portable secure phone's transmit-mode switch was still in the Encrypt position. He switched it to Clear. Then, consulting a small notebook he retrieved from his inside jacket pocket, Metz dialed direct to the home of Walter Hoess. A male servant answered in a clipped East Prussian-accented German that annoyed Metz, whose family name was derived from the city his ancestors had helped take from France in 1870. As a result of World War II, Metz was once again in France and East Prussia now in Poland. Where did this flunky get off trying to high-hat people with that accent?

Metz's reverie was interrupted by Walter Hoess. "Yes, Metz?"

"Would it be convenient for you to take this call from your library and use the machine, sir?"

"I am in the library. Switching modes." There was a pause, then Hoess's voice took on a metallic note: "What news?"

"It's worse than I had imagined, sir. Security utterly lax when one considers the consequences of discovery. In my entire conversation with Kramer, he concentrated upon what the woman who penetrated may have seen and photographed, yet it never occurred to him that his own guard, the one who captured the woman and is nothing more than an outside contract employee, saw everything she did! My men with Letzger tell me that when the experiments are going on, all doors are locked and no unauthorized personnel could ever view any actual activities, but—"

Hoess cut him off. "You are taking the necessary measures to correct the situation?"

"Yes, sir. The obvious is being done. Guards no longer have access to any sensitive areas, either in experimentation or production. I am following the penetration business closely. Have I your permission to make Kramer aware of the situation with your son?"

Hoess's voice took on a tone of anxiety. "No! I was to tell no one, remember? Why? Are you having trouble with Kramer?"

"No, no. He is loyal. But, of course, the sudden crash program for the new product and the danger involved I am sure have him curious. He is certainly nervous. I just thought perhaps if he understood the true stakes—"

"No, and . . . you're sure this device is secure?"

"I've bet my life on it a number of times."

"You're betting my son's life on it now."

"We have to be able to communicate, sir. There are always risks. In this instance, I believe the risk is minimal."

There was a long pause, then Hoess said, "I don't suppose you've heard anything new about 'The Man.' "

"Who has your son? No. Only what I told you before I left. 'Al Rajul' translates from Arabic as 'The Man.' All my intelligence-community sources tell me it's part of a longer descriptive name, such as 'the man faithful to the prophet,' or something or other. The point is, it's not a proper name, like Mohammad Abbas. No one knows his true name. There are no photographs of him. Nothing. All that is known is that he is more clever than Carlos and more deadly than Abu Nidal. I got that from the French. They think the Israelis may know a bit more, but not much. Whatever the Israelis know is closely held.

They want to kill him and don't want some idealistic Americans messing it up trying to capture him for a trial."

"I don't suppose," said Hoess, "that you have any Israeli sources?"

"My father was *Gauleiter* of Metz after we took back Alsace-Lorraine."

"Yes. Well, carry on. The sooner I can meet the demands of this 'Rajul,' the sooner I get back my son."

"You have heard further?"

"Just another videotape. He appears well."

"When this is over, sir, I shall take pleasure in killing the swine personally."

Hoess sighed in resignation. "If the Jews can't kill him, it isn't likely you will."

"He's not dealing with the Jews. He's dealing with us. All I need is the slightest slip—"

"And all *I* need is my son, alive and unharmed. You will do nothing to jeopardize that. Nothing! Do you understand?"

"Yes, sir."

Hoess's voice was controlled again. "Very well. Keep me informed."

Michael Stone stood before the closet in his bedroom and eyed his wardrobe. As a result of his years in the navy, he was long on uniforms and short on civilian clothes. He owned exactly two suits. One of them he had on, a brown sharkskin he had worn to court that morning. He retrieved the other from the closet. It was a dark blue wool, a uniform in its own right, what lawyers call their 'Court of Appeals suit.' He slipped it into a garment bag, then added four shirts, two white and two blue, and some conservative ties. That left a gray Harris tweed sport coat and two pair of slacks, both gray, one a light shade and the other dark. He packed the light ones, figuring he could always wear the trousers from the blue suit with the sport coat. Stone wasn't sure just how long he'd be at the hotel, but there wasn't any point in dragging over everything he owned.

Stone took a supply of socks and briefs, then noted with a barely audible grunt that he was short of undershirts. He looked through some of his athletic clothes, found a couple of white navy T-shirts that had some service emblems on them, and packed them on the theory that they'd do double duty; he could wear them to work out or, in a pinch, as underwear—no one could see the emblems through a blue dress shirt, anyway.

As Michael Stone came down the stairs, his aunt May was at the bottom of them, calling up to him. "Michael, we're having something to eat." Stone smiled at her. "You're saving my life, Mazie. What've you got?"

Aunt May turned and led the way into the kitchen, saying, "Tuna-salad sandwiches, potato salad, and lettuce and tomato. Fruit for dessert."

As promised, it was all laid out on the kitchen table. So were eight Polaroid color photographs. Sara Rosen, in her new jeans, was leaning over them. Her face was triumphant. "I got them! Ziegler chairs, Blaylock press, Collison cannulas, Noble-Collip drum, even a Horsley-Clarke stereo-taxic device. I'll wait till you've finished eating before I tell you what they're used for."

Stone took a large portion of potato salad and offered some to Sara Rosen. She wrinkled up her nose at it, reached for the lettuce and tomatoes, and said, "Sandwiches *and* potato salad? Keep that up and you won't fit in that little car of yours."

The reference to his brutish Mustang as a 'little car' did not sit well with Michael Stone. His displeasure took the form of a lecture on the virtues of potato salad. "The trouble with you people who subsist on a diet of rabbit food is that you tend to be moody." Stone waved his salad fork up and down in the air describing an invisible graph with large swings. "Your blood sugar goes up and down, up and down, and so does your strength and your mood. This stuff," he said, indicating the potato salad, "is a starch—a complex carbohydrate. It breaks down slowly, over a period of time, and you keep a level blood-sugar rate. That gives you continuing stamina and a calm, level personality."

"Hah!" exclaimed Aunt May. "Your uncle Harry *loved* my potato salad, and he had a temper like I've seen in someone *else* around here!"

"Mazie," said Stone, "how can you say that about Sara? You've hardly met her."

"You dreadful creature," said Aunt May as she cleared away Stone's dishes.

Sara Rosen thought it a good time to change the subject. "Okay," she said, indicating the photographs, "let's look at the evidence." She picked up the first print. "Blaylock press. Know what it's used for?"

Stone looked at the device shown in the photograph. It looked like an old-fashioned printing press. The top and bottom plates, which looked as if they were made of heavy steel, had ridges running the length of their opposing surfaces. "Haven't any idea," said Stone.

Sara pointed to what looked like an automobile spring compressible by tightening four nuts. "That spring can force those ridged plates together with a pressure of five thousand pounds per square inch. They use it to crush the muscles in an animal's legs without crushing the bone. Nice, huh?"

Stone concealed his discomfort with a question. "Why is it called a Blaylock press?"

"All these things are named after the bastards who invented them. They insist upon it. They're proud of the efficiency of their torture devices. They write them up in the medical journals!" Sara glanced at Aunt May. "Excuse the language please, ma'am."

Aunt May was bent over from putting the last of the dishes into the dishwasher. She straightened up, then said, "Judging from your description of what they do with those awful things, I'd say your choice of words was appropriate." So saying, Aunt May pushed herself through the swinging door to the hall, leaving Stone and Sara alone in the kitchen.

Sara handed Stone another photograph. In it was what appeared to be a small, completely enclosed Ferris wheel. "Noble-Collip Drum," said Sara. "Works like a big exercise wheel. You know, like they have in squirrel cages. Only all over the surface of the raceway are knobs and bumps. They put an animal in there—anything from a dog to an ape, say—and turn the damn thing on. The drum revolves and the poor thing inside it has to run at whatever speed the operator sets it. The only thing is, it's hard to do because the projections keep banging into the victim. They try to jump over them at first, but after a while they're exhausted and the machine does its work—produces traumatic shock without hemorrhage."

Stone looked grim. "What's the excuse for a thing like that?"

"There isn't any."

"Yeah. But what do they say it's for?"

"I told you. Produces traumatic shock without hemorrhage—so they can 'study' it. They've been 'studying' it since 1942."

"Why?"

"Because the government and foundations keep giving them grants to do it. Good as that thing is at producing trauma, it's even better at producing money!"

Sara handed Stone another Polaroid print. "Ziegler Chair. You can fasten a monkey or an ape into that steel seat so that it absolutely can't move any part of its body—but large parts of the body are still exposed for you to do anything you want to them, no matter how much pain they feel or how much they scream and try to escape. They're completely helpless. Except maybe for the head. They can wriggle their heads a little. So"—Sara produced another photograph and handed it to Stone—"we have the Horsley-Clarke stereo-taxic device."

Stone examined the collection of connected rods adjustable by thumbscrews. Their chromium finish shone brightly, and the device gave the impression of being a precision instrument.

"I can't figure it out," said Stone.

"Say you've got an ape, or a monkey—or even a cat, like my Romeo," Sara said, her eyes misting and her breath starting to be irregular. Michael Stone caught the signal of Sara's emotion and quickly moved to get her mind off her lost cat. "What," he asked, "is the difference between an ape and a monkey?"

Sara snapped out of it. "Not to bore you with a lot of biology, monkeys have tails and apes don't. Gibbons are little things, so people call them monkeys. But they have no tails, so they're apes. People are *always* calling chimps monkeys. But they have no tails, either, so they're apes. *You*'re an ape, unless you've got something in your pants I don't know about."

Stone smiled. "Want to check?"

"No, thank you," Sara replied. "I'll take your word for it."

"So, how does this thing work?" Stone asked, handing the photograph back to Sara.

Sara looked straight into Stone's eyes and spoke slowly, for effect. "First comes blinding, 'enucleation,' they call it. Removal of the eyeballs. Then two steel rods attached to a steel frame are stuck into the empty sockets. Two more are inserted into the mouth and attached to the same frame. The whole head is then clamped into the rigid frame, eye sockets, mouth, and skull all held tightly in the grip of those finely adjusted steel rods. Any movement is impossible."

"But what is it *for?*" asked Stone, the revulsion clear in his voice.

"Well," said Sara, "for one thing, for these." She produced another photograph. Stone studied it. The objects depicted in it were small and round in appearance. Stone shook his head.

"I know," said Sara, "it isn't very clear. They're Collison cannulas. With the head clamped in the stereo-taxic device, they put a hole in the skull, insert the cannula, and then they can repeatedly pass anything they want through it directly into the brain—electric stimulation, hypodermic needles, stuff like that."

"The other three photos?" Stone inquired.

"Just a couple of other views of the same things."

Michael Stone stared out the kitchen window for several moments, digesting what Sara Rosen had told him. Finally, he said, "Those are very sick people. Very sick."

"And all to no good purpose!" Sara exclaimed. "It's not just that animal experimentation doesn't achieve anything for the benefit of man; it's actually counterproductive! In the first place, after a new product has been tested out on animals, they have to test it on humans before it can be used. That's the law. Human testing is required for FDA approval. And the animal testing is useless. I know the FDA requires that, too, before human testing, but it's stupid, unscientific. There are too many fundamental differences between humans and other animals. The date gathered are just not validly transferable from animals to humans. Or vice versa, for that matter. Ask a vet. It's *stupid.* Now do you see why I want to show those pictures at a press conference?"

"No," said Michael Stone, "I don't. *That* would be stupid."

"What!"

"And, to coin a phrase, 'counterproductive.' "

Sara Rosen looked hard at Michael Stone. He was serious. "You want to explain that?" she asked.

"Item one," said Stone, "your self-interest. You produce those photographs and claim you took them inside Riegar, and you might just as well plead guilty at your arraignment tomorrow. You make the prosecution's case for them. And I remind you that we're not dealing with turning left from the right-hand lane here. You're charged with Burglary Two, for which you could get real time. And giving you real time could be a smart thing to do politically around here right now. You may not know it, but in the state of New York, judges are elected like aldermen in Chicago.

"Item two: your cause. The devices shown in those photographs are empty. For there to be any shock value to what's in them requires your description of what they're used for. But, as they stand, from the point of view of the press, they aren't very sexy. On top of that, the appeal you make with the pictures is to the emotions. Aren't you the one who said to me something like 'everyone thinks our position is based on emotion and bleeding-heart-fuzzy-good-for-animals shit'?"

Sara Rosen looked down at the table. Stone, she knew, was right.

"One more thing," Stone said, "you use those photographs, and I'll withdraw as your counsel. I've got better things to do than waste my time."

Sara Rosen blew up. "Don't give me ultimatums!"

Stone realized he had gone too far. He should have quit while he was ahead. He waited a minute, then said, "Ultimata."

Sara stared at him, then started to smile. In unison, they both said, "The plural of *ultimatum* is *ultimata*." The tension between them dissolved in laughter.

"You feel up to making a report on your apartment to the police yet?"

Sara Rosen shrugged. "Sure," she said, "why not?" Then, gathering up the Polaroid photographs, she asked, "What should I do with these?"

"Give them to me," said Stone. "I'll put them in the office safe."

As Michael Stone escorted his client in through the front door of the Rhinekill police station, he gave her some last-minute counseling.

"Remember, you're here to report a burglary. A *new* burglary. You have nothing whatever to say about the one you're charged with."

"*I* know that," said Sara, annoyed.

"Fine," said Stone, "just don't forget it. I wouldn't put it past them to try to slip in a question that, if you answer it, will be an admission against interest."

Immediately inside the entrance to the station was a large two-story-high room. Only near the corners of the room was there any varnish left on the hardwood floor. To the right, a heavy banistered stairway led to the floor above. Directly across from them, against the rear wall and dominating the room, was a platform, almost a stage. Across the front of the stage and around the sides was the only clean thing in the room, a brightly polished brass rail. Behind the rail sat an immense desk and behind it an almost equally immense man, dressed in the uniform of a sergeant of the Rhinekill police department. He had been sitting behind the desk in the fetid atmosphere of the un-air-conditioned room for hours, and his uniform had a wrinkle for every minute of every hour. The sergeant's face matched his uniform, wrinkle for wrinkle. He recognized Michael Stone as he and Sara Rosen approached the desk and gazed upward at him.

"Yessir, counselor, how can I help you?"

"Thank you, Sergeant"—Stone read the sign on the edge of the middle of the desk—"Caughlin. My client, Sara Rosen, would like to report the burglary of her apartment."

Sergeant Caughlin looked down at them benignly. "Seems every time I hear your client's name, it's in connection with a burglary, counselor." As Stone started to respond, Caughlin held up his hand as if to fend him off. "Yeah, yeah, I know. Take a seat over there." Caughlin gestured toward some ancient benches lining the wall to his right. "I'll see if I can get someone down to take your complaint." He picked up a telephone, pushed a few buttons, and spoke into it in a low voice, turning his head far around away from them as he did so, effectively keeping his conversation private.

Michael Stone ushered his client over to a bench, where they sat down to what Stone was certain would be a long and boring wait. To his surprise, within minutes a stocky middle-aged man with a florid face and equally florid sport coat and clashing trousers came down the stairway and walked over to them. He held out his hand, first to Stone, then Sara, and introduced himself in a smooth voice that belied his rubelike appearance.

"Walt Fisher," he said, "detective division. Why don't you folks follow me, and we'll get you all fixed up." With that, Fisher turned and led them across the room, up the stairway, and into a small room bearing the soiled sign INTERVIEW ROOM NO. 3. Inside the room was a wooden table in the middle of the floor. There were four chairs arranged around the table and another two, one each in the far corners. The rest of the room was bare except for a single light bulb, suspended high up toward the ceiling in the middle of what to Stone looked like the same kind of green enameled shades used to shield the lights on the outdoor platforms of the railroad station.

Fisher annoyed Stone by adopting a familiar tone in addressing his client. "Now, then, Sara, tell me about it," Fisher said, pencil poised above a notepad.

Sara Rosen had seen a lot of movies and television. "My name is Sara Rosen . . . Sara without the *h*. I reside at 1337 Clifton Avenue, apartment 5-B. About noon today, when my lawyer here, Mr. Stone, drove me home from court, I went up to my apartment and found it had been broken into and trashed. Everything all over the place. Like it was searched. The place is a complete wreck. I want you to come with me and see it."

"I'll take your word for it," said Fisher. "Let's see. You say you discovered this about noon. It's now . . ." Fisher glanced at his watch and wrote the time down. "Five thirty-four. Seems to me that if someone had done this to *my* place, I'd have been down here on the double."

"You mean," Sara burst out, "you're not going over to take pictures and fingerprints and everything . . . !"

"Ms. Rosen," said Stone, "had spent the night in the county jail and had not had the opportunity to either eat or bathe. She was exhausted from being driven all over hell's half acre last night. She has been with counsel and is here as soon as counsel thought it appropriate." Stone looked hard at Fisher. There was something about him that looked familiar, but he couldn't place it.

Fisher put his index finger into his left ear and wiggled it around, trying to scratch an itch he couldn't reach. "You have a list of what was taken?" he asked.

Sara looked down at her hands. "The only thing missing is my . . . my dirty laundry and . . ." She thought of the douche nozzle but couldn't bring herself to mention it. "And some personal items of no value."

"That's it?" said Fisher. "That's all that's missing?"

Fisher made a last note on his pad, then raised his eyes and said, "Okay, I'll have some men over to photograph and dust the place first thing tomorrow morning. How's eight o'clock?"

"Ms. Rosen," said Stone, "has a court appearance tomorrow morning. Plus, she'd like to get her apartment cleaned up. Could you send over some people now?"

"Now?" Fisher looked at his watch and frowned. "I dunno . . ."

"They'd be over there in a flash if there'd been a murder," Stone said.

"This ain't no murder, here, counselor. You weren't there. I wasn't there. No one knows what really happened over there—"

"Well, *I* wasn't there, either!" Sara exploded. "I don't know what you're trying to imply, but—"

"Okay, okay. *I'*ll grab a camera and a dusting kit and go over with you now, all right?" He got to his feet. "I'll meet you over there."

Stone and Sara Rosen rose to leave. "Oh," Fisher said, as if it was an afterthought, "we'll need your fingerprints, Ms. Rosen . . . to eliminate them from whatever we find."

Sara's voice was scathing. "You already *have* my prints, remember?"

"Right," said Fisher. "I forgot." He looked speculatively at Stone. "Anyone else's prints we should have . . . for elimination purposes?"

Stone could sense what was going through Fisher's mind, and he didn't like it. "When I looked at her apartment at my client's request, I touched the front doorknobs, the open window shade, and the bathroom door. If you need my prints, just call my office and I'll come right down." He took Sara by the elbow and guided her out of the room, down the stairs, and out to his car, expressing his contempt for Fisher's speculations by being careful not to glance back even once to see whether the detective was following.

6

ON STEPHANIE HANNIGAN'S SALARY AS AN ASSIST-
ant public defender, a Honda Prelude was sheer extravagance. The
payments, even on a five-year note, left little over for her other needs.
Nevertheless, she never regretted buying the first new car she had ever
owned. She rationalized that its front-wheel drive helped her get
through winter snow to make court appearances when a postponement
would mean extra days in jail for those too poor to make bail, but the
truth was that she enjoyed the attention her little yellow coupe drew
as she darted about the county. This morning, for the first time,
Stephanie wished she had a nondescript car.

This late in May, at shortly after 6 A.M., it was already bright
daylight, and the Honda's yellow paint glowed in the morning sun.
Stephanie Hannigan was sure that the few people on the streets of
downtown Rhinekill noticed her as she drove past and made mental
notes to tell everyone they knew. Although she had the right to park
in one of the spaces designated PUBLIC DEFENDER ONLY directly in front
of the entrance to her office, Stephanie parked blocks away and walked
to it. Not until she was inside, and her guess that no one else would

be in the office that early had proven correct, did she relax somewhat. Stephanie was not used to clandestine activities, even of the most innocent kind.

The big electric clock on the wall of the main file room of the public defender's office said 6:12 as Stephanie opened the drawer marked PRECEDENTS. She looked through them quickly, removing now one, then another copy of pretrial motions filed in past cases by her office, motions that had been successful in seeking suppression by the courts of alleged confessions, or of evidence seized by police in a manner contrary to the Fourth Amendment to the Constitution. That done, she selected motions that had been used to compel the district attorney to reveal and produce evidence that was exculpatory of the defendant and inconsistent with the theory of guilt. For good measure, she threw in some motions to dismiss the prosecution's entire case for various reasons, then, tiptoeing although there was no need to do so, she moved to the copying machine and turned it on.

The noise of the copying machine in the empty office seemed to Stephanie Hannigan loud enough to attract attention from outside the building. In addition, it masked her ability to hear anyone entering. Consequently, as she copied each page, Stephanie became ever more anxious. Nevertheless, she proceeded steadily until her task was finished and, with a sigh of relief, she could turn off the machine and return the material she had copied to its proper place in the files, slip the new copies into her briefcase, and make her way out of the building.

It was, Stephanie noted to herself as she sank into the bucket seat of the Prelude, the second time in as many days that she had made off with precedent files from her employer's office, and both times for the sake of a man she hardly knew: Michael Stone. Better not analyze that too closely, she thought, just go with the flow.

Michael Stone was "always exercising down at the athletic center," Stephanie had recalled from the remarks passed at city court the day before. That would be an ideal location, she had thought, to effect the covert transfer of the purloined precedent files, if only she knew when Stone would be there. That problem had been solved last night by a telephone call to her friend Naomi Fine. Naomi, the deputy county clerk, had custody of all the real estate—transaction recordings in the county. That was her job. Her hobby was the informal tracking of those few unmarried males in Rhinekill over the age of puberty and not yet senile who had what Naomi considered "prospects."

"He has prospects only because he's a lawyer, and with them you can never tell . . . no offense. He doesn't make much, but he's going to inherit a nice house. You could do better."

"Naomi! I just want to know when he exercises at the athletic center."

"Sure. And I've got a date Saturday night with Clyde Beatty."

"That's Warren Beatty."

"Whoever. He should be there tomorrow morning, six to eight. But don't try to swim with him. You'll drown, and he won't notice. It's been tried."

"Naomi!"

Stephanie Hannigan's glasses fogged immediately when she entered the fifty-meter indoor pool area at the athletic center. She had to take them off to make her way to the grandstand, where she sat in the first row and surveyed the pool. It was divided into lanes by lines kept on the surface by buoyant plastic floats that resembled multicolored beads as they shimmered in the water. Men and women swam back and forth in the lanes.

There was only one swimmer in the lane closest to Stephanie: a large male wearing a faded racing swimsuit, goggles, and a dark blue rubber cap. He was swimming an odd breaststroke, his legs just dragging behind him, supported by a float between his ankles. When the swimmer stopped to put aside the float, resembling a white dumbbell, he removed his goggles, and she recognized Michael Stone.

Stephanie resisted the impulse to wave to attract Stone's attention. Instead, she watched him, quietly. There was a battery-operated electric clock with a sweep second that had been set up on the deck at one end of Stone's lane. It must have been, Stephanie estimated, almost three feet in diameter. Stone glanced at it, waited until the second hand was straight up, then launched himself into a powerful butterfly stroke.

Stephanie wiped off her glasses and put them back on. Adjusted to the temperature now, the lenses stayed clear. As he passed directly beneath her, she could see the muscles in Stone's back ripple like a little wave from the base of his neck and shoulders, down the broad planes of his back, through the narrows of his waist, to disappear into tight buttocks more revealed than concealed by his wet and nearly transparent skintight racing suit.

Although she knew it was the long, loose muscles of his arms and legs, moving in what seemed an effortless rhythm, that propelled Michael Stone at speed through the water, it seemed to Stephanie that he really moved through that sensuous ripple like a marine mammal she had seen once at an aquarium in her childhood—the one all the other children called a dolphin but, she remembered her teacher saying, was really a porpoise. As Stone passed back and forth beneath her, Stephanie became mesmerized by the ripple, her concentration on it unbroken until he changed his stroke to freestyle, swimming powerfully past her ten more times as he warmed down for a final five hundred meters, then propelled himself out of the pool with an easy push of his arms against the deck. Only then, as he stood, water sheeting off his body, breathing as if he had just walked across a room, not put in ten thousand meters of hard swimming, did Stephanie call out to Michael Stone.

"Mr. Stone!" Her voice reverberated throughout the cavernous pool enclosure. Stone gave no sign that he had heard her. Instead, he peeled off his cap; then, one by one, he removed plugs from each ear. Stephanie tried again, her voice lower this time, and accompanied by a vigorous wave.

Stone glanced up at her, hesitated a moment, then recognition swept across his face and he smiled. Stephanie gestured toward the door. Stone looked puzzled. Frustrated, and not wanting to call out yet again and attract unwanted attention to the two of them, Stephanie held her arms out straight in front of her, fists gripping an imaginary steering wheel, which she proceeded to rotate right and left rapidly, then gestured again toward the door and the parking lot. Stone nodded, acknowledging her message, and, with a wave, entered the men's locker room.

As Michael Stone walked out into the athletic center's parking lot, Stephanie Hannigan was sitting in her car, looking into her rearview mirror and putting the finishing touches onto her mouth with a dark pink lipstick. She squeezed her lips together, nodded approvingly at her reflection, put the lipstick back into her purse, then returned her attention to the building's door.

Stone, seeing no one waiting in the lot for him, concluded he had misinterpreted Stephanie's signal, shrugged, and was about to enter his car when he heard a horn blow. He looked toward the sound and there was Stephanie, waving wildly from the window of a yellow Honda Prelude. He walked over to her, smiled, and said, "Your car or mine?"

"Hop in," said Stephanie.

Stone settled into the right bucket seat of the yellow coupe and asked, "Where're we going?"

Stephanie produced her briefcase. It was awkward getting it open in the small confines of the front seat, but she managed it. "Nowhere," she said. "I just didn't want anyone seeing me give you this stuff."

"What . . ."

"Precedents. Should be just about everything you'll need to get your burglary client a fair shake."

"You sure we both don't go to jail if I use this?"

"You're welcome. And not if you keep your mouth shut about where you got it, if the subject ever comes up."

Stone tried to cover his embarrassment by leafing through Stephanie's offerings, then he turned to face her squarely. "This is good stuff. I really appreciate it. Thank you."

Stephanie looked away and stared at the dashboard. With a small voice, she said, "It's okay."

Stone felt decidedly uncomfortable. He noticed Stephanie's thigh straining against the cloth of her white linen suit and he guiltily shifted his glance upward to her face. Its troubled expression saddened him. He felt as if he'd just blown something important. He wanted it back.

"Look," he said clumsily, "I've got an indictment and pleading this morning at ten, then a press conference to monitor that I'm not at all happy about. It would be a late one, but could I buy you lunch? There's a little place across the bridge overlooking the river I've been meaning to try out. How about it?"

Stephanie faced him. "Okay. Thank you. But let's make it dutch. Give me a call when your press conference is over."

"Deal. But I wish you'd reconsider the dutch thing. I'm not trying to compromise your independence. You've done me a hell of a favor, and I'm in the middle of making a mess of trying to say thank you."

Stephanie smiled. "Oh, you're not doing such a bad job. I'll think about it. Give me a call when you're ready."

Stone got out of the car. "Thanks," he said, "see you later."

Stephanie started the Prelude and drove away. Stone watched her go. He felt something in the pit of his stomach that he hadn't felt for so long, he had thought it was a part of youth one grew out of and he'd never feel again. Distracted, he turned and walked back to his car.

"What's going on out there?" Judge Louis Carlini of the Mohawk county court was leaning through the doorway of his clerk's office and gesturing with his head toward the hallway outside.

"It's the television people, Your Honor. They're setting up for a press conference in the hall after the plea to the Rosen indictment. The rest of them—there's a lot—are in your courtroom to cover the plea. Then they all move out into the hall."

"Not *my* hall, they're not. What, they think the Rosen indictment's the only one we've got this morning? And the motions afterward? The court's supposed to conduct its business with a circus going on outside in the hall? You tell them to go downstairs and make arrangements— no, send the bailiff. Tell them if nobody objects, they can use the downstairs lobby; otherwise, they're out in the street. This is a court of justice, for Christ's sake!"

Some twenty minutes later, the bailiff in Judge Carlini's courtroom intoned "All rise" and Judge Carlini, to his surprise, took the bench of a packed courtroom. There was not another seat to be had, he noted. Only trials of the most bizarre murders, usually with a twisted sexual angle, had drawn this much attendance in the past. Like the rest of the seats, the press section was filled.

"Will the district attorney and"—Carlini looked down at some papers on his desk—"Mr. Stone approach the bench."

Stone and a graying man of forty rose and walked up as close to the front of Judge Carlini's desk as they could get. To the judge's left front, a small middle-aged man at a stenotype machine leaned forward to catch the conversation and record it. Judge Carlini leaned forward and said, in a voice cast to travel but the necessary few feet, "Mr. Holden, who's handling this matter for your office?"

"I'll take it myself, Your Honor."

Michael Stone was taken aback; the district attorney rarely handled a trial himself unless it was a notorious murder. It was unheard of for him to handle an arraignment. He must be responding to all the press interest, Stone thought.

"All right," Carlini said, "I think most of the people in the room are here for the Rosen plea, so I'm going to take it out of order so we can clear these people out and handle the rest of today's matters without all the potential for commotion. Any objection?"

"No, Your Honor," the two men said in unison.

"All right, then," Carlini said. As the two lawyers returned to their seats, the judge waved over the court clerk. "Call *People* v. *Rosen.*"

"*People* v. *Rosen,*" the clerk called out dutifully.

The district attorney rose. "Warren Holden for the People."

"For the defendant, Michael Stone."

"All right," said the judge, "will the defendant please rise?"

Sara stood up next to Stone. "Sara Rosen, you are accused in an indictment handed down by the grand jury of Mohawk County of one count of burglary in the second degree in that on or about—"

"May it please the court," Michael Stone said, "defendant waives further reading of the indictment and is ready to plead."

The request was so routine, Judge Carlini didn't wait to hear whether there was any objection from the district attorney. "Without objection, motion to waive further reading granted. How does the defendant plead?"

"Not guilty, Your Honor."

"A plea of not guilty will be entered," chanted the judge.

"On the matter of bail," offered the district attorney, "People recommend twenty-five thousand dollars."

Michael Stone could barely conceal his anger as the audience gasped in response. "Your Honor, defendant has twice appeared to answer this first-offense charge. She has a local address and has been on her own recognizance as set by another judge of this same court. Request defendant be continued on her own recognizance."

"This is a felony charge, Your Honor," said the district attorney. "There is substantial exposure to a prison term. To be fair to the people of this community—"

"All right, all right," said the judge, his mind making rapid political calculations and judgments. He didn't want to offend his senior colleague, yet there *was* substantial political interest here, and he had his own future to consider. "The People want twenty-five thousand dollars' bail, and the defendant wants no bail at all. In view of all the circumstances, court sets bail at one thousand dollars." The district attorney looked miffed and the audience sighed in release of tension. Judge Carlini decided it had been a good call. Time to clear out his courtroom. "Court will take a ten-minute recess," he said and, banging his gavel, rose to leave.

"All rise," responded the bailiff.

As the judge left the courtroom, Sara looked at Stone and said, "What now? I don't have a thousand dollars. I could get it from my grandparents but it'd take—"

"You don't need a thousand. A bail bond costs ten percent. I'll lend you another hundred."

"A hundred, I can handle. Will they take a check?"

"A bail bondsman? Not from his mother, from what they tell me. If it'll make you feel better, *I*'ll take a check."

A sheriff's matron came up to Sara's elbow to lead her away. "Do me a favor," Stone said to her, "hold her back in the jury room a couple of minutes while I get bond posted, okay? We're talking a hundred dollars here. Do me two favors. I'll bet you know every courtroom personality in the building. There should be a bondsman hanging around looking to pick up some business, am I right?"

The matron, who liked what she saw in Stone's broad shoulders, said, with a nod to a sour-looking man sitting in an aisle seat in the last bench at the rear, "Right back there. Name's Murphy. We'll be in the jury room."

The door to the jury room was just across the hall from the courtroom door. As uniformed deputies blocked off the few steps between the two and Sara and the matron walked past, the press barraged Sara with questions. The matron kept her moving and the distance was so short, she didn't have a chance to respond, much to Stone's relief. Murphy in tow, Stone told the waiting crowd that his client would be released on bond in a few minutes. The deputies herded the crowd of reporters downstairs, where arrangements had been made to hold the press conference in the main lobby. Two reporters eluded the deputies dragnet and attached themselves to Stone. One was Terry Caulfield of *The Wall Street Journal*. The other, a man of medium build, in his late thirties to early forties, with raven-black hair and eyebrows set off by skin so white it seemed never to have seen the sun, introduced himself to Stone in a lilting brogue as "Brian Sullivan, sir, Reuters. Would y'be mindin' if I tagged along till we get to the conference?"

"I would still like," said Terry Caulfield, clearly annoyed by the entire turn of events, "to speak with your client privately, if that can be arranged."

"As would I," Sullivan chimed in cheerfully, his dark brown eyes probing Stone's blue. Stone held both hands up in a placating gesture as they reached the clerk's office, answering neither directly. He handed Murphy a hundred-dollar bill and Murphy, with a swiftness born of years of doing the same thing, got from Stone the basic information on his client, executed the bond, pocketed his money, and left rapidly to get back upstairs to resume his seat in the hope of picking up some more business. Stone now could not put off dealing with the two reporters any longer.

"Reuters and *The Wall Street Journal*," Stone said. "I'm sure my client will be impressed. *I*'m impressed. I know the *Journal*'s interest, but Reuters? From the cut of your jacket, Mr. Sullivan, I'd say you were just over from Europe. That's a lot of interest for a place like Rhinekill."

Sullivan smiled. "Dublin, sir. That's where both the jacket and I came from, seven years ago. This piece of cloth is m'last link with home. Been working out of New York and, when the fuss started up here, they sent me to cover it. Riegar is very big in Europe, mind you, and this animal business strikes a sympathetic chord in doggie and pussycat lovers the world over. It's universal, it is."

They approached the gathered press and sightseers in the lobby.

Stone addressed them all: "Ladies and gentlemen, my client has made bail, and I'll be bringing her down in a minute. I want you all to know that I have advised my client that for her to respond to press inquiries in her circumstances is not advisable from a legal point of view. She has agreed not to discuss her case, just her position on the controversy with Riegar over the experimental use of animals. Now, I know I cannot control what questions you ask my client. But I hope to control her responses. Meaning if you ask her a question I think gets into the facts and circumstances of her case, I am going to try to have her keep her word to me not to answer. Fair enough?"

There was a general murmur as Stone, not waiting for an answer, and seeking to shake Caulfield, Sullivan, and any others trying to follow, sped up the stairs, two at a time. He was successful and was able to speak privately with Sara as he escorted her down, emphasizing the same things he had just told the assembled press. He stood right beside her and said, "My client will have a brief statement and will then respond to questions."

Sara stepped forward. The television lights blinded her to much of the crowd as she spoke.

"First of all," Sara said, "I want to make it clear that I am speaking only for myself. I don't claim to represent any organization or movement, formal or informal, for animal protection or animal rights. Okay? I have a point of view. It's shared by some and some disagree—"

"Is it the group that agrees with your viewpoint," said a young woman holding a microphone out toward Sara as a cameraman snapped on yet another light and filmed her reaction, "that is behind the anti-Riegar demonstrations?"

"No," Sara said, turning to face her questioner, "just about every point of view is represented down there."

"Are you their leader?" asked a man holding out a tape recorder.

"No. As I said, I just represent myself here."

"Then why are we all here listening to you?"

"Because, I suppose, I'm the first demonstrator to be charged with anything more than disturbing the peace."

"Just what were you charged with?" asked the woman television reporter.

Michael Stone edged right up next to Sara and grasped her elbow. Sara glanced down at his hand and frowned her annoyance. "Burglary," she said.

"Why were you singled out for such a charge, especially if you're not the leader?"

Stone squeezed Sara's elbow hard and said, "I'm Michael Stone, Ms. Rosen's attorney. I have advised her not to discuss her case while it's pending. There is, however, no legal reason why she may not discuss with you her views on the treatment of animals." Stone made the statement, which was a repetition of his remarks to the press earlier, less for them than for the benefit of Sara, whom he wanted to warn discreetly and remind of their agreement back in Aunt May's kitchen. Sara understood his meaning clearly.

"I think it might be more efficient if you'd let me just state my views and then I'll be happy to answer any questions not related to my case. Okay?" The response was silence, which Sara took as assent.

"The people out in front of the Riegar plant are there because Riegar is a worldwide operation that experiments on animals for profit. All animal experimentation is, of course, for profit. The so-called pure research people are in it for the grant money. In the case of Riegar, it's more obvious. They're not in the drug business to allay suffering. If they wanted to do that, they'd stop experimenting on animals. They're in it to make money for their shareholders." *The Washington Post* stringer liked that one. He underlined the quote in his notes as Sara continued.

"Now, some of the people demonstrating believe the rights of animals are being violated. I disagree."

Heads popped up from notebooks at that. "You disagree?"

"Yes. If animals had any rights, these things wouldn't be done to them. Our law doesn't recognize any rights for animals. Even the laws governing cruelty to animals are completely silent on that subject."

"Are you saying that animals shouldn't have any rights?" The "let me make my statement first" idea was eroding fast.

"No. I'm just saying they don't, in fact, have any that the law recognizes. Now, if you'll just hold your questions, please, until I finish. Most of the demonstrators are upset by the cruelty that's going on, not just at the Riegar plant but everywhere animal experimentation is carried out. It's hideous, I agree. But the point *I*'m trying to make is that not only is it cruel, it is unnecessary. Actually, not only does it *not* benefit humans, it's *dangerous* to human beings. Not just because it misleads researchers down false trails and delays the development of new medicines. If that's all that happened, we'd be lucky. Thank God Fleming didn't have any guinea pigs handy when he discovered penicillin; it's a deadly poison to guinea pigs. And it's a good thing they didn't test out strychnine on guinea pigs—or monkeys, for that matter—they can eat it safely. Any of you want some? Chloroform is so poisonous to dogs, for years they wouldn't use it as an anesthetic for humans. Give the *Amanita phalloides* mushroom to a rabbit and you've got a happy rabbit, but *you* take one bite and you're dead. Test cyanide on an owl—no problem. On humans, we use it as a substitute for the electric chair. It's insane!"

Terry Caulfield spoke up. "Assuming everything you say is true, Ms. Rosen, isn't it a fact that animal testing has been valuable in discovering, for example, that various food additives, like cyclamates, are carcinogens, leading to their being outlawed and thus saving countless lives?"

"You're with *The Wall Street Journal,* right?" Sara asked, then kept speaking without waiting for Caulfield's answer. "How much do you think it was worth, in billions of dollars of sales, to the sugar industry to get an artificial sweetener thirty times stronger than sugar that cost five times less banned from the market?"

"But the fact remains, doesn't it," Caulfield pressed, "that cyclamates *have* been proven to cause cancer in animals?"

"Sure," said Sara, "cancer and a lot of other diseases. You know why? They pumped so much of the stuff down animal throats, it's a wonder they didn't suffocate under it. You want to know how much of that stuff you'd have to ingest to be exposed to the same amount? How'd you like to drink eight hundred cans of diet soda every day for the rest of your life? You'd *drown* in it!"

Someone called out from the gloom at the rear of the group, "Was that eight or eight hundred cans?"

"Eight *hundred.* A day. For the rest of your life. Look, it should be obvious all animals are not the same—they are very different in many ways—even rats and mice. It follows that people, humans, are also not the same as other animals. Herpes B virus is harmless to Old World macaque monkeys, but it kills seventy to eighty percent of humans exposed to it. Your paper, Ms. Caulfield, reported just last year that a monkey handler working for a lab in Michigan died of Herpes B when one of the monkeys bit him. His death was called an 'occupational hazard'! The point is, not only is there nothing to be gained here, there's a lot to lose—like your life."

"So why do it?"

Michael Stone, who from his position at Sara Rosen's side was equally blinded by the television lights, recognized the Irish accent of Brian Sullivan, the man from Reuters.

"Well, for one thing," said Sara, "the United States Government requires it. The Food and Drug Administration insists on the testing of any new drug on animals *before* it can be tested on humans, the only valid kind of test. So what happens? They test it on a being that reacts differently from a human, certify it safe for humans, and then, when it eventually proves harmful to humans, the cop-out is that it was safe for animals. Remember Thalidomide? Metaqualone killed three hundred sixty-six people; stilbestrol gave women cancer; isoproterenol killed thousands of asthmatics. Eraldin was another killer. Tuberkulin, a vaccine that cured tuberculosis in guinea pigs, *caused* it in humans. This didn't happen yesterday; it's been going on for years. Where have all you hotshot investigative reporters been?"

Sara's barb drew instant retort from the woman behind the television microphone. "Was it that passion for your cause that led you to break into the Riegar laboratories?"

The party, Michael Stone thought, was getting rough. He squeezed Sara's elbow so hard, the pain made her wince. "Thank you very much," he said, then wheeled his sputtering and protesting client around and propelled her out of the lobby and down the street.

"But I wasn't finished, damn it!"

"Either you were or I was. You go back in there, you go alone. You had your say, and you stayed out of trouble. Be grateful, not greedy. How much of what you said do you think they're gonna publish, anyway?"

Sara looked at Stone sharply. "All of it. Why not? It's all true and a matter of life and death. And that's news!"

"No it isn't. You said so yourself back there. If they've been sitting on the story for years, what makes you think *you*'re gonna turn 'em around?"

They were back at Stone's car now. He looked back. No one was following. "You don't get the point, Sara. Who are you, the Wizard of Oz giving out guts, brains, and heart to people without any?" He opened the car door for her.

"Okay," said Sara, "so I'm not the Wizard of Oz. That makes me a failure?" She got into the passenger seat.

"No. But you're a long way from Kansas, kid."

Stone flipped Sara's door shut. Through the closed window glass, he could see her exaggerated lip movements as she mouthed "Fuck you."

Something about Stephanie Hannigan seemed different to Michael Stone as she descended the steps of the public defender's office to the street. Stone was leaning against the passenger side of his Mustang, waiting for her, trying to figure out what it was. Her dress and hair were the same. She wasn't carrying her briefcase, but that wasn't it. Stone was distracted for a moment by the strong sun backlighting Stephanie briefly as she walked through the reflected glare of the glass doors behind her. It made her hair form a golden halo and, even more diverting, rendered her skirt unexpectedly translucent for a flash outline of parted thighs. Although the effect vanished a step later, its effect on Stone was such that she was almost upon him before he realized what was different about her appearance: she wasn't wearing her previously ever-present glasses. "Hungry?" he asked, opening the car door.

"Very! How far away is this place of yours?"

Stone shut her door and climbed in behind the wheel. "Worth the wait." The car interior had heated up under the sun as he waited for her. "This car has no air conditioning," he said, "helps keep the weight down and the speed up. How do you feel about top-down travel? It could blow the hell out of your hair."

Stephanie smiled, turning her head toward him. "Let 'er rip, counselor. I brought a comb." Inside the Mustang, the distance between them was small, and Stone noticed the outline of a contact lens in Stephanie's eye. He found himself wishing she'd kept her glasses on. The contacts made her eyes seem smaller. Maybe the glasses magnified them. Anyway, he thought, she had the pure blue eyes for which Ireland was almost as famous as its emerald green shamrocks.

Stone flipped the catch at the upper left of the windshield, then leaned past Stephanie to do the same on her side. As he did, the right side of his body brushed her left breast. "Sorry," he said.

"It's okay," Stephanie said softly. Stone noticed that she didn't pull away.

As the top whined to a stop in its retracted position, Stone depressed the throttle to set the choke and twisted the ignition key. The engine caught, and he blipped the throttle. "Light off all eight boilers, aye, aye. Ready to launch!"

"What?" shouted a mystified Stephanie as the engine's bellow enveloped the Mustang's open cockpit.

"I'm mixing navy metaphors," Stone answered, pulling out into traffic. "In the days of steam, for maximum speed the skipper ordered all boilers lighted to produce the most steam possible. 'Ready to launch' comes from the carrier fleet." He turned right onto the bridge over the Hudson River. There was little traffic at that hour and Stone mashed the throttle. Stephanie grabbed the door grip with her right hand and held the back of her head with her left in a vain attempt to keep her hair from streaming out in front of her from the backwash of the windshield as the red convertible accelerated.

"Bullitt!" she shouted above the roar.

"What?" Stone shouted back. The noise of the exhaust now was deafening as it was compounded by ricocheting off the concrete railings of the bridge.

"That's where I heard that sound before," Stephanie shouted. "The car Steve McQueen drove in the chase scene. It sounded like this one."

Stephanie couldn't have said anything to please Michael Stone more. He grinned. "Mustang! Made before the government screwed up the auto industry along with everything else it touches."

There are no tolls going west across the Hudson, so Stone didn't slow as he took the sharp right at the other end of the bridge and screamed up the hill to the top of the rocky palisade.

"I thought you said 'lunch,' not 'launch,'" Stephanie yelled into Stone's ear.

Stone took the hint and slowed down. They had reached the narrow two-lane road running south overlooking the Hudson far below, and it was the view he had wanted to show off to Stephanie, in any event. They drifted along at forty-five miles per hour, the big V-8 barely registering on the tachometer. The sun warmed them and shone brightly off the surface of the river.

"It is beautiful, counselor, isn't it?" said a now-relaxed Stephanie.

"Counselor," said Stone, "is not the name on my birth certificate."

Stephanie's blue eyes flashed warmly. "Michael," she said.

"Michael is what my Aunt May calls me," said Stone, "and she doesn't approve of me. Try Mike."

Stephanie looked impish. "I'm not sure I approve of you, either. You drive like a maniac. Think I'll stick with Michael, at least until I see if I make it back alive."

Stone's foot came off the gas. The car fell silent and coasted as he looked intently at Stephanie and said, "No harm will come to you while you're with me."

Stephanie could tell instantly by Stone's expression and tone of voice that she had stumbled into a sensitive area. It probably had something to do with his masculine pride. She wished she hadn't been an only child. If only she'd had a brother—even an older sister who dated a lot—she wouldn't be so damned ignorant about men. She always had to be so . . . on guard. She hated having to apologize for a perfectly innocent remark, but she did so again, for what seemed like the thousandth time. Stephanie concealed her resentment: "Hey"—she smiled—"I'm sorry. I got in the car, didn't I? Besides, I'm not wearing the right shoes to walk back."

Stone was embarrassed. He'd overreacted again. "I keep screwing up with you," he said. "Sorry."

Stephanie leaned over and put her finger against his lips. The pit of Stone's stomach reacted again, and he felt as if he'd stopped breathing.

The distraction caused him to interrupt his long-ingrained driving habit of scanning the road, his instruments, and the rearview mirrors, so his first indication that they were not alone on the road was a deep rumbling sound that he identified instantly.

"What's that?" Stephanie asked, trying to turn around far enough to see behind them.

"Only one thing in the world makes that sound," said Michael Stone, "a Harley-Davidson."

Stone saw the motorcycle in his rearview mirror for only a moment and then it was alongside of them as if to pass on the left. As the big machine drew opposite Stone's car door, it slowed and stayed there a few moments. The rider, a heavy man with a beer gut, clean-shaven head, and full dark beard, stared at Stone and Stephanie intensely then, shovel-head engine thundering from a two-into-one exhaust, pulled ahead, and disappeared around the next bend. The last thing Stone saw was the bright red tilted and double-overlapping *H* insignia on the rider's back.

"What was *that?*" Stephanie asked.

Stone had a pretty good idea, but there was no sense alarming Stephanie unduly. The bike had a rigid frame and had been built up from parts to suit the rider. The insignia had been the colors of the Heads from Hell gang, as described to him by Ira Levin. It could have been a coincidence, or the rider could have been a scout, now going to report to his buddies on some prospective fun—a lone man and woman, a seldom-traveled road, a couple of Yuppies ripe for robbery and a gang bang. Worst-case scenario, he had been recognized as Sara's lawyer. Worst case, that was, because of Stephanie's presence.

"Dunno," Stone answered Stephanie, "maybe a little local color. We turn off up here, anyway."

Stone turned left down an even narrower road that led as close to the cliff edge as the road department deemed safe, then widened to accommodate a small building between the road and the cliff. A sign in front of the building announced that this was the site of Van der Meer's Stage Stop Tavern, established 1663 and open for business without interruption ever since.

Stone pulled in and parked the Mustang as far to the rear as he could get it, hoping it would be more difficult to spot from the road. To Stephanie's unspoken inquiry, signified by a quizzical glance, he responded, "Can't lock an open car. Wouldn't want some teenager to go joyriding in it off the cliff."

Stephanie nodded her approval. "You're a thoughtful man, Michael. You'd have trouble living with something like that, wouldn't you?"

Stone feigned incomprehension. "Damn straight," he replied. "I can't afford another car right now. I just got finished paying off this one."

Stephanie looked shocked for a moment, then realized she'd been had and, grinning sheepishly, swatted Stone on the buttocks with her pocketbook.

The inside of the tavern had original-looking dark post-and-beam load-bearing walls with patched, rough sand-finished plaster in between. Against the far wall were small, two-person tables beneath a series of plate-glass windows that gave a spectacular view of the valley and the Hudson, far below. The rest of the small room had round tables seating six. To the right was a bar. To the left was a door, over which was a sign that read, in carved wooden letters, REST ROOMS. Except for a middle-aged bartender, the place was empty, the lunch hour having passed and the cocktail hour still the better part of an afternoon away.

"Not too late for lunch, are we?" Stone called to the bartender.

"No, no. Sit anywhere you like, folks. I'll be right over."

"What d'you say we sit at the historic plate-glass windows and enjoy the view?" Stone asked Stephanie.

"Sure," she answered, "that way we won't have to use the Colonial electric lights. Go ahead," she said, heading for the rest rooms, "I'll be back in a minute."

"We'll both be back in a minute," Stone called to the bartender, and followed Stephanie through the rest rooms' door. Inside was an anteroom. A pay telephone was on the wall. Two doors led off from the anteroom, one marked HERREN, the other, DAMEN.

"I wonder," said Stephanie, heading for Damen, "what happens when some dropout thinks *Herren* means her'n and goes through the wrong door?"

"You guys get another win on a Peeping Tom case. If high school graduates can't read English anymore, no jury's gonna believe a drop-out can read Dutch."

As Stephanie disappeared into the bathroom, Stone went to the pay phone, picked up the handset, unscrewed the mouthpiece, and turned it over in his hand. The microphone, an inch-and-three-quarter disk with round holes arranged in a circle and one in the middle, fell away into his palm. Stone replaced the screw-on mouthpiece quickly, dropped the microphone into his outside jacket pocket, and entered the men's room.

Michael Stone and Stephanie Hannigan exited their respective rest rooms at almost the same time. "Perfect timing," Stone said as he held the door into the restaurant open for Stephanie. They took their seats and the bartender stood over them, pencil poised over pad.

Stephanie looked up at him. "Do you have a house white wine you serve by the glass?"

"We got a Taylor Chablis," said the bartender. "That's a New York company," he added helpfully.

Stone smiled at him. "So's New York Oil and Gas. And," he said to Stephanie, "they've got a diesel number two I think you'd like better." He turned to the bartender again. "Could I see your wine list? I was told you had a—"

Stone was interrupted by the rumble of a big Harley just outside the tavern. The engine went quiet and in came the skinhead biker who had passed them on the road. The biker glanced over at Stone, then headed for the rest rooms' door.

"He a regular?" Stone asked the bartender.

"Never seen him before," the bartender protested. "This ain't that kind of place. I'll getcha the wine list."

As the bartender was retrieving the wine list from behind the bar, the biker came out of the rest rooms' door and yelled over to the bartender, "Yer phone don't work right, mister. Ya can hear, but they can't hear you!" He headed for the door, and a moment later, the Harley boomed into life, exhaust sound receding as it moved off down the road.

"Excuse me a moment," Stone said to Stephanie. He rose and walked over to the bar and spoke softly to the bartender. "Kind of badass lookin' guy. You got anything back there in case things get exciting?"

"Uh-uh. I told ya, mister, this ain't that kinda place. We don't have no trouble here. We ain't even open after ten-thirty. What's more, I ain't no hero. Anything *did* start, I mean serious shit, I'd sit down back of the bar an' stay there till it was over an' let the cops an' the insurance company straighten it out. I ain't gonna go to no hospital for what I make in this place in a week."

"Makes sense to me," said Stone. He picked up the wine list and returned to Stephanie. As he looked over the list, Stone asked her, with an elaborate casualness not lost on a woman used to reading juries, "Would you do me a favor?"

"Sure, if it's reasonable. What?"

"If that beer belly on a bike comes back in here again with some of his buddies, would you mind going back to the ladies' room and staying there till I come knock on the door?"

"What? You know that guy? I mean, are you expecting trouble? If you are, let's just leave now and avoid it."

"No, I'm not expecting trouble. I'm just anticipating. Force of habit. Old navy training. If there's no trouble coming, we might just as well stay here and enjoy lunch. That's what we came for. On the other hand, if trouble *is* coming, it won't be from one biker, or he'd have started it when he was here. That being the case, we're better off here than on a narrow road surrounded by a swarm of—"

The growling, revving, booming roar of a squad of Harley-Davidsons arriving rendered the rest of Stone's sentence moot. He slipped off his suit coat and handed it to the startled Stephanie, then went to work on the knot of his necktie. As he was handing it to her, the front door burst open and half a dozen big bald bikers entered and crossed to the bar.

"Beer!" demanded the leader. He was six feet two and nearly three hundred pounds of muscle and blubber in dirty jeans, a sweat-stained black T-shirt, and a vest bearing the HH symbol of his gang on his back. Tattoos covered his arms and the lower portion of his neck. Three more bikers, one of them the man who had passed Stone on the road and later complained about the telephone, were given to fat. One, the youngest in appearance, had the body of a muscle-building weight lifter. The sixth was thin and rangy, with the eyes of a serious doper. All sported shaven heads, tattoos, and "colors" on their backs.

The bartender brought up multiple beer bottles in each hand, holding them by their narrow necks between splayed fingers. "Now," said Stone softly to Stephanie, "would be a good time for you to excuse yourself. Take it easy. Be cool and casual. Don't come out till I knock."

"I can't leave you here like this!" Stephanie whispered urgently. "There's no point to it. The phone doesn't work, so I can't get help. Maybe they won't do anything as long as I'm here as a witness."

Stephanie was shocked at the transformation that came over Michael Stone. His face became blank, cold. His voice was flat, utterly devoid of emotion, as if some inner switch had been thrown. It hadn't changed his personality so much as eliminated it. She felt as if she were facing a machine.

"You don't understand. I disabled the phone. I don't need any help, *they* do. And I don't want any witnesses. Now go."

Without another word, Stephanie rose, turned, and made for the rest rooms' door. As Stone's last words to her sank in, she realized that their impact had been extraordinary. In a moment, the source of her fear had been transferred from the menacing biker thugs to the now-cold, emotionless man who had sat opposite her—a man who was now a total stranger.

By the time the rest rooms' outer door had shut behind her, Stephanie's shock had dissipated enough to allow her curiosity to assert itself sufficiently to disobey Stone's "no witnesses" injunction. Ever so slowly, Stephanie eased the door open a crack, just enough for her to see and hear what was going on in the main room of the tavern. Which, for the moment, was nothing much.

The skinheads continued to swill beer, joking among themselves. Stone quietly studied the wine list. Then, raising his head, he called out to the bartender:

"If you've got a minute, I've picked out a wine."

"Wine!" bellowed the huge biker leader.

"Wine!" chorused his five companions dutifully.

"Only pussies drink wine!" snorted the leader.

"Only pussies drink wine!" came the echo from the other five.

"Number twenty-seven," Stone called out to the bartender, ignoring his tormentors, "chilled if you have it."

"Chilled if you have it," mimicked the bodybuilder, trying his best to sound effeminate. The others joined, each trying to sound more airy-fairy than the last.

"Hey, bartender. Forget the twenny-seven. Give 'im the sixtynine!" the thin one shouted, then doubled up in laughter at what he was sure had been a devastating display of wit. He stopped in midlaugh, frozen by the sudden change in the tenor of events signaled by the venomous tone of the leader's voice. "Nobody in this fuckin' joint drinks nothin' who ain't wearin' colors." He turned to the bartender. "Hold that bottle of piss." Then, staring right at Stone, he said, "Lessee yer colors, buddy. If ya got any."

Michael Stone turned toward the big man and rose. Stephanie could see when he turned that he was smiling. It was a small smile and, she thought, not one that she would ever want directed at herself.

It was one of those situations, Stone thought as he rose, in which totally unrelated events just seem to fall fortuitously into place. He remembered the T-shirt that he had substituted for an undershirt that morning as he had dressed for court, the one with the military emblem and motto that couldn't be seen through his blue dress shirt. Stone unbuttoned his shirt cuffs first, then started on the front as he said, pleasantly, "Okay. You want to see my colors? I'll show you my colors."

This unexpected event brought the proceedings to a temporary halt as the bikers stilled, watching Stone like stalking predators waiting for their prey to decide in which direction to bolt before they gave chase. Stone's fingers moved deliberately from one button to another until, the last removed from its buttonhole, he took off his shirt, dropping it over the back of Stephanie's chair, and stood facing his would-be assailants. In blue, across Stone's deep and expansive chest, was an eagle, wings spread, head bent down to its right, talons clutching an antique flintlock pistol and Neptune's trident, superimposed over an anchor. Beneath the emblem was the legend: *The Only Easy Day Was Yesterday*.

There was a moment of such absolute stillness that Stephanie was sure everyone had stopped breathing. A biker, whose arms were covered with nautical tattoos, broke the silence with an awed whisper that penetrated every corner of the room. "Jesus," he muttered, "the *Budweiser!*"

What?" barked the leader, snapping his head around to address him.

"That thing on his shirt looks like a Budweiser label? That's what they call it. I seen it before once, when I was inna navy. Inna Philippines. Special Warfare." He raised his voice to address Stone. "Hey, sorry, man. It's cool."

Furious at this challenge to his authority, the leader turned on the speaker, thrust his chest against him, and said, "Hey, you cocksuckin' wimp. No Head backs off other colors. 'Fucks the matter with you?"

Chest-to-chest, the smaller man made a pleading gesture and dropped his voice to a half-whisper. "For Chrissake, Tiny, I'm tellin' ya, that guy ain't no pussy. He's a fuckin' maniac is what he is. They all are. Knows all kinds a shit. Rather kill than fuck. I ain't goin' near that motherfucker. You wanna fuck with him? Go ahead. He'll tear your head off and shit'n your chest cavity fer openers."

Tiny grabbed the smaller man under both arms and hurled him against the front wall. He hit with the back of his head first and slumped down to the floor, unconscious. Tiny, like any leader, knew fear could be contagious.

Stone, the wine list held firmly in both hands, walked slowly toward the bar. Good as his word, the bartender disappeared slowly beneath it: "Rice-burner-ridin' little shit." Tiny muttered toward the unconscious figure on the floor, then he turned and strode toward Stone.

"Hey, asshole," he called to Stone as he approached him, "where the fuck ya think you're goin'?"

Stone made no reply. He altered his stride imperceptibly to time and position himself precisely as the two men came together, Stone still holding the wine list in both hands.

Stephanie Hannigan held her breath. Tiny arrived in front and slightly to the right of Stone, blocking his path to the bar. If Stephanie had blinked, she'd have missed it. Hands never leaving the wine list, Stone's right elbow came up and his whole upper body twisted to the left and back with strobelike speed. The motion was accompanied by a sound that reminded Stephanie of her girlhood, when she accompanied her mother to an old-fashioned butcher shop where meat was cut to order on a block before the customer, the sound of a leg of lamb being slammed down on the block prior to trimming. Jawbone fractured and completely dislocated as it was driven with terrible force out of its socket and into the nerve ganglia behind it, Tiny fell, mercifully unconscious, to the floor. Stone kept walking.

The bodybuilder snapped out of it first. He pulled a boot knife and, holding it out in front of him, pointed at Stone, said, "There's four of us, for Christ's sake!" and led the charge.

Stone dropped the wine list and turned toward the knife-wielder. Pivoting to his right to avoid the blade point, he brought the heavy long bone on the underside of his left forearm down with some forty pounds per square inch of concentrated force on top of the wrist behind the knife-holding hand. The radial nerve in his right arm paralyzed, the bodybuilder stared in disbelief as the knife fell from his lifeless fingers, now powerless to hold it. Retaliating, he swung hard with his left fist at Stone's head, but Stone merely stepped back easily to let the blow pass, then caught the inside of the wrist of the extended arm and, in a repeat performance of his upper-body twisting motion, drove the base of the palm of his right hand as hard as he could directly into the back of his opponent's elbow. The bodybuilder screamed as both forearm bones popped wide apart in a dislocation that tore out his ligaments and shattered his rotator cuff.

Stone never stopped moving. But such was his grace, economy of motion, and precision that he seemed to Stephanie to be moving almost in slow motion as he pivoted back to his right, right hand forming a fist with the second knuckle of his middle finger projecting outward sharply. He deflected a left hook from the biker to his left with the underside of his own left arm, then drove the projecting knuckle of his right fist unerringly into the man's left floating rib, severing it cleanly. The skinhead gasped, curled over to protect his side from further damage, and rolled out of harm's way. In doing so, he temporarily blocked biker number five, the man who had originally passed Stone and Stephanie on the road to the tavern.

The fourth thug thought to exploit his one-time ability as defensive tackle on his high school football team before he was sidelined for academic failure and dropped out of school. He hurled himself low and hard in a classical football hit, but Stone wasn't there when he arrived. Off balance, the ex-tackle hurtled forward and slammed his shaven skull, which in his enthusiasm he had forgotten was not protected by a helmet, into the wall behind Stone.

Stone eyed his remaining opponent, who was still trying to negotiate his way around his broken-ribbed biker brother in an effort to get at him. The beer-belly blubber that made the bearded gang member so awkward also served as a kind of armor over his vitals that would be difficult to penetrate. Stone, seeing that he had plenty of time, decided to try. He wound up like a baseball pitcher with no one on base and, using his right fist as the ball, hurled it overhand with a perfect follow-through directly into the bloated biker's sternum. The man's chin fell, and he bent over sharply at the waist. Stone took aim, then drove his right knee directly into the big biker's face, pulping his nose and breaking both cheekbones, to the accompanying sound once again of a slab of meat hitting the block of Stephanie's mother's butcher. Stone stepped over him and headed for the man who had recognized his insignia, now fully awake and cowering at his approach.

"Man," the biker protested, "don'tcha remember? I'm the one told them not to fuck wit' you. Please . . ."

Stone held his hand out to the man, who looked at his face carefully, then took it. Stone lifted him to his feet with ease and led him over to the bar. The biker jumped in reaction when Stone slapped the bar, leaned over it, and said, "Okay. All clear. You can come up for air now."

Slowly, the bartender arose from the floor behind the bar. He looked at Stone, then, incredulously, at the carnage Stone had wrought.

"Jesus!" said the bartender.

Stone took out a five-dollar bill and put it on the bar. "This is for beer for my old shipmate here. He needs it."

Stone turned toward the rest rooms' door. Stephanie scurried into the ladies' room. Stone saw the outer door swing back the one inch from Stephanie's peeking position. He went through it, walked up to the ladies' room door, knocked on it, and said, "Ally ally in free."

The door opened slowly, and Stephanie emerged. She looked at Stone and said, "You're back."

"Yeah," said Stone, "I said I'd come knock."

"That's not what I meant," Stephanie said as they walked into the dining room.

"I know," Stone said.

Stone retrieved his clothing while Stephanie stood looking at the now-groaning bikers. "God," she said.

As Stone and Stephanie walked out to his car, she said, "Where were you back there?"

"It's a long story."

"Want to talk about it?"

Stone didn't answer at first, pondering the question. He helped Stephanie into the car, got in himself, and sat for a moment more, hands in his lap. Abruptly, he said, "Yeah, I guess I owe you that."

"No, you don't," Stephanie said as Stone drove slowly out onto the road and headed back toward Rhinekill. "You owe me a meal. The talk is purely voluntary, or I don't want to listen."

Stone was silent again for a while; then, as he turned toward the bridge, he said, "Okay, I want to talk about it." He turned to face her directly. "Not because I have to. And not because I'd even want to to anyone else. But, for some reason, I want to talk about it to you."

Stephanie turned to look out the window to keep Stone from seeing her eyes. "Thank you," she said. Then, turning to look at him, she said, "That's the nicest thing anyone's said to me in a long while."

Stone shifted out of fifth for fourth to take the downhill onto the bridge. The V-8 burbled, accentuating the silence between them. Stephanie came to a decision.

"Tell you what," she said, "it's closer to dinnertime than lunch, and with all that energy you just expended, you've got to be even hungrier than I am. And I'm hungry. I'm also a good cook, if I say so myself. You seem to be in a trusting mood. Trust me enough to try my supper?"

Stone grinned at her. "Geeze, I dunno. The contents of my soul is one thing. But my stomach? Are you as good a cook as I hope you are a listener?"

"I'm a *damn* good cook," Stephanie replied with vehemence. Then, gently, "I'm an even better listener."

Stone just nodded in reply. They were both silent for a time, but neither was bothered by the fact. It was, thought Stephanie, a comfortable silence and, between men and women, that was rare in her experience.

Stephanie guided Stone to a small, neatly kept two-story house in an older part of town. He pulled into the curb directly in front of the place, because there was no driveway. The front yard was defined by a low white picket fence that wouldn't keep out a determined dachshund. Behind it was a beautiful confusion of multicolored rambler roses, then a neat lawn.

"My mother planted that garden," Stephanie said.

"It's beautiful," Stone replied.

Unaccountably, the events at the tavern coursed through Stephanie's mind as they walked toward the front door. She paused there, fumbling to get her key from her purse. She found it, then gave an involuntary shiver and said to Stone, "You're not a porpoise at all, are you?"

"What?"

"You're a killer whale!"

Stone regarded her calmly. "Actually," he said, "I'm a SEAL."

● THE MASSACHUSETTS INSTITUTE OF TECHNOLOGY
graduate student lay in the powder-fine burnt sienna–colored sand of
the Mexican desert seven miles south of the United States border at
the state of Arizona. His clothes, like those of his much older companion, consisted of jeans tucked into athletic socks; worn, cloth-topped
jogging shoes; a long-sleeved shirt with the collar turned up; and a soft
tennis hat, brim down all around. All of it, from shoes to hat, had been
dyed with cheap red wine and coffee to blend into the sun-seared,
boondocked, wash-scarred landscape.

From behind one of the boondocks, the young man peered through
a pair of ten-powered, lightweight, roof-prismed binoculars at a railroad tank car. It sat alone on a crude trestle that took a short spur track
from the main line over a wash, only to end at a pile of cross-ties a
few hundred yards farther out in the desert. The area was halfheartedly
fenced off by barbed wire bearing a sign reading PELEGRO!

The binoculars came into focus on the largest feature on the side
of the car, a stylized logo of an *N* inside a *B*, then moved to the
next-largest, the capital letters *BN*, followed by a serial number. Next
was a warning stenciled in white paint:

Warning *CORROSIVE* liquid
Oleum
Hot, concentrated, fuming sulfuric acid

Below that was a diamond-shaped sign depicting two test tubes being poured out onto a human hand and a flat object. The word *Corrosive* appeared again, and the legend "UN class 8."

The MIT man let out a low whistle.

"What?" asked the man lying next to him.

"That stuff's got an equivalent acid concentration greater than pure H_2SO_4—pure sulfuric. It's much stronger-acting."

"What d'they use it for?"

"Make explosives, for one thing. Or dyes, drugs, petroleum refining . . ." He took the glasses away from his eyes and glanced upward. "Light looks to be right now," he said. "Try to get it all, but focus on the serial number. That's the most important. Then the DOT number. The rest of those are just weights and capacities and stuff."

"Gotcha covered," said the older man, bringing to bear a single-lens-reflex camera with a 135 mm lens attached. *"You* make sure no rattler comes easin' up behind us and bites my ass."

"I told you, no rattler's gonna come near us. They're as afraid of you as you are of them. Their first line of defense is retreat. You get 'em where they can't retreat, they'll try intimidation—that's what the rattles are for. A strike is his last resort if you keep after him, or his first if you surprise him by not being careful when you move around out here. After he strikes, it takes him awhile to replace his venom. Which means he goes hungry in the meantime. Now, a scorpion, that's something else."

"Great," said the cameraman. "All I gotta worry about is a scorpion up my ass. For a while there, I was concerned. Ready to copy?"

The young man put down his binoculars and twisted to remove a small pad and pencil from the buttoned breast pocket of his shirt. The back of his shirt, heated by the fierce sun, burned him, but so rapid was its evaporation in the 4 percent humidity, there was no trace of sweat. "Go," he said.

Through the 135 mm lens, the cameraman read off the serial number, then the Department of Transportation number. It could have been done more easily through the binoculars, but this way served as a check on the focus of the camera.

"Got it," said the MIT grad student.

The cameraman fired off several exposures.

"Jesus, that thing's loud!" the young man said in a forced whisper.

"It's the motor drive and the mirror banging up out of the way. You want quiet, there's only one way to go, an M Leica. It's a range finder, for one thing, so there's no mirror. And a leaf falling makes more noise than the shutter."

"So, how come we don't have one?"

"How long you been with Clean Earth?"

"Four years. Why?"

"They ever give you a Porsche to run an errand?"

The question didn't call for an answer and none was offered. Instead, the younger man put down his notebook and picked up his binoculars, scanning. Presently he said, "Uh-oh. Company."

The two men waited in silence as a battered old step-side pickup truck churned up a long dust trail approaching the wash at a leisurely pace. It pulled to a stop next to the railroad tracks before the trestle and two men wearing faded coveralls got out. They walked on the railroad ties through the fence opening for the tracks and out onto the trestle over the wash. As they did so, they pulled what appeared to be paint sprayer's masks up over their faces. When they reached the tank car, the two men steadied themselves against its side, placing their feet carefully on the ties outside the rails until they reached the middle of the car. There, a metal ladder ran from wheel level up to a catwalk along the top of the car. One of the men climbed up toward it while the other waited below.

The catwalk ran the entire length of the car. It consisted of open steel gridwork, designed to be nonslip to the sole of a shoe. The users were protected further by low steel handrails on both sides of the catwalk. The man on the ladder reached the top of the car and turned left on the catwalk. The man left below reached into the front of his coveralls and withdrew a pair of heavy gauntlets, which he proceeded to draw on.

Both the MIT student and his companion followed the actions of the two men as best they could, the student through his binoculars, the other man through the telephoto lens of his camera.

"What're they up to?" asked the cameraman. "You can see a lot better with those things than I can with this camera."

"I don't know," said the student. "The guy on top is fooling around with that turretlike thing on the top right. The other guy's just hangin' out."

"Hell, I can see *that.* I mean what's he doing with the turret?"

"I can't tell."

The man on the catwalk left the turret and proceeded along the top of the car to a similar turret at the other end of the car, then leaned over and waved at his coworker below. The man left his post at the middle of the car and walked along the ties, holding on to the side of the tanker, until he came to a spot approximately below the position of the man on top. Then, cautiously, he edged under the car, positioning his feet as far as he could safely on the inside of the rail, because the center section of all the cross-ties of the trestle beneath the tanker had been cut out so as to leave an opening to the floor of the wash below. There the smooth, rounded river rock and sunbaked sand had been stained a foul, sticky, malodorous yellow-brown. Nothing grew. Nothing lived. No snake, lizard, scorpion, or tarantula, however venomous, could match the lethal toxins wrought by man that waited in the wash like a cocked pistol for the cloudburst that would release the trigger, sending death randomly down the wash as far as the floodwaters would take it.

"The guy underneath is doing something to that thing sticking out from the bottom of the tank," said the MIT man.

"You want me to photograph it? We could blow up the picture and see what he's doing."

"No. Sound travels over the desert almost as well as over water. Too risky."

"Whatever it was he was doin', he finished, anyway," said the cameraman. "He's headed the hell out of there. The guy on top's turnin' something."

A puff of hot wind blew a tumbleweed down the side of the wash. It came to rest under the tanker, below the projection from which the ground-level man had retreated. A hot, dirty-colored liquid gushed from the belly of the tanker. It hit the tumbleweed, first charring, then dissolving it. The worker on the top of the car walked quickly to the ladder, descended it, then, coughing, followed his companion back along the side of the car and then to their truck. Behind them, the discharge from the tanker bubbled and hissed as it spread, gallon upon gallon, foul and fuming, through the wash.

At the exact moment the liquid had started to splash from the valve, the MIT student had depressed the button of a stopwatch. He watched the continuing flow through his binoculars, and when the volume fell abruptly, indicating the mere draining of residue, he depressed the button again, read the elapsed time, frowned, and made a note in his little book.

"Somethin' wrong?" the older man asked.

"Not sure. I'll need to make some calculations later. One thing, though, that stuff coming out of the tanker wasn't pure. I was wondering why anyone would dump that stuff. It's toxic but it's not waste."

"How d'ya know it's not pure?"

"Wrong color. That stuff was yellowish gray, almost brown. That's the way it looks when it's used, contaminated."

"Figures. That's why they're dumpin' it."

"Uh-uh. It's usually recycled. Used for something else. You know, if they use it first for making explosives, the recycled stuff might be used next for, say, petroleum refining."

"They're comin' back."

The two workmen left their truck again and returned to the tanker car. This time, the man who climbed to the top went directly to the forward turret and the ground man to his position underneath him.

"Closin' her back up," observed the older of the two watchers. The workmen retreated carefully, coughing through their masks, to the truck, then drove away the way they had come.

The sun was lower now, headed down behind a low mountain range to the west. "You 'bout ready?" he asked.

The MIT student pocketed his stopwatch and notepad. "No. I want to wait until dark."

"Yeah. I guess it'd be safer that way. We got enough water?"

"Yes. But that's not why I'm waiting. I want to get a sample of what's in that wash."

"A *sample?* Hell, you said yourself it looks like used. And it says what it is on the side of the tank."

"Yeah, that's what it *says* it is. But how do we know? And why get rid of it in a toxic-waste dump? Why not recycle? What's it contaminated *with?* We get a sample, we analyze it later, we *know.*"

"You gotta be nuts. You goin' down in that wash in all that toxic shit?"

"It's called commitment, man."

"It's called *lunacy,* man. I knew guys like you in Korea—all balls and no brains. It takes a certain amount of intelligence to know when to be scared, you know. Not one of those guys came back. What happens if you get overcome by some gas or something and croak? Then I gotta go down there, retrieve your fuckin' body, drag it seven miles to the border, then try to exfiltrate without gettin' my ass shot off by the Border Patrol, the INS, Customs agents, and Christ knows who all else, who will then proceed to indict what's left of me for murder. I don't think yellin' Clean Earth is gonna do any good. They'd be easier on me if I claimed to be with a Satanic cult. A sample wasn't in the plan. We're down here to survey illegal toxic dumps being used by American companies payin' off the locals, expose it, and make 'em stop."

"Yeah, I know. But something screwy's going on here, and it's not just not recycling. I timed how long it took to empty that tanker. We know its capacity. Even without calculating it, I can tell you it should have taken twice as long."

"So it was only half full. So what?"

"So what company sends half-full tanker cars to Mexico to dump toxic waste? It doubles the cost. And the farther away it comes from, the more it costs in the first place. With what we've got, we can find that out exactly. Just punch that serial number and the initials in front of it into the railroad's IBM Compass system and the UR code'll tell us every place that car has been in the last thirty days: where and when it stopped, was spotted for loading and unloading, when it was released, where it was going and for whom. And the photograph proves we've got the right number. But it *doesn't* prove what went into it was what was supposed to."

"How we gonna get access to a railroad's computer system?"

"You think there aren't railroad people who care about the environment?"

The older man pondered that, then said, "Okay, I'm with you. But how we gonna do it? These clothes can't handle acid, if that's what it is. And what are you gonna put the sample in? The acid'll eat up the container."

"The thermos. We pour out the coffee, rinse it out with a little water so it's clean. The inside of the thermos is glass. It'll handle the acid. We get some uncontaminated rock from another wash to step on and manipulate the thermos with some mesquite branches."

"Sure. An' while we're stumblin' around in the dark pickin' up rocks and wood, the scorpions and Gila monsters and diamondbacks are gonna give us a pass because they appreciate all we're tryin' to do for the environment, right? I mean, they know we're the good guys."

"Jesus, Charlie, you went through a war in Korea."

"I was a lot younger then."

"So then what the hell are you doing out here in the desert now?"

"I forgot something I learned in Korea."

"What's that?"

"Never volunteer."

Moonlight was spilling under the trestle and across the wash as Charlie, the Korean War veteran, stood uneasily on newly placed rocks, hanging on to the MIT student's belt as the young man leaned out over the poisonous muck trying to get the last of it he could into the neck of a thermos bottle he was maneuvering with two sticks.

"You know, if he's really lucky," Charlie said, his voice muffled by the neck cloth he had tied over his nose and mouth against the stench, "by the time he finishes his teens, an American male is familiar with certain odors he'll never forget: burnt gunpowder, a wet dog, a sweating horse, and an aroused woman—not necessarily in that order. But some things, *no* kid can't identify by the time he absolutely has to shave: gasoline, sweat socks left in a locker too long, and battery acid. And right now I feel like I'm standing inside the world's biggest car battery."

"Yeah," said the young man, "but battery acid is only fifty-percent-strength stuff—and it'll burn your clothes. Pure sulfuric is in the high nineties—strong enough cold; hot it's ferocious! This stuff wasn't pure, but it was hot. It's been used to dissolve something, then *kept* hot, all the way here. Why? That's what I want to know. What . . . were . . . they . . ." he continued, struggling now with his task, "trying to get . . . rid of? Dioxin? PCBs? Infectious . . . medical wastes?"

"God, you've got some imagination. Suppose it's just old battery acid collected at gas stations, like used crankcase oil?"

"Then it . . . wouldn't be . . . hot. There. Got it. Ease me back."

As the two men picked their way up the side of the wash, Charlie said, "You carry that thing back, okay? It ain't what it used to be, but I'd just as soon not have my dick burned off just yet if it's all the same to you."

The younger man started to laugh, then said urgently, "Hold it!"

"What?"

"There. Get down." He pointed toward a flashing light moving east.

"Locomotive," said Charlie, "coming on the main line, moving slow."

"They usually rip through here. It may be stopping to pick up the tanker. Keep down. The switch for the spur is just a couple of hundred yards up ahead, and they'll drop someone off to throw it after the train passes and stops to back up."

"What're you worried about?" Charlie whispered. "Someone comes after us, just throw the sample at him. That'll fuck him up for good."

Two General Motors diesel-electric locomotives, coupled back-to-back, drew past slowly, pulling twenty-six freight cars, a modest load. The caboose had been put in the middle rather than its traditional last-car place, giving its occupants easier access to the length of the train. Duly, the train stopped when the last car, a hopper, was twenty feet beyond the switch. In the moonlight, it was easy for the two activists to see a brakeman drop to earth, throw the switch, then signal with an electric lantern. The locomotive engines gave a short rumble, then subsided as momentum carried the train backward slowly onto the spur. The hopper car coupled with the tanker, and the brakeman waited until it had cleared the trestle and stopped again before he dropped in the safety pin and attached the air-brake hose. It was while the train was stopped dead that Charlie grabbed the MIT man and squeezed his arm. There was no need to have done so, because there was no way the other man could have missed the alarming sight.

Seemingly from all around the two men, the distance appearing closer than it actually was because of the moonlight, human outlines rose to a half-bent posture from behind boondocks and crept toward the train. Within moments, while the brakeman's back was turned, they swung aboard. They did so in an orderly fashion, as if led or rehearsed. Moments later, the brakeman signaled and the diesels responded, pulling the train and the newly acquired tanker car and clandestine passengers slowly out onto the main line.

The two environmentalists hugged the ground until the train was well away, then Charlie said, "Jeeesus! Did you see that? Those guys were all around us. No way they couldn't have spotted us!"

"I dunno. We didn't spot them."

"Yeah, but they weren't moving. We were all over the place gettin' those rocks, goin' in and out of the wash. We're lucky we didn't get our throats slit!"

"Why? We weren't interfering with their plan. They may have figured we were going to try our luck sneaking into the U.S., too. What the hell, it was a big enough train for everybody." With that, the graduate student stood up, saying, "Well, we've got seven miles to do before—"

MIT never finished that or any other sentence. For the first time since 1953, Charlie heard the sound of a high-powered rifle bullet slamming into flesh right next to him, a split second before the crack of the weapon. As he died, MIT motioned with his hand that Charlie take the sample.

Charlie did more than that. Moving imperceptibly, never lifting himself from his ground-hugging position, Charlie eased the notebook from his dead partner's pocket, substituted the thermos for the camera he now abandoned, the film safely in a plastic canister in his pocket, and tied his neck cloth tightly around the dead man's wrists. That accomplished, Charlie lifted the body's arms over its head, slid his own head up between the tied arms, rolled it over onto his back, and, moving on his hands and knees, started to crawl forward toward the north. Moments later, two more bullets smacked home into the back of the dead man on top of him.

Charlie dropped flat and remained motionless, hoping against hope that the shooter would have such confidence in his marksmanship that he wouldn't bother to check what he had every reason to believe was another dead tribute to his ability. An hour later, as the moon went down, Charlie concluded that he had won his gamble and resumed his crawl. "There are no ex-Marines," he thought, "only former Marines. And Marines always bring back their dead."

As Charlie resumed his crawl, the twin-diesel train remained halted on the U.S. side of the border for the usual checks and inspections. A small knot of men stood to one side, talking. One of them held a Belgian shepherd on a leash. He was a Customs inspector. "Find anything?" an Immigration man asked him.

"Ha!" snorted a Border Patrol member. "He couldn't find piss in a boot if'n he held it upside down. What d'ya think they give 'im the dog for?"

"Bite his balls off, Sam," the Customs man said, smiling, to his dog. The dog, who had heard this line of banter from these old friends daily for years, paid no attention to the mock command.

"No shit on this one," the Customs man replied, "least as far as me'n Sam can find. How 'bout you guys?"

"Come up with four wets," said Immigration.

"You mean," said the Border Patrol man, "un-doc-u-men-ted a-lee-uns?"

All but one of the group laughed at this sally. The dissenter was a young, earnest-looking man who said, "Listen, I know I'm new here and all, and I know the dog's good. But he can't smell what's inside the tanker car, and no one looked inside it."

The Customs man grinned at his buddies, who did not include the new representative of the much-resented upstart Drug Enforcement Agency. Customs and the DEA had been battling over turf since Lyndon Johnson took the DEA's predecessor out of the Treasury Department and put it under the Department of Justice. "He wants to look inside the tanker. He's absolutely right. Get the man a measuring stick and a rag."

With elaborate politeness and solicitude, another Customs man brought over a long measuring pole such as those used to measure the contents of underground oil-storage tanks. With it, he brought a dirty rag to wipe it. "Right this way, sir," he said, leading the way to the tanker, then up the ladder to the catwalk and over to the rear turret.

The turret was ringed with dogged-down toggle bolts. "What's that?" the DEA man asked.

"That there's the manway. You undo the toggle bolts and flip 'em all back, an' you can get a man down into the tank to inspect it, repair it, or what have you." He proceeded to loosen the bolts and flip them to the open position.

"You'd think," said the DEA agent, "that if you can get a man in through that manhole thing, the INS would be up here, too, looking for aliens."

"You'd think so, wouldn't you?" said the Customs man. He handed the DEA agent the pole, then tied the rag to the end of it. "Now," he said, indicating the cover plate over the manway, "just lift back the plate, stick your head down in there, and look. Use your flashlight."

Gripping the beragged pole in one hand, the DEA agent lifted back the manway cover plate with the other. He got his head as far as over the opening when he reeled back, dropping the pole, clutching his chest, and coughing furiously. "Gas!" he gasped.

"Acid. Sulfuric acid. Just like it says on the sign on the side there. You should try that when it's full."

"You . . . knew!"

" 'Course we knew. It's our job to know. Here, watch."

The Customs man picked up the pole and then, saying, "You think maybe they're hidin' drugs or people down there?" he lowered the pole, rag end first, until it hit the bottom of the tank, then swished it around in the residue and drew the pole back up. The rag was gone and the end of the wooden pole was smoldering. He held it out to the DEA agent, who gagged further as the acid-eaten end approached his face, then turned, ran down the catwalk to the ladder, down to the ground, and off toward the small administration building.

"Hey!" the Customs man shouted after him. "You were right. They were trying to bring in a load of acid. Street value in the millions.

You'll get a medal for this!" He intended to say more but he was laughing too hard.

"Hey!" shouted the other Customs inspector, still holding the dog. "Don'tcha wanna check the other hole?"

"Mother . . . fuckers!" choked the DEA agent. "Mother . . . f . . . fuckers!"

His voice was drowned out by the sound of the train leaving.

As Michael Stone stepped behind Stephanie Hannigan into the small living room of her home, he draped his suit jacket, shirt, and tie over his left forearm and asked, "Where's your head?"

"Screwed on nice and tight in the usual place, last time I looked," Stephanie answered. "Why, were you afraid I'd lose it in a delayed reaction to your little contretemps with the motorized morons back there?"

For a moment, Stone looked puzzled by Stephanie's response. Then he looked aside with slight embarrassment, chuckling in an attempt to conceal it. "Sorry, force of habit. Navy usage. I'm liable to call your floor a deck, stairs a ladder, ceiling an overhead, and so forth."

"So, what's a head?"

"Bathroom. I'd like to freshen up a bit."

"Aye, aye," said Stephanie, pointing to what looked like a closet under the stairs. "You'll find the bare minimum under the ladder there. For more fully equipped facilities, you'll have to go up the ladder and take the first door to your right."

Stone cast a calculating eye on the space beneath the stairs and said, "I'm not sure I could stand up in there." He headed toward the stairs, saying, "I'll be down in a little bit."

"Wait!" Stephanie exclaimed, darting in front of Stone and holding up her hand. "I've got some female things flying from the yardarm up there."

"I'll keep my eyes closed," Stone said, pretending to move around her. Stephanie scurried up the stairs, saying, "Sorry, classified!" and disappeared.

Stone smiled to himself as he settled into a sofa that faced a fieldstone fireplace. Inside it, the winter's accumulation of ash had been removed and replaced by an arrangement of dried flowers. He looked at the coffee table in front of him and concluded that Stephanie had two passions: the law, as evidenced by the latest issue of *The Fordham Law Review* lying facedown, opened to a discussion of cases in which plea bargains had been held not binding by reason of failure of performance by the defendant; and gardening—witness the current issues of just about every one of the many magazines devoted to that subject.

"All clear," Stephanie called from the bottom of the stairs, then made for the kitchen down the hall at the rear of the house. Stone rose and walked easily up the stairs to the bathroom. It was large, feminine, and decorated with living green plants that thrived on the warm, moist air generated by bathing. Whatever Stephanie had been concerned he might see was gone. Instead, fresh towels and soap had been laid out invitingly.

A few minutes later, Stephanie eased her way down the hall from the kitchen and listened intently at the bottom of the stairs. Presently, she heard the shower start in the upstairs bath. Smiling at winning her gamble, she trotted back to the kitchen, confident she had enough time to lay on a decently prepared meal.

When Michael Stone, now feeling fresh and relaxed, arrived at the top of the stairs to start down, he paused to make a last-minute adjustment to the knot of his necktie and was reminded suddenly of how hungry he was by the delicious combination of cooking odors wafting upward from below. He moved down the stairs eagerly, to find Stephanie waiting for him with a confident smile. "Supper's ready, Michael," she said, and led him down the hall.

An archway on the left, between the living room and the kitchen, opened into a small dining room. The double-hung windows in the opposite wall let the shadowy light of late afternoon slant through the evergreen bushes into the room. It was paneled up to a chair molding on all four walls. Above that, the walls were covered with a wallpaper depicting fox-hunting scenes. One end of the room was dominated by a curved glass antique cabinet that contained a collection of cranberry glass, porcelain figurines, and gold pocket watches. Above the cabinet was a large, ornate, gilt-framed beveled-glass mirror. At the other end of the room, a Sheraton piece contained dining room linen and silver.

In the center of the room, an oval dining room table was covered with crisp linen. There were place settings at each end, and a floral centerpiece was bracketed by single sterling candlesticks. The candles were alight and their flames reflected in the mirror and the glass. Serving dishes sat on the table and awaited them.

Stone assisted Stephanie to her chair and took the one at the opposite end of the table. Stephanie's eyes picked up the candle flames. They crinkled in laughter as Stone held his hand above his eyes as if to shield them from the light and mock-shouted, "Ahoy, passing vessel!"

Stephanie picked up the filled wineglass before her and raised it to Stone in a toast. He lifted his glass in return. "To ships that pass in the night," Stephanie said, and sipped her wine. Stone sipped his and found it to be an excellent cabernet sauvignon. "Well done," he said as Stephanie filled his plate with a broiled sirloin steak, small red-skinned new potatoes, and peas, passed it to him, then filled another plate with a mixed green salad topped with a honey-mustard dressing.

Stone waited until Stephanie had served herself, then cut into his steak. Stephanie was perfectly still until Stone had placed the first bite into his mouth, chewed it, smiled, and said, "You've put me in an awkward position."

Stephanie was apprehensive but, reassured by Stone's smile, said, "Oh?"

"I'm not sure how to break it to my aunt that there dwells in Mohawk County a woman less than half her age who is her rival in the kitchen."

"On the evidence of one bite?" Stephanie replied, obviously pleased.

"Save your summation until all the evidence is in, counselor."

It seemed to Stephanie all too soon that their plates were empty, the wine bottle down to but an inch remaining, and the candles, now the only light in the room, near guttering. Stone caught her look of wistfulness and said, "I was wrong, and you were right. I should have waited until all the evidence was in. You are not Aunt Mazie's rival."

"Oh?"

"You are her peer."

Stephanie smiled. "Records are made to be broken, counselor."

Stephanie excused herself and returned in a moment with a warm apple pie in one hand and a pot of coffee in the other. As he finished his pie and sipped his coffee, Stone said, "Did you hear that?"

Stephanie, having heard nothing but the increasingly loud beating of her heart, said, "No. What?"

"That's funny," said Stone, "I heard it clearly. The unmistakable sound of a record breaking."

Stephanie gave Stone a warm, approving look, rose, and said, "Bring your coffee cup. In the living room, I have a really good Armagnac."

"I don't know," Stone protested halfheartedly, but he rose and picked up his coffee, nevertheless. "I don't drink much, and I've had half a bottle of wine already."

Stephanie led the way back into the living room, now lighted solely by two table lamps at either end of the room, their peach-colored cloth shades causing the room to glow softly. The sofa, and the area between it and the fireplace, were in gold-tinged shadow. It was there that Stephanie chose to sit, on the far end of the sofa. The bottle of Armagnac and two snifter glasses were on the table. Stephanie put her cup and saucer down next to them and turned her attention to the brandy. Stone followed suit and sat on the opposite end of the sofa.

Stephanie poured Stone a brandy and handed it to him, then did the same for herself. This time, Stone gave the toast. "Thanks for turning what could have been a disaster into something memorable."

"Thank you, counselor."

"Mike. Please. Remember?"

"HMmmmmm, as long as you call me Stephanie, I'll stick with Michael. I'll call you Mike when you call me what people who . . . know me well . . . call me."

"What's that?"

"HMmmmmmmmmm, I'm not sure I'm ready to tell you that yet. You're a nice man, Michael. And certainly attractive. But you're kind of scary, too. It's not just what you did back there, although if I'd read it in a book, I wouldn't have believed it. It's *how* you did it. I mean, you weren't angry. You weren't . . . *anything*. It's like you went away and a machine took your place. Then, after it was all over, you came back. That's scary."

"Yeah, I suppose it was, from your point of view. Funny thing of it is, you didn't see it the way it *really* is. Or can be. Fact is, I was scared back there. Not in the way you'd expect or maybe even understand. And I *was* angry. At myself. Still am. It's hard to explain. No, that's not true. I can explain it. But that might scare you more, and I don't want to do that."

Stephanie was silent for a moment. Then she said, "You liked my cooking?"

"You know I did. It was great."

"But you didn't know that when you sat down at the table, did you? You trusted me. I told you I was a damn good cook, and you trusted me. Remember what else I told you, Michael? I'm a *great* listener. But you'll never know unless you trust me."

Michael Stone stared into the depths of his glass. He took one more sip, then, very deliberately, he placed it back on the coffee table, leaned back into the sofa, and continued to stare at his glass, averting his eyes from Stephanie as he spoke:

"I've been trained as two things in this world. The first, when I was very young, was as a lawyer. Between my second and third years of law school, I married a classmate. She was in my study group. Smart. Good-looking. Very committed to the law. Within a year, we were fighting over the Vietnam War. I supported it; she was dead set against it. We agreed to disagree. Then she met some professor of journalism at Columbia and ran off with him. Never even told me, just did it. I had to find out from friends. I tried to stop the hurt through study. It worked, and it didn't. I graduated and passed the bar, but the hurt didn't stop."

Stone faced Stephanie for the first time since he had begun and gave her a mirthless smile. "My first case was my own divorce. Then I joined the navy. I figured if she was doing all she could against the war, I'd do all I could to win it. I was NCAA champion swimmer at fifteen hundred meters and swam water polo for the New York Athletic Club. So it was a natural for me to volunteer for the SEALs—Naval Special Warfare. Stands for Sea, Air, Land. It's hard even to get a chance to try out for it. The basic training is six months long. In a class of, say, a hundred and twenty-five, twenty-five might make it through. They give you more pain than a human being is supposed to be able to stand to try to make you quit. I substituted one kind of pain for another and made it.

"In Nam, I got lucky and fought with Scott Lyon. We both ended up with commissions and stayed on after the war because we loved operating. You didn't really see me operate in that tavern. What I did was right for a lawyer. I didn't kill anyone, although I was afraid I would. That's why I didn't want any witnesses. That's why I waited until I was attacked first and then pulled all my punches. I never really 'clicked on'—what you described as going away and becoming a machine. I was afraid I would. If I had, none of those guys would be alive. I'd have attacked *them*. I'd have gone for the first thing that moved and killed it. From the point of view of an operating SEAL, my performance sucked."

"But," interjected Stephanie, "you're *not* an operating SEAL. You're a practicing lawyer. You handled it beautifully."

"I was lucky."

"Why are you so down on yourself? Your performance was correct for who and what you are now."

"Because I'm in the wrong culture. And it's my fault. Look, I'm not a good lawyer. Without your help, I'd still be driving around Mohawk County trying to find my client, for Christ's sake. In the SEALs, I was an operator's operator."

"What happened?"

"I blew it. My last physical, they found an insignificant hearing loss. I mean I can hear any sound anyone else can, but I'll sometimes mix up *thigh* for *sigh*. Stuff like that. They said I could keep my Trident— what that guy in the bar called 'the Budweiser'—but they wanted to make me a support guy. I blew my stack and resigned my commission. Stupid, stupid, *stupid!*"

Stone's vehemence took Stephanie aback. "What choice did you have?"

"I should have kept my cool and appealed. All the way to Bethesda. I should've taken it to a board. Trouble was, it could've taken me two years to win. Two years of being a support guy instead of an operator in the teams. I was too proud to do that, so I screwed myself. Now I'm neither fish nor foul, and because I owe a guy a favor from combat,

I'm representing his sister when I'm not qualified to. Christ, I don't know whether I should be representing her even if I *was* qualified!"

"Why do you say that?" Stephanie leaned over toward Stone as she spoke, her interest engaged even more.

"Someone who's information I respect says the Riegar people knew she was coming and expected her."

"What does she say?"

"I haven't asked her yet. I didn't want to confront her while she was a guest in my home. I just don't know who I can trust in this thing."

Stephanie took his hand. "You can trust me."

Stone held Stephanie's hand and squeezed it. "Thanks . . ."

"Neffie," said Stephanie. "My friends call me Neffie . . . Mike."

Maybe, thought Stephanie, it was the wine. Or maybe it was the combination of his scent and that of the roses drifting through the window from the front yard that made her feel dizzy when he kissed her. She held him tightly, then returned his kiss with passion. He put his hand on her breast and, for the briefest moment, her body tightened with indecision. Then Stephanie remembered the time when she was eleven and she finally swung out over the pond on the same rope as the boys, but instead of swinging back to shore, she abandoned fear and let go, splashing into the water for the first time. She had never regretted that moment, and she didn't think she'd regret this one. Stephanie let go. "Upstairs," she whispered. "In my room. In my bed."

Stone's hand never lost contact with Stephanie's body as it slid off her breast, went under her arm, then around her back to grip her securely beneath the opposite arm. His other arm caught her beneath her knees and he rose, cradling her easily. Stephanie felt utterly secure in his strength and, reaching around his neck to hold him around his shoulders, she tucked her head into the side of Stone's neck, closed her eyes, inhaled his scent, and hung on.

As Stone climbed the stairs to her room, Stephanie could feel the muscles of his back move under her hands and her mind's eye saw the sensuous ripple that had fascinated her when he swam beneath her gaze at the pool that morning—a morning that now seemed very long ago. She felt his breath penetrate her hair to warm her scalp, and the warmth flowed down throughout her body.

At the top of the stairs, Stone paused, unsure of the way to Stephanie's bedroom. Stephanie lifted her head, kissed his chin, then pointed to the door straight down the hall. Then Stephanie let her head fall back, hair swaying, as she watched the ceiling pass by, then the top of the door frame, and, finally, the light fixture above her bed, which, she hoped, Stone wouldn't turn on. He didn't.

As Stone started to lower Stephanie onto her bed, she eased herself to her feet deftly, said, "Be right back," then slipped out the door and down the hall. Stone started to undress, folding his clothes neatly and placing them on a skirted, slipcovered chair that went with the feminine decor of the bedroom.

Stephanie went into a spare bedroom and directly to a closet, where she stored clothing she used infrequently. A quick hunt uncovered what she was looking for, a negligee/peignoir combination purchased impulsively several years ago while accompanying her friend Naomi on a shopping trip. "If it's your size, Neffie, grab it. Guaranteed hormonal storm in any man you wear it for, even the duds around here."

"Naomi! I've never met *any*one I'd let see me in *that!*"

"Hey, kid, the Boy Scouts got it right. And you never know. Besides, it's forty percent off."

Well, thought Stephanie as she donned the filmy outfit, now we'll find out whether Naomi knows what she's talking about.

Stone watched Stephanie enter her bedroom from his position in her bed, half his body under the covers, the other propped up on an elbow. She seemed to glide, and now the faint outside light that made its way in through the hallway behind her outlined her figure through her barely there gowns. *Lush,* he thought as she crossed the room before him to her bureau. *Ready* came to mind as she paused to light two candles at opposite ends of the bureau, which quickly became four flames as the mirror above it reflected them back into the room, casting over it a glow reflected more softly by Stephanie's skin. *Nubile,* Stone decided as she slid under the covers beside him.

Stephanie's hair shone, backlit by the bracketing candle flames. Tentatively, she reached out and brushed her fingertips through the hair of Stone's chest. He held himself motionless, as if confronted by a beautiful wild animal, lest any movement frighten it away. She leaned toward his chest, inhaling his scent, as if trying to identify this new being in her bed. Finally, Stephanie raised her head and looked at Stone directly. His eyes shone in the direct light of the candles, watching her intently as she stood, removed her peignoir slowly, then the negligee, to stand golden, her secrets in shadow before him.

Stone's chest swelled as he tried to control the intake of his breath. His eyes now glowed more brightly than the candle flames. Stephanie Hannigan was a good lawyer, smart enough never to ask a witness in court a question to which she did not already know the answer. "Do I please you, Mike?" she whispered as she came to him.

Michael Stone's answer was a primal groan, to which he added the unnecessary translation, "God yes, Neffie." His strong suit might not have been the law, but Stone shared the SEAL heritage of legendary self-discipline, enabling him to deny lust in favor of love. He took her with a patience and gentleness that demanded all his strength of will.

"UMMmmmmmmmmmmm," Stephanie responded. Eyes closed, she began to nod her head affirmatively, as if in answer to a series of questions only she could hear. "Uh-huh," she nodded, wearing a half-smile of pleasure and anticipation. "Uh-*huh.*" As Stephanie's affirmations increased in frequency and intensity, Stone's loving was drawn into and captured by their rhythm. A moist mist shone candlelight gold on her face as Stephanie lifted it to him. He tasted its sweet salt as he kissed her eyes. "Yes!" she said, turning her head to bring his lips on hers. *"Yes!"* The kiss dissolved what remained of Stone's self-discipline, and he gave himself to her with uncontrolled strength.

"Oh, *God!*" said Stephanie. Her hands balled into fists, and her head rolled violently from side to side until she stopped suddenly, shook both fists, and shouted, *"Make me pregnant!"*

The words that had escaped from somewhere deep within her were even more shocking to Stephanie than to Stone. She lay beneath him, wet, exhausted, sobbing. "Oh, God, Mike, please believe me. I have no idea where that came from. I mean . . . you don't have to worry. I used pro—"

"It's okay, it's okay," Stone said, easing aside. But from the hint of strain in his voice, Stephanie knew it wasn't okay. She turned her head away from him, despair on her face.

Inside Stone, embarrassment and apprehension mingled and fought with compassion and love. The conflict unresolved, he tried to relieve Stephanie's misery and forced a laugh. "You really know how to crush a guy, kid. I mean, here I thought I had a shot at the anodized aluminum medal for barely adequate performance, and you take all the credit."

Stephanie turned her head back to look at him. Whether her look held disgust or contempt or both, Stone couldn't be sure. Whatever it was, he withered under it. "Bad joke, counselor," Stephanie said.

Stone hung his head. "Yeah."

● TWO MEN STOOD BEFORE THE COUNTER SUR-
rounding the nurse's station at Immaculata Hospital in the U.S. border
town of Santa Rosa, Arizona. They both cast an appreciative glance
at the young woman behind the counter, then the older of the two
said, "Hi, remember me from last night?"

"Sure," said the young nurse, "you're the Customs—"

"Special agent, right. Ed Nutting. So, how's he doing this
morning?"

"Much better. He was exhausted and dehydrated. He's had a night's
sleep under mild sedation, and we've been rehydrating him by I.V. He's
a tough old bird. Yelling this morning about getting out of here. He'll
be okay."

"Must still be delirious if he wants to get away from you," said
the blond young man standing next to Nutting. The nurse smiled
up at him.

"I'm sorry," said Nutting. "Ms. Rosario, Phil Dahl, EPA. Charlie—
Mr. Bates—asked to see an EPA representative before he passed out
yesterday. Can we see him?"

Ms. Rosario consulted a chart. "Yes," she said, "it's okay. He's in Three fourteen."

"Thank you." The two men walked down the hall, found the room number, knocked, and, at a cheery "C'mon in, Honey!" entered.

"Oh," said Charlie Bates, slumping back into the pillows that held him propped up in bed, "I thought you were—"

"Yeah," said Nutting, "I know. Even my wife's stopped calling me Honey." He turned to Dahl. "This is Phil Dahl, EPA. We got him for you."

"Hey, thanks. You tell him what it's all about?"

"Just that you and the guy whose body you brought in are with Clean Earth and your buddy got shot while you were checking out toxic dumps on the other side of the border."

Charlie's face darkened. "Anything on the bastard killed him?"

" 'Fraid not. Like I tried to tell you yesterday, we've got no jurisdiction over there. We reported everything you told us, but you've gotta understand; we can't even get satisfaction on a DEA agent tortured to death down there. It was probably a 'coyote,' a professional who runs wets over the border for a fee, protecting his operation. What you said checked out. Immigration found four of them on that train."

"There were a lot more than four got on."

"Yeah. But sometimes they drop off just before the border an' sneak back on later. The border's a sieve. Anyway, Phil's here, for anything you want to give him."

"We already ran the information in your partner's notebook," said Dahl. He took out a notebook of his own and consulted it. "The BN before the serial number on the tanker car stands for the Burlington & Northern railroad. The car's leased to a pharmaceutical company to haul oleum; that's the best way to haul sulfuric acid. Oleum is H_2SO_4 plus some SO_3—sulfur trioxide. Has a low enough freezing point to be transported practically—the pure stuff freezes at about fifty-one degrees—and it's easy to turn it into pure sulfuric when they get it to where they need it. Sulfuric acid's the most commonly used chemical in industry. They use a lot of it to make drugs; that's probably why the pharmaceutical company rents its own car.

"The UN class 8 sign is what we require on anything hauling that stuff internationally. Oleum—fuming sulfuric—is real dangerous, much more violently active than even pure sulfuric acid. Usually they reuse it after a first run, but, eventually, you get toxic waste. It's a lot easier to dump it in Mexico. And a lot cheaper, even after payin' off. You know how it is in this country, no one wants a toxic dump in the same state. Anyway, it doesn't look very mysterious to me."

"What about the tank was only half full?"

"Still cheaper in the long run. Besides, your buddy's notes said it was a two-holer. That means two tanks. The time would work out if they only drained one."

Charlie grunted, digesting the information. Then he asked, "You find out the name of the company rents the tanker?"

"Riegar. The car was on its way back to a plant in Rhinekill, New York."

"Long way to haul that shit." Charlie looked away into a distance only he saw. Suddenly, his memory brought him back to the room. "Y' analyze the stuff in the thermos?"

"Yeah. Sand. Powdered quartz, mostly, some pebbles, little piece of charred bone—all that's left of a jack rabbit, probably—all soaked in sulfuric acid. A *lot* of sulfuric acid."

Charlie sighed and sank back into his pillow. "God," he said, "all that education and the kid dies to be sure what's in some industrial sewer in Mexico."

"Bullshit!" said Dahl, the anger in his voice snapping Charlie's head around. "In the entire fucking universe, there's only one place we know of has life. We're killing it. He died trying to stop us."

Charlie nodded slowly, resignation on his face. "One thing I figured out a long time ago," he said.

"What's that?"

"Nothin' serious ever gets accomplished in this world less'n someone's willing to die for it."

Sunday mornings Michael Stone slept in. It was the only day of the week he didn't start off with two hours of rigorous exercise. The omission wasn't motivated by sloth; Stone knew that he had to give his body at least one day a week to rest, heal, and rebuild. He had found, however, that if he didn't set the alarm on Saturday night, he would awaken at the usual time, anyway. If, on the other hand, he did set the alarm, and then, as the realization that it was Sunday hit him, he gave in to the luxury of shutting it off, he could sleep to an extraordinary hour, once as late as 8:50 A.M. This Sunday was no exception.

At 8:24 A.M., Michael Stone was home in bed, Sara Rosen having returned to her own apartment after her news conference. The aroma of Aunt May's percolator coffee and blueberry-pancake batter coming to perfection on a hot griddle woke him with a ravenous appetite. Then he thought again of the fiasco with Stephanie Hannigan, and the edge came off his feeling of well-being. But only the edge, such was the power over him of Aunt May's cooking.

Shaved and showered with the practiced speed possessed only by a military veteran, Stone was in the kitchen within a quarter of an hour. "Everything I own for a cup of that coffee, Mazie," he announced as he entered, "and my soul for the pancakes."

"Humph," Aunt May snorted. "All you own would shame a beggar. And the soul you offer is no doubt blacker than the coffee!"

"Aw, Mazie," Stone said, bending down to kiss her cheek, "I admit to honest poverty, but how can you say such a thing about my soul?"

"Don't take it personally. There isn't an unmarried man on the face of the earth not destined to burn. Pour yourself some coffee. Pancakes'll be ready in a minute. The Sunday paper's on the table in the library."

Stone poured himself a mug of steaming coffee and walked with it to the library. He picked up the heavy newspaper and carried it back with him to the kitchen. There he fished out a section that reviewed the news of the past week and started to read.

"Damn!" Stone exploded, spilling his coffee.

"You mind your tongue in this house, young man!" said Aunt May. "What's the matter?"

"Sara. She gave *another* interview! Look, this is the weekly news review section. See this article, 'Animal Activists Continue Upstate Protest'? They summarize her indictment and plea. Then her news conference, where she went into all the different reactions to poisons and things between humans and animals? And nailed that *Wall Street Journal* reporter on their own article about the monkey handler dying from a virus that didn't bother the monkey, remember?"

"Yes."

"Then listen to this: 'Meanwhile, as police estimate that animal welfare protesters are increasing by more than twenty per day "from all over the country," in an interview given a Reuters reporter yesterday, Ms. Rosen is quoted as asserting that "photographs exist [depicting means by which] animals are subjected to horrible experiments [which are] not only useless in attempting to improve human health, but outright dangerous [to it.]" Ms. Rosen refused to state how the photographs came to exist "on advice of counsel," and refused to respond when asked whether she took them.' "

"Well," protested Aunt May, "the girl told the truth, didn't she?"

"That's not the point, Mazie. She gave *another* interview, without consulting me, and I'm supposed to be her lawyer. That's bad enough. But she confirms that there are pictures of the inside of the plant and that she's seen them. She doesn't *have* to admit she took them; that's the clear implication of what she said. The DA's gotta be licking his chops!"

"Someone *else* could have taken the pictures," Aunt May said. She had become fond of Sara during her stay.

"Who?" Stone asked sarcastically, "Her missing cat?" He slapped the newspaper down, picked up his cup, guzzled down the coffee, then rose.

Hands on hips, Aunt May demanded, "Just where are you going?"

"See Sara," Stone replied, his voice muffled by the napkin he was using to wipe his lips. "That was a summary. I've got to know exactly what she told that guy from Reuters."

"At eight-fifty Sunday morning? Have you lost your mind? You think I'm going to eat all those pancakes? You sit right back down and have your breakfast like a civilized human being, then see if you can act like a lawyer instead of a teenager whose girl's going to the prom with someone else. Go on, sit!"

Michael Stone did as he was told.

Fifty minutes later, calmed by a full stomach and the grudging recognition of the need to conduct himself professionally, he drew the Mustang to the curb across the street from Sara Rosen's apartment, locked it, then surveyed the sleepy Sunday-morning neighborhood. The only sign of activity was an elderly couple walking a small dog. Stone crossed to Sara's building, entered the vestibule, and pushed her bell.

To Stone's surprise, Sara answered after the first ring. Although it was 10:00 A.M., he had expected her to be asleep.

"It's me, your lawyer. At least for as long as it takes to have one more conversation with you."

"Oh, Michael. For heaven's sake. Come on up."

Stone took the steps to the fifth floor two at a time, not because he was in any particular hurry, but to waste the opportunity for the exercise would have been unthinkable. At the fifth-floor landing, breathing rate unchanged, he walked to Sara's door and knocked.

Moments later, Sara's apartment door opened just far enough for her hands to slip out. Her left hand was extended flat, palm down. Under it, her right hand formed the classic middle-finger gesture, tip of the extended finger touching the palm of the hand above it.

The hair on the nape of Stone's neck rose. He flattened himself out against the wall to the side of the door, scanning for danger. A moment later, the door was thrown full open. A man jumped out, shorter and lighter than Stone but with a strong, wiry build. He landed in a martial arts "horse" stance, legs open and bent, hands in guard position, white teeth flashing in a broad grin. "Gotcha!" he said.

The smaller man's defensive posture was prudent because Stone had started to strike when, relief and chagrin flooding through him at once, he cried out, "Saul, you *fucker!* I oughtta kill you for that!"

"You can try, sailor boy, but better men than you haven't been able to do it yet!"

The two men embraced, pounding each other's backs. They were still laughing as they walked into a smiling Sara Rosen's apartment.

"Where the fuck did *you* come from, and how long've you been here?" Stone demanded.

" 'Bout an hour. Drove up from Washington early this morning.

No traffic on a Sunday. Just snap on the ol' radar detector and cruise."

"Washington? What the hell you doing in Washington?"

"A little more respect, please. You're in the presence of the new Israeli military attaché's first assistant, *Lieutenant Colonel* Saul Rosen. I outrank your ass. Anyway, read in the paper about some fiery young activist getting busted for breaking into a laboratory and, whatta you know, it's my little sister. So here I am, see if I can do anything to help."

"Wait a minute," Stone said, "Sara told me you said to call me the night she was arrested."

"No, I didn't," said Sara, "I told you Saul said you were the only one I could trust up here, to call you if I ever got in trouble. He told me that when we were both visiting our grandparents in the city. What is this, anyway. Why are you cross-examining me?"

"Because little things like this keep happening. I came over here to check out another one. How come the Germans working at Riegar knew you were coming here? They were expecting you, you know."

"What?" said Sara.

Saul Rosen's face lost all conviviality. He stared at Stone and said, "Explain that."

"What's to explain? According to a source I consider reliable, the German workers at Riegar were expecting Sara to arrive."

"That's a conclusion," said Saul. "What are the facts that led you to that conclusion?"

"Hey," said Stone, "who's the lawyer around here? The Germans are quoted as talking repeatedly about 'when we get Sara' or 'when we have Sara.' "

"But that's not possible!" Sara protested.

"It's possible," Saul muttered darkly, "but not probable." He looked directly at Stone. "So, in spite of everything in the past, you suspect not only my sister but me?"

Stone returned Saul's glance levelly. "When things look funny, they look funny. When they don't add up, they don't add up. I mean, the Germans are expecting her, and here she is. *No* one's expecting you, and here *you* are."

"Look," said Saul, "we're talking trust here. I told my sister she could trust you. In Nam, you trusted me with your life. Now you don't trust *us?*"

"Tell me," Stone said intently, "that neither of you is with the Mossad."

"The *Mossad?*" Saul Rosen spit it out with half a laugh and half a snort. "The Mossad *hates* me, for Christ's sake. For reasons I can't go into." He paused, then said, "How 'bout this?" Saul Rosen raised his right hand and said, "I swear by all we've been through together, I am not now, nor have I ever been, a member of the Mossad."

"What about her?"

"I dunno," said Saul. "What about you, sis? You with the Mossad?"

Sara looked at both of them with disgust. "I wouldn't know the Mossad from B'nai B'rith! What is it with you people, anyway? I mean, first my brother shows up, out of the blue, at *the* most inopportune time on a Sunday morning," Sara said, rolling her eyes upward in a 'Why me, God?' expression, "then, here comes my lawyer, who my brother makes me give the finger to through the door, and who then accuses me of being a Mossad agent. I mean, shit, guys, what's going on here? What'd that crazy finger thing mean, anyway? That's how the Mossad people identify each other?"

Stone grinned, and Saul broke into laughter. "The signal," Stone said, "comes from Nam. You won't find it in any squad-tactics manual, but what it means is, 'I'm fucked, cover your ass.' You give it, for example, when you're on point, and you walk into an ambush. You see the bad guys, and they see you. Only they're waiting for the rest of the patrol to walk into the trap with you. Saul gave me that signal once, and it saved my life. He took a round through his lung."

"I never could figure out," Sara said to Saul, "what you were doing in Vietnam."

"I was in the Israeli Defense Forces, full of piss and vinegar, and volunteered for a counterterrorist group working the beach approaches and operating by small boat in and out of hostile territory in Lebanon. They sent me to cross-train with the U.S. Navy SEALs, best in the world at that stuff. That I was also a U.S. citizen gave me an in. It also got my ass in trouble. Someone in the IDF with a weird sense of humor figured the best training is combat. Got me attached to this beach hopper's unit in Nam. I didn't get to go home until I took that round and my lung collapsed."

Stone, who had been mentally filling in Saul's bare-bones tale with his own recollections of close-quarter battle they had shared, suddenly turned to Sara and said, "What was so awful about Saul's showing up this morning? Something going on here I don't know?"

As if in answer to his question, Stone heard a key enter the lock of Sara's front door. He looked and saw the knob turn. The door opened and a very tall, very thin young man stood there with a bag full of groceries. The expression on his face was intense and unpleasant. His eyes fixed on Stone. "Him, I know," he said, nodding toward Saul. He nodded toward Stone and looked at Sara. "Who's he?"

"It's Michael Stone, Eddie. Remember? My lawyer. I told you about him. Eddie Berg, Michael Stone."

"Hi," said Stone, putting out his hand.

Eddie Berg ignored Stone's proffered hand. He kept both of his firmly on the bag of groceries and headed for the kitchen. "Hi," he said in passing.

Stone turned his hand over and scrutinized his palm. Sara, whose arms were at her sides, spread her hands out, dipped her head, and headed for the front door, saying to Stone, "Could I see you outside for a minute, please?"

"Sure," said Stone. He followed her out the door.

"Let's go for a little walk," said Sara. "I need to talk to you."

"Same here," said Stone. "You gave another press conference—this one without me there—to the Reuters guy. I need to know exactly what you said in addition to what was in the Sunday paper. And I want to know *why*."

"First," said Sara, "I want to talk to you about Eddie."

"He's the raptor guy you had a thing with."

"Right."

"I can't see why you broke up with him. He's such a very pleasant person. Gotta be great at parties."

"There's no point being sarcastic. Eddie has his faults, completely unjustified jealousy being one of them and a single-minded devotion to his causes being another. I broke up with him because of the jealousy. He's here, in spite of his pride, because of what's going on at Riegar. And, I guess, my telling him about what a great guy my lawyer is wasn't a smart move. You're just going to have to make allowances to get along with him."

"*I'm* going to have to make allowances? Why? I'm not *his* lawyer. And I'm not going to be, either. He gets his devoted ass busted, fuck him. He's on his own. And something tells me with *his* attitude problem, he's gonna *get* his ass busted."

"Oh, Michael, please. This whole thing down at Riegar is a mess. Completely unorganized. And Eddie's an *incredible* organizer. That's why I'm putting up with him. I'm not asking you to like him, just don't do anything to screw things up."

They were downstairs by now and out on the balmy Sunday sidewalk.

"*I* shouldn't screw things up? What do you call giving that Irish reporter an interview without your lawyer present? And admitting, goddamn it, that the pictures exist?"

They turned back toward the building. "Michael, don't you see? The pictures don't really show anything. The apparatus was empty. But Riegar doesn't know what isn't in the pictures. Maybe you can make a deal—"

"Damn it, Sara, the only deals I'm going to make are with the prosecutor—to try to get you off. And you've just made that much harder."

"I'm sorry, Michael, I just thought—"

"Well, *stop* thinking, okay? When it comes to this stuff, you're not good at it. And another thing. I don't care if you fuck Eddie Berg, but don't fuck *around* with him. Get that? Guy looks like a fanatic. He's gonna go down in flames, and I don't want you along for the ride."

Sara flushed. "Who are you to talk to me like that!"

"Your lawyer. Or do you want to get someone else?"

"No . . . no . . ."

They reached the door to Sara's apartment. "Okay," said Stone, "I want to know *everything* you told the Reuters guy."

"Other than the stuff about the pictures that you read, it was pretty much a combination of a rehash of the press conference and me dodging his questions—'Was I in there?' and 'Did I take the pictures?' I remembered what you said. Believe me, if I'd admitted anything, you'd have read that, too."

"What's your take on the guy?"

"The reporter? That's what he is. Asks questions. That's what reporters do. Why?"

"I dunno. Too many coincidences, too many little things. I just remembered why that detective, Fisher, looked familiar. He's the guy was hanging around the water cooler when we left the courtroom. Snoopin'."

"You're getting paranoid, Michael. Reporters ask questions. Detectives snoop."

"Yeah, maybe you're right."

The two of them reentered the apartment. Saul was seated, eating a bagel and cream cheese. Eddie Berg was pacing up and down, fuming. As soon as he saw them, he opened his mouth to speak.

"Don't start, Eddie," Sara said, "just don't start."

Stone ignored Eddie Berg and spoke to Saul. "I don't think either one of us is exactly welcome here just now. Got plenty of room over at my place. Cooking's great, and the price is right. Whatta 'ya say. Grab your gear and let's launch."

"Thought you'd never ask," said Saul, swallowing his last mouthful of bagel. He got up and picked up a suitcase. "Ciao, everybody," he said to his sister and Eddie Berg. Then he grinned at Stone and said, "Good to go."

Helmar Metz was angry. "I tell you she knows something!" He held a newspaper in front of the seated Georg Kramer and pointed to a line of text. " 'Monkey handler,' she used the term *monkey handler*. Isn't that the exact term you told me is the . . . How do you call it? Nickname used by your employees for the men I provided Letzger? That's inside information! She didn't come by *that* in a late-night intrusion."

"I saw that article." Kramer was trying to calm Metz with a

moderate tone and reason. "You'll note that the article deals with the employee of another company who actually *was* a 'monkey handler.' That's what he did—he handled monkeys, and one of them bit him in the chest. He caught the disease that was harmless to the monkey, and because he was a human, not a monkey, he died. That's all there was to it. It was just a coincidence."

Metz slapped the paper down on the top of the desk that now belonged to him and sat down. "I don't like coincidences," Metz said. "Not when so much is at stake. We must know everything that woman knows. She must be working for someone, someone she reports to. That means she must prepare reports—"

"You're thinking like a German," said Kramer, "very logically. Americans are not always so logical—" He was interrupted by the ringing of the telephone on the desk. Helmar Metz, leaning back in the spring-loaded chair behind it, checked his instinct to pick up the phone, motioning instead to Kramer, who was sitting in the wing chair. Kramer dutifully got up and answered his own telephone, listened for several moments, then said, "I'll be back to you," and hung up.

"Well?" said Metz.

"That was Fisher, the local detective I told you about who moonlights for our security company."

"Moonlights?"

"An American expression for a second job. He's my contact with the motorcycle thugs. One of them is an informant for him on drug matters. He reports that a half dozen of them beat up the lawyer for the Rosen woman, but that he gave a good account of himself. He has physical courage."

"His present condition?"

"Fisher says the gang members he talked to said they were careful not to put him in the hospital or damage him where it could be seen. Face is okay, for example. Oddly enough, Fisher's informant says a couple of the attackers needed medical attention."

"All right," said Metz, "he has physical courage. We'll see if he has moral courage. With your other idea, you may go forward."

Kramer picked up the telephone again. He punched in a number from memory and said, "It'll just take a phone call."

* * *

With the longest day of the year only twenty days away, at a little after 8:00 A.M. on Monday, the first of June, sunlight already flooded Aunt May's kitchen as Stone and Saul Rosen were finishing breakfast. "So, how long can you stay?" Stone asked.

"Within reason, as long as I want."

"Got a ton of annual leave stored up, huh?"

"Yeah, but that's not the reason. I'm under the ambassador, and he can do pretty much what he wants with his personnel. I'm just an assistant to one of his assistants, remember. When I told him my sister was in trouble, he said to take off and not worry about it. You know how Jews are about family."

"Something everyone could take a lesson from," Aunt May interjected. "Speaking of family, a man your age, which is about the *same age as my nephew,* should be married and having one of his own by this time, wouldn't you say?"

"Are you sure," Saul asked Stone, "your aunt isn't Jewish?"

"Worse," said Stone. "She's Irish Catholic. They *really* know how to lay a guilt trip on you. I'll put Catholic guilt up against Jewish guilt and spot you five any day."

The telephone interrupted simultaneous attempted rebuttals from Saul and Aunt May. Eager to get out of the hole he was digging for himself, Stone scooped it off the kitchen wall, said, "This is he," then listened for a minute and said, "Yeah, I mean, yes, sir. Your office at eight forty-five. Yes. I could do that . . . right."

"I'll be damned," said Stone.

"You will, indeed," agreed Aunt May.

"What is it?" asked Saul.

"That was old man Van der Hoven himself. Wants me to meet him in his office at eight forty-five. That's late in the morning for him. I see him going to work when I'm still running."

"Who is this bird?" asked Saul.

"Current senior partner of a law firm that was founded when the first Van der Hoven stepped off the *Half Moon* when Henry Hudson sailed her up the river. Local lawyers in their day to the Vanderbilts, the Roosevelts, and the rest of that crew."

"I wonder," said Aunt May, "what he wants with the likes of you?"

"I don't know," said Stone, "but I'm sure going to find out. Want to ride with me downtown, Saul? It's an easy walk back, and you can get to look the town over."

Saul Rosen grimaced. "Jeeze, Mike! You just got through damn near killing me on that Marine reserve obstacle course this morning. If you don't mind, I'll hang here for a bit and digest this great meal, then I think I'll walk down to the Riegar plant and check it out—see what's going on."

"You one of those animal-welfare people like your sister?" asked Aunt May.

"No, ma'am. Though I'd hate to think those Germans are treating helpless animals like Jews."

Stone checked his watch. "I'm outta here. Tell ya about it when I get back."

As Michael Stone steered the Mustang through downtown Rhinekill, he yielded to an irresistible urge and went two blocks out of his way to drive past the public defender's office. When he saw the yellow Prelude parked out front, he swept his eyes upward to the building's windows, felt an ache deep inside him, then condemned himself for being little boy foolish. That accounted for the stern look on his face as he entered the office of William Van der Hoven.

The man behind the huge mahogany desk looked like a self-portrait of Frans Hals in the latest from Brooks Brothers. The office itself resembled a museum more than a law office. The ceiling was high, the paneling everywhere and almost covered completely by oil portraits of ancient Van der Hovens and seventeenth-century deeds to half the New World. Hidden among all this was the usual in the way of academic and bar-membership credentials. Van der Hoven himself looked as if he wouldn't accept a fee unless it was in gold. "Come in, Mr. Stone," he said with a voice surprisingly firm for someone so old. "Sit down. Good of you to come over on such short notice. Cigar?"

Stone took a seat in a deep maroon leather chair and declined the cigar with a gesture.

"Little early for me, too," said Van der Hoven. Then he said, "I'll get right to the point, sir. You've been following this savings-and-loan mess that's still all over the news?" Van der Hoven assumed Stone had and continued without waiting for an answer. "Bad business, sir. Bad business. But, as with everything, from the point of view of this firm, some good has come of it.

"After all the mergers and reformations have shaken out, the firm has ended up representing several more banks in the area and one savings and loan. The manpower resources of the firm are taken up completely with the banks and our other clients. The savings and loan, under the new federal rules, will be limiting its investments strictly to real estate mortgage loans—what savings and loans were invented to do and did well until they got greedy and went into things they knew nothing about. But they're back on the track now, sir, back on the track!

"To be brief, the firm needs a lawyer with knowledge of the local real estate scene and experience in real estate law to handle this one client. I must tell you that were he still alive, this offer would have been made to your uncle. Outstanding man in his field. But it is your field, too, and from what everyone tells me, you're good at it. Now, do you know what a newly admitted lawyer who graduated from, say, Fordham or Columbia Law as Law Review and in the top ten percent of his class commands in New York City? Ninety thousand a year, sir. Ninety thousand a year."

Stone broke in as Van der Hoven paused for breath in his "brief" monologue. "I think you may have received some bad information, sir. I was never Law Review, and I wasn't in the top ten percent of my class."

Van der Hoven didn't like being interrupted by anyone under seventy. "Let me finish, sir. Let me finish. In spite of his academic performance, a newly admitted lawyer is an unknown quantity when it comes to practicing law. You have experience, sir. In the exact field we need. I'm offering you a position as a senior associate at ninety thousand a year. When can you start?"

"Mr. Van der Hoven, I haven't accepted your offer yet. I'd like a little time to think it over, I—"

"Time, young man, is something that unfortunately we do not have. This client, for all intents and purposes, is a brand-new institution. It must get off to a correct start. The scrutiny will be severe, as you can imagine, in view of the circumstances. I'd like you to start tomorrow."

"Sir, that's not possible. I represent a young woman—"

"Yes, yes, yes, I know all about that. Against Riegar Pharmaceutical—"

"No, sir. Against the state of New York, which indicted her."

"Principle's the same. She's accused of breaking into the Riegar premises. Riegar is a client of the firm. I'm afraid there's a clear conflict of interest here."

Stone stood up. His face was cold with anger. "No," he said, deliberately dropping the *sir*. "There is no conflict, because I am not now, nor will I ever be, representing your firm." He looked at his watch. "You have just wasted a half hour of my time in an attempt to bribe me to discontinue representing my client. I'd have you up on charges before the bar association if I didn't know it'd be a waste of more of my time, the way you guys play cover each other's ass. Which, *sir,* is where I suggest you stick your offer."

Stone turned on his heel and walked out, leaving the door to Van der Hoven's office wide open. "Here!" He could hear the old man's voice shouting as he left. *"Here!"*

9

● SAUL ROSEN WAS STILL RUBBING HIS EYES WHEN he walked into Aunt May's kitchen on Tuesday morning. "Sorry," he announced, "I overslept." His disheveled hair and the stubble on his jaw proved it. The chiming of the grandfather clock reproached him. Saul looked small in Stone's bathrobe, the shoulder seams hanging halfway down his upper arms.

"Just in time," Aunt May said with a hint of disapproval in her voice. "The kitchen was about to close. Sit down, there're still some scrambled eggs left that the disposal there was too embarrassed to finish."

"Ha!" Stone replied. "She's really mad 'cause I *didn't* finish them. If I ate everything Mazie cooked for me, I could work out *four* hours a day and still end up a blimp." He looked accusingly at Saul. "I was looking for you this morning when I started my run."

"Hey," said Saul, seating himself at the table and picking up a brimming cup of hot coffee, "I'm still getting over the Marine 'O course.' I'm the same age you are, and we're both out of the 'Hoo-Rah' business. Only I admit it. I'll work out with you from time to time, but you still go at it like the old days. I'm not getting shinsplints and worn-out knees because you're a fanatic." He sipped some more coffee and picked up a section of the morning paper, saying, "What's new?"

"Eddie Berg's looking for trouble. Got himself arrested down at the Riegar plant yesterday. Violating an injunction not to interfere with employees going to work."

Saul put down the paper and relied on Stone for the details. "What'd he do?"

"Chained himself to the main gate. Five'll getcha ten I get a call from Sara to help him out."

"No deal. She's stuck on the guy."

"Yeah," said Stone, "I can't figure it. Guy's been around raptors so long, he's developed their personality."

"What's a raptor?" asked Aunt May, putting a plate down in front of Saul.

"Bird of prey," Stone answered.

"You mean like an eagle?" The telephone started ringing. Aunt May went to pick it up off the wall.

"Looks and acts more like a vulture to me," Stone said, but Aunt May was listening to the telephone.

"For six months?" she said into the receiver. "All my bills for six months?" She listened awhile more, then said, "Well, how much do you think I'll get back? . . . I see. Well, all right, I'll bring them down this morning."

As Aunt May hung up, Stone said, "What was that all about?"

"New York Oil and Gas. The government says they overcharged customers. Something about counting a tax as an expense in setting the rates or something, I don't know. If I take my bills down for the last six months, they can tell how much I should get back."

"Wonder why they didn't write you a letter."

"I don't know. Everything's different these days. Nobody has any last names. I'm supposed to see Marsha, whoever she is."

"Better take a sandwich," said Stone. "There'll be a line a mile long behind the person who tells you where to find Marsha." Stone got up and pulled down the bottom of his suit coat to make it fit better over his shoulders. "Well," he said, "I've gotta get going. Gonna hit the DA with another motion in Sara's case. Make him work for it." He turned to Saul. "What're you gonna do, go back to bed?"

"Nope," said Saul, lingering over his coffee, "gonna shave 'n bathe and check out the fun down at Riegar."

"Just don't get busted," Stone said, smiling, and was out the door.

As Stone's Mustang pulled out of the driveway at 182 Garden Street, a man in a dark green Chevrolet four-door sedan, parked half a block back on the same side of the street, spoke in German into a transceiver: "I have him."

The transceiver's squelch broke with the reply: "Not too close." The Chevy driver hit his transmit button twice to acknowledge the instruction, then pulled away from the curb.

A little while later, Aunt May, clutching a pocketbook containing six months' worth of heating-oil bills, started walking toward downtown.

Again there was a transmission in German, this one from a Chrysler K car across the street, three houses up, watching through a side mirror. "She's afoot!"

"So? Get out and follow on foot!" The speaker was dressed in coveralls and a paper cap that read DURON, and was seated in the right-front seat of a van with a rack of ladders on the top. The side of the van read CLARKE & SONS, PAINTING CONTRACTORS. It was parked on Blain Terrace, a side street that intersected Garden. "That's both of them," the passenger said to the van driver. "Let's go."

The van pulled out, turned left onto Garden Street, and made directly for number 182. It turned into the driveway and drove under the porte cochere. The man in the right-front seat got out, glanced at the massive front door, and continued along the side of the house to the rear. There, arms akimbo, he looked up at the rear of the house as if estimating the time it would take to paint it.

Inside the house, Saul Rosen rinsed off his razor in the sink of the same second-floor bathroom his sister had used. Face still bearing the residue of shaving cream, he stepped into the bathtub, pulled the curtain, and turned the shower on full blast.

The man in the Duron painter's cap noted with satisfaction that several second-floor windows were open to the balmy early June breezes, then walked back to the truck. He gestured to the driver, then toward the ladders. The driver dismounted, reached around into the club-cab area behind the front seat, and took out two five-gallon paint cans, both labeled DURON, and set them heavily on the ground. Then he went to assist his boss in taking down an aluminum extension ladder from the rack on top of the truck.

The two men carried the ladder to the rear of the house and, holding it upright, pulled the rope to extend it, then set it carefully in place beneath the second-floor hall window. That accomplished, the men walked back and each carried one of the five-gallon paint cans to the base of the ladder. The man with the Duron cap went up first, carrying one of the paint cans, as the driver held the base of the ladder steady. At the top of the ladder, the climber first passed his paint can through the hall window, then himself. He checked quickly, then leaned out and gestured to the man on the ground. The driver picked up the other can and made his way up the ladder and inside.

As he entered the second floor, the driver, the younger of the two, cocked his head and said, *"Wasser?"* The sound of running water somewhere was clear. The first man pointed outside the window toward the rear yard. There, at the right rear of the property, a large water-fan sprinkler was soaking Aunt May's early radish and carrot bed. The driver grunted in reply, then the two men made their way downstairs, carrying the paint cans with them.

On the first floor, the men split up, methodically searching each room, looking behind paintings on the wall and anywhere else it would be logical to hide a safe. When the driver entered Stone's office, he saw immediately that his search was over. In the right-front corner of the office stood an ancient Mosler that housed the wills that Stone's late uncle Harry had drawn and held for safekeeping against the deaths of his clients, clients now inherited by Michael Stone. "Here," the driver called. The older man joined him, then slipped a screwdriver from a tool loop in his overalls and used it to pry the lid off one of the five-gallon paint cans.

There was no paint inside the can. Instead, the man withdrew a portable cellular telephone and walked over to Michael Stone's office desk. It was still furnished with Harry Stone's old leather blotter holder and onyx desk set: double set of Parker pens on an onyx base, matching windup clock, onyx-based letter holder stuffed with bills to be paid and correspondence that could be put off, and a "perpetual" calendar that had not yet been switched from May to June. He set the phone down on the desk and the two then conferred about the safe. "Old," said the younger man. "Should be easy to cut through with the torch."

"No. This is a lawyer's office. The principal hazard is from fire. That box probably has alternating layers of steel and copper to draw off the heat. To burn it will take too much time."

"Drill, then?"

"Not necessary. As you say, it is old. We pull the spindle." He turned to pry off the lid of the other paint can.

Upstairs and on the other side of the vast Victorian house, Saul Rosen shut off the water to his shower and fished around on the rack for a bath towel.

A quarter of a mile away, Aunt May, disgusted that the personnel at the offices of New York Oil and Gas had never heard of Marsha and didn't know what she was talking about when she proffered her bills for a refund, declined to wait around until the manager had time to see her and walked out the door in indignation, convinced that the state of the world was even worse than she had suspected. Her surveillor, startled to see her emerge so soon, took refuge behind a parked car and rapidly punched a number into his lightweight cellular telephone.

The cellular telephone on Michael Stone's office desk rang, and the leader picked it up, saying, "Ja, ja."

"The old woman," said the voice on the telephone, "is returning."

"Delay her. We need more time."

Saul Rosen, dripping water onto the bath mat, pressed the towel hard to his face to absorb the water from in and around his eyes. It was then that he heard the telephone downstairs. Because of the distance, the sound was faint. He decided not to try to answer it and take a message. It would undoubtedly stop ringing just as he got there. Suddenly, Saul Rosen's skin started to tighten at the base of his spine, the way it tightened in Vietnam when he walked into the tall grass and first suspected he had entered an ambush. The telephone had rung just once. Sure, someone could have changed his mind and hung up after the first ring, but that was unusual. More important was the fact that it was an *electronic* ring—and there were no electronic telephones in Michael Stone's house. Very slowly, Saul wrapped the towel around his dripping waist and eased through the bathroom door into his bedroom.

Saul wiped his hands carefully along his thighs to towel them dry, then slowly reached into his suitcase to withdraw a Browning P-35 Hi Power 9 mm semiautomatic pistol. A small hole directly behind the trigger betrayed the fact that the magazine safety had been removed. He depressed the safety on the left side of the frame and the hooked top of it slipped out of a notch in the bottom of the slide, freeing it. Saul eased back the slide, checking to ensure that there was a round in the chamber. That brought the hammer back into the cocked position. He left it that way, and left the safety off as he made his way carefully down the hall toward the stairway.

Downstairs, in Michael Stone's office, the man in the painter's cap froze abruptly.

"Was ist . . . ?" the younger man started to say, only to be hushed by the movement of a finger to the lips of his leader.

"Das Wasser," the leader whispered. The younger man cocked his head. The sound of running water was greatly diminished. He looked out the window toward the garden. The sprinkler fan was still oscillating.

The two men, moving as slowly and silently as they could, both reached into the second paint can and withdrew identical .22-caliber Walther PP semiautomatic pistols to which slides had been fitted from the PPK model. Because the PPK slide was shorter, the PP barrel protruded five-eighths of an inch from the shorter slide. The protruding part had been threaded and a six-inch tubular-steel sound suppressor screwed onto it. Both men carefully checked for a round in the chamber, then proceeded out of Stone's office.

As Aunt May walked down Albany Street away from the New York Oil and Gas offices, her step was sprightly enough for a woman twenty years younger. She threw her head back to inhale the scent of late spring, then blew it out sharply as her lungs took in more auto exhaust than fresh air. With an alternating roaring and hissing of air brakes, a diesel-powered bus turned onto the street at the other end of the block. Aunt May wrinkled her nose in disgust. More pollution. A body couldn't even enjoy a springtime walk through town anymore, what with all the smelly machines. And the people! Time was when people stopped to say hello to friends and were at least courteous to women. Now a woman was lucky not to be bowled over by some fresh child in a hurry.

Aunt May felt a presence behind and to her left. It was a man, she could tell, much larger than she. He was too close for comfort, invading her personal space. Probably, Aunt May thought, trying boorishly to get through the crowd ahead of everyone else so he could push his way first onto the bus, now headed for the curb.

As the man started to thrust her toward the street, Aunt May's eyes blazed with indignation. She started to turn toward him, and said, "Now, see here!"

As Aunt May turned, the man, his body now directly against hers, swept her up in a running push. "Oh!" she cried, her legs trying but failing to keep up with her motion and starting to trip. She turned away from the offending man to see where she was going and try to regain her balance. Too late, she realized her right foot was out over the curb. It came down nearly a foot farther than she expected, pitching her violently forward. On the startling blast of an air horn, she looked upward. *Oh, dear God!* May thought as the blind eye of the bus headlight swung inexorably toward her in what seemed like slow motion. *It's going to hit me!*

Instinctively, Aunt May threw up her right arm and turned her face away as the right-front corner of the bus struck her all along her body. She lost consciousness to the sound of her own cry being drowned out by the screech of air brakes and the descending howl of the bus's turbocharger. As the asphalt rose to meet her, Aunt May was furious at the thought of dying because of the rudeness of the kind of man who probably wouldn't give up his seat to a pregnant woman on crutches.

* * *

Moving silently on his bare feet, Saul Rosen, pistol held at the ready in both hands, made his way farther down the hall. He stayed along the wall until he came opposite the long banister that protected the stairwell, and eased over to it. Saul positioned himself at the edge of the stairwell, taking care not to expose any part of his body to anyone who might be watching below, and listened for any sound that might betray an intruder. In the silence of the great house, all he could hear was the faint running of water and the slow ticking of the grandfather clock in the hallway below. Slowly, a pool of water gathered below Saul's left foot as the bathwater on the inside of his legs slid downward. The water dripped off his big toe onto the small space between the carpeting and the edge of the stairwell, left bare to the hardwood floor because of the difficulty of fitting carpeting around the rails of the banister. The water pooled, then started to drip over the edge.

The first drop of water fell onto the face of the bareheaded gunman as he was looking upward through the stair railing toward the first landing. He froze, then moved back gingerly to find and inform his superior, who was in the kitchen doorway. The man in the painter's hat smiled mirthlessly at this intelligence, then gestured silently to his subordinate. The younger man carefully made his way back to Michael Stone's office and repositioned the cellular telephone, glancing as he did toward the large overstuffed leather wing chair, intended for clients, that sat to the right front of the office desk. Satisfied with the position of the phone, the man crouched down behind the big chair, invisible to the office door.

Saul Rosen, hearing nothing after a period of intent listening, descended the stairs slowly, his back to the wall, keeping his pistol close so as not to "flag" his approach. From the cracked-open kitchen door, the senior intruder watched the reflection of the bottom of the stairs in the glass of the cabinet of the grandfather clock. Silently, Saul Rosen's bare lower leg appeared, then he swung suddenly left, pistol outstretched, to cover the living room. At that moment, the man in the kitchen finished pushing the last button on the kitchen telephone. A moment later, the portable telephone on Michael Stone's desk broke the silence with its startling electronic ring.

Saul pivoted expertly 180 degrees and covered the open door to

Stone's office. The telephone continued to ring. Saul crossed quickly to the doorway and glanced between the rear edge of the door and the frame to satisfy himself that no one was hiding behind the door. He checked again to see that the safety was off the Browning, then slowly approached the cellular phone.

As Saul Rosen reached the phone, his back was to the empty chair. At that moment, the younger burglar rose silently from behind it and, with one smooth motion, slammed the suppressor-equipped barrel directly behind Saul Rosen's right ear. Blood running from behind his ear down his neck, Saul Rosen collapsed into a limp, wet pile on the Oriental rug. A hand reached down, took the Browning from his reach, removed the magazine and ejected the cartridge from the chamber, then threw the piece back down on the floor six feet away. Immediately, the two burglars turned to their task. With a cold chisel and hammer taken from the paint cans, they knocked the dial off the front of the safe, then mounted a screw-operated extractor device to the spindle and pulled it from the opening in the safe door.

. The man in the painter's hat operated the handle, and the safe door swung open with a squeak that asked for oil. He opened, then cast aside the petty-cash box and scooped out an accumulation of wills, all neatly enclosed in paper pockets that proclaimed in Old English script "Last Will and Testament of . . ." followed by handwritten names in the older documents, typewritten in the more recent.

Sara's photographs were not apparent. The leader picked up the will packets and, holding them by their closed ends, flipped them downward sharply so that the documents flew out onto the floor. No photographs. *"Scheiss!"* he muttered, then checked his watch. "We go," he said.

"But—" the younger man started to object.

"The intelligence is bad. There was a third person where there were supposed to be two. Who knows whether there's a fourth about to return? The whole house is left to be searched. There is no time. We go."

The men put their tools and weapons back in the paint cans and left, this time by the front door. They had retrieved their ladder and were gone by the time Saul Rosen, head throbbing and feeling nauseated, returned to consciousness.

* * *

It hadn't taken Michael Stone long to serve the district attorney personally with his writ, then walk over to the office of the clerk of the court to file a copy there for the judge. That accomplished, there were still some papers left in his undernourished briefcase, some title searches that were long overdue, thanks to his preoccupation with the troubles of Sara Rosen. He went upstairs to the great room, where all the deeds recorded in Mohawk County since the time of the Dutch colonists were entered on great two-and-a-half-foot-square ledgers, and methodically went to work.

Stone finished his stint in the record room just before noon. He hadn't seen Ira Levin for a while and thought to drop in on him for the latest, be it solid information or mere gossip. Whatever Levin had to offer, it would at least be entertaining.

The door to Levin's cigar store was propped open to take advantage of the beautiful day. However, it served its most important function, as far as Stone was concerned, by venting to the outside the large concentration of lethal cigar smoke in which Ira Levin, like some alien creature that breathed another gas, seemed to thrive. Stone was expecting Ira's customary enthusiastic greeting, so he was surprised when a look of sorrow crossed the man's face when he saw Stone and said, "Aw, counselor, I'm so sorry. How's your aunt?"

"May? Fine when I left her this morning. Why the long face, Ira? What's there to be sorry about?"

Levin guessed immediately that Stone hadn't heard about his aunt's accident. "Come in the back, Michael, come in the back." His voice and face were grim.

"What is it?" Stone asked, standing with Levin in the back storeroom cum office. "What's going on?"

Ira Levin spoke as calmly and reassuringly as he could under the circumstances. "I hate to be the one to tell you, counselor, but your aunt had an accident earlier this morning. She was walking on Albany Street and, I dunno how it happened, but, maybe she was tryin' to get on a bus or something—"

"Ira, for Christ's sake, what *is* it!"

Ira Levin drew a deep breath and ran it all together: "Your aunt was hit by a bus at a bus stop. They took her down the hospital. She's hurt, I dunno how bad—"

"Thanks, Ira. Jesus!" Michael Stone turned to run out of the store, Ira calling out after him, "Come back and lemme know how she is, okay?"

Stone sprinted to the parking lot, burned rubber to the exit, shoved a five-dollar bill at the startled lot manager, and, without waiting for change, roared off down the street toward the hospital.

The emergency-room nurse directed Stone to the intensive-care unit, telling him only that his aunt was alive and insisting that only the attending physician in intensive care could give him any further information. Frustrated, concerned, and angry, Michael Stone burst into the intensive-care unit, confronted the chief nurse, and demanded to see the attending physician: *"Now!"*

The chief nurse was accustomed to dealing with distraught relatives, but nothing in her experience ever before had exposed her to anything like the cold and deadly eyes of the Michael Stone who stood before her. "One moment, sir," she said, then picked up the phone and said, "Dr. Heller, come to the station, please, right away." Then, to Stone, she said, "He'll be right here." Her voice was frightened.

There was the sound of a pneumatic-mechanical slam, and big double doors from the main hall burst open. Through them, white coat and stethoscope flying, came a young man with dark wavy hair, wearing wire-rimmed glasses. "Yes?" he said to the nurse. She just nodded her head toward Stone.

"I'm Michael Stone. I understand you have my aunt, Mary Stone— she goes by May—here. Accident case. I'm next of kin. I want to see her. How is she?"

Dr. Heller looked Stone right in the eye and said, "How she is depends upon whether you're one of the people who sees a glass of water half full or half empty. The half-full guy sees good news. Your aunt's alive and gives every indication of staying that way. The half-empty part is that she's hurt. She's got a fractured rotator cuff of the right arm, broken right rib, lacerated right kidney, and a hyperextension of the tendon inside her right knee. The most serious is the kidney. She has blood in her urine. But all her injuries should heal. The knee will probably bother her for a year. Have to wear a brace. You can look in on her for a minute if you want, but you'd do better coming back late this afternoon. She's out of it. Under sedation."

"What time?"

Heller looked at his watch. "Try after four. Anything else you want to know? I'll be off duty by then."

"Yeah. How'd it happen?"

"For that, you'd need the police. Or, after four, she may be able to tell you herself."

"Right," said Stone. "Thank you, Doctor. I'll just look in her door for a moment." He turned and left.

Ten minutes later, Stone turned the Mustang left off Blain Terrace onto Garden Street and was surprised to see Stephanie Hannigan's yellow Prelude starting to turn into his driveway at number 182. He gunned the Mustang to come up behind her, and both cars were still moving down the driveway when he blipped his horn to draw her attention.

Stephanie stopped under the porte cochere and stood by the door of her car, waiting for Stone. As he approached her, she said, "Oh, Mike. I'm so sorry about your aunt. I heard it on the radio while I was driving to lunch and came over to see if there was anything I could do."

Stephanie's use of "Mike" wasn't lost on Stone. He took it as a peace offering and accepted it gracefully by returning the favor. "Thanks, Neffie. I just came from the hospital. She's hurt, and it'll take her some time to heal—especially at her age—but they say she'll be okay. I can't talk to her until after four. She's under. C'mon in. I'll introduce you to my new roommate."

The word *roommate* sent an icy knife into Stephanie's stomach. Determined not to show the hurt, she affected nonchalance with an airy "Sure." Then she said, "What an extraordinary house! If it's as interesting inside as it is out, I'd love a fifty-cent tour."

"You got it," Stone said as he hit the doorbell. "If you'll take potluck, I'll throw in lunch—though it may be a peanut butter and jelly sandwich and glass of milk."

"Brought up on them," Stephanie said as the front door swung open. To her immense relief, Saul Rosen was standing there, left hand on the doorknob, right holding a kitchen towel full of crushed ice to the back of his right ear. He was dressed in jeans and a khaki military-style shirt, and he had the Browning pistol tucked into his waistband.

"The hell happened to you?" asked Stone. Then, remembering Stephanie, he said, "Saul Rosen, Stephanie Hannigan. Saul's my client's brother. We're rooming together for a while. Stephanie, here, is the mainstay of the public defender's office."

"Which," said Stephanie as they all moved inside, "will come as news to the public defender. Oh, Mike, the place is fabulous!"

"Thanks," said Stone. Then, addressing Saul, he said, "So what happened? And what's with the nine mil.?"

"What," Stephanie asked, "is a nine mil.?"

Saul answered her by pointing to the Browning, then said to Stone, "I'm afraid I've got bad news for you, ace. Your ol' combat buddy screwed up. While I was taking a shower just after you and May left, someone got in here. I heard him—or rather his goddamn portable phone—got the 9 mil., and went down to take him for you. Only he took me. Damn near took my head off. Then ripped off your safe. Sorry, guy. Shit."

They walked into Stone's office and surveyed the ravaged safe, its contents strewn over the floor. Stone carefully avoided stepping on them as he went to both windows and pulled the shades all the way down to cover them completely. Then he moved to his desk, took a torn-open business-sized manila envelope out of the letter rack, looked inside it, and announced, "It's okay. They're still here."

"You mean, what they were looking for in your safe was in the letter holder on your desk all the time?" Stephanie asked.

"Yup. Last place they'd have looked for it."

"Where in your misspent youth," asked Saul, "did you pick up that bit of trade craft?"

"In my misspent American Lit class sophomore year in high school, when we studied Poe."

The Purloined Letter. " Stephanie said it slowly, her look at Stone appraising. With a new respect in her voice, she said, "And I'll bet you just pulled down the shades because you read Conan Doyle, didn't you?"

"Uh-huh."

"Wow."

"Would somebody mind telling a young Jewish boy raised in a kibbutz what this conversation's all about?" Saul pleaded. "I mean, I spent most of my time studying the Torah and the rest of the Old Testament, but I don't go around using a sling when I can get an Uzi."

Stephanie smiled at Saul. "In the nineteenth century, two great writers, Edgar Allan Poe, an American, and Arthur Conan Doyle, an Englishman, wrote mystery fiction on a common theme—finding the hiding place of something very important. Poe wrote about a stolen letter, and the detective he created reasoned that it would be hidden best in plain sight, where no one would expect to find it. That's what Mike did with whatever it was the thief who hit you was looking for. Years later, Conan Doyle had his great detective, Sherlock Holmes, looking for the hiding place of a compromising photograph. He created a disturbance, a fire, then watched to see where the person who had hidden the photograph rushed to save it. That's why Mike pulled down the shades—in case the attack on you and the safe was a use of the same ploy."

Stone grinned. "You got it, kid."

"So," asked Saul, "what'd you save by being so well read?"

"Something belonging to my client."

"Oh, for Christ's sake, Mike," said Saul, "I'm her brother. You can say what it is."

"Mike's right," Stephanie said, defending Stone. "It's privileged. He's behaving like a lawyer."

"Yeah, well a lot of good it's doing him and my sister, his client. First her place is ripped off and now your own office. . . . I'm sorry, Mike. That was outta line; my brains are still a little scrambled, but I took leave to help the Mike Stone I knew in Nam, not a lawyer."

"Forget it. You're right."

"No, he isn't, Mike," said Stephanie. "In the restaurant, you didn't have much choice. Here the choice is clear. You handle it like a lawyer. Call the police."

"Call them about my aunt, too?" Stone's voice was cold.

"What about your aunt?" Saul asked.

"In the hospital. 'Accident.' "

They walked to the kitchen. "Party's getting rough," Saul said, holding out the ice-filled towel. It was soaked with his blood.

"You better get that attended to," Stephanie said.

"I'll be all right," Saul grumped. He was still upset with himself for having been bested.

"I don't guess you saw the guy?" Stone asked Saul.

"Nothing. Got a great look at the phone, though. When they try the phone, I'll make a great witness."

Stephanie looked in the refrigerator and overhead cabinets, then busied herself making salad and sandwiches. The peanut butter and jelly she made for herself, for the men there was cold roast beef and some sliced boiled ham and Swiss cheese. As she worked, she listened to the two men talking.

"You still didn't tell me what you're doing with a nine mil.," Stone said to Saul.

"Hey, I told you. I'm stationed in Washington, D.C., the murder capital of the United States. Only a lunatic would walk around town without a gun when every twelve-year-old has a piece."

Stephanie put the salad bowl and dishes out on the table, then handed Stone the roast-beef sandwich, Saul the ham and Swiss, and put the peanut butter and jelly at her own place. She was about to sit down when she suddenly said, "Oh, how stupid of me!" and switched the peanut butter and jelly over to Saul and took the ham and Swiss for herself. "No problem," said Saul. He grabbed Stone's roast beef and gave him the peanut butter and jelly. Quickly, Stone switched his peanut butter and jelly for Stephanie's newly acquired ham and Swiss.

"That was quick!" said Stephanie.

The three of them started to laugh. "Which sandwich has the pea under it?" Saul challenged.

"Quit changing the subject!" Stone laughed. "What are you doin' packing?"

"Ah, come on, Mike. I'm the assistant military attaché, an active-duty Israeli Defense Forces officer with diplomatic immunity, which is almost as much immunity as being twelve. The P-Thirty-five is our issue sidearm, you know that. It's the best nine mil. ever made."

"What about the new stuff with double action?"

"You know better'n that, too. Two completely different trigger pulls for the first and second shot. No offense to you and Stephanie, here, but none of the new stuff is designed by gunsmiths. These days, they're all designed by product-liability lawyers. Look at all the crap they've got stamped on the sides of the barrels: 'Do not stick in your mouth and pull trigger; it could be hazardous to your health.' That's why the new iron's loaded down with all those bells and whistles—so you don't shoot yourself. Trouble is, you can't shoot anyone else, either. Not for half an hour while you screw around with all the stuff they've put on there to defend against lawsuits. Christ, they've got regular safeties, magazine safeties, grip safeties, ambidextrous safeties, extended safeties, hammer-lowering levers, hammer blocks—"

"This conversation," interrupted Stephanie, "is way over my head and makes me nervous. Someone said something about a tour?"

Stone drained a glass of milk, checked his watch, and said, "Sure. Plenty of time. Go lie down, Saul. When I go the hospital to see Mazie, you're coming along to get that head looked at, not that they'll find much inside it."

Saul waved them out of the room. "What's a matter? Afraid I'll sue? You should've told Charlie in Nam you were a lawyer and threatened suit. Would've scared the shit out of him."

As they toured the old house, Stephanie was struck by the beauty and craftsmanship that were products of an age that had more time to devote to handwork, and in which things were expected to last and were built that way. She stopped at the windows to admire the different views, especially Aunt May's carefully tended flowers, and she hovered over the antique furniture pieces, displaying a knowledgeable appreciation that impressed her host. It was the latter interest that led her to discover which room was Stone's.

To Stephanie, there was something remarkably out of place in one of the bedrooms. At the foot of the bed was a massive chest, of obviously recent and relatively crude construction. "What's that?" she asked.

"What? Where?"

"There, by the foot of the bed."

"Why? What about it?"

"Well, the whole house is filled with fine old and antique furnishings. That looks like it was made last week, and not by Chippendale. It just looks a little out of place, that's all. What is it?"

"A sea chest. My sea chest. That's genuine teak. Had it made for me in P.I. The Philippines. It's got my gear in it, my old navy gear. This is my bedroom."

"I'm sorry, Mike. I'm sure it's a wonderful sea chest. You just don't expect to see one in a room like this. Why do you keep your navy things in it? I mean, why not put them away and keep your current things in it, where they're handy, at the foot of your bed?"

Stone stared at the chest with it's heavy padlock, then turned to look Stephanie in the eye. "I haven't opened that chest since the day I took off my navy uniform," he said softly, adding almost as an afterthought, "I feel more comfortable with it right where it is."

"Could I see them?"

"What?"

"Your uniforms."

"Sure." Stone laughed. "They're in the closet, there. Plenty of uniforms, no suits!"

"In the closet?" Stephanie's confusion showed in her look. "Then what's in the chest?"

"I told you. My gear. Tools of the trade."

Confusion left Stephanie's face and somberness moved in. "You just can't let go of it, can you, Mike?"

"I don't know. Maybe I just don't want to."

"Why haven't you opened it since you left the navy?"

Stone thought for a minute. "It's a tool box. I haven't had a need for those tools since then. What's the big deal, anyway?"

Stephanie felt uneasy. "I don't know. I guess it's the significance what's in there seems to have for you. I mean, if you follow your own analogy further, the whole law library over at the courthouse is one big set of tools, too. But you don't seem to feel the same way about it."

Stone's voice took on a note of exasperation. "So, how am I supposed to feel? Look, I'm one of the best there is at using what's in there. I can't say the same about what's in the law library, okay? What's more, the stuff in there works. And I can't say *that* a lot of the time about what's in the law library, that's all. I mean, I don't see the problem here."

Stephanie's legs felt weak. She was reacting emotionally, and she hated it. In an effort to recover, she sat on the end of Stone's bed and faced him, then forced herself to speak calmly and rationally. "The problem," she said, "is that you're not being fair with yourself. You've only been practicing for a relatively short time. There's no objective reason you can't be as good a lawyer as you are a, a—"

"SEAL," Stone interjected.

"Right. But you're never going to do it if you keep disparaging your legal abilities and persist in these . . . mystical feelings about what you used to do. That's over, Mike. You've got to keep this box closed, actually and psychologically."

"Why?"

"Why? I just told you. You'll never—"

"I know what you just told me. Now give me the real reason."

Stephanie seemed to wilt. She struggled with her emotions for a moment longer, then gave in and said, "Because I'm afraid, Mike."

"Of what?"

"Of you. Of what I saw in the restaurant. God, Mike, you didn't have any of your 'tools' there, and look what you did. What would have happened if you had? I guess . . . I guess I don't ever want to see what happens to you when you open this box."

Stone put his head back and drew a long breath through his nose, held it, then let it out slowly. He lowered his head and looked directly at Stephanie. "When a SEAL goes on an op," he said, "he goes into isolation for from twenty-four to ninety-six hours. In isolation, he clicks on. When he comes back, he goes into isolation again, for debrief, after-action report and to click off. You're right. You don't want to see a fully rigged-out, clicked-on SEAL. You don't want to be *near* one. But, so what? You could be married to one and never have occasion to see it. The only people who see it don't live to tell about it. I told you before. I wasn't clicked on in that restaurant. And that's no box. It's a chest."

Stephanie rose. "Freudian slip," she said.

"You think it's Pandora's box, don't you?"

Stephanie's legs were trembling. Presently she said, "I know it's an unfair comparison. When Pandora opened the box Zeus gave her, all the ills of humanity escaped. I just have this feeling that you've put every bad thing that ever happened to you in there. The other night, you told me some of those things. I know there must be more, especially from the war. I won't ask you about them, Mike. It was curiosity that led Pandora to open the box." She looked up at Stone. She was composed as she said, "So, please. Let it be. Don't open it."

Stone regarded Stephanie quietly. "Well," he said, "I haven't yet, but if I ever do—and I'm not saying I will—but if I do, try to remember the rest of the legend."

"The rest of the legend?"

"Yes. There was one thing, remember, that didn't escape from the box."

"What was that?"

"Hope."

10

● "I WANT YOU TO *SUE* THEM, MICHAEL. SUE THE pants off them!"

Aunt May, speaking from her hospital bed, was very much awake as Michael Stone and Saul Rosen, his head newly bandaged, walked through the door to her room.

"Never mind all that, Mazie," said Stone, going over to her bed to plant a kiss on her forehead, "first things first. How do you feel?"

"How do I feel? How would you feel if you were hit by a bus? I feel rotten, thank you—hello, Mr. Rosen, thank you for coming—that's why I want to sue!"

"I don't know, Mazie. The bus was right where it was supposed to be, and you weren't. The question of liability here—"

"I don't mean the bus company, you young puppy! I mean whoever it was pushed me in front of the bus! And what happened to you, Mr. Rosen? Were you two boys horseplaying around in my house?"

"No horseplay, ma'am. An uninvited guest slugged me while I was trying to chase him out of your house. Not to worry, I'm fine. Got an X ray says so. More important, what does the doctor say? How much more vacation is he gonna give you?"

"He won't tell me, but I told him I want to go home as soon as . . . *In my house?* Someone broke *into my house?* And what were you doing, Michael, while your nice young friend was getting his head knocked to protect my house?"

"I was at work at the courthouse, Mazie. I'm sorry."

"It's all right, ma'am," Saul said, "I carried him all the way through Vietnam, too. I'm used to it."

Stone's reaction to Saul's needle was to sound a bit testy when he asked his aunt, "Can you describe the person who pushed you, Mazie?"

"How can I describe him? I never saw him. He came from behind. But he must have been good-sized; it was a hard push! There were all kinds of people around, Michael. Someone must have seen him. The police will catch him, and you can sue."

"Maybe if we tell the police we think the guy was a client or a friend of mine, they might go all out and catch him," Stone answered. "Otherwise, I wouldn't hold my breath."

Aunt May grimaced as she pushed the button to raise her bed to a higher position. The intravenous tube feeding into the back of her left wrist swung wildly. "Did the man who hit you damage my house, Mr. Rosen?"

"Saul. Please. And no, aside from damaging Mike's safe, everything's okay."

"Needed a new safe, anyway," Stone said quickly. Then he said, "Mazie, you don't worry about the house or anything else. Just do as the doctors tell you so you can come home soon. We're starving to death without your cooking. You don't behave and do as the doctors say, Saul and I are gonna bring a bunch of girls in and have an orgy all over the place."

"Ha!" Aunt May sniffed. "Probably already have. Go on, get out of here, and let me have some peace while I can before I have to go back to putting up with the two of you."

Saul Rosen laughed, and Michael Stone bent down and kissed his aunt goodbye. Then, waving, they left the hospital room. They were barely out of earshot of Aunt May when Stone said, "Goddamn it, Saul, there's a lot more going on in that Riegar plant than someone abusing a bunch of monkeys. The prosecutor's going after Sara like she's a Colombian drug lord, complete with ignoring the trashing of her apartment. My livelihood's been threatened, and a bunch of motorcycle cretins set on me. Then they tried to bribe me. When that didn't work, they ripped off my safe. There's at least one detective in with the show—clumsy son of a bitch was even spying on us in the courthouse—and now they try to kill my aunt! They could've killed you, but didn't, but they did try to kill her. I don't know what I'm dealing with here. I need some intel, ol' buddy, and I need it fast."

The two men left the hospital and headed for the parking lot. Saul said, "Well, I know a few electronic tricks I picked up when I went to the Hebrew equivalent of TACSIGINT school in Tel Aviv. We studied both communications and electronic intelligence. Sort of a combination of COMINT and ELINT. I could give it a shot."

"Wiretapping?"

"No, their commo's probably protected by encryption—proprietary drug research leads to patents worth billions worldwide. Best bet'd be to go after their computers."

They got into the Mustang, and Stone started the V-8. "So you're a hacker? Always thought you looked a little nerdy."

Saul laughed. "I'm barely computer literate. Wouldn't get past their password system."

"So what are you gonna do?"

"Not even going to try to crack them. Let them do it for me. I'm gonna see if I can record what's on their screens on videocassette, then we can read it at our leisure."

Stone pulled into his driveway. "How're you gonna do that?"

"I've gotta buy some stuff first, then see if I can put it together right. We used to have to put field-expedient stuff together on our exercises. If it works, I'll show you how."

As the two men went into the house, Stone was troubled. Saul had just given him a pretty good layman's description of TEMPEST technology. Stone wasn't all that long out of the navy, and TEMPEST was the acronym for the highly classified Transient Electromagnetic Pulse Emanation Standard. One of the last locked-door briefings he'd had was on NACSIM–5100A, a National Security Computer Information Memorandum. That was BUBERE, "Burn Before Reading" stuff. What was Saul Rosen doing knowing about something like that?

Stone covered his concern by saying to Saul, "Better call your sister, and let her know her stuff's safe. Better yet, have her come over so I can show it to her, so there won't be any question. I've gotta clean up the mess in my office."

"Gotcha covered."

As Stone laboriously picked up the wills and matched them with their jackets to reinsert them, he decided that he might be overreacting. After all, Israel was pretty advanced when it came to technology. He'd withhold judgment until he saw what Saul came up with and how well it worked.

Saul stuck his head through the door. "No answer. She's probably with Eddie Berg raising hell outside the Riegar plant. I wanted to catch their act anyway; if I see her, I'll tell her."

"Take my car if you want, this is gonna take me some time."

"Nah, it's not that far, and I want to be able to mingle and check things out. Walk'll do me good."

"Just don't *you* get busted."

"Not a chance, ace. I've got diplomatic immunity, remember?" Saul left and Stone was alone with his wills and his thoughts.

Stephanie Hannigan arrived back at the public defender's office feeling depressed. She'd been down at the county jail interviewing her latest client, a young man charged with burglary, who insisted upon going to trial with the defense that the reason he'd been caught inside the house was that he was homeless; he thought the place was vacant, and he needed a place to sleep. Why that required him to unplug and move to the back-door area two television sets and one electric typewriter, he handled by telling Stephanie, with a straight face, that that was the way he found them.

Another winner, she sighed to herself as she picked up her message slips. They were all routine except for one, "Brian Sullivan, Reuters. Please call. 471-3400." Probably a hotel, the defense lawyer in her speculated on the double-zero ending of the telephone number. Her curiosity placing the Reuters reporter's message at the top of the list, Stephanie sat down and picked up the telephone.

Sullivan's Irish accent betrayed him even on a single word—"Hello."

"Mr. Sullivan? Stephanie Hannigan, returning your call."

"Ah, yes, Miss Hannigan, and I thank you. I know anyone named Hannigan will be immune to me Irish charm, so I'll get right to the point. I'd like to take you to lunch or dinner, your choice, as soon as is convenient. Before you say no, I'll admit that I wouldn't blame you; reporters in your country being held in less esteem than abusers of horses in mine. And, lovely as you are, I'll admit that 'tisn't that on me mind. I'll be after cultivatin' you as a source. Which means if you'll put up with me for the length of a meal, it'll at least be a good one, for it's Reuters'll be payin' for it. What d'you say?"

"I say you've definitely kissed the Blarney stone, Mr. Sullivan, and I have no idea why you'd want me as a source, but a good meal is worth finding out. When did you have in mind?"

"Why, I imagine a handsome women like yourself is booked solid for months, but I'm sure from time to time you have a cancellation from a death in the family or such. But, if not, that's why I suggested lunch as an alternative."

"As a matter of fact, Tom Selleck's great-grandfather died just this morning, so Tom had to cancel for tonight."

"Rest in peace. Five-thirty at your office?"

"Ha! With our caseload and budget, the public defender's office is no nine-to-five job."

"Six-thirty, then?"

"You're on, sir. See you then." So saying, Stephanie scooped up the motions that she had dictated for typing in her absence and headed for the district attorney and county clerk's offices at the courthouse.

At the clerk's office, Naomi was up to her usual form. "So, what's new at the public defender's office, kiddo?"

"Very funny, Naomi. As a matter of fact, I've been asked out to dinner by a foreign correspondent, Brian Sullivan, of Reuters."

"Is he cute?"

"Well, he's not *not* cute. I've seen him around town a bit. More . . . intense than anything else. He talks like a professional Irishman and says he wants me for a source."

"Source of what? That's always the question, honey."

"Oh, Naomi, you're such a cynic."

"Realist, when it comes to men. How're things with your friend the fish?"

"SEAL. Not so hot. We both blew it, and we're both dancing around trying not to make things worse. He's got a lot of problems with his identity, I think, and, I mean, how can you get to really know someone when he doesn't know himself or what he wants in life? How can I relate to that?"

"Sounds like you want to, anyway. What's he trying to choose between?"

"The law and the navy."

"So why not become a navy lawyer?"

Stephanie thought about her answer for a moment. She wanted the benefit of Naomi's counsel, but not at the expense of betraying Stone's confidences.

"No. Not that simple. It's not so much the navy per se, as what he did in the navy. He obviously loved it. But it's more than that. It was a way of doing things that, I'm sure, was completely different from the way a lawyer does things."

"You wouldn't be trying to nudge him one way or the other, would you, kiddo?"

"Naomi, he already *is* a practicing lawyer. The other's in his past. It's time to move on!"

"How much do you know about what he did in the navy?"

"Very little. Just that he was a SEAL, and he seems to think that was tremendous."

Naomi paused to accept and block-stamp some papers from another lawyer. When she was finished and he had moved out of earshot, she replied, "You see what you're doing? You're trying to get him to choose between two alternatives, but while you know all about the first—being a lawyer—you know beans about this SEAL business. And it's none of my affair, but it sounds to me as if you'd like him to choose you, too. Lemme tell you something, honey; before you start influencing someone about a choice, you better know all about *both* alternatives—otherwise, you're flying blind. And another thing, you hook up choosing you with one or the other of those alternatives—especially when you don't know much about one of them and how strong a pull it could have on him—you better be ready to settle for a calico cat and a lot of flannel nightgowns."

Stephanie sighed, looked down, and picked at a button on her suit. Abruptly, she raised her head, looked straight at Naomi, and said, "Okay. So what's the plan?"

"First, find out what you're dealing with in this SEAL business. Research it in the library if you don't want to bring it up with him. I'll tap into the state library in Albany with the computer 'n see if I can come up with anything, all right?"

"Thanks, Naomi." Stephanie turned to leave.

"Hey!" Naomi called out to her in a hoarse whisper. "Lemme know how it goes with the Irishman, okay?"

A little after 6:00 P.M., Saul and Sara Rosen, accompanied by Eddie Berg, all three carrying groceries in brown paper bags, entered the Stone home in high spirits not shared by Michael Stone. The look on his face, reflecting his frustration, caused Sara to grow serious immediately and ask, "Michael, I was so sorry to hear about Aunt May. Anything new?"

"No, no. Nothing since she threw Saul and me out of her hospital room this afternoon. You guys are all sure charged up. What've you been up to?"

"We got *great* coverage this afternoon!" Sara said. "Eddie had photographs of some experimental rats; some the military dipped into boiling water to test burns and some hairless ones taped down to boards and fried alive under sunlamps until they died, just to test suntan lotion. He got to show them on television—network, not just cable."

"Riegar's doing military work and making suntan lotion?" Stone asked.

"No," said Eddie Berg, "but these things, and a lot worse, are being done by the military and in the LD-Fifty tests for consumer products, like force-feeding helpless animals shampoo, even oven cleaner, until they die from hemorrhage and convulsions. It's got to be brought to the attention of the public. We don't get many chances like this Riegar thing. I didn't say Riegar was doing it."

"But that," said Stone, "was the clear implication."

"You saw the photos Sara got," Berg rejoined. "With that kind of equipment, they're doing a lot worse!"

"Speaking of which," Sara said, "I remember specifically you told me you were going to put my photographs in your safe. But Saul said the safe was ripped off and they're still here. How come?"

"Suppose," said Stone, "someone threatened to kill a little kid if you didn't tell them where the pictures were. What would you have told them?"

"In the safe."

"Right. And you'd have been convincing, even under Pentothal or a polygraph, because you believed it to be true. My way, the stuff was safe."

"But, what," asked Eddie Berg, "if they came back empty-handed from your safe? They'd kill the kid and maybe Sara!"

"Uh-uh," Saul jumped in. "Like Mike says, you'd have convinced them with your answer because you thought it was true. They'd have killed you and the kid before they left."

"Could I see them?" Sara asked.

"Sure." Stone slid the manila envelope out of the letter-holding rack on his desk and handed it to Sara. She shook the photographs out into her hand and studied them, then smiled. "Eddie got busted yesterday for chaining himself to the Riegar fence," she said.

Stone turned to frown at Eddie Berg. "What charge?" he asked him.

"Disorderly conduct," Eddie answered.

With Stone thus distracted, Sara slipped the photographs into her pocketbook, then returned the manila envelope to the letter holder on the desk.

"Well," Stone continued to Eddie, "they obviously didn't jail you."

"Hundred-dollar bond. I'll forfeit. The movement needs me more than the hundred."

Saul turned his head away to hide his smile. Sara glowed in silent agreement. "Thanks for the groceries," Stone said. "We gonna eat them or save them for the class picnic?"

The Surf & Turf restaurant in Rhinekill was lighted just above dim. What it saved in electricity, it spent for top quality in its steak and lobster. The decor was ersatz Chaucerian England, and the ale was served in chilled pewter mugs by costumed barmaids. "You've got to try some of this raisin bread," Stephanie said as she sliced a thick piece off a loaf next to the salad bar. "You'll love it."

"On your say-so, Miss Hannigan," said Brian Sullivan. He added a piece to his salad plate, then led Stephanie back to their table. They were seated in the rear of the restaurant, near the completely unnecessary fire that fought the air conditioning, itself unnecessary if the windows had been openable to the rain-cooled June evening, which was all the "air conditioning" anyone could want.

The table was lighted by a candle in a glass chimney. It increased, by its reflection, the intensity of the dark eyes of the Reuters correspondent as he lifted his mug to Stephanie and said, "Your health, Miss Hannigan."

"Mud in your eye," Stephanie answered. She took a drink, then said, "I'm really curious about your saying you want me for a source. I mean, what could possibly interest Reuters subscribers about the goings on in the Mohawk County public defender's office—assuming that I could tell you anything without breaching the attorney-client privilege or some other aspect of legal ethics?"

"My dear lady, I assure you there isn't a thought in me head about asking you to compromise your principles in any way. You're quite correct. I have no interest in the operations of your good office. I'm here to cover the Riegar animal-experimentation dispute, which, if I may say so, has taken on an importance in the press out of all proportion to its merit as news. But, as we both know, these things happen from time to time, and we must deal with what we have."

Sullivan looked up to greet their waitress, who arrived at that moment bearing sizzling skillets of steak and lobster, large baked potatoes, and sides of drawn butter. "Ah, thank y'lass," he said.

"Sour cream?"

"No, thank you," Stephanie said.

"If you please," said Sullivan. When the waitress retreated, he said, "As you might expect from me heritage, I've visited every pub within miles. It's also a good source of information, tongues loosening as they do with a bit of liquor across them. In one place, across the river, the bartender told me that you were there with a man who gave quite a good account of himself in a fight with a gang of ruffians. Bested the lot of them and made it look easy, the bartender says. Now, even allowin' for the usual exaggeration, that was quite a feat. But the reason for me interest is that this man's picture was in the paper over there as the lawyer defending Miss Sara Rosen, La Pasionaria of the Riegar affair. It's him I'd like to be finding out about, for what we call a 'sidebar' in the newspaper business. A color piece, you might say. What can y'tell me about him?"

Stephanie put a big piece of steak into her mouth and chewed it slowly to give her time to think over Sullivan's request. Her first thought was to wonder how the bartender knew who *she* was, then she remembered that her picture had been in the paper when she was appointed, and a few more times when she had handled newsworthy cases for the office. She decided it wouldn't be right to tell Sullivan as much about Stone as she had told Naomi. Naomi might be expected to share her information with a lot of her girl friends, but that was a far cry from publication in the international press.

Stephanie swallowed. "Well, Mr. Stone's a navy veteran of the Vietnam War, specializes in real estate law, and is quite an athlete."

"Interesting," Sullivan observed. "A real estate lawyer defending a woman in a criminal case. How did that come about?"

Stephanie lied. "Not sure. Sara Rosen's from out of town and wouldn't know Mike's—Mr. Stone's—specialty. And it's not exactly Sacco and Vanzetti, you know. He can handle it."

"If it's a slow enough summer for news, it could run Messrs. Sacco and Vanzetti a close second, the way things are going. You wouldn't be givin' the lad a few pointers, now, would you?"

"Lawyers talk shop, bounce ideas off one another all the time."

"Ah. And what kind of ideas might Mr. Stone be bouncin' off your lovely head?"

"That, I'm afraid," Stephanie said, "would be privileged information."

"Unfair to Mr. Stone?"

"Unfair to his client."

It was Sullivan's turn to chew on steak while he thought about the conversation. Presently, he said, "As devoted as you are to the law, do y'not think you might be suffering from what the religious call 'scrupulosity'?"

"No. I went to Catholic schools, too, Mr. Sullivan, and I know the meaning of the word. Let me put it to you this way: The law is all that stands between us and the world of Thomas Hobbes."

"Well, now," said Sullivan, taking a long draft of ale, "let us not be unfair to Mr. Hobbes. He was *describing* life in its natural state, not *advocating* it. What's more, he was right. You're privileged to live in the richest country in the world. But I assure you, my dear, that for most of the rest of it, including places right here in your own country, there are 'no arts, no letters, no society' or what there are are mockeries of the words. There is nothing but 'continual fear and danger of violent death, and the life of man—' "

" 'Solitary,' " Stephanie interrupted, " 'poor, nasty, brutish, and short.' Well, that's one firm *I*'ll never join!" Stephanie's cheeks flushed with anger. "You should be having this conversation with Michael Stone, not with me."

"Oh? Now, that is a very interesting observation, Miss Hannigan. Very interesting indeed."

Stephanie, a knot in her stomach, wished she hadn't made it.

As Saul and Sara Rosen and Eddie Berg went off after dinner to celebrate the media coverage they monitored on the network evening news, Michael Stone went to the hospital to visit Aunt May. She was asleep when he arrived, and he chose not to wake her, sitting quietly instead at her bedside.

Aunt May looked small and vulnerable in her hospital bed, and, it seemed to Stone, she had aged years in the few hours since she had been struck by the bus. Presently, he slipped out of the room and made his way to the nurse's station, seeking any new information available on his aunt's condition. In the absence of the attending physician, all he could get were guarded generalities and euphemisms. In disgust, he went back and sat down next to his aunt. Her eyes opened and fixed on him.

"Did they catch him yet, Michael?"

"No, Mazie, not yet. You go back to sleep and get some rest. I'll be right here."

Aunt May's eyelids drooped. Probably sedated, Stone thought.

"Since my Harry's been gone," Aunt May said, her breath thin, "you're the man, Michael. And the man is supposed to take care of things when something happens. The man . . . is supposed . . . to . . . do something."

Aunt May's eyes closed completely. She was asleep, Stone knew. He'd seen enough death to know that, had she died, her eyes would have remained open. He rose, bent to kiss his aunt, and then, in spite of his promise to remain, left, her words preoccupying him as he drove home: "The man is supposed to take care of things when something happens. The man is supposed to do something."

Stone entered the empty house and went straight upstairs to his room. He went down on one knee before his sea chest and worked the combination lock, then set it aside on the floor. He stared at the chest, Aunt May's voice still reverberating through his mind: "The man is supposed to do something." Slowly, Michael Stone the lawyer raised the top of the chest he had closed the last day of his naval service and looked again upon the instruments of sophisticated death.

"Fuck it," he said aloud to himself as he reached into the chest. "I need the goddamn intel." At that moment, the voice of Aunt May was stilled within his mind. Michael Stone, SEAL, had clicked on.

11

THE LITTLE QUARTZ ALARM CLOCK AT MICHAEL
Stone's bedside blipped electronically at 0100 hours, and he silenced
it immediately. He had slept soundly for four hours in preparation for
the night's mission. Now he was fresh, alert, and utterly calm; cold and
machinelike. He rose and moved over to the chair that held the
clothing he had selected for the night's work.

Over his underwear, Stone drew on a black-dyed sweatshirt, then
a pair of straight-cut jeans so new, their original blue registered nearly
black. They had been washed with a fabric softener for maximum
flexibility and an absence of static electricity. The jeans had no rivets
that could either reflect light or cause noise if scraped along a hard
surface. Olive drab athletic socks covered his feet and were themselves
covered by calf-covering black dress socks. The boots he selected were
combat, well broken in by many miles of running. He bloused the jeans
into the boots, then took a roll of black duct tape and made that
juncture and the laces secure. While he had the tape in his hand, he
put some over the metal tip end of a black-dyed web belt, then did
the same with the slide buckle; only then did he don the belt.

Stone used a red-lensed mini-flashlight to preserve his night vision as he moved to his sea chest and pondered his choice of weapons. This was to be a recon op. All he needed was something to defend himself with if necessary; ideally noiseless so as not to attract further attention. He picked up a knife in a black plastic sheath that bore the legend "USN MARK 3 MOD 0," grasped the black handle, and withdrew the blackened blade. The withdrawal caused a noise as the metal of the blade scraped along the plastic sheath. The weapon had a blade six inches long and one and a quarter inches wide, with a two-inch, false-edged, dropped Bowie-style point. Along the top of the blade was a two-and-a-half-inch saw edge capable of cutting through aircraft aluminum in an emergency. Stone was familiar with the navy-issue knife and respected its all-around utility; nevertheless, he rejected it in favor of another.

The knife Stone chose was a Gerber variant of the Fairbairn-Sykes pattern used by British commando forces in World War II. The all-black, rough-finish, aluminum formfitting handle had a skull-puncturing projection at the butt. A hole had been drilled through it for a lanyard if desired. The blade was essentially a stiletto: slender, double-edged, only fifteen-sixteenths of an inch wide and six and three-quarter inches long. Along both edges, starting one and a quarter inches from the hilt and extending forward two inches to end three and a half inches from the blade point, were fourteen scallop-cut, surgically sharp teeth. The blade had been covered entirely in black Teflon except for the hair-thin glisten of razor edges. Stone drew the blade from its black leather sheath quickly. It was whisper quiet. Satisfied, Stone slipped his belt through the sheath, then tied the thong hanging from the end of the sheath around his right thigh, securing it with more black duct tape. As he walked back and forth, there was no sound.

Once more, Michael Stone reached into his sea chest. He brought out a metal tube about as thick around as the opening in the top of a soft drink bottle. The tube itself was olive drab. Printed in black along the side were the words PAINT, FACE, CAMOUFLAGE. There was a military specification number, then LIGHT GREEN AND LOAM. Stone twisted off the two metal ends to see which was which, found the loam, and pushed on the opposite end to make the loam color project from the tube. He applied the substance to his face to break up its outline, concentrating on the prominent features—the nose, cheekbones, and chin. He wished he had black, but the loam was a very dark green and would do well enough. When he finished with his face, Stone spread the coloring on the backs of his hands. The camo paint was dull and nonreflective, and it would not run from sweat.

The last thing laid out on the chair was easy for Stone to find under the red light of his flash: a black bandanna. He rolled it flat, messed up his hair to break up his head outline, then tied the cloth band around his forehead. Then he put the flashlight back into his chest, locked it, and left.

The rain had subsided into heavy fog as Stone ran lightly down toward the river and the Riegar plant. He followed the path he had taken numbers of times before, so as to arrive well ahead of what he now knew from observation would be the usual time of arrival of the switch engine and tanker car at the plant. Had anyone else been abroad on the streets at that hour, Stone would have appeared as a ghost, looming out of the fog, vapor swirling in his wake. He arrived at the river before 0200 hours.

The Riegar plant rumbled and hissed into the fog-shrouded darkness, its sodium vapor lamps producing a hellish yellow glow. Stone moved carefully, staying in the darkness, examining the plant from all angles, probing for any weaknesses in security. He decided that the arriving train was his best opportunity and prepared for it by going over the river-side fence and down to the railroad tracks, taking up position by lying flat on the roof of a small maintenance shed from which he could see but not be seen.

Stone almost missed the telltale mutter of the diesel-switch engine in the rumbling from the plant, but soon the rhythmic murmur distinguished itself as it drew closer. Stone moved to the ground, sheltered in the lee of the shed, and waited. Shortly, the switcher's diesel engine revved higher, and emerging from the fog came a large two-holer tank car. Behind it, pushing, was the small engine.

A brakeman had positioned himself on the leading end of the tanker, holding on to a railing and guiding the engineer by the slow waving of a lantern. A fireman, Stone could see, was watching ahead from the other side of the engine cab. Fog or no fog, if he tried to hitch a ride on the tanker, they might see him. The only blind spot was the rear of the engine. As the little train proceeded dead slowly through the fog, Stone detached himself from his hiding place, sprinted, then leapt onto the rear of the double-ended switcher. Ahead, even over the noise of the diesel engine, he could hear the whine of the motors as the plant doors opened; then the light flooding from within reminded him once again of the old SEAL saying: "Gettin' in is easy. It's gettin' out that's the trick."

As the engine entered the cavernous, lighted interior of the railroad car—receiving building, Stone squinted his eyes to slits against the glare and peered forward around the engine housing. He needed a place to hide.

On both sides of the immense enclosure were loading docks. To the left, they served the plant itself for the loading and unloading of cargo. To the right, on the river side, they served the cranes that were used to load the oceangoing freighters for overseas transportation of pharmaceutical products. The docks were a good four feet high and their overhangs blocked the ceiling-mounted lights. As soon as the engine cleared the great entry doors, Stone sprang from the rear of it into the darkness underneath the river-side loading dock and lay completely still.

Stone could hear nothing over the din of the diesel and the motors driving the doors closed behind it. He couldn't tell at all whether he had been seen. Were fifty men headed toward him in his hiding place, he couldn't have heard them. He had relied on surprise, mere fleeting movement and subsequent stillness, blending into the blackness, for protection against discovery.

The diesel stopped, its engine idling, and Stone could see the men move to uncouple it. After some clanking, a snap and hiss of steam, the doors whined open again and the diesel moved out. The doors kept on going until they were fully open, then moved closed again. Stone concluded that they were on some kind of automatic mechanism that protected the gearing from being stripped by requiring the doors to open fully before they could be reversed and closed.

The moving out of the switch engine cleared Stone's view of the interior. The tanker car was to his right. He saw legs approach it from the other side, then mount the car. Some men were speaking German. There was the sound of metal upon metal, but he couldn't see the top of the car where it was coming from. To improve his field of view, Stone moved left and toward the tracks, taking care to remain in shadow and move slowly enough to avoid hitting anything that might make a sound and betray his presence. The place was remarkably clean, Stone thought, considering it was an industrial area. There was an occasional discarded spike between the cross-ties supporting the rails, some cigarette butts, an old railroad flare that must have fallen from an engine utility box, and a polystyrene wrapper for a piece of fast food; not bad, in view of the vastness of the place.

Two men were atop the tanker on the catwalk. One was a powerfully built, sandy-haired man in his early forties. The way he stood indicated dominance. The man with him, nearly equal in size but with a dark crew cut, was deferential as he pointed things out to the sandy-haired man. They spoke in German, and all Stone could learn was that the dominant man was named Metz. The man with the crew cut brought Metz to the far manway cover of the tanker and proceeded to loosen the dogs that held it in place, as if it were a large porthole on a ship. Then he leaned over and spoke down into the manway. To Stone's surprise, instead of German or English, he spoke in Spanish—a language Stone understood from having attended the military's language school at Monterey, California.

Slowly, six men, their legs unsteady from days of disuse, struggled up through the manway in response to the order in Spanish. They were joyful at the prospect of their release, as would be anyone who had spent much time inside a railroad tank car, Stone thought. All, that was, but one. He had changed his mind. He didn't want to work so far away from home. He'd had no idea how far from Mexico they were going.

The man was told to wait, the *patrón* would come and talk to him about it. In the meanwhile, the others were to go inside. There was the sound of the opening of doors and footsteps on steel stairways, doors closing, and the dissenter was alone with the men who had released him from the tank car. He sat down on his haunches and, patiently, waited as he had been told. Stone could see him from under the tank car. The man was young, with a four- or five-day growth of beard. And he was dirty—as might have been expected from his recent confinement.

As the unhappy Mexican national waited, a large hose was fitted to the washout outlet beneath the tank, directly under the manway in the top. Other men appeared and manned a steam hose that was played inside the still-open manway. Stone guessed they were sterilizing the interior. All spoke German. The man named Metz did nothing to assist them, and only the man with the crew cut spoke to him, answering questions and, from time to time, apparently offering information.

Presently, there was the sound of a door opening and another German speaker arrived. There followed a consultation among them and, whatever the decision taken, it was clear to Stone that Metz had made the determination as to what to do. The young Mexican was told that he could, indeed, return home, upon his promise to say nothing of his trip. The young man promised on the soul of his dead mother to say nothing. He was grateful. How was this to be accomplished? Why, in the same way he had gotten here, of course. But, as the man could see, the part of the car that he had been using would have to be cleaned and made ready. In the meanwhile, he could wait in the other section of the car.

The grateful Mexican agreed. Together, he, Metz, and the Spanish-speaking German climbed the car and mounted the catwalk. They moved to the other manway, which was closer to Stone's position. He watched as the Germans spun the toggle dogs, then lifted the cover back. The Mexican recoiled, saying something excitedly about a bad odor. Abruptly, the Germans seized him and dropped him through the hole. He hit with the dull sound of the ringing of a large cracked bell, then started to scream.

Metz laughed, and the crew cut signaled the others. A boom carrying a large-diameter hose lowered toward the manway hole. The crew cut donned heavy work gloves he pulled from his waist and guided the hose ending into the hole, then stepped back, motioning Metz back with him. The Mexican screamed some more. His cries made a hollow sound as they echoed through the manway hole after reverberating around the inside of the great metal tank. About all Stone could tell was that the man was in great pain. Every other word seemed to be *favor!*

The man with the crew cut who'd given the signal that brought the giant hose down gave another and a moment later there was the sound of a huge volume of liquid, boiling, bubbling, hissing, and fuming as it poured, roiling and splashing, into the tank.

The Mexican's screams rolled into a single long and agonized wail, then died under the thundering influx of liquid. Fumes filled the air and Metz and his guide scrambled back away from the top of the tanker as fast as they could. The stench made its way quickly to Stone and scalded his lungs. It was as if all the battery acid in the world had been concentrated and brought to a boil. He fought to avoid coughing, then pulled the bandanna down from his forehead to cover his nose and mouth. As quickly as he could without giving himself away, Stone made his way forward, toward the hangar doors, scanning to find the controls that operated them. Almost to the doors, still under the dock, Stone spotted the control panel. It was all the way on the other side of the vast enclosure and the distance in between was lighted brightly. Even more difficult was the fact that the controls were manned by a heavyset, bull-necked man wearing a beer-ad T-shirt that revealed his powerful musculature. A pistol of some sort was enclosed in a covered holster at his waist.

The acid fumes were heavier than air. That meant that the men above him were relatively unbothered by them and, perhaps, protected to some degree by the forced ventilation system of the building. Unfortunately for Stone, that system did him little good. He knew he could suffer lung damage if he didn't get out of there soon. He needed a diversion.

Stone looked about him. There was an empty beer can, but with all the noise from the acid flow into the tank car, even if he was to throw it hard, no one was likely to hear it. Then he remembered the railroad flare. Stone worked his way back opposite it, then slowly reached out, exposing himself as little as he could, and caught the flare end between two fingers. He worked it over toward him slowly, then grasped it and brought it to him beneath the dock.

The flare was simple to operate—just scrape the striking end against something rough. The problem was its age and exposure to moisture. Stone used the underside of the dock to scrape it. Nothing. He tried again. Again nothing. The fumes were getting to him now. On Stone's third attempt, the flare sputtered, then caught and ignited. He hurled it up, over the tanker and toward the opposite end of the building.

There were shouts as Stone sprinted across the open area toward the control panel. The controls operator had seen and followed the arc of the flare, then traced it back and spotted Stone's black figure, almost upon him. Frantically, the man reached for his pistol. But before he could get it out of its covered holster, Stone's left hand had grabbed him, pinching his nose and closing over his mouth. The attempted warning shout was stillborn. The black blade of the Gerber rose and fell with precision at the left side of the operator's thick, sloping neck. Stone rocked the knife grip forward and backward swiftly, then slid the slender blade up and out. The heavy body collapsed and Stone supported it as he sheathed his knife and hit the control switch. The motor whined and the massive sheets of corrugated metal began to move. Stone dropped the carcass of the slain guard and, to shouts in German echoing behind him, darted through the opening doors to escape into the enveloping darkness.

Seventeen minutes later, as Stone washed the soap-soluble camouflage paint from his face and hands and scrubbed the blood from the blade of his knife, the sound of the water running in the bathroom awakened Saul Rosen. Saul wondered where his friend had been, then decided that it was none of his business. Stone returned to his bedroom and reset his alarm for his usual early-morning wake-up time. He would put in his full workout, keeping to his established pattern. In his SEAL culture, he'd have had a beer with Saul and talked over the op. Clicked off now, Stone was back into the lawyer culture, in which an after-action report to Saul was unthinkable. Instead, he started pondering ways and means of avoiding the legal consequences of his night's activities.

Georg Kramer, hands stuffed into his pockets, was staring moodily out the window of his office at the Hudson, watching it flow past the

Riegar dock facilities, when the speaker on his desk projected his secretary's voice throughout the room: "Dr. Letzger is here."

Helmar Metz, seated behind the desk, pushed a button and said, "Send him in."

The office door opened and Letzger advanced directly to the desk and, without a word, handed Metz a manila folder. Metz opened it, took out several black-and-white eight-by-ten photographs, and set them aside, then read the typewritten report also contained in the folder. Georg Kramer walked over to try to read it over Metz's shoulder. Metz glanced upward in annoyance and Kramer retreated. Letzger continued to stand before the desk, almost at attention.

"You are a skilled forensic pathologist, Letzger," Metz said. "The detail here is excellent. It is also very troubling." He picked up the photographs and studied them carefully. The first depicted the nude full body of the controls operator Stone had slain. It was laid out on a standard stainless-steel autopsy table, complete with sink. The head was propped forward on a block. The second photograph showed the same body in the same position, but with the difference that the chest had been opened with a Y-shaped incision and the ribs separated and peeled back to reveal the internal organs—heart, lungs, liver, gallbladder, kidneys, and stomach. The next photograph was of the removed heart. A retractor was displayed holding apart the top of the organ where it had been sliced nearly in half.

Metz picked up another photograph. It showed a section of the upper spine. It had been severed cleanly. Finally, there was a close-up picture of the left side of the corpse's neck. A small slit appeared just inside the clavicle, in the hollow depression near its joint with the sternum. "Yes," Metz said, putting the report back together and returning it to Letzger, "very troubling."

"What's the problem?" Kramer asked. Metz ignored him and addressed Letzger: "Correct me if I'm in error, *Herr Doktor,*" Metz said. "Your man was killed by sliding a stiletto downward into the chest cavity through the depression between the neck and the clavicle. The blade was then rocked"—here Metz held out his arm, fist gripping an imaginary knife, and shoved it forward and back—"causing the blade to arc back and forth in the chest cavity, slicing the heart while moving in one direction and severing the spine in the other, *nicht wahr?*"

"Ja, ja."

"I understand," said Kramer, "why it is troubling that one of Dr. Letzger's men was killed by an intruder, but why the concern over the method?"

"Because," Metz answered, his voice using the elaborate patience one would with a pesty child, "it is clear the killer was a professional. Moreover, he was skilled in a method known only to those highly trained in special warfare techniques. Not only that, I saw him. He did it under stress and at great speed, which means that he is not only specially trained, he is very experienced. He has killed that way many times before." Metz's voice grew loud and angry. "What was such a man doing here? *Who sent him?"*

The question was answered by silence. Neither Letzger nor Kramer had anything to offer. Indeed, Kramer secretly took pleasure in Metz's frustration. First the bungled attempt to obtain the Rosen woman's photographs from the lawyer's office—proving Letzger's people no more competent under Metz than they had been under Kramer—and now it was apparent there were a few things Mr. Know-It-All did not, in fact, know.

Metz calmed down. His voice was completely controlled when he said to Letzger, "Disposition of the body?"

"He is with the Mexican. By now, there is no body."

"Explanation to the family back home?"

"Virulent disease contracted in the course of praiseworthy work in aid of humanity. Cremation—we'll send the ashes of something— substantial check from the company. No problem."

"Sehr gut, Letzger. *Danke."* Letzger understood the thanks as a dismissal and left. Metz checked the time, then picked up his secure telephone and looked pointedly at Kramer, who excused himself reluctantly and left the room. Metz then placed a call to Hoess. He would have to report this disturbing development, for which he had no explanation, and he might as well get it over with. At least the old woman that fool Hartmann had pushed in front of a bus in an effort to delay her had not died, and Schmidt had had sense enough not to harm the man found in the lawyer's office. Bad enough that they hadn't found the photographs.

"Yes, Metz," Hoess said as soon as the secure connection had been made. "I was about to call you. I have heard informally from GSG-Nine." Hoess was referring to the West German government's counterterrorist organization. "According to an unconfirmed report from a source that has proven reliable in the past, 'Al Rajul' is believed to be currently in the United States for purposes unknown. *I* suspect he's there to check up on us. What is the progress on the product?"

Metz was silent as this new intelligence sank in.

"Metz? Are you there?"

"Yes, sir. What you have just told me may very well explain something that has just occurred. There has been another intrusion. This time through the railroad entrance. The man was detected, but escaped after killing one of Letzger's men. The method used makes it almost certain that he was a highly trained and experienced commando type. He could well be working for this 'Al Rajul.' If he is as wily as he's said to be, there is no reason 'Rajul' would trust your assurances in spite of the hold he has over you through your son. He might well be trying to assess our progress independently. When we are successful, we shall have something possessed by no one else in the world—and many would want it badly."

"He cannot believe I would sacrifice my own son to double-cross him for profit!"

"Why not? Such people have no honor; they are completely depraved. *He* would do something like that; why not you?"

"Good God! What do you suggest?"

"If he's here, we don't know what assets he has with him. His capabilities and intentions are unknown. Press your GSG-Nine contact for as much information as possible. In the meanwhile, send as many of my men over here as you can spare. Keep just a skeleton crew. The action will be here in any event, not where you are."

"But my son!"

"We can only keep our end of the bargain and hope for the best just now."

"Very well. But keep after Letzger. The product must be completed and tested as soon as possible. Have them work shifts throughout the night."

"That is already being done."

"All right, all right. But from now on, when something happens like that intrusion, I want to know about it *immediately*, do I make myself clear?"

"Yes, sir." The telephone went dead in Metz's ear.

At 7:30 A.M., Saul Rosen left a note on the kitchen table for Michael Stone, who had not yet returned from the athletic center.

> Heading for Riegar to check things
> out. Coffee's hot. Best to Aunt May,
>   Saul

By 7:45, Saul was seven blocks away from the Riegar plant. Although the words were still unintelligible, he could hear clearly the echoing of a loudspeaker. As he rounded a corner, Saul was surprised to see a group of highly modified Harley-Davidson motorcycles lined up, front wheel to curb, in the middle of a quiet street of middle-class homes. He counted them. Thirteen.

Rosen entered the street in front of the plant at its easternmost intersection, still three blocks from the plant entrance. Even there, the street was filled with people. Some carried signs denouncing animal experimentation in general; others denounced Riegar in particular. The people were of all ages. Little old ladies wore sweatshirts with a representation of a fur coat on the front. Superimposed over it was a red circle with a bar slanting across the coat. There was nothing festive about this gathering; the people were angry. Saul spoke to one of the anti-fur-coat women:

"I just got here. How's it going?"

"They say the whole police force is out this morning. They used to just keep the gate area clear for the employees, but the word coming back is they're pushing and shoving people. Getting nasty. There's no excuse for that. Everybody knows we're nonviolent; but people are getting upset."

Rosen nodded his thanks, then retreated to the intersecting street. He circled several blocks and came in on the railroad side, close to the gates. He went over the same fence Stone had the night before, the fence holding back the crowd, and he walked along the concrete foundation on the other side of it to get close to the plant, then climbed to the top of the fence for a better view. Saul didn't like what he saw.

A cordon of police, facing the crowd, arms linked, were shoving it back from the entrance. The crowd was offering no resistance, but the sheer mass of humanity—Saul estimated that there were fifteen hundred people in the gathering—led to continuing body-to-body contact with the police.

About twenty people deep into the crowd, and up against the plant fence not far from where Sara had gone over it the night of her arrest, Eddie Berg was standing precariously three-quarters of the way up a seven-foot stepladder, holding a portable loud-hailer in front of his mouth with one hand and some papers in the other. Saul was disturbed to see his sister at the foot of the ladder, trying to hold it steady against the jostling of the crowd that was being pushed toward them by the police. Even more disturbing was the sight of shaven-headed, heavily tattooed men, about a dozen of them dressed nondescriptly in blue jeans and a variety of T-shirts and sweatshirts, who were slowly working their way through the crowd toward Eddie Berg and Sara.

Eddie, reading from the papers in his hand as he spoke, was oblivious to all else. As he read, he got more and more emotional. "Right here, Alstone Chase in *The Wall Street Journal,* listen to this: 'Nearly half the six-billion-dollar budget of the National Institutes of Health subsidizes research on vertebrate animals"—he paused for dramatic effect, looking directly into the lenses of the television cameras and emphasizing his next words—" '*killing around twenty million,* among them one hundred seventy-four thousand dogs, fifty-three thousand cats, one hundred eight thousand five hundred wild animals, and nearly fifty-five thousand primates.'

"In one experiment, blinded cats were made to jump into pails of water. In another, rats were fed gin and vodka to determine which got them drunk faster. In still another, dogs were drowned in various saline solutions, to see if the amount of salt in water affects the rate of drowning. Several veterinary schools break the legs of dogs and cats to teach students how to mend them. . . . 'Much research,' noted biomedical researcher Dr. Henry Heimlich told me, 'is cruel and unnecessary.' "

"Cruel and unnecessary!" Berg shouted over and over as the television cameras zoomed in. *"Cruel and unnecessary!"*

Rosen swept his gaze over the assembly. To the left, at the intersection being kept clear by police so that Riegar plant workers could park in the company lot and walk across the street to enter the plant, an unmarked police car was parked. Two men in civilian clothes occupied the front seats. From time to time, the driver would pick up a microphone and speak into it.

"Cruel and unnecessary! Cruel and unnecessary!" The crowd was picking up Eddie Berg's chant and shouting it in unison at the plant workers as they filed through the police cordon. More and more of the crowd picked up the chant as the words worked their way back through it, block after block.

Inside the parked unmarked police car, Detective Sergeant Walter Fisher spoke to the assistant district attorney seated next to him. "He don't have no permit for that loudspeaker. I checked. That's a violation of a city ordinance. We could bust him right now. Then we show the judge he's just out for Discon an' ask him to keep him locked up."

"Locked up?" asked the young prosecutor. "For failure to get a loudspeaker permit? C'mon, Walt, the judge'd have me committed for observation."

"So, how about RICO? I read all ya need is two priors and it's a racketeer-influenced criminal somethin'. I mean, they busted half of Wall Street for a couple phone calls."

Assistant District Attorney Mark Cole laughed. "You mean the Racketeer Influenced and Corrupt Organizations Act. Yeah, well, you've got a point there. Discon and failure to get a loudspeaker permit is a lot more than what they busted some of those Wall Streeters on. Two problems, though. One, RICO's a federal beef. Two, the courts don't like it. Comes sentencing time, instead of giving out telephone numbers, they're giving 'em what you get for Failure to Keep Right." Cole patted Fisher on the shoulder. "You're a good cop, Walt, but better let me do the legal thinking." He looked out the windshield. "Things look like they're getting kinda nasty out there. Now, if there's any violence, that's a different story. Lock up all you can grab. There's no First Amendment right to violence, and it really pisses off the judges. Know what I mean?"

Fisher smiled. He glanced out at the crowd and noted the skinheads getting closer and closer to Berg. "Way ahead of you, counselor, way ahead of you."

As Fisher spoke, Saul Rosen went back along the fence, then over it behind the crowd. He bolted to the parking lot and joined the Riegar workers walking toward the gate protected by the police. As he arrived in front of the gate, Rosen eased over to his left as close as possible to the police line and slowed, watching for an opportunity. It came when an officer got into a shoving match with a demonstrator who was trying to hold his footing. In the brief moment that the officer had his arms unlinked and raised, Saul Rosen dropped and charged, football lineman–style, between the officer's legs, which were spread wide for maximum stability. In a moment, Rosen was two-deep into the crowd. He wriggled to his feet and pressed his way over to his sister. "C'mon!" he shouted to her over the bellowing of the loud-hailer and the chanting, shouting crowd. "Trouble! You guys gotta get out of here. Follow me!"

Eddie Berg was oblivious. He was caught up in the hypnotic trance of his own voice and the crowd's mass response.

"I've got to stay with Eddie," Sara shouted to her brother, gripping the ladder. "He needs me!"

"He needs a fucking straitjacket!" With that, Saul Rosen used a military come-along move to break his sister's hold on the ladder, threw his arm around her shoulder and over her mouth to stop her shouts, and, bending the two of them over, began to worm his way toward the outside of the crowd, shouting, "Look out! She's gonna be sick!" Pressed as they were, the crowd found a way to avoid what it was sure was the imminent projection of vomit in an unpredictable direction.

As Sara and Saul Rosen arrived at the fringe of the crowd, three skinheads made it to the foot of Eddie Berg's ladder. Two grabbed him by the legs to drag him down while a third shook the ladder violently to throw him off it. Berg used the loud-hailer to bash the heads of the men who had his legs, and their scalps spouted blood from deep gashes. The blood ran down into their eyes and, partially blinded, they instinctively dropped their grasp to feel for the source of the bleeding. With a shout, the third hoodlum put his shoulder to the ladder and gave it the same thrust he had the training sled when he was on his high school football team. The ladder went over and so did Eddie Berg—right over the fence and onto the grounds of the Riegar plant. Before he could catch his breath and get to his feet, plant guards had swarmed over him, cuffed him, and hustled him over to the police stationed inside the gate. "Got him trespassing," said the guards.

"You sure did," grinned the senior officer. He triggered his transceiver and reported the good news to Fisher. The report squawked through the speaker in the detective's police car. As the static burst of squelch terminated the message, Assistant District Attorney Cole looked over at Fisher and said, in a voice heavy with scorn, "I'm supposed to prosecute a guy for being knocked over a fence?"

"Yeah," said Fisher, "I know. . . . Shit!"

Four blocks away, as Saul Rosen continued to struggle with his sister, a mid-sized Ford sedan bearing a rental-car bumper sticker pulled over to a stop beside them. On the top of the dashboard, a portable scanner radio, its red diode blinking disconcertingly back and forth, stopped every time a police or fire frequency was triggered and blared out whatever was broadcast. Brian Sullivan turned down the volume and said, "Miss Sara Rosen, we meet again. Are ya in distress, lass?"

"Oh, hi, Mr. Sullivan. No, it's just my stupid brother playing big brother, little sister. I was with my boyfriend, you know, Eddie Berg? The guy who's leading the rally? And asshole here just fucking kidnaps me! You wanna help, tell him to let me go. Eddie needs me."

"Ah, lass, I'm afraid you can't be much help to him now—"

"What? What happened? Is he hurt? I swear, I'll kill—"

"No, no, no. Not to be worryin'. He just got knocked off his ladder and inta the hands of the guards on t'other side of the fence. 'Tis in the hands of the constables he is, arrested for trespass and quite safe. Listen, hear it for yourself." With that, Sullivan keyed a tape recorder on the seat next to him and played back the report to Detective Fisher.

"So," he said, "can I be givin' you two a lift?"

Sara opened the rear door for herself and said, "Thanks. I'd better tell Michael . . . Mr. Stone, my lawyer. He's at One eighty-two

Garden." Saul climbed in on the other side and introduced himself: "Saul Rosen, many thanks."

"Not at all," said Sullivan. "Just doing m' job. I earn me living talking to people in the news. I don't suppose you'd care to comment on this latest development, Miss Rosen?"

"No," said Saul, "she wouldn't. Her lawyer'd fire her as a client."

"Damn you, Saul, I can speak—"

"Now, now," said Sullivan, "let us not resume the internecine warfare. How about you, Mr. Rosen. You're new on the scene. Where do you fit?" He pulled out from the curb and headed for Garden Street.

"Just a nice Jewish boy trying to keep his sister from going to jail over some reform-nut-case animal-rights fanatic—"

"You bigoted bastard!" Sara shouted. "Who gives a shit if Eddie's reform—?"

"All right, all right," said Saul. "We'll talk about it later. Mr. Sullivan wouldn't know what we're talking about, and I'm sure could care less."

"On the contrary," said Sullivan, taking a turn, "the Catholics are as divided as anybody. How d'ya think a real Irish Catholic takes to the bishops over here backin' Maryknollers runnin' with the Commies below the border? Next thing y'know, the Little Sisters of the Poor'll be callin' themselves the Marxist Sisters of the People!"

"Hey," said Saul, "I thought the IRA was Communist."

"Glory be to God, no," said Sullivan. "The original organization did go that way years ago—that's why there's so few of them left. The IRA that you're hearin' about these days is the Provisionals. They're *socialist,* yes, but not Communist. They owe no allegiance to the Soviet Union." Sullivan pulled into Stone's driveway. "Well," he said, "from the look of his digs, it's a good lawyer you've got! Good luck to all."

"If you don't mind," said Saul as his sister got out of the car, "I'd appreciate a lift downtown. Got some shopping to do."

"At your service, Guv'nor," said Sullivan, backing out. Saul waved to his sister. Still angry, she stalked away without reply.

It was twilight when the telephone rang in Stephanie Hannigan's office. She took off her glasses and rubbed her eyes before answering it.

"Public defender's office," she said, giving the after-hours reply that office protocol specified, "Hannigan speaking."

"All work and no play," said the voice of Naomi Fine, "and you'll never make it with Jack."

"Naomi"—Stephanie laughed—"you're impossible. Right now, I couldn't make it with anybody. I'm so tired, I can't see straight."

"That's probably a good thing, considering who you're thinking of makin' it with. You find anything at the library?"

"Haven't had a chance to try. I've got a caseload here—"

"Spare me, kiddo. Save it for the board of supervisors at raise time. Besides, on account of you, I'm in my office, too. Didn't want to get caught printing out personal stuff from the computer on taxpayers' time."

"You found something?"

"Yeah. But don't sound so eager. I don't think you're gonna like what I found. If you do, you're probably into whips and chains."

"What?"

" 'Devils with green faces.' That's what Vietnamese on *both* sides called the SEALs. They were organized in 1962 on orders from President Kennedy, using Navy frogmen volunteers. SEAL stands for Sea, Air, and Land. They pick from the strongest there are, give them special training to get them *ready* for the six-month course, and even then about seventy percent don't make it through. In one week during primary training, called 'Hell Week,' they never get to sleep *at all.* It's constant training, day and night. They put them naked into the cold Pacific surf at dusk. There's a doctor on shore with a stopwatch and an ambulance. He knows the temperature of the water—say in the fifties. When the doctor says they're in danger of death from hypothermia, they let them out of the water and sit them in a circle on the beach around a fire—close enough to see the flames but too far away to feel any heat. When the doc says they're no longer in danger of death, back in they go. Sometimes they're cycled in and out like that over *twenty times* before dawn, trying to break them psychologically. They take them over five miles out to sea and throw them overboard. They don't just have to make it back—they have to do it in fast time! Listen to this. They take their primary parachute training after they complete the basic SEAL training, called BUD/S. They take it at Fort Benning with the rest of the airborne, and they always get in trouble. Once, when they were on one of those two-mile runs, the SEALs pulled out as a unit and literally *ran circles around the other trainees* for the entire two miles! There're not many of them, and no wonder. They're the most elite military unit in the world, quote, 'often referred to by other military personnel as super commandos,' unquote. Those few who make it through the training and long probationary period after that are reviewed by a confirmation board and 'only those who are perceived'—I'm still quoting—'to perform at optimum level are awarded the coveted SEAL Trident . . . the right to pin the infamous "Budweiser" badge above the left breast pocket. A SEAL is an individual by nature who has learned to submit his ego, desires, and needs to that of the team. At the completion of his training, a SEAL *exceeds the medically accepted limitations of human physical and psychological strength by a factor of ten.'* Jesus, Neffie, you want to go to bed with that? What're you, Lois Lane?"

"Naomi, I—"

"I mean, I'm not reading you half this stuff. This guy's a stone killer—"

"Damn it, Naomi, that's enough! That's all in the past. He's a lawyer now. People change."

"Sure," countered Naomi, "you remember Freckles, the dalmation used to live down at Hook and Ladder Number One over on Crawford Street? To the *day he died,* he'd leave a bitch in heat to jump on that goddamn truck when the siren went off. Listen, honey. You asked for my help, I gave it. I'm not saying another word. Bye!"

The telephone clicked, and the dial tone came on. Stephanie just held it for a minute, then quietly put the receiver back in its cradle.

"You know anything about that van outside in the driveway with the big ice chest inside?" Michael Stone was looking down at the kitchen table where Saul Rosen was stripping the insulation off wires and making connections between a mysterious-looking black, cracklefinished, vented metal box, a small black and white television receiver, and a videocassette recorder. To the side lay a citizens-band radio antenna, the kind with a black rubber-suction-cup base for mounting on the roof of an automobile.

"Well," said Saul, "most of it is just what it looks like. The black box here is what's called a synchronizer. I built it from parts. If I remembered right and cobbled this stuff together correctly, starting this afternoon we might just get some intel out of Riegar. You know, from their computer screens, the way I told you."

"I've already got some, never mind how. Either Riegar's using undocumented alien labor, or someone down there's running a wet-back distribution system on the side, which I very much doubt. The people doing it are Spanish-speaking Germans." Stone deliberately left out any mention of the lethality of the Germans or their method of disposing of a body. He was puzzled by the fact that there had been no report in the press of the death of the control operator, nor, in view of the hullabaloo over Sara Rosen's cat-rescue attempt, any mention of his intrusion. On the one hand, the report might have been sup-pressed as part of the investigation by police; on the other, the Riegar people might not have reported it for reasons of secrecy.

"Who gave you that information?" Saul asked. "Ira Levin?"

"What do you know about Ira Levin?"

"Hey, I've been here a few days now. Everybody knows about Ira Levin. He's a local legend. You ought to get out of the house and into the gin mills more. Be surprised at the intel you can pick up. Here, help me get this stuff out to the truck."

Stone grunted in reply and picked up the television, then put the VCR on top of it, being careful not to stress the wiring. Saul did the same with the synchronizer and the antenna, and together they walked slowly out to the van. Saul had the lighter load, so he stuck the antenna under one arm and opened the van doors. "Put 'er down here," he said, indicating the floor of the rear of the van.

Stone watched as Saul opened the ice chest and motioned him to take a look. Inside was a gasoline-powered portable electric generator. A rubber hose had been affixed to the muffler with an insulator against the heat and it ducted the exhaust out the side of the box and through a hole in the van floor.

"Cost no more to rent than a full-sized car," said Saul. He moved the electronics up to just behind the seats, placed the television on the floor in front of the passenger seat, then mounted the antenna on the roof. Through a cutout in the side of the ice chest, he plugged his jury-rigged electronics into a standard 110-volt outlet in the generator, then started it up and replaced the lid of the chest. "See?" he said. "Can't even hear it much in here, let alone outside."

"It's not gonna work," said Stone as the generator engine died.

"Why not?"

"You ducted the exhaust all right, but you forgot the intake air. Gotta run another hose from the outside to the air cleaner. Hope you know more about electronics than you do about internal-combustion engines."

"Yeah," said Saul, "so do I."

12

● AS MICHAEL STONE STEPPED OUT INTO THE HOSPItal parking lot after visiting Aunt May, his mood was darkening as rapidly as the remainder of the day. Aunt May was taking longer to heal than anticipated, and in her frustration, she was increasingly insistent upon going home. As he drove home, the sun dropped completely behind the hills on the other side of the Hudson and Stone switched on his headlights. He was driving too fast, overdriving his headlights' reach, and the Mustang's tires screeched in protest at the way he was taking corners he saw too late to slow down for sufficiently. Stone was frustrated.

The source of Stone's frustration was his feeling of impotence in dealing with the whole Riegar matter. His attempts to practice criminal law had exposed only how little he knew of its practical aspects. Without the help of Stephanie Hannigan, Sara might still be languishing in jail. He had attempted to cross back into his special warfare culture with similarly little effect. He had killed a man without much to show for it by way of information. The situation was deteriorating, and he didn't know what to do. Lone wolfing it the way he had the other night went against all his training. SEALs operated as members of a team, and Stone had no team. He was no longer a SEAL. He wasn't a very good lawyer. On top of all of that, the solitary and feelingless life he had nurtured carefully, in a Faustian bargain with himself to avoid emotional pain, was now in ruins, along with what had been a promising relationship with the only woman he'd cared about in a long time.

As the Mustang turned into the driveway at 182 Garden, Stone wondered where Saul was, and how much, if anything, he should tell him. He parked the car, entered the house, and went straight to the kitchen. There, he took out a frozen steak and put it into the microwave oven for a quick thaw, then made himself a large salad.

While the steak thawed, Stone went through his mail. It was mostly routine: bills, bar-association notices, solicitations, and a notice that his college reunion was coming up. That reminded him of something, but he couldn't place it. He tossed the mail aside.

As Stone prepared his solitary meal, his mind conjured up memories of the meal Stephanie Hannigan had prepared for him. It would be nice to come home to that. He thought of the way Metz laughed at the agony of the homesick Mexican, dissolved alive under a flood of scalding sulfuric acid. He thought of the motorcycle hoods, of the attempts to bribe him and the veiled threats to his livelihood. And he thought of what happened to Aunt May. There was just no way he was going to get to the bottom of all this as a lawyer—hell, he couldn't even protect his aged aunt. To Stone, his course of action was obvious—recruit a team and go operational against Metz. Stephanie Hannigan would probably never forgive him. But, then, Stephanie wouldn't understand. How could she? The motto of the Special Operations Association to which he belonged said it all:

> *You have never lived until you have*
> *almost died. Life has a special*
> *meaning that the protected will*
> *never know.*

The memory that had eluded him when he was going through his mail suddenly returned. He went into his office and searched through the letter holder on his desk. There it was, right where Aunt May had put it the day he'd made a fool of himself with what he'd thought was a letter bomb; his navy-reunion final reminder. No wonder he'd forgotten it. His unconscious mind must have been protecting him. Even now, Stone felt a sense of loss as he unfolded it.

Inside, on the upper-left-hand corner, was a cartoon of a frog wearing a navy enlisted man's white hat. Beneath it were the initials UDT/SEAL. Stone pursed his lips and blew through them softly. The reunion was being held at Little Creek, Virginia, this coming weekend; Friday through Sunday. Figure a day to make the drive . . . if he was going to get there in time, he'd have to leave in the morning.

Without even a reserve commission, Michael Stone couldn't use the Bachelor Officers' Quarters at the Norfolk, Virginia, naval base to put up overnight, so he chose a motel in the resort community of Virginia Beach, right next to Little Creek, site of the Naval Amphibious Warfare Center. He got up early, but exercised lightly, just enough to work out any kinks after the long drive down from Rhinekill. Among the features of UDT/SEAL reunions were serious athletic contests and part of Stone's recruitment plan was to enter and do outstandingly well. No worthwhile recruits were going to join a would-be leader who couldn't demonstrate that he still had the tremendous physical and psychological prowess of an active-duty SEAL.

After breakfast, Stone went over to the athletic field cum park where the festivities were to be held. The June day was fair, cooled by an onshore breeze—perfect for athletics. Wall-less tents were already set up against the midday sun, for while mad dogs, Englishmen, and SEALs might go out in it, the same could not be expected of their women and children. The atmosphere was half twenty-year high school reunion and half carnival.

There are fewer than three hundred active-duty SEAL officers and, in the course of a career, they serve in several teams. Thus, nearly all the men in attendance knew Stone, and those few who did not, knew of him. The vast majority of those at the reunion had retired as enlisted men, many as master chief petty officers. Stone, whose career had been cut short, was thus about the same age as the recent retirees; enlisted men entered the service at seventeen and were eligible to retire in twenty years.

Stone headed for the table set up to receive entries in the athletic contests, seeking to be early. It was not to be. "Mr. Stone!" he heard behind him as he was shouted at by someone who wasn't aware he'd made lieutenant commander just before his resignation and so therefore used the form of address naval courtesy accorded junior officers. Stone turned his head around to his right to see who it was. He needn't have. A giant hand slammed down from behind on his right trapezius muscle and squeezed. "Monster" Malone, who had no idea at all of his strength, had struck again with his patented, paralyzing greeting.

"God *damn* 'Monster!' " Stone protested, ducking around and out of Master Chief Malone's grip. "I was going to enter some of the events. Now I think I'll head for the nearest corpsman! Uh-oh. Who's this?"

Stone suddenly discovered a very pretty tiny woman of about four feet ten in the lee of Malone's six-foot-six, 240-pound body. Grinning sheepishly, the huge master chief said, "This here's the little lady. We been married six weeks!"

"Well," Stone said, "congratulations. I can see she is a little lady."

Malone popped the top on a can of beer and handed it to Stone, who didn't want it before exercising but took a swig just to be sociable and not offend the newlyweds. At that moment, the bride chose to say, "I can tell what you're thinking. Everyone does. But don't worry, those big gorillas in the zoo have dicks only two inches long."

Stone sprayed beer all over the infield as Malone and his 'little lady' roared. He was spared further embarrassment as two older men, one a veteran of World War II and the other of the Korean War, hailed him. "Hey, Mike!" said a seamed-faced man who'd scouted the beach at Iwo Jima. "You gonna enter anything?"

"Yeah, if I can ever get over to the damn table."

"Good," said the Korean vet, "we'll bet on ya."

Stone finally made it through to the entry table and looked over the contests available. It was difficult because people kept interrupting to greet him, calling him everything from "ol'buddy" to "old fuck" with equal affection. In between, he ran his finger down the table of events to keep track of what he had read. He skipped the parachute accuracy jump and several runs and swims. He was looking for a contest that would demonstrate the highest degree of practical fitness. He found it in the obstacle course. As in BUD/S, it was to be run in boots and soft sand and was followed immediately by a three-mile run, in still more sand.

Stone entered, then wandered the field, greeting friends, some in the same superb condition as himself, others grown overweight and still hung over from drinking the night before. He visited tables that displayed and sold reunion memorabilia and turned down countless proffered beers from the free-flowing kegs. Steers and huge hogs were already roasting on great spits being hand-turned slowly over fires in large, hot coal-packed pits. Farther out in the field, some naval security types were giving a proficiency demonstration of attack-trained dogs: shepherds, Dobermans, and Rottweilers. One dog was demonstrating his drug-sniffing prowess. Off to the side, for those who couldn't wait for the noontime feast, hot dogs and hamburgers were being cooked over a grill fed by a large bottle of propane gas. Everywhere was the aroma of cooking food and the sound of beer-enhanced laughter.

The obstacle course run was scheduled perfectly—1100 hours— plenty of time for breakfast to digest beforehand and, afterward, to cool down before the big noon meal. Stone gravitated back to the contest table and searched the entries for contestants he knew. He nodded with satisfaction when he saw the name "Wings" Harper. His endurance and upper-body strength were legendary, even in the SEALs. His real name was Herman, but no one ever called him that. He was a hell of a runner, but that wasn't how he acquired his nickname. Harper's body was so dense, he was a "sinker." He had gotten through the swimming requirements on sheer guts. The name "Wings" referred to the apocryphal story that he had made it through BUD/S by using water wings.

Stone didn't recognize the next five names, but he certainly did the sixth. It was Master Chief Virgil "Pappy" Saye, so called because he had managed to stay in an operator's slot in the teams until he felt forced into retirement at the age of forty-seven, after thirty years in the navy, rather than accept transfer to a nonoperational billet and become what he referred to as a "support puke." Saye was black, had a completely shaven head, and a lean, well-developed body that looked thirty. Master Chief Saye was said to be furious about what he viewed as unfair treatment at the hands of Pentagon brass, and would be out to prove something on this run.

As eleven o'clock approached, a crowd gathered at the obstacle course to watch. The course was notorious for its difficulty. Some years ago, a West Coast SEAL training officer, the much decorated Scott Lyon, had pronounced the East Coast "O" course a "kiddies playground" and proceeded to make it as tough, if not tougher, than the one he had designed for the West Coast at the Naval Amphibious Warfare Base at Coronado, off San Diego. Each man was sent off separately, at one-minute intervals, and his start time noted. The contestant having the fastest time won. This was necessary because the first obstacle—parallel bars that inclined upward, then straightened out—had to be mounted one at a time. Any obstacle missed had to be done over again from the beginning.

As Stone's name began with an S, he started way back, right after Pappy Saye. He didn't watch those taking off way ahead of him. He wouldn't be able to follow their progress anyway, and he wanted to spend the time before his own start productively by doing stretching exercises.

When Pappy Saye's name was called, Stone made his way forward to watch his start. Cheers went up from the crowd as Pappy took position facing the parallel bars. He was a legend. The parallel bars were "walked" up and across on straightened arms. The exercise was designed to burn out all but the strongest triceps and deltoid muscles. Straight off the end of the parallel bars were the "lily pads." These were pilings of differing diameter, set vertically into the ground at differing height and spacing, taken at a dead run and missed at bodily peril. They led to a sixteen-foot wall. If he could hit the right lily pad, Stone knew, the leap to the top of the wall would be only twelve feet.

Pappy Saye tensed as the timer got ready to start him. He was as focused as anger could make him, his concentration fierce. His advantage, Saye knew, was that he had run this course more times than any man there. Hell, maybe more than any man, *period*. Pappy took the starter's signal and was off the mark and onto the parallel bars in a flash, putting to shame Olympic gymnasts as he nearly ran across the bars with his supple, powerful arms. In moments, he was on the lily pads, hit the correct one, and vaulted the wall, buoyed by a great start.

Stone watched Pappy and knew he was in a real race. At the starter's signal, he was up on the bars as quickly as Pappy, but not quite as fast over them. He hit the right pad and vaulted over the wall, then sprinted through the soft sand to a wall twenty-four feet high. Pappy, already over it, could not be seen. Stone went up this second wall with the aid of a hanging rope, "walking" his way to the top with his feet as fast as he could.

On the other side of the wall, Stone crawled on his belly, using elbows and knees, under ten yards of barbed wire. This got sand all over the inside of his clothes. It was planned deliberately so the sand would chafe and sting when mixed with his sweat. Out from under the barbed wire, Stone sprinted to a sixty-foot-high cargo net, sweat starting to let the sand in his crotch do its dirty work.

Pappy Saye drove himself with such intensity that his feet skidded in the soft sand. It held him up a moment, like an automobile spinning its wheels. As a consequence, he and Stone arrived at the cargo net at the same time and Saye felt challenged by more than time and himself. Stone, allowing for the difference in ages between himself and Pappy, expected to arrive on the other side of the net ahead of the powerfully muscled black man with the shaven skull now gleaming in the sun from sweat.

Both Stone and Saye went for the sides of the net, where it was attached to the sixty-foot uprights. It wouldn't sag as much there and slow them down. Stone took the left side, Saye the right. Both men, to Stone's surprise, reached the top at the same time, climbing hand over hand, foot over foot, using the net as a rope ladder. At the top, they both risked death by diving over the crossbar to snare the net on the other side with one hand, then began a rapid descent. They both hit the sand running at the same time and sprinted to the twenty-foot-long rolling logs—so named because they were set up horizontally, in the direction of the course, unfixed, so as to be allowed to roll and throw a man off as he tried to run along their length. The way to stay on was to do it fast, and Stone and Saye did. Then, side by side, now directly competitive, they sprinted to the log barrier.

The log barrier was built by placing a large number of pilings horizontally on the ground, perpendicular to the path of the contestants. Then a row with two fewer logs was set atop the first layer and so on until there was room for just one at the top of the pyramid. The men had to go over it, touching every log on the way up and again on the way down, then race through the sand to the rope swing. They brushed each other doing it and the physical touching added to their sense of personal rivalry.

The rope swing was built of two pilings twenty feet high, with a crossbar piling that extended several feet out over each vertical support. From the extensions hung ropes, one on each side. From the middle of the crossbar was suspended a steel ring. Stone and Pappy each grabbed one of the ropes and climbed, hand over hand, opposite each other, then let go with one hand and reached for the center ring to swing over to the opposite twenty-foot rope and down to the ground. The two men reached for the ring at the same time, banged into each other, exchanged ropes, and made it to the ground at the same time.

They sprinted up and over another log barrier like the previous one, then ran to the Belly Buster.

The Belly Buster was so named because it consisted of two logs, each set horizontally across the path of the contestants. One was set five feet above the sand, the other at eleven feet. The correct way to take the obstacle, Stone had been taught, was to run as fast as one could and leap up onto the first log, then mount the second and go over. That was the theory, but Stone had found that, invariably, on the first leap, the log hit him right across the abdomen, thus earning its name. Those not in the best of shape were struck across the chest. Either way, the blow is jarring and takes the breath out of a man. Stone, to his disgust, got it in the belly again. To his surprise and envy, the more experienced Pappy made a "school solution" mount and was ahead of him by a few feet on the other side and even farther in the lead after they went over yet another piled log barricade. Pappy, therefore, made it first to the Weaver.

The Weaver resembled a large ladder, about five feet across and made of smooth metal pipe. One end of the ladder was inserted in the earth at a steep angle, then, at the middle, the ladder was bent so that the other end was in the earth at an angle of the same degree. The crossbars laddered up, then down. The device had to be negotiated by "weaving" the body through the crossbars, or rungs of the ladder, over and under, over and under, four rungs up and four down. The lithe Pappy Saye was still ahead of Stone at the other side of the Weaver and, angry at himself for being bested by the older man, Stone said, sharply to himself but out loud, "Come on, Stone, you love this shit!" He drove his body mercilessly as he and Pappy Saye raced to the rope bridge. As they ran, the two men heard the crowd in the background give a collective, "Oh!" followed by clapping as a contestant fell from another obstacle and rose, uninjured, to repeat it. Such was their focus on their own performances, however, that the sounds barely registered in their minds. Stone reached the next obstacle first by a hair.

The rope bridge was reached by climbing fifteen feet up a tiny flexible ladder designed for exploring caves, using the hands and boot heels. That brought Stone to the top of a pillar. Pappy Saye, his waist and crotch now raw flesh from the sand and stinging from the salt in his own sweat, was so close to Stone he was tempted to grab him by the leg and throw him off the caving ladder. Instead, he vented his frustration by saying, "Let's go, let's go, let's *go!*"

From the top of the pillar extended a bridge consisting of three ropes, arranged in the shape of a V. Balancing on the outstretched strands that formed the widest part of the V, Stone, closely pursued by Pappy, walked rapidly across the lower rope. Once at the other end, he slid down a rope to the ground and sprinted to the Tower, arriving just two steps ahead of Pappy.

The Tower was square-shaped and consisted of four storys, each eight feet high. In the top story, at the very center, was a shoulder-width hole. Not permitted by the rules to use the corners, Stone and Pappy hit the first story on the run and leaped up to the floor above, grabbing it with their hands, then using upper-body strength to lever themselves up to the platform that formed the first floor. They repeated the process until, at the third floor, Stone found that the lighter-weight Saye had beaten him there by a fraction and was already on his feet. Saye got to the space under the hole in the fourth floor first, jumped up, planted his hands on either side of the hole and, pressing his body weight firmly and swiftly, rose up through the hole to the top of the tower. While Stone was coming up through the hole, Saye was already descending from the tower, using the Crawl for Life.

The Crawl for Life was a forty-foot-long rope that slanted down at a broad angle from the tower to the ground. Saye followed the rules, negotiating it by a commando-crawl downward along the top of the rope. He dropped to the ground as soon as he safely could and ran to the bottom of another rope, arriving there just as Stone hit the ground from his own crawl for life.

Saye used the rope to swing up to a supported beam and ran along a twenty-foot-long horizontal telephone pole. As soon as Saye dropped the rope, Stone had it and was up on the beam, chasing Saye down the telephone pole. He was right behind him when Saye jumped to the ten-foot-long overhead Monkey Bars, and Stone, arm muscles burning, followed immediately behind Saye, hand over hand, to the end, where they both jumped down onto another set of lily pads. At the other end of the lily pads, the two men were even again as they ran through the sand, its softness dragging at their boots at every step, to the Rooftop wall.

The Rooftop was a wall inserted into the ground at a severe angle so that the far side was pitched downward like half a pitched roof. Stone and Saye raced to the high edge, exposed to them, leaped upward onto it, then slid down the sloping far side to the ground, then sprinted, matching each other pace by pace, to the Wall Scale.

Stone reached it first by half a stride. It was a wall, thirty feet long, set vertically into the ground. Along the sheer face of it were small strips of wood placed from four to ten feet high with which a man could cling with fingertips and boot-sole edges. Saye crowding him from behind, Stone inched along the wall's face for thirty feet and dropped to earth to sprint to the Hurdles.

The Hurdles were just that: eight telephone poles set horizontally across their path, one after the other, at hurdle height. Under the rules, they had to be negotiated using the hands only. If a foot touched a hurdle, the entire obstacle had to be renegotiated. As Saye and Stone hit the ground on the other side of the hurdles, Stone was only a footstep ahead. But, because he had started a minute behind Saye, he was now ahead of the other man by a minute. The watches timed his completion of the obstacle course, in six minutes, nine seconds, then started again as he launched without stopping into the three-mile run, still in his boots, entirely through soft sand, flesh from waist to thigh chafed and raw, soaked in stinging sweat. Pappy Saye swung into the three-mile run fueled by sheer willpower and guts, but it wasn't enough to overcome Stone's age advantage.

Stone completed his run in nineteen minutes, sixteen seconds. As he crossed the finish line, he raised his fist and shouted, "I *love* this shit!" Cheers from the crowd answered him. His performance was good enough to beat Pappy Saye, but not Wings Harper, who beat him by twelve seconds. The fact that Wings would have drowned trying to beat him swimming was little consolation, and the performance of the forty-nine-year-old Pappy Saye was astonishing. There were other finishers not far behind, but Stone didn't know any of them. One thing he did know: He wanted Wings and Pappy for his team. The trick was how to recruit them.

It was easy enough for Stone to fall in with the two men as they walked to cool down. It was Pappy Saye who gave him the opening he wanted. Wiping his sweat-shining shaven skull with his pulled up T-shirt, he muttered, ". . . not just your *hat* made a brass. Whole muthafukin' *head* solid brass tell me too old t'operate. Take a look at *them* times, baby, then stick 'em in your *ass.*"

"Tell 'em, Pappy," Stone said. "Bastards did the same thing to me."

"T' *you,* Mr. Stone? No way. You not that old, man."

Stone wiped his face with his forearm. "Didn't use age. Used a bullshit hearing degrade. Wanted to make me a support puke; 's why I resigned."

"So *that's* what it was," said Wings Harper. "I heard it was physical but didn't believe it. Not with the shape you're in. You should've fought it, man. I got the same thing from stuff going bang in my ears in Nam."

Stone looked at him, "Why didn't *you?*"

Wings kicked the dirt in front of him. "Oh, figured it wasn't worth it. Hell, I had my twenty in; got my retirement. So's Pappy. But you don't. That's the difference."

"That," said Pappy darkly, "an havin' to be a support puke!"

"You really miss operating, don't you, Pappy?" Stone said.

"Do the fish miss water?"

"Yeah." Wings laughed. "Sometimes I think if I could have just one more op, maybe the itch would go away."

"Bullshit," said Pappy. "Itch ain't *never* gonna go away."

Stone made his move. "How'd you guys like to scratch it just one more time?"

Wings stopped walking. "You know something we don't know?"

"It's not official. You could get killed or arrested, and I couldn't help you because I'd be killed or arrested right along with you."

"I'm in," said Pappy.

"You've got two," said Wings.

"You haven't even heard what it is yet!" Stone protested.

"Don't try to get out of it, Mr. Stone," said Pappy. "It ain't like you."

"We need one more guy," Stone said.

"Won't be so easy," Wings said. "A lot of these guys were SDV and SBU people—unless you've got water ops in mind?"

"Not sure *what* we're going to end up having to do," Stone said, looking around at the other contestants. The SEAL Delivery Vehicle and Special Boat Unit guys were good men and the best at what they do. They all knew that, but still . . . "I need *operators*—the more experienced the better."

Pappy turned to Wings. "How 'bout Arno?"

"He here?" asked Wings.

"Saw him last night. Said he was gonna enter the five-thousand meter and, naturally, the jump accuracy."

"Which he'll fuckin' win."

"No contest," agreed Pappy.

"I've heard of him," said Stone, "but I never worked with him. He ended up teaching HALO and that stuff, didn't he?"

"And HAHO," Wings said, differentiating between high-altitude jump with a low-altitude parachute opening after a long free-fall, and high-altitude opening with a long glide of up to a hundred miles, both methods of clandestine insertion into hostile territory.

"Saw him once win over a thousand bucks usin' a square chute.

Landed on a quarter, stepped right fucking on it, from six thousand feet. Then he bet he could do it on a dime. There were no takers."

"Plus," said Wings, "he's almost as good a shot as you, Mike. You can work with him."

"Sounds good. Let's see if he's interested."

"They did the five thousand earlier this morning," Wings said, glancing at his watch. "We get our ass in gear, should be able to see the jump contest over at the ball field."

The three men walked toward the field, only to stop suddenly at the sound of an explosion, heads snapping around in unison toward the blast. The cause was obvious. Fifty yards away, the propane tank that had fed the hot-dog grill was describing a lazy arc sixty feet in the air above a fireball at the grill site. Women and children in the area were either running or on the ground with fright. The former UDT/SEALs were all standing, admiring the display.

"Someone screwed the bottle on wrong," Pappy commented.

"Screwed the pooch is what they did," Stone said. "Beer and propane don't mix."

"Sounds just like an officer," Pappy said, grinning at Wings.

"Absolutely," Wings agreed. "Always tryin' to fix responsibility."

"Gimme a break!" Stone pleaded, laughing.

The ball field had a white taped cross just outside the infield. A crowd was around the field, looking upward, straining to see what appeared to be small multicolored dots that grew larger as the contestants, already out of the aircraft, fell to earth in jumpsuits of a variety of colors. The chutes flared after a free-fall, and an official pulled the pin on a smoke grenade and set it off near the cross marking the target on the field. The thick orange smoke indicated the direction of the wind for the jumpers, a factor critical to their ability to maneuver for accuracy.

One by one, the nine contestants descended, the interval determined by when they opened their chutes. They landed, softly, after nearly flying their highly maneuverable square chutes, by stepping lightly onto the ground. The skill of the parachutists was displayed by their ability to judge the wind and guide themselves accordingly as they "flew" in slow, large circles above the field, trying to position themselves so that they could step down with one foot as close as possible to the mark. All but one were within the X formed by the cross, and he was still within the circle defined by the spectators.

The last contestant alighted like a blue heron, his long legs extended until the last moment. Then he pulled one up slightly so that the other would step directly on the center of the cross.

"Way to go, Arno!" Wings Harper cheered, his words drowned out by the appreciative roar of the crowd. The three men waited until the contestants had gathered up their parachutes and been congratulated by their friends; then Pappy and Wings walked up to the winner. Wings said, "Hey, Arno, how much you make on that one?"

The jumper peeled his helmet off to reveal light red hair, and smiled slyly at Wings. "Who, me?" he asked in mock innocence. "Gamble?" Then, spotting Pappy Saye, he said, "Pappy, you know me like a brother. You know I'd no more gamble than ol' Wings here would jump in the water without his inner tube."

"Sure," said Pappy, "and I'm Snow White." He jerked his thumb at Stone. "Meet a friend of ours, Mike Stone."

The raw-boned redhead put out his hand and smiled. "Arno Bitt," he said. "Heard about you in the teams. Always wanted to shoot with you. Say you're real surgical."

Stone smiled at the compliment. "Surgical" shooting had a precise meaning in the SEALs. It meant the ability to fire in a close-quarter battle situation, such as hostage rescue, with the ability to unerringly score two lethal hits to the head of the hostage takers without endangering either the hostages or other rescuers, all that in a crowded room in the heat of a life-and-death battle with desperate men.

"Well," said Stone, "maybe you'll get the chance. What're you doing these days?"

"I'm in between divorces. Had a parachute school going, nice little business. She got it in the settlement. Started another. I think it's gonna go the same way. It's like they say, 'lucky in cards . . .' "

"Gotcha," said Stone. "Think you could work with these two beach-hoppers again?"

"Work with the devil if the price is right."

"It's not. It sucks. But, who knows? You might get to shoot with me."

"C'mon, Arno," said Pappy. "All you got to lose is your ass, and most of that's gone already."

"You might get laid," Wings Harper added helpfully.

"Lemme think about it," Arno said.

"Sure," said Stone. "Let's get something to eat."

As the three men crossed the field back to where the propane tank had blown, they were greeted by the sounds of gasoline-powered chain saws. At the cooking pits, people were lined up with plastic plates as the "chefs," all volunteer former SEALs, carved the roasted carcasses with chain saws, then used pitchforks to heave the chunks of meat onto wooden tables for slicing and distribution to the waiting diners. Beer flowed copiously from innumerable kegs. The sea stories got wilder and wilder and the eyes of the children wider and wider until their mothers herded them out of earshot at "Aw, Mom, just when they got to the good part!"

It was late in the day when Stone, cold sober, helped Pappy Saye and Wings Harper, slightly inebriated, carry a thoroughly drunk Arno Bitt off the field and back to Stone's motel. "He'll be okay," Pappy slurred, "ish just Germans can't hannel beer. Not used to it." They placed Arno on the second bed in the room, then left with the promise to come by in the morning. Stone took off Arno's shoes, loosened his belt, and covered him with the bedspread, then turned in himself.

In the middle of the night, Stone awakened the moment Arno Bitt rose from his bed and lurched into the bathroom. He listened as the man got thoroughly sick. Then, when Arno failed after a period of quiet to emerge from the bathroom, Stone realized he had passed out. Many a man, he knew, had choked to death on his own vomit. He got up and went in to check on Arno and found him unconscious, head, shoulders, and one arm down in the bathtub. The tub was sprayed with a thick layer of vomit, the combination of partially digested meat, potatoes, and corn, and what seemed to be half a keg of beer. Stone sighed, then went to work.

Arno Bitt wakened shortly after 8:00 A.M. His head ached the way it had the day that he was next up in a baseball game, the batter took a vicious swing for a third strike, and the bat slipped out of his hands and hit Arno in the forehead.

Arno lay still on the bed. He wasn't dizzy. That was a plus. He didn't feel sick. Another plus. He might live. Then he remembered the middle of the night and knew why he didn't feel nauseated anymore. He looked over at Stone, who appeared to be asleep.

Painfully, but with a sense of obligation and embarrassment, Arno Bitt got up and went into the bathroom to do his best to clean up the mess he'd made before Stone, whom he hardly knew, got up to find it. To Bitt's astonishment, the bathroom was immaculate—albeit, there was a sour odor that the wide-open window had still not fully dispersed.

Stone was stirring when Arno came out of the bathroom. "Listen, Mike," he began, sheepishly.

"Forget it." Stone cut him off, his voice kindly.

"Yeah, but—"

"Arno, in BUD/S, when both my knees gave out the third day of Hell Week, the guys in my boat team virtually carried me all the rest of the week when we weren't in the water. It's what it's all about, Arno. You know that. You wore the Budweiser."

Bitt thought about that for a minute, then said, "Mike, yesterday when I said I wanted to think about your thing—you know, goin' in with you? It was because . . . well, I knew Wings and Pappy real good. I operated with them. But I didn't know you, know what I mean? But what you said . . . about the Budweiser. I mean, you're right. You wore it, too. And if that ain't good enough, nothin' in the world is. I mean—"

"I know what you mean, Arno. Thanks. Welcome aboard."

Arno smiled ruefully and held his head. "Besides," he said, "maybe I can steal something."

Stone grinned and frowned at the same time. "Jesus," he said, "I didn't hear that."

13

"DOCTOR, I DON'T MEAN TO SOUND LIKE I'M QUES-tioning your judgment, but the fact of the matter is my aunt said nothing about going home until I mentioned that I'd put up three old navy buddies at the house. That makes a total of five men, including me, that she considers to be just out of adolescence, with nothing better to do than rip up her house while screwing our brains out with every teenage girl we can lure in there from the local junior high. She'll go nuts home."

Dr. Heller looked Michael Stone in the eye and spoke with the effort at control of someone who's just been insulted by an idiot: "The facts of the matter are, there has been no blood in your aunt's urine for days now; the rotator-cuff fracture was hairline and responded well to healing by electrical stimulation—a relatively new technique. Ditto the broken rib. We don't tape them up anymore, and it's healing just fine. The problem is the knee. She's got an orthopedic brace. *I*'ve been urging her discharge for days, because unless she uses her legs, the muscles will atrophy. I don't care that she'll be a problem to you at home. You're not my patient, *she* is. Bring her back in two weeks for a checkup. Now, if you'll excuse me, I've got to finish my rounds."

So it was that Stone found himself, the day after returning from the SEAL reunion, cautiously driving Aunt May back from the hospital. He hoped fervently that his new allies would remember his urgent warnings against profanity and off-color sea stories. Seeking any advantage in a bad situation, he had told his aunt that his friends were there to help him find out who had injured her, all hope of effective action by the police having been abandoned.

Stone turned into the driveway at 182 Garden, stopped under the porte cochere and "accidentally" hit the horn. It was an arranged signal to let everyone know he had arrived. By the time he had helped his aunt up the steps and opened the door, Pappy Saye, Wings Harper, and Arno Bitt, freshly shaven, scrubbed, and dressed, were lined up on the other side of it as if ready for inspection. Only Saul Rosen, out in the van monitoring the computers at Riegar, was missing.

Heaving a sigh of relief, Stone made the introductions. His friends "ma'amed" Aunt May to death, as if she were the Queen of England and they local yeomen. Aunt May bought their act so thoroughly, Stone was astonished to hear her say, "Well, now, Michael, it's nearly noon and we can't have strong young men like these standing around starving. You take my things up to my room and I'll just get lunch started. You do have food in the house, don't you?"

The four men protested at once, citing her injuries, but Aunt May would have none of it. "The doctor said if I didn't use this leg, I'd lose it," and off she limped to the kitchen.

"Oughtta make her an honorary SEAL," growled Pappy Saye.

Lunch consisted of sandwiches and caused Aunt May to hand Stone a long grocery list before she allowed herself to "rest a bit upstairs." He pocketed the list, then the four of them crowded into the Mustang for a familiarization trip around Rhinekill, with emphasis on the Riegar plant and the athletic center, where, Stone emphasized, he expected to be joined for PT in the morning. His mandate drew no objections, but there were a couple of bets back and forth between Arno Bitt and Pappy Saye as to the number of laps Wings Harper would cover before he drowned.

At Goldberg's card shop on Main Street, Stone left the engine running to run inside to purchase three Rhinekill street maps. After paying for them, he opened each on the counter and made two X marks, one showing 182 Garden, the other the location of the card shop. Back in the car, he passed them out and said, "Okay, guys. As you can see, this is a small town. Use the maps, recon further on foot while I go get the groceries. Meet you back at the house."

As Pappy, Wings, and Arno went off in different directions, Stone parked and walked the short distance to Ira Levin's cigar store.

"You got some nerve!" Ira Levin said as Stone walked through the open door to his shop. "You were supposed to come back and tell me how your aunt was an' I haven't seen you since. Good thing people in this town tell me things so I can keep up. I just wish you was one of them. So tell me, counselor, how's . . ." The plump shopkeeper's hand came up and clutched at his chest. His face looked striken and his legs started to give way. Stone thought the old fellow was having a heart attack and rushed toward him, intending to ease him to the floor.

Before Stone could reach Ira Levin, the ever-present cigar fell from the fingers of Ira's right hand as he put it out against the counter to support himself. The hand at his chest reached out as if to point to Stone, and it was then that Stone noticed the blood. It was seeping from a tiny hole in Ira's left side—above the heart but not above the lung, Stone recognized. He knew a sucking chest wound when he saw one.

"The . . . man . . ." Levin said, and fell to one knee. Stone glanced behind himself at the open door. There was no one in sight. He knelt, put his arm around Ira and, supporting him, lowered him to the floor. Levin's chest was wheezing through the hole and the bloodstain was growing.

"Rosen . . ." Ira rasped. "Saul. Not what you think . . . but . . . okay . . . Riegar . . . Sar . . ."

"Don't talk, Ira," Stone commanded. "I'll get help."

With one hand, Ira Levin grasped Stone's shirt, as if to detain him. With the other, he fumbled in the pocket of his cardigan sweater. "The . . . man . . ." Ira Levin coughed up blood from his lung. His mouth moved a bit more, but he said nothing. The hand clutching Stone's shirt relaxed. His pupils dilated. Ira Levin was dead.

Michael Stone looked at the dead man's right hand. As he died, it had fallen out of his sweater pocket. Still in his fingers was a scrap of paper with something, appearing to be in shorthand, written on it in pencil. Stone knew he should leave everything as he found it and call the police. Instead, he took the piece of paper, rose, went to the door, and looked. No one. He walked toward his car. If he was seen, Stone would say he was going for the police. He wasn't seen.

Stone rationalized that he had witnessed Levin's death but had not seen the shooter. There was nothing, really, he could tell the police, and he couldn't afford to become involved in what he knew would be a fruitless investigation that would tie him up in knots at a time he most needed to be free to act. He drove two blocks toward a nearby supermarket, then changed course abruptly for a more distant neighborhood mom-and-pop grocery where the proprietors would know him.

"How's it going, Tony?" Stone asked the man behind the counter, who had been a classmate in high school. His parents had opened the store and turned it over to Tony Lorenzo when they retired.

"Good, Mike. How's your aunt? She home yet?"

"Brought her back today. Gonna be okay."

"Thank God. What can I do for ya?"

"Mazie gave me a grocery list as long as your arm. I don't get the right brands and stuff, she'll have my ass."

"Let's see 'er."

Stone handed over Aunt May's list and browsed at the magazine rack while Tony filled his order. Finally, Tony called out, "There you go," and Stone returned to the counter. "What do I owe you?"

"Eighty-three, sixty-seven. Watcha gonna do, open a restaurant?"

"Nah, got a bunch of old navy buddies visiting. Eat me out of house and home." Stone faked looking for his wristwatch, then said, "Forgot my watch. You got the time Tony?" He handed him five twenty-dollar bills.

"Sure. Two-forty. And, your change: sixteen thirty-three. You need some help with them bags?"

"Nah. I got it. Thanks, Tony. See ya." A harried young woman with three young children in tow approached the counter and Stone left, his arms full of groceries. He could hear sirens in the distance.

When Michael Stone arrived back home, none of his retired SEAL friends had returned from their familiarization tour of Rhinekill. He put away the groceries, then tiptoed upstairs so as not to awaken his aunt. To Stone's astonishment, she was up and dusting his bedroom.

"For heaven's sake, Mazie, that sort of thing can wait until you're up to it!"

"I *am* up to it, as any fool can plainly see. Besides, I can't have your friends, who came all the way up here to help me, think I run a pigsty of a household."

Stone threw up his hands and said, "All right, but don't carry on when I have to bring you back to the hospital." Searching for some excuse to get his aunt to sit down, Stone thought of the slip of paper he had taken from the dead hand of Ira Levin. He fished it out of his pocket and said, "Mazie, what shorthand system do you use when you take my dictation?"

Aunt May stopped her dusting, turned to him, and said, "Pittman. That's what they taught at business college in my day. Nobody uses it anymore; they use Gregg—that is, those who don't use that clumsy machine. Why?"

"Oh, I found this old piece of paper when I was cleaning up the mess the burglar made of the safe." Stone put on an innocent face. "Did you write this?" He showed the paper to his aunt.

Aunt May took the piece of paper from her nephew and looked at it, frowning. "I certainly did not. I don't know *what* system this is. It certainly isn't Pittman, and I know enough Gregg to tell it's not that, either. You say you found this in the safe?"

"Yeah. Well, it's not important. Thanks, anyway. Here, I'll finish up in here; you go rest."

"I've had enough rest for a week, thank you. Did you get the groceries?"

"Yup. Tony had them all. And I put them away."

"Humph. There's hope for you after all." She started to limp out of the room, hand against her skirt to hold her thigh. "This devil's device," she said, "is too tight."

"Mazie, those people know what they're doing. They measured it carefully."

"They made a mistake," Aunt May said, and was gone.

Stone puzzled for a moment over the paper he had taken from Ira

Levin, then shrugged and put it into his wallet. The doorbell rang, and Aunt May went to open it, admitting Pappy Saye. He'd have to get his friends their own key, Stone thought, as he went downstairs to greet Pappy.

"'M I the first back to the hooch?" Pappy asked.

"Looks that way," Stone said. Stone might not be Clarence Darrow, but he knew enough law not to make admissions against interest to anyone about witnessing Ira Levin's death. He would share information on a need-to-know basis, but not sources. His intelligence training taught him that.

Stone was impatient for the return of Saul Rosen. It was time for a confrontation. Ira Levin had died with Saul's and Sara's names on his lips, and Saul had some explaining to do.

"I'm gonna hit the head," said Pappy as he headed upstairs. "It's been a long walk."

Arno Bitt and Wings Harper, having arranged to meet before returning to base, arrived together. Stone let them in the door. "Well," he said, "whatta you think?"

"Calling this place a city is stretching it," said Wings. "Not that much to cover, really. Think I've got a pretty good handle on the layout."

"Went back down to that Riegar place and did some surveying on foot," said Arno. "The place is weird. Looks like something out of Batman."

"That's because it's a combination of something built a hundred years ago and modern stuff. See anything interesting?"

"Mixed with the crowd when the four-o'clock-shift change got under way. Tell ya one thing, got some hostility goin' there."

"Yeah," said Stone, "some of those animal-rights people get really worked up."

"I don't mean them," Arno said. "A couple of the guys at the gate were speaking German, and one of the guys coming off shift went by, talking to his buddy, and called them 'fucking monkey handlers.' Might be able to use that. You know, get 'em in a bar or something, work on the resentment, pick up some intel."

"Speakin' of which, wish you spoke German. It'd be interesting to know what those guys were saying."

"We spoke German all the time at home. My grandmother never did learn English. The one German called the locals lazy and sloppy and the other guy agreed with him. That was all. But you can see there's no love lost."

Wings Harper, trying not to look as impatient as he felt, said, "When you gonna brief us on this op of yours?"

"This evening, right after chow. I need to get whatever intel Saul Rosen's been able to come up with first. Catch you later."

Stone went into his office and closed the door. He wanted to collect his thoughts before confronting Saul. There was no local television— all the stations were out of New York City, so he turned on the FM receiver of his stereo system and tuned in to the local talk-radio station. The host was taking calls. The subject was local crime in general and the murder of Ira Levin in particular. Preliminary police reports said that the shopkeeper had been shot once, fatally, with a small-caliber weapon, probably a handgun, in what was presumed to be a robbery attempt he resisted. Fearing discovery, the killer apparently fled without taking anything.

The grandfather clock was just chiming five when the doorbell added a few notes and Saul Rosen, carrying several videocassettes, entered. Stone intercepted him and steered him into his office.

"Sit down, Saul."

Saul could tell by the look on Stone's face that something serious had occurred. "Sara—she's okay?"

"Sara's fine," said Stone. Then he hit him with it cold. "Ira Levin's dead."

Saul didn't bat an eye. "When?" he asked flatly. "How?"

"This afternoon. One shot from a suppressed subcaliber weapon. He thought you and your sister important enough to be the subjects of his last words on this earth. Now, tell me again how fucked up I am to be suspicious of the guy who saved my life. I'm gonna ask you again, Saul. Who are you with and what the fuck's going on here?"

Saul Rosen's voice was level and calm as he replied: "I'm a lieutenant colonel in the IDF, assigned as the first assistant to the military attaché at the Israeli Embassy in Washington."

"That was very good, only a bit too practiced, as a first cover story tends to be. Now let's remember who you're talking to and forget covers number two and three and get to the truth. Who're you with?"

"Hey, listen, Mike," Saul said with some heat, "I told you—hell, I *swore* to you I'm not with the Mossad."

"And I believe you. But that doesn't answer the question, does it, Saul?"

Saul said nothing, and Stone let the silence just hang there, getting thicker and thicker. Then he said, "I'm the guy you told your sister she could trust. I'm the guy who's trying to keep your sister out of prison, in the course of which I've been attacked physically, my office burglarized, my livelihood threatened. I've been the subject of an attempted bribe and had my aunt thrown in front of a bus. The Germans at the plant were talking about your sister before she got here, and now a cigar-store owner who gets popped with a suppressed weapon dies talking about Sara and says you're okay—but that you're not who I think you are. And I never told him who I thought you were. Now, *who the fuck are you?*"

For a few moments, Saul Rosen struggled, like a man trying not to throw up. "I swear, Mike, I don't know why this guy, the Germans, why anybody would be talking about Sara. I mean, Sara's just . . . Sara, that's all."

"Okay. I believe you. Or at least that you don't know. Now, how about you?"

Saul Rosen said the hell with it and threw up. "I'm what I told you I was, but you're right, it's a cover. But I'm not with the Mossad." He gave a small, mirthless laugh. "Why is it every *goy* thinks half the Jews in the United States and everyone in Israel is Mossad?"

"I don't know. Maybe because Ira Levin was Mossad?"

What little color was left in Saul Rosen's face drained from it. "What do you know about that?"

"Nothing. I'm guessing."

Rosen heaved a deep sigh. "You're real close. Back during the war for independence in 'forty-eight, Ira Levin used his New York mob connections to help out the *Irgun*. When this Riegar business came up, the Mossad remembered that and tapped into him for whatever he could come up with for them. I mean, he was already here, had connections . . . I knew about him, but I didn't think he knew about me. They must have briefed him on me."

Saul paused, looking off at the wall without seeing it, then said, "Mossad simply means 'institution' in Hebrew. The full name is *Mossad le Aliyah Beth*. Central Institution for Intelligence and Special Assignments. Or, you could translate 'assignments' as 'services.' They're good. Real good, but their interests are still relatively provincial, generally Middle East, compared with the more worldwide interests of other pro-Western nations. And my outfit."

"Which is?"

"I'm with the LAKAM. It's an acronym for the Hebrew, *Lishka Lekishrey Mada;* the special division of the Defense Ministry in charge of acquiring scientific and technological intelligence. Historically, this has made for somewhat tense relations with the Mossad—kind of a rivalry. That's why I was told about Ira Levin. He was the Mossad agent-in-place, keeping tabs on Riegar for them, when that's really not their business. It's ours.

"For reasons I can't go into, we've targeted Riegar. And our interest, I think, is the source of the Mossad's interest and their use of Ira. I came up really to take on the local operation here. I swear Sara's got nothing to do with us and I'd know if she was with the Mossad. They're pissed because the U.S. press put the onus on them for the Jonathan Jay Pollard spy case—you remember, the U.S. citizens who gave national security secrets to Israel from July of 'eighty-four to November 'eighty-five. Pollard worked for us, LAKAM, not the Mossad."

"Shit," said Stone. "You telling me an outfit like the Mossad can't take a little heat in the U.S. press for an op it didn't run? C'mon, that goes with the territory."

"You don't understand. The real embarrassment was in Israel. When the Pollards first volunteered to pass U.S. secrets to the Israelis, the Mossad *turned them down*. They didn't want to pull clandestine ops against the United States because it would endanger their close relationship with the CIA. Ironically, the relationship was built up by

James Jesus Angleton, then the Agency's top counterespionage official. He'd been using the Mossad to do things for the CIA domestically that it was prohibited by law from doing itself.

"Now, the guy running my outfit, LAKAM, had once been a high official of the Mossad who was passed over for the top job. He knew all about the CIA-Mossad connection, but was still pissed at not getting the number-one spot a decade before, so he didn't give a shit. He took the Pollards on and embarrassed the Mossad with the intelligence coup they gave Israel. Then the shit *really* hit the fan: just months after the Pollard conviction, the Iran-Contra affair blows and the American administration and the Israeli government are trying to deny the U.S.-Israel link in the swapping of arms for hostages. Believe me, there's no love lost between the Mossad and the LAKAM!"

"So, what are you after Riegar for?"

"I can't tell you that because I really don't know much myself. I don't need to. That gizmo I told you I learned to put together in school? That's bullshit. I brought that synchronizer with me. I'm just supposed to tape their computer screens and send the tapes back by diplomatic pouch to Israel. The guys wearing thirty pens in their plastic shirt-pocket protectors will figure out what it means. But I'll let you review them first for whatever help it'll give you with your op to help my sister. All you need is a TV and a VCR."

"Okay, Saul. Fair enough. I'll keep your cover at the briefing tonight. Thanks for leveling with me."

"Okay to ask a question?"

"Shoot."

"Just what, exactly, did Levin say?"

"I'm not saying I was there and heard it. Right?"

"Sure." Saul smiled.

"Understand," said Stone, who had committed the vital words to memory, "the man was dying. There were . . . gaps. The first thing he said was 'the man.' He was pointing behind me—probably trying to call my attention to the man who shot him. It was no robbery attempt or he'd have hit me, too. My back was to the son of a bitch, for Christ's sake. I don't know why Ira was hit, but it wouldn't surprise me if it was to silence him before he could talk to me. The next thing he said was 'Rosen, Saul.' He inverted your name, like he was reading from a military personnel list. Then he said, 'Not what you think, but okay.' He was gasping pretty badly now in between words. Then he said, 'Riegar,' then 'Sara'—or," Stone thought a minute, "at least the first part of it, like 'Sa . . .' or 'Sar . . . .' You know, he's gasping for breath, shot through the lung."

"I know just what you're talking about," said Saul. "I remember."

"Yeah, I guess you tend not to forget something like that. At any rate, the last thing he said was the same as the first: 'the man.' Then he died." Stone withheld any mention of the piece of paper with the unusual shorthand on it. He didn't know what it meant, and Rosen had no need to know.

Saul Rosen seemed lost in thought. "What is it?" Stone asked.

"Oh, nothing. . . . I'm sure you're right."

"About what?"

"Well . . . this is pretty farfetched. Look, you're sure that when Levin first said 'the man,' he was pointing at somebody behind you? Like the guy who shot him?"

"Sure. That's exactly the way it happened."

"Then why did he say it again, after the guy is long gone, and it's his final effort, his *last words?*"

"I don't know. He was dying, for Christ's sake. People say strange things when they're dying. The brain's going, you know."

"Yeah. But not usually really focused people like Ira. Suppose he was trying to tell you something he considered more important than anything else he had to tell you—about me, or Sara, or anything?"

"Like what, for Christ's sake!" Stone's voice was irritated, impatient.

Rosen ignored the tone of voice and continued in a measured way. "It may be a helluva coincidence, but there's a terrorist, who's number one on just about everybody's list, who's name is Al Rajul. In Arabic, that means 'The Man.' "

Stone considered what Saul had said for a moment, then nodded his head and said, "You're right, that is a helluva coincidence. But what would a top Palestinian terrorist be doing in a place like Rhinekill, New York?"

"Who said he was Palestinian?"

"You said the name was Arabic."

"Correct. But it's not a proper name. More like a description, if anything. Nobody knows this guy's real name, or nationality, or even what he looks like."

"Still, what would he be doing here?"

"Hey, Mike. There's a thousand people here weren't here a month ago. Why am I here? Why is the international press here?"

"Riegar?"

Saul Rosen raised his eyebrows and shrugged his shoulders.

"You get a better answer, tell me."

"But what . . . ?"

"Who knows. One thing's for sure."

"What's that?"

"We're not gonna find out sittin' on our ass around here."

Michael Stone got up out of his chair. "Yeah. Let's go to chow."

Stephanie Hannigan was frustrated, annoyed, fearful, and perplexed to the extent that her uncharacteristic mood swings were drawing comment among her colleagues in the public defender's office. The memory of the intensity of her arousal frustrated her and the fact annoyed her with herself. What she had learned from Naomi led her to be fearful—both of the future she still longed to have with Michael Stone, and of the man himself and his capabilities. Her perplexity arose from not having the slightest idea what to do about all this.

Pride had dictated that Stephanie avoid locations and occasions where she might run into Stone again. She had carried off the last meeting rather well, she thought, but it had been excruciatingly difficult, requiring a self-control she was unsure she could repeat. Nor, damn it, was she sure she wanted to.

Nature, however, was uncooperative with Stephanie's intellectually taken decisions. Gradually, subtly, her resolve was subverted by her human instincts. She started to rationalize. There could be no harm, temptation whispered, in just physically *seeing* the man; especially if he did not know about it. Seeing him might help to clarify her thoughts about him; one must be careful in important matters such as these to avoid fantasizing and be certain one was dealing with reality.

At the athletic center, Stephanie recalled, the layout—high spectator seats above the line of sight of those in the pool—as well as Stone's use of goggles while swimming and his general preoccupation with the details of his exercise program had made it necessary for her to call attention to herself at the pool and again later by blowing the horn of her car. What better place to observe the man discreetly? Never intruding into her consciousness was the thought of her reverie as she sat mesmerized by the sinuous, rhythmic rippling of the muscles in Stone's back as he swam beneath her gaze.

Shortly after 7:00 A.M. of the morning following Michael Stone's briefing of his small former SEAL unit, Stephanie Hannigan slipped into the athletic center. This time, to be on the safe side, she took a seat on the highest row, back in the farthest corner. Stone, she could see, was present, but something unusual was going on. The routine was markedly different from that which she had observed previously.

No one was swimming in the pool at all. A number of men and women in wet bathing suits, obviously just out of the water from the way it still dripped from their bodies, were clustered at the near side of the pool like so many spectators. Four men, one of them Stone and one of them black, were stripping off one of the two racing trunks competitive swimmers typically wear to increase drag when practicing, the same psychology that prompts baseball batters "on deck" to swing several bats at the same time. There was an air of expectancy in the vast area that Stephanie could sense all the way up in her high perch. Curiosity gnawed at her, but she dared not get closer, where she might have been able to find out what was going on.

To Stephanie's relief, several people who had been down on the pool deck came up into the stands to get a better view. Instinct again overruled Stephanie's caution, and she moved unobtrusively down behind them, seated herself, then leaned forward and whispered to a bathing-suited young woman who was shivering under a large bath towel. "What's going on?"

The woman turned around and, with excitement in her voice, said, "That's Michael Stone behind the block in the outside lane. He's a local lawyer who's a member of the New York Athletic Club water-polo team. He works out here all the time. The other three guys are members of the team, too, up visiting from New York. They were working out together when the tall guy—the one with the red hair?—kept teasing the other white guy that he was a sinker an' all and couldn't really swim. I don't know why, the guy was doing great in practice. Anyway, he got the others betting about it, and they're gonna have a race. The redheaded guy wanted a two hundred IM. That's an individual medley; two laps 'fly, two back, two breast, and two free. But Mr. Stone, he said that wouldn't be fair—why, I don't know—so it's going to be two hundred breast. I—"

Someone blew a whistle and called out, "Swimmers on the blocks!"

The four men stepped up onto the blocks, raised boards that slanted downward to the front, leading edge even with the side of the pool. The men moved to the front of the board so that their toes hung over it. Then they curled their toes to grip the forward edge tightly and leaned forward, gently shaking their long, muscled arms as they hung loosely before them.

"Take your mark!" Stephanie could see the man who was speaking now. He was a balding senior swimmer, who spoke with the authority of an experienced swimming judge and had positioned himself at the near end of the pool, slightly to the front of the racers so that he could sight down the line they formed. At his command, Stone and the others had leaned down and placed their hands on the boards next to their feet, gripping the edge hard enough to whiten their knuckles. They seemed to be pulling with their hands and pushing with their feet. As Wings Harper gripped the board with his hands, his body didn't stop moving. As if in slow motion, it pivoted on the board edge he was gripping with hands and feet until his center of gravity was well over the water. He let go with his hands and waved his arms in a vain attempt to restore his balance, failed, and fell into the pool.

"False start on number one!" shouted the man serving as the official. Wings Harper, sheepish under the leer of Arno Bitt, climbed out of the pool and back onto his block. Four spectators equipped with varying kinds of stopwatches and standing behind the blocks rechecked their watches as the other three contestants used the interruption to relax.

"Take your mark!" the bald man repeated, then brought the whistle up to his mouth. Again the four former SEALs leaned forward and gripped the board edges with hands and feet. The official checked that none was moving, then, using his tongue to start and stop it, produced a short, sharp note from the whistle.

Michael Stone, Pappy Saye, Arno Bitt, and Wings Harper launched themselves like F-14s from the steam catapult on the deck of an aircraft carrier. They entered the water several yards out from the pool wall with remarkably little splash, then glided at speed like so many porpoises, arms outstretched. They rose to the surface as one, Michael Stone slightly in the lead, then dug their arms downward into the water, hands cupped and whipping upward toward their chests as their legs, seemingly loosely hinged at the knee, whipped together to propel them forward with a smooth, froglike, repetitive power.

Stone hit the far wall first, then pushed off in his turn. He was followed in quick succession by Arno Bitt, Pappy Saye, and Wings Harper. The four men stayed in the same relative formation through the first and second laps, Stone slightly lengthening his lead, their times causing rising comment from the small crowd.

Stephanie leaned forward and addressed the young woman again. "What is it, what are they saying?"

The woman held up a stopwatch so Stephanie could see it. It was electronically operated with a number of sets of liquid-crystal display numbers, some running, some motionless. The numbers meant nothing to Stephanie. "Look at those splits," said the excited young woman. "They're fast! I can't believe it; those guys are *old.*"

Up yours, kid, Stephanie thought, but said nothing.

As the four men hit the far wall for the last time prior to the final lap, Michael Stone was pulling away by two body lengths, and Arno Bitt, perhaps still feeling the effects of his recent overindulgence in alcohol, had fallen slightly behind Wings Harper, who, sensing moral victory, started to pull farther away until he was even with Pappy Saye. It was proving to be one helluva race, and the crowd was cheering.

At that critical moment, a young woman, fully dressed, burst onto the pool deck and shouted, "Michael! MICHAEL!" It was Sara Rosen.

Sara's shouting to Michael Stone, who was clearly winning the race, caused but a minor stir among the audience. It was engrossed in the drama of the finish, and the fact that a young woman was shouting what was taken as encouragement and approval to the apparent winner seemed not at all unusual. Sara's cries did not penetrate to the hearing of any of those in the water, much less break through their concentration to register on their consciousness.

Stone touched the poolside, the winner, and threw his head back, clearing his throat for more air. He was followed by Pappy Saye and a jubilant Wings Harper, who was enjoying payback for years of needling, and then a crestfallen Arno Bitt, who didn't like losing bets, especially in public when he was a subject of the wager. The men moved to the lane edges and shook hands, stripping away their goggles. It was then that Sara Rosen registered on the crowd as rude and pushy.

Sara pushed her way to the head of Stone's lane, leaned over, and shouted at him. "Michael, I've got to see you right away!"

Stone became aware of her presence for the first time. "Later, Sara, in my office, okay?"

Oblivious to her surroundings, Sara shouted back at him. "Damn it, Mike, you don't understand. Eddie didn't come home last night. He's disappeared!"

Michael Stone sucked in more air. Shit, he thought, now I'm not only her lawyer, I've gotta be counselor for her love life. What he actually said was, "Not here, Sara. You know my car; it's in the lot outside. Wait for me there." To avoid argument, he pushed off to do a warm-down lap.

Up in the stands, Stephanie Hannigan had been watching all this. She recognized Sara Rosen from her photograph in the newspaper, but this was the first time she had seen her slender young figure. Under her breath, but right from her gut, she said, "You bitch."

14

● "I DUNNO," SAID MICHAEL STONE. HE WAS STAND-
ing next to his car in the athletic center's parking lot. "This is gonna
look like one of those circus clown acts. Mustangs just aren't built for
five people."

"She can sit on *my* lap anytime," Wings Harper offered hopefully.

Sara's tone was acid. "I have my own car, thank you." She pointed
to a vehicle in the opposite row of parking spaces, even with the
Mustang. An old slant-six-engined Plymouth sedan, its rocker panels
rust-digested, slumped between the white lines. Stone regarded it
briefly. "Someone die and leave you a fortune?" he asked.

"Very funny. The engine's reliable and it's paid for, which is more
than most people can say. Now listen. Eddie's gone, and I think they've
got him. I—"

"Not here in the parking lot, for Christ's sake. Follow us back to
the house. We'll talk there."

The clapped-out slant-six couldn't hope to keep up with the Mustang, and Sara Rosen didn't try. Stone and his friends were already in
the house when she arrived. Stone and her brother let her in and

ushered her into Stone's office. "Take it from the beginning," he said.

"Eddie's been acting funny—"

"That's a switch," Saul interjected. Stone, annoyed at the interruption, waved him off. "Go ahead, Sara."

Sara glanced at her brother and continued. "As I said, he's been acting funny; cross-examining me about what I saw inside Riegar; going over the Polaroids again and again—"

"What?!" Stone moved rapidly to his desk and pulled the manila envelope out of the letter holder. From its weight, he knew it was empty. "If that asshole—"

"Eddie had nothing to do with it, Mike. I slipped them out of there when you weren't looking. I'm sorry."

Stone sighed in resignation, then shrugged his shoulders. "They're your pictures. Why didn't you just ask me for them?"

"I didn't want another hassle. It was on the spur of the moment, Mike. I didn't mean anything by it."

Stone shrugged again, dismissing the issue. "Anyway," Sara continued, "Eddie made me keep trying to count the floors I ran up after I got out of the elevator that night, trying to pin me down about how many there were. He wanted to know the exact floor I was on when I was caught."

"Why?" Stone asked.

"Look at this." Sara passed Stone a piece of paper. It was a sales receipt from Paul's Camera Shop, South Road Mall, Rhinekill. Stone squinted at the clerk's handwriting for a moment, then recognized the words. "Minox!"

"Right."

"Let me see that," Saul asked. Stone gave him the paper.

"Two hundred fifty bucks. The price is low."

"C model. Used. Hell, spies've been using 'em since World War Two. Price works. What else you got?" Stone asked.

"Nothing. Just a hunch. Eddie's impulsive. And he's dedicated. I think he may have gone into Riegar to get photographs showing the animals actually in the apparatus in the labs. He's been unhappy with the way things are going. I mean, we're getting lots of press and all, but none of it seems to be affecting Riegar. Business as usual, you know?"

"All right," said Stone, "but we're gonna need more to go on than we've got so far. Go back out there and talk to your movement people. They know you're tight with Eddie. Ask where he is. Someone may know what he's up to. We'll do what we can to find out from this end."

"What are you gonna do?"

"Whatever we have to. Now go on, get out of here."

"And, sis," Saul said.

"Yes?"

"Don't *you* go disappearing, okay?"

Sara gave a disgusted wave and left.

"Herr Kramer is aware of this development?" Helmar Metz was speaking in German.

"No, sir," answered Rudolf Letzger. "The capture was made by my people—yours really—not the building guards. I thought it best to come straight to you, especially after the fiasco when the woman was turned over to the police without the opportunity to interrogate her. And, of course, the disaster the night we lost Olaf and failed to catch the man who killed him; to say nothing of the fact that the killer must be assumed to have witnessed the disposal of the Mexican."

Metz rocked forward in his chair behind what had been Kramer's desk. "You were correct in coming directly to me, *Herr Doktor.* Where is he now?"

Letzger remained at near attention in front of the desk. "We cleared out a small storage room on the primate laboratory floor. He has been in isolation there since capture."

"He was armed? I'd like to see the knife he used on Olaf."

"No weapon. But he was carrying this." Letzger produced a small, black-finished, rectangular object. An eighteen-inch beaded chain was attached to the bottom end. He handed it to Metz.

"Minox subminiature," Metz observed. He pulled at both ends of the object and it extended, revealing a tiny lens. Metz snapped it shut and handed it back to Letzger, asking, "The film?"

"We have already processed it. Nothing. He was intercepted before he could use it. You want him brought here?"

"No. Take me to him. I don't want him seen, and I certainly don't want him heard when I interrogate him." Metz rose, and the two men left the room.

Getting off the elevator after traveling down from the eighteenth to the twelfth floor, Metz, still speaking German, asked, "This storage room, it is soundproofed?"

"Yes, sir. This floor and everything on it, even the closets."

"Good."

The two men reached a door and entered. It was the outer room of Dr. Letzger's office. A woman sat behind a desk with a computer and a telephone in front of her. Letzger nodded to his secretary and, without speaking, took from her hand several proffered messages. After a quick glance, he stuffed them into his pocket, turned, and, Metz still in tow, went back out into the elevator hall. He passed several doors, then entered another that led to a hallway, walked down it, and nodded to Metz at another door. Letzger fished a key out of his pocket and was approaching the door when Metz stopped him. "Careful," Metz said. "He could be waiting to attack the first person to enter."

Letzger smiled coldly. "We used the primate restraints. I assure you, he is secure." Using his key, he unlocked and opened the door.

The supply closet was six by ten feet in area, but that was reduced by shelving that extended a foot inward from each wall. The shelves were empty. The room was not. A single overhead fluorescent light fixture cast a cold light on the figure of Eddie Berg. He was on the floor, dressed in unfaded blue jeans and a dark blue turtlenecked shirt, an old jacket, black basketball shoes on his feet. Eddie was lying on his side, cap fallen off his head to the floor beside him, his hands secured behind his back at the wrists and his legs fastened at the ankles by tapered yellow plastic strips with a series of zigzag projections along both edges. The strips diminished to a point at one end. The pointed end had been slipped through a slit in the broad opposite end, in a manner similar to the fastenings that accompany plastic trash bags to seal them after filling.

As Letzger and Metz entered the room, Eddie was in the process of rolling over onto his other side to ease the strain on his muscles. His thinness made for little padding between his bones and the hard floor and, coupled with his height, made him appear even more awkward in his bound state. Eddie looked up and said to Letzger, indicating Metz with a nod of his head, "He the police?"

Letzger laughed. "There is plenty of time for that, Mr. Berg." Then, in German, he said to Metz, "He had no wallet, but my men recognized him immediately. He has been outside the gates for days with a loudspeaker, inflaming the crowd."

"Inflaming the crowd your ass, schmuck. Yeah, I know what you said, it's close enough to Yiddish for me to make out. *Verstehen sie 'schmuck'?*" Eddie didn't wait for an answer. "The crowd was inflamed before they even got here by what you guys are doin' to the animals. That's why they're here. Now quit fuckin' around. I know my rights. Turn me over to the cops or let me go. And I want a lawyer."

"Ah," said Metz, "Mr. Stone, perhaps?"

"Stone!" Eddie Berg's contempt knew no bounds. "I want a *real* lawyer!"

"A wise position for a murderer, Mr. Berg."

"Murderer! What the hell're you talking about?"

"I'm talking about the employee you killed making good your escape from here the other night. So, you are returned to finish the job. You are incorrigible, Mr. Berg."

"And you're a fuckin' lunatic. I've never been in here before! I've never killed anybody in my life. I was a conscientious objector, for Christ's sake!"

"We shall see," said Metz, "we shall see." He motioned to Letzger to accompany him, then withdrew, leaving Eddie Berg alone on the closet floor.

"Hey!" Eddie called after them. "I told you. I want a lawyer!"

Outside, in the corridor, Metz turned to Letzger and asked, "How many from the last shipment left unused?"

"Two, sir."

"Put our prisoner in with them. It is more secure. I want to wait a bit. It is possible he told someone where he was going. I want to be able to produce him unharmed if necessary. If no one comes soon, we can assume his whereabouts are unknown and proceed with the interrogation."

"With your permission, the reason I put him in the closet instead of with the Mexicans immediately was in case you did decide to release him. If we put him with the Mexicans, he will know about them, and they might tell him how they got here, and so forth. He will be quite safe in the closet until you take a decision on his fate."

Metz had a low tolerance for suggestions from underlings that his might not be the best way to proceed. It crept into his voice as a hard edge when he said, "Those Indian peasants speak neither English nor German. They can tell him nothing. He will assume it is a workman's dormitory. Do as instructed."

"At once, sir." Letzger peeled off toward his office to carry out his orders. Metz took the elevator back up to his office.

Within minutes, two of the Germans Stone had seen in the railway-receiving hangar entered Eddie Berg's closet, gagged him, freed his legs, and lifted him to his feet. The circulation in Eddie's legs had been impaired, so they buckled. The two men walked him in circles until his legs were secure under him again, then led him out and down the hall, through a series of doors, until the three of them entered a windowless, fluorescent-lighted dormitory with bunks, shower, and toilet facilities for twelve men. The gag was removed from Eddie's mouth and the plastic binder from his wrists. Then he was shoved down on a bunk and left there.

As soon as his guards left and locked the door, Eddie Berg looked about him. Two men in rough work clothes lay listlessly on bunks. The rest of the bunks were empty. The room was curiously empty of any personal property belonging to either man. "What's it like in this joint?" Eddie called over to his fellow prisoners. There was no answer. Eddie got to his feet and went over to the nearest man. He looked young, strong, but worn and defeated. In his career as an activist, Eddie had seen the inside of some local and county jails. He had been in a lot worse than this place, and to have three men sharing space for twelve was unheard of in a nation of overcrowded jails. "Hey," Eddie asked, "when's chow in this joint?"

"No habla ingles, señor."

Eddie Berg, a native of Imperial Beach, California, had no problem with that. In fluent Chicano dialect, he launched into conversation. "What is this place, a private prison? What are you two in for?"

The young man let out a bitter laugh. "On the Virgin Mary, I wish this were a prison, señor. We two are all that is left of six. We paid the coyote to smuggle us into the United States and get us jobs so we could send home money to our families. We traveled in the dark a long way—there was no way to count the days—to this place. When we got here, Pablo, my cousin, said he wanted to go home, is too far away here. I pray to God they let him go, but I do not know. The rest of us they put in here. The food is good. We are warm. They take us one by one through that door over there." He pointed to a door at the opposite end of the room from that through which Eddie had entered.

"Yes," joined in the other Mexican, lying on his back and not looking at Eddie, "we leave one by one. But no one ever comes back."

"What happens to them?"

"I do not know, señor, but sometimes, late in the night, when it is very quiet—my ears are very good, you know?—I hear sounds."

"What kind of sounds?"

The young Mexican sat up and looked penetratingly at Eddie. "When I was a little boy, the priest told us all about the damned souls in hell. He was a very talented storyteller, our priest. When I was little, I had nightmares about hell. I could hear the damned cry when the devils tortured them. In my sleep, the cries were very clear. One never forgets something like that. Now, when I lie awake at night, I hear cries, very faint, from in there. They are the same as I heard in my dreams."

"You're sure it's not another nightmare?"

"Then," said the other prisoner, "we are both having the same nightmare, señor. I hear them, too."

"Animals," said Eddie. "That's what you hear. That's what they do here. Torture animals to make money."

"No, señor," said the first Mexican, still sitting up, his eyes boring into Eddie's. "When I was a small boy, I had a puppy. A truck ran over his hips. It took him some time to die. I took him to the priest for burial in consecrated ground so he could go to heaven. The priest said animals cannot go to heaven. Neither do they go to hell. I heard my puppy scream as he was crushed. And in my dreams, I have heard the damned in hell. The puppy was the better off, señor. God was merciful to him. Where there is no God, there is no mercy. And there is no God in hell."

The other prisoner finally sat up. His face was gaunt, his eyes hollow. "Yes," he agreed, pointing to the far door, "and there is no God in there."

At 1:00 P.M., Stephanie Hannigan nosed her yellow Prelude into a parking space in the lot of the new Rhinekill Holiday Inn, got out, and entered the lobby. Brian Sullivan was waiting for her and, with Continental flair, escorted her into the dining room to the table he had reserved. It was in an ersatz solarium, a greenhouselike extension of the front of the building, abundant with hanging asparagus ferns. Their table was at the very front, with a view of the mountains to the south and west.

"I must say," said Stephanie, "that being a source of yours could prove very damaging to my waistline." She picked up the menu, examined it, then ordered a Caesar salad. "Discipline," she said, smiling, "I've got to exert discipline."

"You're sure?" asked Sullivan. "Reuters c'n affard all y'want."

"Yes," said Stephanie, "but *I* can't afford all I want."

Sullivan ordered a flank steak and an Irish whiskey, neat, for himself. Stephanie acquiesced to a Chablis. "Well," she asked, "what can I probably not help you with this afternoon?"

"There has been an interestin' tarn of events in the Riegar matter, my dear. A mister Eddie Berg, who has been makin' himself prominent in front of the factory gates with his loud-hailer, exhartin' the protesters to ever-more-vehement denunciations of the devil, did not show up at his post this marnin'. No one knows what's become of him, or, if they do, will not tell me. I thought y'might have heard somethin' about that from your laryer friend. Y'see, if I repart to me editors that the leader of the Riegar protesters has pulled out, they will not be satisfied with that as the story. They will want to know *why* he abandoned the cause. *That* is the story."

Stephanie waited until she had chewed the heart of lettuce in her mouth thoroughly before she said, "Why do you think Mr. Stone would know that?"

"Because Mr. Berg is living with his client, Sara Rosen."

That statement was news to Stephanie, and she was unable to keep some of her delight from being reflected in her face.

"Ah," said Sullivan, "y'were not aware of that, then?"

"It shows, huh?"

"Yes."

"No, I wasn't. So, obviously, Mr. Stone hasn't taken me into his confidence in the matter. Nor is there any reason that he should."

"Of course," Sullivan observed, "but there'd be no harm in askin' the man, would there?"

Stephanie blushed. "Mr. Stone and I are not on quite the familiar terms you assume."

Sullivan took a sip of whiskey and said casually, "Lovers' quarrel?"

"What?"

"I'm a reporter, Miss Hannigan. I hear things. No offense."

"No offense taken. But I thought you were from Reuters, not the tabloids. Anyway, in the unlikely event I learn what you want to know in a manner that wouldn't be unethical to reveal, I'll tell you. I appreciate the meals, and we Irish have to stick together."

"I'll drink to that."

"I suspect you'd drink to anything," Stephanie teased.

"Because I'm Irish?"

"Because you're a reporter."

"Touché. Breakfast tomorrow?"

Stephanie's bantering tone turned resentful. "I won't be seeing Mr. Stone this evening."

"No, no," Sullivan protested. "No quid pro quo. Strictly social. And early, won't interfere with your schedule. Pick you up at five-thirty."

"Five-thirty! For breakfast? That's insane!"

"The reward'll be breakfast with a view of the Hudson I guarantee you'll not have dined to before."

"I wouldn't get up at five A.M. for a view of heaven. Where is this place?"

"Ah, lass, the mystery's part of the allure. I'll give y'a hint. It has to do with the angle of the sun in the early hours at this time o' year. Are y'game?"

Stephanie, challenged, paused only for a moment. "You're on!"

"Fine. Five-thirty, then."

"Won't you need my address?"

"Oh, I already have that." Sullivan smiled.

"You *do?*"

"I'm a reporter, remember?"

Eddie Berg tried to stay awake and alert. To that end, he undertook to review the events that had led to his present unpleasant circumstances. One of his most valuable assets in life was that he never kidded himself. He might not show or admit them to others, but he knew his strengths and weaknesses. He had undertaken this mission with no more idea of how to go about it than could be gleaned from reading novels and watching motion pictures. The only uniform Eddie Berg had ever worn was that of the Boy Scouts of America.

Eddie was scared. His bravado with his captors was an attempt to mask it. It did not occur to him that his fear was a demonstration of his bravery. He had entered the dread confines of the gloomy and mysterious, hissing and rumbling Riegar plant in spite of his fear. He was also resourceful, to a point. Eddie had gained entry by mixing with the personnel entering for the next shift personnel. When he found them all punching their cards in the time clock, he just shuffled by with the rest of them, wearing an old jacket and cap, used his height to reach up to the top row of cards, plucked one at random, stamped it in the machine, and put it back where he found it. From there, it was just a question of finding a place to hide until the last employee had left, then making his way to where the animals were being experimented upon, photograph them with the Minox, hide again until the next mass exodus, and make his escape. It had not occurred to him that double punching time on shift would lead to the interrogation of the employee whose card he had appropriated, and then a search for an intruder.

The security-service guards had been no problem. It was the others who found him. He knew when he heard the words from behind him, *"Hände hoch!"* that he had been detected by those the locals so resented and the animal activists had come to hold in particular contempt: the torturers themselves, the feared and hated monkey handlers. He was determined to remain awake and alert but, despite his resolve, he finally fell asleep.

They came for Eddie Berg late at night. The Mexican prisoners, who slept much of the day, were awake and watched a now-familiar routine: four large muscular men approached Eddie's bunk. One leaned over and shook him gently. His eyes opened, and he stared upward for a few seconds before comprehension hit him and he started to bolt upward.

Two sets of exceedingly strong hands gripped Eddie's upper arms and wrists so tightly that they became numb almost at once. Another hand held his jaw with such strength, it felt on the verge of dislocation. The man held the forefinger of his other hand in front of his mouth and shook his head. Eddie felt completely helpless and decided to obey instructions in the hope that a slip in his captor's alertness might give him an opening to—do what? Eddie wasn't sure, but he was confident he'd think of something. He'd gotten in, hadn't he? No one had ever told Eddie Berg that getting in was easy, that getting out was the trick.

To his surprise, the men did not walk Eddie through the door referred to with such fear by the two Mexican prisoners. Instead, they took him out the way he came in, then into another room that he recognized from Sara's description as the one in which she had hidden herself, the computer-monitoring room. The two men who had visited him in the closet were waiting for him.

"Good evening, Mr. Berg. You slept well, I hope?" It was the big one, the one so thick in the shoulders, who spoke to him.

"Where's my lawyer?"

"You have a one-track mind, Mr. Berg. I have told you that I want to know what you came here to do, both last night and the other evening, when you so skillfully killed one of my employees. Now, then, there are two ways we can go about this: the intelligent way, which is for you to acknowledge your situation and just tell us what we want to know, or the difficult way—difficult, that is, for you."

"Next thing," said Eddie Berg, "you're gonna tell me I have relatives in Milwaukee, and you have ways of making me talk, right? I'm surprised you haven't asked to see my papers. I knew I was in the hands of a bunch of lunatics when you started talkin' about my having been here before and killed somebody. Now I find I'm in the middle of a fuckin' World War Two movie. I don't believe this."

"You will be a believer very shortly, Mr. Berg. And my congratulations. You are about to complete your mission. You came twice to see what we do here. Miss Rosen photographed certain of our equipment while it was not in use. Now you shall see it *in* use. I think Dr. Letzger would be able to explain it best. *Herr Doktor . . .*"

Letzger took the lead in walking over to the computer banks. Metz followed at Eddie's side, and the four guards followed behind. Eddie glanced at them. They were alert to his every move. The party stopped before the row of elevated cathode-ray-tube terminal screens.

There were twelve screens. All but three were dark. The lighted screens bore the captions "Primate No. 1," "Primate No. 2," and "Primate No. 3." All three carried physical descriptions by length and weight in centimeters and kilograms. Next came vital signs: blood pressure, pulse, and respiration rates. Then the more sophisticated measurements, an apnea monitor that read leads to the diaphragm to measure chest movement. It determined whether the subject's breathing had been interrupted or stopped altogether. An oximeter measured the amounts of oxygen and carbon dioxide in the blood; an electromyograph measured the strength of particular muscles. An echocardiogram kept track of the T and S waves causing the ventricles of the heart to contract, and an electroencephalogram measured the alpha and delta brain waves. There was a mark to show when the delta wave was slow enough to indicate coma.

There followed data that varied, such as "reaction, positive/negative, rejection, time to rejection, and test substance." These were followed by times, chemical formulas, and more data that was meaningless to Berg.

"It is here," said Letzger, "that we monitor each primate. All are connected to the computer. There is a display terminal for each. Because of the hour, there is no one here to observe the terminals—all the desks, as you can see, are empty—but the computer, fortunately, does not sleep. It continues the monitoring twenty-four hours a day and stores it for our examination and evaluation later. The information monitored is, as you can see, quite complete."

"Like hell it is," said Eddie. "Where on your screens does it monitor pain?"

"Very observant of you, Mr. Berg. Believe me, if we could, we would. Unfortunately, no one has yet devised a way to do that. Perhaps you will be able to help us in that regard. Come. The subject primates themselves are in here."

Letzger led the way to the door through which Sara had entered the room from the laboratory. Eddie recognized that they had come in somewhat of a circle. The door they were approaching led into the room so dreaded by the Mexicans. Letzger paused before it. "Correct me if I am wrong, Mr. Berg. It is the position of the animal-welfare activists that there is such a difference between the physiology of humans and that of other animals that product testing, for example, or drug testing on animals for human efficacy is, essentially, useless. Correct?"

"Correct."

"Then you will be happy to learn, sir, that we are in complete agreement."

On Eddie Berg's astonished *"What?"* Dr. Letzger opened the door.

15

⬤ THE M.S. *AKA MARU*, TOTALLY UNLADEN, HER FUEL and freshwater tanks empty, rode at her mooring at Albany, New York, so high out of the water as to appear ungainly. Actually, she was anything but. One of the very latest high-technology freighters produced by the shipyards of Japan, *Aka Maru* made money for her owners because, thanks to computerization, she could be operated by a crew that would have left a good-sized rowboat undermanned. Just who the fortunate owners were was lost in the fog of interlocking corporations chartered by such major maritime powers as Ghana. Her flag of convenience was Panama, which took care of any union and safety problems. The "M.S." before her name stood for "motorship," meaning that her propulsion was diesel.

The scribe marks running down from *Aku Maru*'s waterline to the Hudson River grew fewer as she took on sufficient fuel oil to navigate halfway around the world; then she cast off and headed south in the channel, only to halt again and anchor off Hyde Park, New York, to let down hoses that would pump aboard the potable fresh water available there at no cost from underground springs feeding into the riverbed. More scribe marks had settled into the water when she finished, hauled anchor, and proceeded the short distance farther south to Rhinekill, where her captain steered her skillfully into the dock at the Riegar pharmaceutical plant.

The nighttime mooring was watched intently by an observer posted on the road above the railroad entrance to the plant. The dark was no inconvenience because the viewer watched through binoculars equipped with an ITT F4937/Generation III image-intensifier tube, a commercial variant of the military model. Through it, he took in every detail of the vessel and counted the few crew visible helping with the mooring lines. A sound below on the railroad tracks distracted him.

A diesel-switch engine pushing a two-manway tanker car huffed to a stop, and a brakeman carrying a lantern and a ball-peen hammer walked up alongside the car. He tested the wheels for structural integrity by tapping them with the hammer. The singing ring indicated there were no cracks in the steel. As if on impulse, the brakeman swung his ball-peen at the great tank itself. The deep, hollow, gonglike sound left no doubt that it was empty. As he put down the night-vision binoculars and brought up his left wrist, Brian Sullivan looked at his watch and noted the time.

Georg Kramer knocked at the door of his own office. It was well after hours, but Helmar Metz was using the place as living quarters. There was no answer. Kramer entered and went straight to his desk. He activated the LPC-10 secure telephone that was still housed in Metz's briefcase sitting on the desk, then, consulting a card taken from his wallet, he dialed Germany, where it was already business hours. Walter Hoess answered his LPC-10 himself. *"Ja."*

Kramer spoke English. Those sons of bitches Metz and Letzger had tried to keep it secret from him, but by God he hadn't been running this plant for seven years without being wired into what was going on. This was the news Hoess had been waiting for, and, as it should be, it would be he, Kramer, who conveyed it. "I wanted to tell you immediately, sir. It's been done. We have it."

"It has been tested?"

"Chemically, sir. The proof test will be run tonight. But it's just a matter of form. The manufacture has already begun. The ship is here to receive the order. We shall make the deadline you set."

The sense of relief in Hoess's voice puzzled Kramer, who was unaware of the hostage situation. "Well done, Kramer! Put Metz on. I want to be sure the shipment leaves without a hitch."

"I'm not sure just where he is at the moment, sir." Kramer couldn't keep the resentment out of his voice. "It's after hours here. I'll leave a message for him to contact you as soon as he returns. But you may rest assured I will see to it that—"

"Yes, yes. Of course, Kramer. You have my complete confidence. Nonetheless, I want to speak to Metz as soon as possible."

"Certainly, sir. I . . ." But Kramer was speaking into a dead telephone.

"See you a minute, Saul?"

"Sure, Mike." Saul Rosen got up from in front of the television set, grateful for the break in his seemingly endless staring at video-tape of the Riegar computer screens. The recordings were not ex-actly high-definition, and from screen to screen were uncoordinated. There was no one to tell Saul what the data meant. He was bored, and his eyes were tired.

Michael Stone led the way into his office, then said, "Saul, in a minute I'm going to call the rest of the guys in and ask them what stuff they brought from home—personal weapons and such. I don't want to blow your cover, so I'm asking you privately. What else did you bring up from Washington with that synchronizer thing?"

"Hell, Mike, I've got the Browning Hi-Power. You saw it almost as soon as I got here."

"I know. I don't mean that. What other electronic assets have you got?"

"Not much. I told you straight what my mission was. I've got some tapping gear, but as I said, Riegar's overseas commo's gonna be en-crypted. I don't have anything to deal with that, just phones like you've got here in your office. Other than that, I do have some ultrasensitive hard-wire listening gear, mikes, amplifier, and, of course, I have the layout of the plant and offices, floor by floor, to help select what to try to zero in on. I'm supposed, for example, to try for the computers in the research labs, but it's not easy. I pretty much take what I can get. I mean, I wasn't sent up here to go to war, you know. Shit, I've got only one spare mag for the Browning!"

"Okay, thanks, Saul. That's what I'll limit myself to when we have the meeting. The Browning. Do me a favor. Call the others in, okay?"

"You got it." Saul left to assemble the others, and Stone stared out of his office window into the darkness. They would be light on assets, his little band. No one would have anything like the material he had in his sea chest upstairs.

Saul returned with Pappy Saye, Arno Bitt, and Wings Harper in tow. They sat around the office, looking at Stone expectantly. "Okay," he asked, "who brought what to the party?"

Saul Rosen, who knew the question was coming, spoke first. "Nine mil. Browning Hi-Power. Two loaded magazines."

The other men looked at him respectfully. All were familiar with the high reputation of the last modification John Browning had made on his famed short-recoil-operated semiautomatic pistol. They knew the staggered box-column magazines held thirteen rounds each. With one in the chamber, that totaled twenty-seven rounds, usually more than ample for resolving serious differences of opinion with persons not prepared to be reasonable.

Pappy Saye spoke up next: "A three-fifty-seven Magnum. Smith & Wesson, large frame, five-inch barrel. Box of shells. An oldie but goodie; cylinder's got recessed chambers for the cartridge heads. Don't make 'em like that anymore."

"Sounds like a self-description, don't it?" asked Wings Harper. They all laughed. They laughed even harder as Pappy retorted, "Yeah, 'least I don't have to blacken my face to keep from shinin' like the full moon hanging' over a ridge line."

"All right, Wings," Stone asked, "what've *you* got to offer?"

Wings smiled. "Little souvenir from Nam. Chicom AK in good shape. Four loaded magazines. That's twelve hundred rounds, cousins."

"Which, if you treat it like a seven-point-six-two garden hose," said Pappy, "won't last long."

"That got that little pigsticker triangular folding bayonet?" asked Saul.

"Right. Type fifty-six-slash-one. Ain't so little. Near nine inches long."

"Man," said Pappy. "That's as long as my dick."

"Don't you fuckin' wish!" said Wings.

"Anything else? Handgun?" Stone asked.

"Sorry," said Wings.

"I've got one," Arno Bitt offered.

"What is it?" asked Stone.

"Ballester-Molina."

"What?"

"Forty-five ACP. It's an improvement on the Colt government model. Y'know how the forty-five auto has that U-shaped straight-back two-rail trigger? The Ballester has a trigger pivots on a pin. Better trigger pull. Browning himself went to it with the Hi-Power. Even better's the metal it's made of. Best steel in the world. Listen." Arno reached under his shirt and pulled what appeared to the others to be a big Colt .45 auto from his waist. He dropped the magazine and pulled the slide back to clear it, then let the slide slam forward and racked it back and forth again. The clash of metal on metal rang like a bell.

"Man, what makes it do that?" asked Pappy Saye.

"You like that, huh?" Arno answered. "Any of you guys ever heard of the *Graf Spee?"*

"I did," said Stone. "She was the state-of-the-art German pocket battleship slipped out into the Atlantic in thirty-nine, just before the start of World War Two. Roamed all over the ocean sinking British shipping left and right until damaged in a terrific battle with three Brit cruisers off South America. Took refuge in the neutral port of Montevideo, but the Uruguayan government forced her to return to sea unfit for battle, so her skipper scuttled her just off the River Plate. What's that got to do with anything?"

"Everything, man, everything," said Arno. "The Brits got the salvage rights to the *Graf Spee.* They were after the electronics. When they finished, two brothers, named Ballester, teamed up with a guy named Molina and bought the rights from the Brits. You wanna know why the metal of this piece sings? 'Cause it's made out of the armor plate of the *Graf Spee,* that's why. It's not only an improved design over the Colt, it's made of prewar German *Kruppstahl* armor. The best there ever was."

There was a moment of silence while the four other men, all experienced warriors of the highest skill, appreciated what Arno Bitt had just told them of his weapon. Then Stone asked, "How many magazines do you have for it?"

"Just the one that came with it. But it's interchangeable with the G.I. Colt. Should be able to pick up more anywhere."

"No time for that," said Stone, "but we're in luck. My field gun was a Colt government built up for me by Jeff Cooper out at Gunsite in Arizona. I've got half a dozen mags upstairs, along with a lot of G.I. hardball ammo for it; boxes of nine mil. and some other gear left over from my misspent youth with guys like you, keeping the country safe for Eddie Berg and assorted other assholes."

While Stone was speaking, Arno had handed the Ballester around to the others to let them inspect it. As Pappy Saye handed it back to him, Stone asked, "Anything else?"

"Just my personal chute."

Stone acknowledged that with a nod, and Pappy Saye asked, "What do we do now, boss?"

"We still don't know for sure that the Berg kid is in there. I want to wait for Sara's report. Meantime, Saul's gotten hold of the plant layout. I'm gonna do some contingency planning. Saul, how many more of those tapes do you have to go through yet?"

"I dunno. A bunch."

"All right, brief the others here on what to look for. Use both televisions. Start with the latest tapes first, the stuff you just brought in, then you go back out there and start monitoring directly for the very latest. Stay in touch by telephone. I'll let you know what Sara has to say soon as she checks in. Drop in after you get the guys set up before you take off."

"Aye, aye," said Saul as all but Michael Stone rose. "I'll bring the plans in first."

"Do that, please," said Stone.

It took Saul Rosen less than a quarter of an hour to set up and brief the others on the TEMPEST tapes and get back to Stone's office. "What's up?" he asked.

"I know you can't do any good on the encrypted phones, but I don't want to leave anything uncovered. Intel is everything when you're planning. How hard is it—how long would it take—to tap the regular phones in and out of that place?"

"Well, probably a number of trunk lines in a place of that size, but they probably all run together. I spotted the junction box while I was down there. Fortunately, it's a block away—won't have to worry about plant security. This time of night I'll probably be taken for a phone company guy doing emergency work if anyone notices. Gimme half an hour once I get there. Stuff's all in the van ready to go."

"Okay," said Stone, "go."

"What about your aunt?"

"What d'you mean?"

"All this coming and going. The televisions and everything. She wakes up and all this going on in the middle of the night . . ."

Stone smiled. "Don't worry about it. When I gave her her medication this evening, I slipped a little extra in. Banged her right out. The Second Coming wouldn't wake her up before tomorrow."

"Yeah," said Saul, putting the heels of both palms to his eyes and rubbing them hard to relieve their fatigue. "Let's not be in any hurry for that."

"Huh?"

"The first coming caused my people enough grief, thank you."

Stone grinned. "Get out of here."

Saul left, and as the door closed behind him, the smile slipped from Stone's face, to be replaced by a sober look. The closed door seemed a metaphor for what he had done. He could justify the killing of the German in the Riegar plant as self-defense. Sending Saul in to wiretap was something else, a clear violation of federal and state law. However good his reasons for doing so, he had closed the door on his attempt to live according to the culture of the legal profession. Even were he not discovered—as he sincerely hoped—he had taken a decision akin to Caesar's crossing of the Rubicon. Stephanie would never understand and, even if she did, could never approve. He had committed himself to resolving the Riegar problem within the rules and using the means of the Special Warfare culture. In his heart, the door was truly closed to the practice of law and, quite possibly—no, probably—any future with Stephanie Hannigan. It was the latter loss that distressed him most.

So be it, he thought. What was it Caesar had said? Half-aloud, he repeated it: "The die is cast."

"Naomi, I wish you wouldn't—"

Naomi Fine used her free hand, the one not holding the telephone, to wave off Stephanie Hannigan's objections, then placed it over the mouthpiece as she said, "You hardly know this man. And he's a foreigner. You can't be too careful." Then, uncovering the mouthpiece, she said, "Fine. F-I-N-E, as in dandy. Clerk's office, Mohawk County. I want to check on the credentials of a man who says he works for you. I—"

Naomi sighed as she was placed on hold yet again. "Really," said Stephanie, "this is completely unnecessary. I've seen Reuters quoted in New York papers about this Riegar business—"

"Fine," Naomi started again, speaking into the telephone, "Naomi Fine from the Mohawk County clerk's office. A Mr. Brian Sullivan has been representing himself as one of your reporters, and I wanted to check—Sullivan, Brian. Right . . . yes, I will . . ." Naomi put her hand over the mouthpiece again and said, "Checking the computer. But I don't know, none of the people I've talked to has an English accent."

"It's the New York office," Stephanie said. "I don't think you'd find the Paris Bureau of *The New York Times* full of Americans, certainly not the telephone operators and personnel department."

"Uh-huh," said Naomi. "What's a 'stringer'?" She listened some more, then thanked whoever it was at the other end of the line and hung up.

"Well?" said Stephanie.

"Yes and no," said Naomi. "He works for them, but not as a regular employee—doesn't get health benefits and a pension. He's kind of what they call a 'stringer,' except a stringer usually sends in stories from just one place on an as-needed basis, or sometimes they'll just send in something and hope they print it, like a free-lance. Brian Sullivan sends in stuff from all over. Been doing it for several years now, from whatever is the hot spot of the moment. One hand washes the other; he gets Reuters credentials, and, they say, they get good stories, often from where other reporters can't seem to get access. So I guess it's all right, but five-thirty in the morning for breakfast. . . . I dunno. You sure can pick 'em."

"What do you mean?"

"First this local lawyer who's going nowhere, now a roamer without a steady job who wants you to go on a date while they're milking the cows."

"Oh, Naomi, I don't feel that way about him at all. It's not like it was with Mike. It's just that he's . . . interesting."

"Remember the old Chinese curse, kid."

"What's that?"

"May you live in interesting times."

There was a brief knock on the door of Michael Stone's office, then Pappy Saye put his head in before Stone could react.

"Sara Rosen's back, Mike. Wants to see you right away."

"Send her in."

Sara started talking as soon as she crossed the threshold: "Four different people said Eddie told them he was going into Riegar—one of them said he was going in sometime today or tonight. I'm worried, Mike. You've got to go get him out right now!"

"Anybody see him actually go in there?"

"No, but it all adds up. He's *got* to be there. Where else *could* he be? You're wasting valuable time. God knows—"

"What is it with you, Sara?" Stone interrupted. "You don't listen to me when I'm acting as your lawyer, and now you won't listen when I'm trying to run an op for you. And I know a hell of a lot more about this business than I do about criminal law. Ease off. I've got a plan, but I don't have the equipment to implement it. I mean these guys I've talked into helping us out are used to high-speed, low-drag stuff you wouldn't believe if I could tell you about it, but we're going to have to make do with what we can go out and buy. And the stores don't open until tomorrow. And another thing, no way we're gonna launch until we *know* Eddie's in there. Assumptions don't cut it."

The telephone on Stone's desk rang before Sara had a chance to reply. He picked up the receiver and waved Sara into the big leather armchair. It was Saul Rosen. His speech was guarded. "That new thing you wanted me to do for you is up and running, but there's no traffic yet. I'll keep you posted." Nothing like placing a tap on someone else's line to remind one of the vulnerability of one's own telephone conversations, Stone thought, and he was careful himself with his reply. "Good. Thanks. What's new on television?"

"Just we've got a new network to add to the big three, with a big new star."

Stone didn't have a clue to what Saul was talking about. "You're gonna have to be less obscure, Saul."

"All right." Saul's tone was grudging. "When I started on the new job, there were three displays active monitoring primates. Your monkey-handler friends are working late. When I finished and went back to check, there was a fourth screen on. I'm sure it wasn't there before. I couldn't have missed it; that was all that was happening. All four of 'em are monitoring primates—they say so—only this last one's bigger than the others."

"Why do you say that?"

"Physical description numbers are bigger, at least in length."

"What are they?"

"Length's one hundred ninety point five centimeters. Weight, seventy-four point five kilos."

"What's that in English?"

"A kilo's about two point two pounds. A meter's not quite a yard. C'mon, Mike, you know this stuff, do your own math."

"Okay, Saul, thanks. Call if you get anything at all new."

"Will do."

Stone hung up the phone. Sara started to speak, but he held up his hand in a decidedly negative gesture as he wrote the figures Saul had just given him down on a desk pad in front of him. "Sorry," he said as he finished. "Needed to get these figures down before I forgot them."

"What figures?" Sara asked.

"Tell you in a minute when I get it figured out." Stone reached for his appointment book. In the back, among the figures for air mileage between major cities of the world, time zones, and other data, were metric to British weights and measures conversion tables. He did some simple arithmetic, then frowned.

"What *is* it?" Sara demanded.

Stone sighed. He knew what he had just calculated would set Sara off again. "The Riegar labs just started monitoring a new primate."

"So?"

"It's six feet three and weighs a hundred and sixty-four pounds."

Sara's shriek brought Pappy, Arno, and Wings into the room.

"They're torturing Eddie!" Sara sobbed.

"We don't know that," said Stone. "We don't know for sure that it's Eddie, although it sure sounds like it. What we *do* know is that whoever it is is alive. You can't monitor a corpse."

"So," Sara confronted him, "what are you doing to do about it?"

"I'd say we have enough information to justify going in there."

"When?"

"I told you . . . when I have assembled the gear to equip my men properly. We're not into suicide missions."

"Oh!" Sara stamped her foot and fled the room. Moments later, the front door slammed. Sara Rosen was gone. To his men's unspoken questions, Stone answered, "Back to work, guys. We go when we're condition one, not before." The three men nodded and left the room.

Some thirty minutes later, Stone's telephone rang again. Again, it was Saul Rosen. He was agitated, trying to control himself as he said, "Mike, we've got big trouble. Sara's in there."

"In where?"

"Riegar."

"Riegar! What . . . tell me what you know."

"I was monitoring the new asset. She *called* them. Said she knew they had Eddie and what they were doing to him."

"What'd they say?"

"Wrong number, no such person there."

"And?"

"Sara's no dummy. She knew they wouldn't admit to having him or talk about it over the phone. She just said, 'I'm coming to the front gate with the pictures. I'll swap you for him.'"

"Did they go for it?"

"She didn't give them a chance to say anything, just hung up. I didn't want to expose the van, so I went over on foot to intercept her—hell, it's only a couple of blocks. I figured Sara called from the apartment, and I'd have plenty of time. Wrong. She called from the pay phone at the parking lot across the street from the gate. I got there just in time to see them grab her and pull her inside, but I was still too far away to help. Ran back here and called you. We've gotta move, Mike, Sara's forced our hand."

"Agreed. Come back here right away." Stone hung up the phone, stared silently at the blueprints of the Riegar plant on his desk, and said, "Shit," then he rose to call the others in to his office.

Pappy Saye was in the kitchen. "I was just gonna make some coffee," he said.

"No coffee," said Stone, "get everybody and assemble in my office." From the way Stone said it, and from long experience, Pappy knew this was it. "Right," he said, and, shutting off the stove, went to get Bitt and Harper.

The three men stood around Stone's desk.

"Saul Rosen is on his way back and will be here in a few minutes," said Stone. "Here's the situation. Sara Rosen, the girl who was just here, has gotten herself captured. She's being held, most probably, with Eddie Berg. That would put them here"—Stone pointed to the Riegar plant blueprints—"in the primate lab on the twelfth floor. This'll be a hostage-rescue op. Unfortunately, we're short military assets, so we're going to have to use field expedients—meaning whatever we can scare up around here in a hurry. Anybody got any problems with that?"

The question was greeted with silence.

"Good," said Stone. Then he looked at Arno Bitt. "We're gonna give you a chance to show how good you are, Arno. Night jump—small, hazardous landing zone with low light conditions. You up for that?"

Arno didn't even wait for the details. "Anybody wanna place any bets?"

There were no takers. "So what do I do after I hit the LZ?" Arno asked. Before Stone could answer, Saul Rosen, who had his own key to the front door, knocked and entered. "Come over here, Saul," Stone said. As Saul took his place around the desk, Stone said, "Saul cross-trained with us as an Israeli Defense Force officer, then got some practical experience with me in Nam, during the course of which he saved my life."

"What'd ya do a dumb thing like that for?" Pappy Saye asked. "Yeah," said Arno, "I dunno if I want to go on an op with someone with such a record of bad judgment."

"Thanks, guys," said Stone, but he had accomplished his intention of establishing Saul's credentials with the others for a combat operation and gained their assent. The next was said for Arno's benefit. "How many hours you got now, Saul?"

"Little over thirteen hundred."

"Think you can handle a Cessna?"

"From a one fifty to a Citation Two."

"A one seventy-two should do it."

"We got a one seventy-two?" asked Arno.

"We will have," Stone answered, "as soon as you and Saul borrow one out at the Mohawk County airport. It's an uncontrolled field, and there are plenty of them there. Should take a screwdriver and a pair of needle-nose pliers, which you'll find in my uncle's toolbox in the shed out back. You're gonna jump out of it, Arno, okay?"

"Lemme take a hacksaw, too," said Arno. "It's all aluminum, should be easy to cut through the hinges and take the right door off. I won't have to fight the slipstream gettin' it open that way."

"All right," said Stone, "I'll buy the poor bastard owns it a new door later. Now, the thing we're short most of is time. Not just because the bad guys are probably working on Eddie and Sara as we speak but because of this." Stone waved the daily paper at them. "Daybreak is at zero four three four, and I don't want Arno hanging from a chute silhouetted against the sky. Make a great shot in a movie, but this ain't Hollywood, and if they spot him, it won't be a camera the hostiles'll be pointing up Arno's ass."

The men all smiled at the thought of Stone's last remark, relieving the tension. He nodded toward Pappy Saye. "Pappy, get a knife from the kitchen. Wings, go down the basement and get the finest file you can find in the toolbox, then you two guys head for the shed out back. Take some newspaper. Pappy, you scrape the rust off everything in sight. Wings, you'll find some aluminum screen frames sitting out there waiting for me to patch them. File the frames. Catch the rust and the filings on the newspaper and fold them up separately and carefully and bring them to me in the kitchen."

"Rust?" asked Pappy.

"You've been too many years outta BUD/S, Pappy. *Rust* is the common term for ferric oxide."

"And," said Wings Harper, "ferric oxide and powdered metallic aluminum in equal parts makes—"

"Thermit," Stone finished for him. "Arno's going to need it. Saul, empty the coffee can in the kitchen. It should hold about a quart of liquid. Keep the press-on lid. Take it to the basement. You'll find the heating-oil storage tank there. There's a spigot on the bottom to drain off water and crap. Let it run until pure oil's coming out, then fill the can. Arno, go out to the shed with Pappy and Wings. You'll find some bags of fertilizer there. It'll have some fancy name on it, but it's just ammonium nitrate. Take the—"

"Hey, my mind's not gone like Pappy's, Mike," said Arno, "I remember. I'll mix the fuel oil into the fertilizer just right. But what're we gonna use to set her off? She needs a hell of a jolt. You got detonators out in your shed, too?"

Stone laughed. "No, but Aunt May'd sure like to. We've got pocket gophers in the lawn. While you're at it, there's some 'Gopher Gas' out there. Looks like miniature dynamite sticks with fuses. Bring that in, too."

"That won't set off no ammonium–fuel oil mix, Mike, you know that."

"That's not what it's for, Arno. It's for you. I'll tell you what to do with it later. Trust me, I've got just the thing for the fertilizer. Okay, let's move. I want to be in and out of that place before the animal-welfare mob assembles for the day. When the word gets out that Eddie Berg's in there, they're liable to try to reenact the storming of the Bastille. It'll be wall-to-wall cops, which we don't need."

"We know what Sara looks like, Mike, but what about the Berg kid?"

Stone produced a newspaper photograph of Eddie Berg. "This is the best we've got. He's a tall, skinny guy. Six three. Sorry about the coffee, but we have to be ready for surgical shooting." Stone smiled at Arno Bitt. "We'll see how good you are with that 'Ballbreaker-Ballerina' of yours."

"That's *Ballester-Molina*," said Arno, "and you promised me ammunition."

"You'll get it."

"Good. The *Graf Spee*'s been waitin' a long time to get back into action."

16

"P'MISSION T'COME ABOARD." JOE CLIFT, LICENSED pilot of the Port of New York, said it with a casual salute as he stepped from the gangplank to the weather deck of *Ake Maru*. The deck officer, an English-speaking Dutchman who recognized Clift from their days together coming upriver from the Atlantic, returned the salute equally casually and made an entry in his log on the small podium next to him.

"You're back early, Joe," the deck officer observed with a smile. "No luck ashore?" He spoke with the British accent he had learned in school. Clift thought he sounded like Basil Rathbone.

"Nah," said the pilot, "small town, not much action. Be glad to get back to the city tomorrow. We all set to go with the tide in the morning?"

"Right. Cargo's all stowed. Just awaiting delivery of some scuba tanks for those rag heads holed up in the two inside compartments down on the number-two deck."

"Who are they? I never saw them."

"Nobody but the captain does. They say there're four of them. Levantines, supposed to be doing some kind of research, but I don't know how. They just sit in those compartments, use portable toilets and have their food brought to them. If they ever do come out, the crew's supposed to let them do what they want. Use a compass to tell them which way Mecca is so they can pray. All very odd."

"They never go ashore?"

"Can't, no papers. Don't seem to want to, anyway."

"Well," said the pilot, "I'm gonna hit the head and crash. Gotta be at work oh-early-thirty in the morning." As the pilot turned to leave, four men appeared at the top of the gangplank. Each pair was carrying an end of a large, single-tank scuba rig. One tank was marked with a painted number 1, the other with a 2. Without a greeting of any kind, the first man said, speaking English with a German accent, "You are to tell us where go these."

The Dutch officer spoke to them in German, which the American pilot didn't understand, then used the telephone on the bulkhead to call a crewman to escort the two Germans. When they were out of earshot, the officer said to the pilot, *"Now* we're ready. Just as soon as those two are ashore again, we just wait for the tide so you can 'do your stuff.' Is that how you say it?"

Clift smiled. "Yeah, that's how we say it. You learn fast."

"Let's hope the captain's guests don't stay late."

"The Germans? Here they come back now." The two men turned to watch as the men who had brought the scuba gear crossed to the gangplank. "Not them," said the deck officer, looking down at a note on the podium next to him that bore his log and instructions. "The captain's having guests for breakfast. You know how polite the Japanese are. He won't say anything even if they make us miss the tide. One of us is supposed to speak up and remind him."

"So, how long does it take to have breakfast?"

"One of them's a reporter. Maybe the other's a photographer, I don't know. The reporter's going to interview the researchers before breakfast. Early. They're supposed to know the schedule."

"Well," said Clift, "thanks for the tip. I'll say something myself if it starts getting late. If the captain gets pissed at me, it doesn't matter. I don't have to spend months at sea with him."

* * *

"I'm here voluntarily, you idiots! Let me go!" Sara Rosen, standing in front of the same elevator bank through which she had attempted to evade pursuit during her ill-fated first visit to the Riegar plant, twisted her slender body from side to side in a vain effort to free her upper arms from the tight grasp of the two hulking laboratory assistants flanking her. The men ignored her, and the nonplussed uniformed security guard, not knowing what else to do, returned to his post at the entrance to the plant.

The red-colored Down arrow blinked off. With a whisper, the number-two elevator door opened before them, and Georg Kramer, on his way home after a very long day that ran into the night, stepped out.

From Kramer's dress and bearing, Sara could tell he was someone of importance. "Hey, mister, tell these goons to leggo of me, will ya? I brought the pictures like I said I would. Are you the one I'm supposed to give them to?"

Kramer stared at Sara. He recognized her at once from her newspaper photograph. "I can't believe you've got the gall to break in here again! What are you talking about?" He gestured to the two men to release Sara. They did so grudgingly but stayed close against her, warily.

"I told you—or somebody—on the phone. I know you've got Eddie Berg in here, torturing him. Well, *he* doesn't have the pictures, I do. So here they are." Sara reached into the side pocket of the light cloth jacket she was wearing, withdrew the Polaroid photographs, and held them out, straight-armed, in front of her so they touched Kramer's suit coat. Instinctively, he backed away from them.

"Go on, take them! They're what you wanted, aren't they? So there's no point torturing poor Eddie to find out where they are. Let him go, and we're both outta here."

Kramer was indignant. "I really don't know what makes you think . . ." Kramer stopped in midsentence, understanding suddenly dawning on him. He stared from one laboratory assistant to the other. "Do either of you know what she's talking about?" Both men, although plainly uncomfortable, remained silent. "Well, *do you?*" Kramer was furious. The accumulated resentment of Metz, the fatigue, the stress all combined in his voice.

The man to Sara's left spoke. "The man, Berg, is with Herr Metz and Dr. Letzger in the primate laboratory. We are the girl to bring."

"And the photographs," the other man chimed in.

"Metz!" Kramer almost shouted. "Letzger! *I* am in charge here!" But he knew he wasn't. He knew that a telephone call to Hoess would only confirm his humiliation. Defeated, he spoke to Sara. "I know nothing of any of this. Remember that. I wash my hands of *all* of you! Of all of *this!*" So saying, he brushed aside Sara and headed for the door.

The elevator door had closed again. The man on Sara's left hit the button. The car was still there, so the door opened immediately. Sara waved the photographs at him. "What am I supposed to do with these?" she asked.

Without speaking, the lab man took the photographs from her hand, regrasped her upper arm, and, together with his partner, half-carried Sara into the elevator, pushed number twelve, and waited impassively for the car to arrive. When it did, the men, never speaking, led Sara down and around several halls until they came to a halt outside the door to Letzger's office. The man to Sara's left entered, looked around, and, seeing that it was empty, went to the telephone console on the secretary's desk and punched in an intercom number. Moments later, he spoke briefly in German, then hung up the phone. In English, he said to Sara, "We wait."

Moments later, Metz entered the room. He looked right at Sara but spoke in German to the man at her left. The man handed over the Polaroid photographs. Metz looked through them quickly but carefully, stuffed them into his pocket, then said to Sara, "Thank you for returning our property to us, Miss Rosen. Now, you wanted to see your friend, Mr. Berg, yes? Very well, you may join him. There you shall have your curiosity satisfied. Our chief of research, Dr. Letzger, will answer all your questions. But, just so you will not feel too harshly about us, I tell you that we are in agreement. We do not experiment on your animal friends. It is quite an expensive waste of time."

"But we *know* you have all kinds of animals here!" Sara protested. "We've traced the shipments."

"Of course we have them . . . rabbits, pigs, mice, rats, dogs, cats, and so on. Your government demands it. So, we buy them, bring them here, kill them—quite humanely, by the way—after the appropriate time has passed. The floor below is filled with them, waiting their turn. We send your government the necessary paperwork certifying that we have done all sorts of terrible things to them, and get the necessary licenses to sell our products in return. But I assure you we never do those things. Why waste the money?"

"But—" said Sara.

Kramer cut her off. "Dr. Letzger will be happy to answer all your questions. Now you must excuse me. Thanks to your Mr. Berg, this has been a very long day for us all. I have a ship leaving in the morning, and I must get some sleep. Good night." Metz spoke again in German to Sara's guards, instructing them to take her to Letzger, and ordering all his personnel not needed by Letzger to stay and sleep the rest of the night on the eighteenth floor. Everyone was on duty until the ship in the Riegar dock sailed in the morning. Then he picked up the telephone and called Letzger to tell him Sara was on her way to him.

Sara's shoulders ached as she was walked down the hall. Her big escort's grip on her upper arms and their half-lifting action put some of her body weight on joints never meant to bear it. With relief, she spotted a white-coated figure down the hall, patiently waiting outside a door. As she drew closer, her relief turned to unease. The man looked like someone she had seen in old newsreels about World War II, a larger-sized version of Dr. Joseph Goebbels, Nazi Germany's Minister of Propaganda. Sara felt a chill in her Jewish bones. Despite Metz's protests, something very wrong was going on here.

There was neither warmth nor humor in the smile with which Dr. Letzger greeted Sara; it was icy. "Ah, Miss Rosen, the clandestine photographer."

"Where's Eddie Berg?" Sara demanded.

"Patience, young lady, you are about to be reunited. I understand Herr Metz has informed you that we are innocent of any mistreatment of animals?"

"I didn't expect you to admit it."

"Then let me prove it to you." Letzger opened the door to his primate laboratory. Sara's two guards took a tighter grip on her and hustled her inside the brightly lit room. The layout was as she remembered it, only now much of the apparatus was in use. She took one look at the closest device and reacted with such horror, she broke the grip of one of her guards. Even as she screamed in revulsion, she struggled to get to the Ziegler chair in which a primate was immobilized, his head held bent backward and rigid in a stereo-taxic device. Wires ran off from sensors taped to his chest and back. An eye had been removed surgically and a steel bar of the head-clamping stereo-taxic device inserted into the oozing socket and tightened against the skull bone behind it. Two stainless-steel clamps held the mouth open a sufficient distance to permit entry of another steel rod that fixed the tongue to the bottom of the mouth, immobile. The primate's other eye was wide open, surgical retractors stretching its upper lid high up to the eyebrow, and the lower down and taut against the cheek. Held in a frame directly above the eye was a glass bottle containing a colored liquid. A metering device caused a drop of the liquid to fall onto the exposed eyeball at regular intervals, where it ran down the eye to pool temporarily in the corners, then trickled down the cheek.

The substance being dripped into the eye was clearly irritating, as the eyeball was inflamed, and, at the impact of each drop, the primate's body stiffened in pain and an agonized cry, unintelligible because of the tongue restraint, issued from the partially open mouth. With her momentarily free arm, Sara brought her hand to her mouth involuntarily as she vomited. The vivisected primate was Eddie Berg.

"Now, now, young lady," Letzger said with sarcastic calm. "You wanted to see what we do here, and when we show you, and you see that we are not touching a hair on the head of your precious animals, you react this way?"

"You filthy Nazi son of a bitch!" Sara shouted. "I brought you what you wanted! The big guy has them. Now let him go! He can't tell you anything; he doesn't *know* anything!"

"Ah," Letzger purred, "but he can tell us something very important." Letzger gestured toward Eddie Berg, tight in the grip of the restraining devices and crying out more loudly in between the drops searing his remaining eye. He was blind, but he wasn't deaf, and he could hear that somehow his tormentors had captured Sara. In mock astonishment, Letzger said, "You think we are doing this just to inflict discomfort on your interfering friend? Such a waste that would be! This is an experiment. It has shown that the substance being tested is not suitable for use by humans. Come now, surely you didn't think we would employ the notorious Draize test? The one that uses rabbits because they are cheap, have big eyes, and are easy to handle? We are not so stupid! The eye of a rabbit is an inappropriate and inaccurate model of human ocular damage. There are fundamental anatomic differences between the human and rabbit cornea, eyelid, and tearing mechanism. No clinician, toxicologist, or ophthalmologist uses Draize data to treat humans. Those so-called acute-toxicity tests used in industry are completely useless. You know it and we know it. Think what you will of us, Miss Rosen, but do not take us for fools! Riegar did not get to be the largest and most profitable pharmaceutical company in the world by the stupidity of trying to apply animal test results to humans. The secret of our success is, as you see, that we use *humans.*"

Letzger said something in German, and Sara's guards relaxed their grip upon her. Immediately, she started toward Eddie Berg. "Ah, ah, ah," Letzger said, "the data we wanted are in our computers. We shall be releasing your young man from the restraints and terminating the acute-toxicity test. I assure you that the next test he and the others here"—Letzger swept his arm to include the room—"will be subjected to will be completely painless." Letzger reached for a paper towel. "Here, my dear, wipe your chin and hands and behave yourself." In German, he ordered one of his assistants to clean up Sara's vomit from the floor. The man took a handful of paper towels and squatted to attempt to clean up the mess. "No, no, you idiot," Letzger said in German, "use a mop with disinfectant. This is a scientific laboratory, not a saloon!"

Sara watched intently as the bottle above Eddie's eye was removed and the retractors holding back the lids taken out. Then the eye was sprayed with an aerosol can. "What are you doing to him?" Sara shouted.

"*Please* stop these silly outbursts!" Letzger replied. "The spray is lidocaine hydrochloride, a topical anesthetic. It will stop the pain. The fluid dripped into his eye was irritating but not destructive. He will be able to see perfectly well from that eye shortly." Then to the assistants, he said, "Continue." The rod was removed from Eddie's eye socket, and it was packed with antiseptic-treated gauze to which lidocaine had been added. Finally, Letzger said, "Mr. Berg, we are about to remove the tongue restraint and take you from immobilization. But, if you do not behave, you shall be restrained again, do you understand?"

"Uuuwaah" was all Eddie could manage. When the tongue restraint was removed, "Uuuwaah" proved not to be "Yes." "You dirty motherfuckers! You'll pay for this! You cocksuckers! . . ."

Eddie turned his head toward the sound of Sara's voice. "Whose fucking side are you on, Sara? I'm supposed to make nice to the bastards who cut out my eye because the next experiment's gonna be painless? What're you, nuts!"

"You were warned, Mr. Berg," said Letzger. Then, in German, he ordered, "Put him in the chamber now and close the door. He can rant all he wants, and we won't have to listen to it."

Struggling, Eddie Berg, his light weight no match for his burly captors, was carried into the Lexan enclosure and fastened into a Ziegler chair, then the door was closed, effectively muffling his shouted invective. Sara ran to the clear plastic wall of the chamber and, stretching her arms out to embrace it and pressing her body against it, shouted, "I love you!" There was no way she could tell whether Eddie could hear her, but she felt better for having tried. She turned away from the plastic wall and faced Letzger. Contempt and sarcasm coated her voice with acid as she said, "Now what, Dr. Mengele?"

"Mengele was a fool who wasted his talents—such as they were— pursuing medical trivia for ideological reasons," Letzger replied affably, "but at least he had the sense to perform his experiments on human beings instead of other animals. Come, let me show you some of our other experiments. We must complete them before the last test of the night, otherwise all the time and expense we have invested in them will be wasted."

"And wouldn't *that* be a pity," said Sara.

The sally was wasted on Letzger. With pride, he displayed a young Mexican male immobilized in a Ziegler chair. His throat was bandaged and his head held rigid in the same kind of device used on Eddie Berg. Both eyes had been enucleated and steel rods pressed deep into the tender sockets. Letzger dropped into a stilted, lecture-like presentation as he said, "Notice the top of the skull. A Collison cannula has been implanted in the brain, permanently attached to the bone of the skull with acrylic cement and four stainless-steel screws. Through it, we can pass anything directly to the living, conscious brain. In this instance, the electrode has been moved several times so as to gather data from different parts of the brain. We are testing a new drug for the suppression of epileptic seizure. The other wire conveys a current to produce seizure on demand, thus—" Letzger pressed a button and, to Sara's cry of *"Stop it!"* the Mexican went into violent seizure, thick drool coming from his mouth. The convulsion stopped immediately when Letzger lifted his finger from the button.

Nausea gripped Sara again, but she had nothing left in her to vomit. She covered her distress by asking, "Why doesn't he scream?"

"Oh," said Letzger apologetically, "of course, I forgot to tell you. You will notice the bandage at the primate's throat. The vocal cords have been removed. We always do that when a tongue restraint is contraindicated and there is—unlike the case of your Mr. Berg— sufficient time."

A buzzer went off and a red light flashed to the left. Both Letzger and Sara turned toward the sound. The flashing light was next to a large revolving drum that was slowly coming to a halt.

"Ah," said Letzger, "I see that another experiment is finished. The light and sound are triggered by the computer monitoring the vital signs. The primate has expired."

"The *primate?*"

"Yes, of course. We humans are no less primates than any other of the apes, monkeys, marmosets, and lemurs."

Two attendants started to retrieve the body of another Mexican from the now-still Noble-Collip drum. Sara could see inside the drum through the open door. The inner circumference was covered with hard rubber-clad bumps and projections. "God!" she screamed as she saw the body, then quickly averted her eyes. It didn't help. She couldn't rid herself of the horror of the image seared into her brain. The corpse was virtually pulped; the bones, even the teeth, broken. The purple-blue bruises on the outside of the body were as nothing to the damage on the inside they concealed from view: ruptured liver, spleen, kidneys, and other vital organs.

Wires from different parts of the body led to a small box implanted in its back. Letzger pointed to it. "My own invention. That is a low-powered transmitter for the collection of data. I didn't invent the transmitter, of course, but the armoring is mine. As you can see, it survived intact after nearly a week inside the drum. Something, unfortunately, we cannot say for our subject. The data will tell us how well the antistress drugs we gave him worked. Come, I'll show you how we dispose of our waste."

"Waste? You call a human being you've just tortured to death for a week waste?" Sara broke down, sobbing uncontrollably as she watched the body of the young Mexican being taken to a door. After a few moments, Sara got a grip on herself. She didn't expect to get out of the Riegar plant alive, but if by some miracle—an earthquake, say—she did, she wanted to be able to give as accurate an account of what was going on there as possible. She owed that much to Eddie and the unknown number of others who had suffered and died in these precincts.

Letzger pushed a metal plate at the side of the doorway and a hydraulic mechanism opened the door for the attendants carrying the body. As Letzger turned, his white coat swung open just enough for Sara to see that he was carrying a pistol in a black holster on his belt. She looked carefully at the attendants and detected the telltale bulge of what she assumed were similar weapons under their white jackets.

In the center of the adjacent room was a large vat, twelve feet in diameter. Five feet above it, a glass-lined, inverted funnel-shaped hood projected from the ceiling and ducted away the furiously hot and corrosive gases given off by the roiling, fuming sulfuric acid. Opposite the door, a metal slab, also glass-coated, projected out from the side of the vat. On the end nearest the door, it was supported by a gurneylike set of folding legs and wheels. The other end was attached to the side of the vat by a piano-type hinge. The attendants placed the body on the slab and looked toward Dr. Letzger.

Letzger waited until Sara had approached close enough to see well, then nodded. At his signal, the hefty attendants gripped the slab at its far end and lifted it easily into the air. The body slid down quickly into the vat. The acid reacted violently to the body's water content, boiling up with a great eruption of fumes. Letzger and his henchmen turned away from the vat to protect themselves from the reaction as the flesh and bone of the corpse disappeared into the seething caldron.

"Jesus!" Sara said, moving back in alarm. "What is that stuff?"

"Oleum," Letzger said. "It is delivered here by railroad tank car, used first in the production of pharmaceuticals, then as you have just seen, for waste disposal. Before you say it," Letzger said apologetically, indicating the duct hood, "yes, we are aware of the air-pollution problem, and we are working on it. I would not want you to think we do not recognize our responsibility to the environment."

Sara looked at Letzger intently, searching for sarcasm or mockery. There was none. Letzger was sincere in seeking to avoid her censure for environmental damage. She shook her head in astonishment.

"You do not believe me?" Letzger asked.

"Oh," said Sara, "I believe you all right. It's just that no one would ever believe *me* if I repeated this conversation."

"You disapprove of us? Even now that you know we do not harm animals? That we employ only humans your own government is at pains to keep out of your country?"

They walked back into the laboratory. Sara said, "I can't believe I'm having this conversation." Again she tried to get through to Letzger with sarcasm. "Why don't you just use the homeless?"

It didn't work. Letzger's reply was matter of fact. "Unsuitable specimens. Eighty percent of the homeless in this country are either severe alcohol or drug abusers. A substantial number of the rest are mentally ill."

"So what do *you* think we should do with them, put them in concentration camps?"

Again the sarcasm was wasted. "There was a time when your government took care of them in institutions, where they belonged. You threw them out in the street to save money and then complain of their presence. Now, look here. Through this plastic window we installed in the abdominal cavity and stomach, you can see at work our new ulcer-suppressant drug."

Sara felt as if she had been captured by the Mad Hatter. It was more comfortable than her previous fantasy, inspired by the acid vat, of being held captive by cannibals. She didn't know how much longer the other experiments in the primate laboratory would take to be completed, and she was ambivalent about it. On the one hand, she wished the sufferings of the tormented be ended as soon as possible. On the other hand, she dreaded the "final experiment" of the evening; the one supposed to be painless for Eddie Berg. It sounded too much to Sara like the "final solution." She shuddered and waited. Even if her captors relaxed their guard for a moment, and she could make a break for it, she wouldn't. Not and leave Eddie Berg behind to meet his fate alone. "Oh, God," she prayed. "Help me, please!"

"The ship sails at seven hours your time, correct?" Hoess's voice sounded tense over the digitized scrambler.

"It is already loaded with what was demanded," said Metz. "It could leave now except that the keel is in the mud because of the load of pharmaceuticals and fuel aboard. It must wait for the tide at seven."

"Good. I am promised my son at exactly that time—one here. As soon as the ship is under way, he will be delivered to me personally."

"Where?"

"They won't say. I am to follow instructions and be led to him."

"I don't like it. They could abduct *you.*"

"You have nothing to say in the matter. I will not hazard the life of my son."

"At least let my men accompany you at a discreet distance. It is for your own protection."

"No. They will have what they want. I could have given them anything, *would* have given them anything, in exchange for my son. There would be no point to taking me. No. *Just you see that that ship sails on time!*"

"The ship will sail exactly as scheduled, sir. You have my word on it. But, when you go for your son, please be care—" Metz stopped speaking when he realized Hoess had hung up. He sighed and walked over to a shipping crate only the day before delivered from Germany. The customs declaration attached to it read "Marine Equipment." He opened it and checked his *Kampfschwimmer* gear. He might never have to use it again, but Helmar Metz felt more comfortable having it close at hand.

The dank, man-made mists that swirled about the Riegar plant shrouded it in an amber glow from the sodium vapor lamps that sought to push back the early-morning dark. The vents that controlled the pressure of the superheated steam from the stationary power plant hissed loudly directly above Michael Stone as he vaulted the fence, then lay motionless in its shadow, watching carefully for any sign of danger. His eyes, long since adapted to the gloom, detected none. Still he waited, using all the time he had, to be certain. Then, with a passable imitation of the call of a mourning dove, he signaled Pappy Saye to join him. Another waiting and watching period, then, finally, Wings Harper joined them. All three then waited and watched, wearing dark jeans, dark sweatshirts, black boots, and bandannas—either covering the scalp completely as Pappy Saye's did, or sweatband fashion, over faces, with the exception of Pappy's, darkened with green camouflage paint. Pappy Saye had his face streaked with it to break up its outlines.

Satisfied that they had not been detected entering the Riegar grounds, Stone started crawling slowly on his belly toward a large vertical steam pipe leading up to the roof, which, at this part of the plant, was twelve storys above the ground and lost in the glowing mist. The men crawled slowly, hugging the ground until they lay in the lee of the building. Stone silently cursed the rumbling mechanical God knew what that caused him to have to strain to hear what he was listening for. Not hearing it, he eased out the hatchet he had taken from among his uncle's tools and duct-taped to him, then he rolled over on his back and stared up at the great pipe, studying it.

The pipe was in eight-foot sections, except for those that branched into the building at irregular intervals. At either end of the sections was a wide flange, drilled for the bolts that around the circumferences of the joined flanges held the pipe sections together against the great pressure of the steam that flowed inside them. Only the smallest part of each flange was visible, because the pipe itself was covered by a heavy layer of insulation for thermal efficiency. Stone wondered how long ago the insulation had been applied and whether it was asbestos. He hoped not, and wished he had been able to get some painter's breathing masks.

Stone's thoughts were interrupted by the sound he had been waiting to hear. Just above the growling of the plant, he detected the unmistakable beat of a four-cylinder Lycoming 0-320 aircraft engine, the chunkety heartbeat of a later model of the classic Cessna 172 high-wing monoplane. Straining through the interference of the noises of the plant, he grimaced as he tried to distinguish the signal he was waiting for from a normal power adjustment. Then it came, a clear "blipping" of the throttle. It was the signal from Saul Rosen at the controls that Arno Bitt had jumped and was away. As if in confirmation, the Cessna's engine sound receded as Saul headed back to the airport and Stone's Mustang to speed to the plant to join the attempt to rescue his sister; the argument against which Stone had known he was going to lose before he started it, then accepted defeat gracefully and offered his fast roadster in exchange for the van so Saul could join them sooner.

Michael Stone eased to his feet and, grasping around the pipe with his left arm, dug his left heel into the insulation around the first flange, then thrust his body upward. As far as he could go that way, Stone used the hatchet to chop a gap in the insulation, then slid the blade back into his belt, grasped the pipe in two arms, raised his right leg and, with his body weight, gingerly tested the strength of the insulation. It held. He hoped it would do so long enough for Saul to be able to use it when he got there. Stone noted the time and thrust himself upward. The pipe, despite the insulation, was quite warm. Sweat formed on Stone's face. His bandanna kept it out of his eyes. He was in his element now. Careful, alert, and determined, Stone was the complete professional SPECWAR operative again. Hanging on to that hot pipe, now lost above the ground in the swirl of mist in the middle of the night, Michael Stone was home. What was even better, he knew in his heart that so were the men who followed him.

ARNO BITT DESCENDED STEADILY THROUGH THE cool dark air at 3,500 feet, body comfortable in the familiar harness below his trademark rectangular black parachute. He steered it easily, like a glider, toward the mottled amber glow below. He knew his target was to the left of the steamy mists that boiled from the production side of the plant and six storys higher. Deftly, he countered the slight breeze from the river that tried to push him to the right, toward the mists, as he watched sharply for his tower-rooftop target. As he glided silently lower, he could make out a dark square, vaguely outlined by the glowing, moving mists on one side and upward-beaming security lights that washed the lower reaches of the office tower on the other. He took one hand off the risers to cinch the sling of Wings Harper's AK-47 to hold the weapon tighter across his chest. He wanted his landing to be as quiet as possible.

The tower rooftop, its square expanse becoming visible enough for him to make out the small shedlike structure directly over the elevator shaft that housed the motors, had a vent to bleed off air pressure from the rising cars, and an emergency escape door. Arno could see now that the shaft house was near the center of the roof, effectively cutting down his landing area to only that space left between the tower's roof edge and any of the shed's four sides. He steered more to his left, against the current of air that kept pushing him toward the mists. Those mists hid the huge tanks, retorts, and piping of the manufacturing process, a twisted maze that extended upward from the twelfth-floor rooftop as high as four more storys. Obscured by the ever-shifting mists, they constituted a potential death trap. As his landing became imminent, Arno steered a spiral path, timing his glide so that he could land into the wind from the river, behind the elevator service shed. He flared his chute and practically walked onto the eighteen-story-high roof of the Riegar tower, quickly spilled the air from the canopy, lest a sudden gust pull him off the edge. Then Arno carefully stowed his parachute for, he sincerely hoped, later retrieval. That done, he examined the shed itself. It was made of steel, painted against the weather. The roof was flat, the entire shed looking like a steel box. On the east-side wall was a vent to relieve the compression of air from the rising cars. Arno inspected it. As expected, Riegar security had welded iron bars across the inside of the vent flange. No entry that way.

From a pocket, Arno took a small two-AA-battery krypton-bulb flashlight. He thrust it into the vent, then turned it on and inspected the interior. The elevator motors were clearly visible, as was a control panel with three large buttons to operate the elevator nearest him from inside the shed in order to assist in maintenance. He played the light to his right. Clearly visible was the door, located on the north side of the shed, on the same side as the front door to the plant so far below. A standard safety push bar operated the latch from the inside. Arno wondered why maintenance men would have a key to get in. Someone caught in a stuck car could go through the trapdoor to the roof of the car, but how then get up to the shed? They certainly couldn't climb up the greased cables. He turned off the light before withdrawing it from the vent, pocketed it, then walked around to the door. It was secured by a Medeco-cylinder lock. The small gap between the steel door and frame, through which one might attack the sliding latch, was protected by a steel plate welded so as to project from the face of the door across the opening.

Out came the little flashlight again. Before switching it on, Arno turned the adjustable lens to pinpoint, then cupping the light to shield it further, he ran it carefully around the crack between the door and the frame. There were no contacts that, if broken when the door was opened, would set off an alarm. Satisfied, he lifted the tiny beam to the joint where the frame had been welded to the roof. The shed was constructed of quarter-inch steel plate. Other than his relief at not having to defeat an alarm, the situation was what Arno had expected from a study of the building drawings Stone had provided.

Arno unslung the Chinese Communist version of the AK-47 and placed it on the roof of the shed, then he did the same with his hands and pressed himself easily up onto it. He crawled to the front of the roof, looked over the edge at the door to gauge it, then reached into his pocket to withdraw a plastic kitchen-wrap package secured with cellophane tape. In the beginning glow of dawn, it looked like a typical package of cocaine confiscated by police. His straight razor-sharp Navy Mark 3 Mod O knife opened the package in one deft pass. From it, he lifted out a lump of dough he had prepared himself in Stone's kitchen from Aunt May's flour and tap water. He kneaded it between his fingers—still moist and pliable, thanks to the plastic wrap.

Each moment increased the daylight, a curse because with it his concealment was vanishing, a blessing because his ability to see improved. Arno made a ring of dough roughly six inches in diameter and placed it on the steel roof in the center, several inches back from the edge of the side where the door was located. He pressed it into the steel, making the inside edge of the dough ring as vertical as possible. Finished, he sat back for a moment and carefully surveyed his work. Content with it, he glanced at his watch and went back into his pocket with renewed urgency.

This time, Arno took out a package made of folded newspaper, taped shut at its seams. He sliced off the point of one corner, and from that crude spout poured the carefully blended fifty-fifty mixture of powdered rust and powder-fine aluminum filings inside the dough-outlined circle. When he finished, he smoothed the fine dust roughly level, then quickly held the newspaper over it as a gust of wind off the river threatened to blow it out of the ring.

From a pocket on the opposite side of his jeans, Arno pulled out a "Gopher Gas" cylinder. In its red-paper covering with a fuse protruding from one end, it looked to him like either the largest firecracker in the world or the smallest stick of dynamite. From his watch pocket, he fished out a battered Zippo lighter that was a World War II souvenir of the late Harry Stone. It had been recharged hours before with charcoal lighter fluid in lieu of the real thing, but he had found it to work reliably with the substitute fuel.

With the Zippo, Arno lit the fuse of the "Gopher Gas" cylinder, waited until it burned down almost to the cylinder, and then plunged the burning end deep into the powder inside the circle of dough. Immediately, he turned his face away to protect himself, first from the intense flaring heat of the ignited Thermit, and second from the deadly fumes of the hydrogen-cyanide gas generated by the still-burning cylinder. The incandescent Thermit, used commercially to weld steel, quickly burned a six-inch hole through the quarter-inch-thick steel plate of the shed roof as molten white-hot steel dripped into the interior and fell away into the elevator shaft. Arno hoped he hadn't started a fire below.

Slowly, the glowing white of the edge of the hole turned to red, but Arno didn't have time to wait until the edge cooled sufficiently on its own to permit him to reach through it safely. A field expedient was called for. Arno stood, opened his fly, and urinated, trying his best to keep the stream on the hot edges by aiming at the residue of the incinerated dough. A fair amount of urine went into the hole. Maybe, Arno thought, it would put out any fire he might have started in the elevator shaft. He watched carefully as the effect of the urine on the steel changed from flash steam to, finally, rapid drying. The stream terminated before Arno had cooled the metal as much as he wished. "Damn," he muttered to himself, "out of ammo." He knelt and checked the rim of the hole with a quick stab of his finger. Safe.

Arno lay down on the rooftop and reached down through the hole he had just made in it toward the emergency release bar on the inside of the door. No good, he couldn't reach it. He withdrew his arm, picked up the AK-47 by its pistol grip, removed the long, curved magazine, and carefully inserted the muzzle into the hole. When he got down to the pistol grip, he had to bend his wrist and rotate the weapon on its longitudinal axis forty-five degrees to get the pistol grip through the hole. Once that was accomplished, he was able to extend his arm enough to get the buttstock through, then his arm up to its shoulder, still holding on to the weapon by its pistol grip. He probed around until he caught the crossbar of the door release between the barrel and the high front sight, shoved it down, and released the door. Then he quickly shoved the door with the muzzle to swing it out as far as he could, threw his leg over the edge of the roof, and caught the door before its spring-loaded hinges could close it again. "Shit!" Arno said aloud as he awkwardly reversed the process to wriggle the AK-47 out of the hole while holding the door open with his foot. A few more colorful expletives and he succeeded.

With one more kick to swing the door wide open enough to give him time to dismount the roof, Arno was ready to enter the shed. He retrieved the AK-47, reinserted the magazine, and moved inside.

When Bitt closed the steel door of the elevator-maintenance shed behind him, he found that the early-dawn light that filtered through the air vent was insufficient, so he broke out the miniflashlight again and inspected the area. The floor beneath him consisted of a metal grating. There was a low safety railing between the edge of the grating and the abyss of the eighteen-story elevator shaft. The powerful motors were directly in front of him, poised over the centers of the two steel-rail frameworks in which the two cars slid vertically on greased rails. Neither car was to be seen. The motors drove the giant pulley wheels from which the cables were suspended. Each motor housing had a control panel with three buttons arranged vertically marked Up, Down, and Stop. The Stop button was in the middle.

As he shone the flashlight around, Arno stopped the beam at the air vent's side wall. There the mystery of why there was an emergency-exit release bar on the inside of the door was solved. He hadn't been able to see it because, looking in from the vent outside, it hadn't been visible. Outside the framework that held the cars was a simple steel-rung ladder set a good six inches into the masonry work of the shaft. It gave about as much protection against a passing car—should a stalled car from which one had escaped through the trapdoor start up again— as the space set into the tunnel walls of the subways in New York. The one on the opposite side had been obscured by the motors when he first looked in, and neither had been shown on the plans. Arno had expected to have to clamber down the framework to a horizontal air shaft, escaping death from a moving car by jumping onto the top of it in the unlikely event of someone using it in an office building at 0445 hours.

Arno slung the AK–47 and used the ladder to start his climb downward. There was, he assured himself, sufficient room for an elevator car to pass him, but he hoped no fat man ever had to use the ladder to escape. He'd lose his ass—literally.

As he descended floor by floor, Arno noted that the floor numbers were painted in large numerals on the outer elevator doors, the ones that protected the opening when a car wasn't there and opened at the same time as the inner doors—the ones for the cars themselves. One story down, he paused to examine one with his flashlight. Seeing nothing of an opening mechanism at door level, he moved down a few feet on the ladder and looked upward from beneath. At the bottom of the outer doors was a striker plate. Obviously, when a car approached from above or below, a projecting striker hit the double-acting toggle switch and opened the outer door at the same time as the inner door. He resisted the temptation to check what he had deduced by operating one of the doors and kept descending.

On his arrival at the twelfth floor, Arno moved down a few feet and over onto the cage-rail framework and unslung the AK–47. With its muzzle extended out as far as he could reach with it, he tripped the switch and the door to the eleventh floor opened. Arno rolled up and out onto the floor and lay very still, looking. No one. At the end of the hall, he spotted what he was looking for, the door to the roof of the manufacturing wing. If all had gone well, Mike Stone, Wings Harper, and Pappy Saye were waiting in concealment on the other side of it. At a crouch, Arno moved swiftly to the door and stood still. Nothing. As he expected, there was another emergency crossbar device that opened the door. As he also expected, a glance upward disclosed the two rectangular blocks of an electrical alarm. One block was attached to the door frame and the other to the top of the door. Break the contact and all hell would break loose.

Arno lifted the duct tape that sealed his breast pocket and removed the twenty-five-foot metal measuring tape he'd taken from Harry Stone's old toolbox. He pulled out a foot of the steel tape. Because it had been formed at manufacture with a slight bend, it stood out straight. Arno held it above him, ready, and depressed the release bar slowly until the latch was freed, then he painstakingly started to push the door outward. As the contact plates moved, but before they had moved far enough for the circuit to be broken, Arno touched the top side of the steel tape to the underside of the upper plate and the bottom side of the tape to the bottom plate. He then lowered his hand slightly to put tension on the tape and slowly, s-l-o-w-l-y, grimacing in concentration, he pressed the door open wider, all the while holding contact between the two electrical plates by means of the tape as it slowly played out from its spring-loaded reel, being pulled by the little tab at its end, which was hooked over the edge of the door top.

Eighteen inches was about as far as Arno could continue the process without risking almost certain loss of contact. He was at that point now, but he dared not speak to hail Mike Stone and the others. Fortunately, he didn't have to. They were waiting in the shadow and, alerted by the crack of light when the door first opened, had waited only until Arno's face had come into view and they could identify him. Slowly, and with great care, each of the three men took his turn ducking under Arno's extended arms and sliding into the empty but brightly lighted hallway of the twelfth floor of the Riegar tower, Pappy and Wings each carrying twenty-five-pound plastic trash bags full of the ammonium-nitrate fuel-oil mixture they had lugged up the steam pipe behind Michael Stone.

As Pappy Saye entered, Arno said, "Where's Saul?"

As if in answer, out of the stillness of the dawn could be heard the screech of tires and the unmistakable "baaruuuup" of the Mustang being double-clutch downshifted twelve stories below.

"That son of a bitch better be able to shinny up that pipe like a fuckin' chimpanzee, goddamn it!" Arno said, his arms still straining upward. "What am I, the Statute of Liberty?"

He was talking to himself, though; the other three had fanned out to clear the area. They returned just as Saul Rosen eased himself under Arno's now-aching arms.

"Here," said Stone, concerned that by now fatigue might have led to a loss of control by Arno in the delicate task of bringing the door back in without breaking the contact, "let me give you a hand with that." He took the outside end, and together the two men got the door safely closed without setting off the alarm. Then Stone took out a section of the plant plans from under his sweatshirt. It had already been folded in such a way as to display the twelfth-floor floor plan.

"Here we are, and here's the primate lab," he said as he pointed to a door down the hall. "But we don't dare make a move until we know for sure that they're there. Saul, got your gear ready?"

"Right here," Saul answered, donning a lightweight set of earphones attached to what looked like, without close inspection, a miniature cassette player popular with joggers. As Saul plugged in what resembled a stethoscope, Stone went into his pocket and came out with a signaling mirror—a hand mirror with a tiny hole in its center through which one could look to direct flashes of sun at a target. He pointed to the area of the door into the primate lab. About seven feet up on the opposite wall was a small video camera aimed at the door area. "I don't know the viewing area of that camera," he said. "One thing's sure: The guys downstairs monitoring the video-cams start seeing moving figures, we've had it on surprise. Gimme a hand."

With a small amount of stiff wire and duct tape, Stone attached the signaling mirror to the camera housing, holding it out in front of the lens at an angle so that it reflected back blank wall.

"What happens when those guys don't see no doors no more?" asked Pappy.

"Sara said there're banks of screens down there, all either doors or halls with blank walls. I'm countin' on the guy monitoring, assuming he's not asleep—par for the course for a rent-a-cop—not to notice one less door or one more wall. At any rate, the shit'll hit the fan anyway as soon as we bust 'em out. And I'm not looking for that to take all day. Let's go."

Saul Rosen started a systematic listening to the stethoscope—highly amplified—as he applied it to the wall. Abruptly he said, "That's Sara!"

"You're certain?" asked Stone.

"She's my sister, for Christ's sake!"

"What about Eddie Berg?"

Saul listened intently, then became agitated. "No. But some guy with a German accent's talking to Sara about some experiment and she can join Berg in a few minutes. They . . . wait a minute." Saul moved the stethoscope. "He's giving orders in German . . . something about 'put them all inside.' From the number answering up, I'd say we got something like six bad guys at least in there." His face turned white.

"What is it?"

"Somebody screamed. God!"

"Sara?"

"No," Saul said, his voice shaky, "a man."

Stone looked at Saul sharply. Saul caught the look and said, "I'll be okay. Only hurry, Mike. My *sister*'s in there!"

Stone looked down at the plans again. "Okay," he said, speaking rapidly, "listen up. Wings, Pappy, leave the fertilizer here; go with Arno. On the floor below's where they keep the animals. Arno'll show you how to get down there. Take some trash bags with you. Use your knives. Be quick and quiet. You know what I want in those bags. Get it back here on the double. Fuck it. Use the elevator. Time is everything. Saul and I'll set up the breach."

"On the way," said Pappy. The others turned to follow him to the elevator bank.

"Okay," Stone said to Saul, "this is an interior, non-load-bearing wall—"

"Mike!" Saul said, his voice forced, urgent. "Skip the fucking engineering lecture, for Christ's sake. Just tell me what to do! They could be doing something to Sara *right now!*"

Stone reached out and grabbed Saul's shirt just below the neck and jerked him so close their faces were inches apart. He spat out his words, hard, fast, and cold. "Listen, goddamn it. You're losing it. I don't give a fuck who's in there or what's going on. I'm telling you what I'd tell any SEAL new to the teams. I don't want to detect emotion one in you. A SEAL team is a machine and we've got no use for weak parts. Now click on or so help me, the next time you break, I'll grease you myself and send your body home to your mother in a rubber bag with a note telling her how you died a hero. Got that?"

Ashen and chastened, Saul said only, "Yes."

Stone let go of Saul and picked up his prior conversation as if nothing had happened. "Okay, we've got drywall over aluminum studs. Insulated. Not for heat and cold but for sound. We'll have to get rid of that, but we've got to be quiet. First hint of trouble, those guys in there'll whack out Sara, Eddie, and any other witnesses. Us, too, and claim the lot of us were burglars. Which, of course, we are. Keep listening with that thing. I need to know if anything alerts them, or if they call in the cavalry."

Stone whipped the slender double-edged Gerber from its scabbard. He put the blade point waist-high against the drywall and pushed it until he felt the resistance stop. Quickly, he slid the blade in until the scalloped teeth could come to bear, then sawed a cut toward his right, trying to find the right balance between speed and quiet. In a few inches, he heard the distinctive sound of the blade teeth hitting aluminum. The Gerber would go through the studding material, but he couldn't risk the sound. Nor did he need to; he just reversed direction and cut over to the adjacent stud two feet to the left. At the stud, he started a cut upward alongside it for about two feet, then across and down again until he was able to remove a rough square of drywall. Then he went to work picking out the sound-deadening material.

As Stone removed it, he discovered the secret of the silence from the laboratory. The plans called for two-by-four-inch studding, as in a normal dividing wall, but the studs had been doubled so that there was eight inches between the Sheetrock of the outside and inside wall. Stone had not only to remove the insulation, eight inches thick, from the hole he had cut, but to dig down and get out another good twelve inches' worth of the stuff below the bottom of the opening. By the time he had done so, the other three had returned, their jeans blood-smeared from wiping off their hands, bearing bulging plastic trash bags.

"Must be gettin' old," Pappy whispered. "Never bothered me to slit Charlie's throat in Nam, but them pigs and rabbits and dogs never did no harm to anybody."

"Think what you were saving them from," Wings muttered.

"All right, tie 'em off and bring them over here," whispered Stone. The three of them followed Stone's instructions and put two bags into the wall opening, starting down below the cut and up to the top. Stone picked up the plastic bag filled with the ammonium-nitrate fertilizer and fuel-oil mixture. "Okay, guys," he directed, "flatten that stuff out as well as you can."

Pappy, Wings, and Arno pressed the plastic bags as flat against the opposite drywall as they could while Stone lifted the final plastic bag—the one with the fertilizer and fuel-oil mixture—in behind them. He broke pieces of the drywall he had cut out to prop the bags in place, then motioned the men out of the way.

Stone turned to Saul Rosen. "What's the latest?"

"They're away from this wall—anywhere from halfway across the room to the other side of it. Least as far as I can judge from listening to them move around and their voices getting louder and softer."

"Okay," Stone said, "according to the plans, we've got a clean wall here, but I've already discovered one modification, so be ready for anything. According to the photographs Sara took, there was no apparatus against this wall. The blast will breach it for us, and that and the little surprise we put in front of the explosive should give us the edge. I'm counting on it to delay any attempt to kill the prisoners and to let us get them first. On the blast, everybody move in and double-tap the bad guys."

Saul Rosen had divested himself of his listening gear and held the Browning Hi-Power in both hands, cocked, pointed toward the floor. Pappy Saye had his .357 Magnum, hammer down because it was a double-action, in a similar position. Arno Bitt had given Wings Harper back his AK-47 and snicked back the hammer on the big .45 Ballester-Molina. "I still wanna see how you're gonna set off that fertilizer–fuel-oil shit," he said to Stone.

"Watch," said Stone. He withdrew a silver cylinder ten inches long and one and a half inches in diameter that had been duct-taped to his thigh. The lettering on it read:

SIGNAL, SMOKE, GROUND, GREEN,
PARACHUTE, MI28A1 WARNING: *Do not
fire this signal if cork sealing disk in
end of barrel is loose.*

"Ooooooh, shit!" said Pappy Saye.

The men moved farther back. Stone angled himself away from behind the plastic bags and against the opposite wall, staying as far away from the hole as he could and still be certain of getting the job done right this first and only time. At one end of the cylinder was a hole. Inside the hole was a primer. Stone slipped off the cap at the opposite end of the silver tube and slid it onto the end with the primer in it, leaving an inch to go. He gripped the tube firmly in his left hand and pointed it at the explosive in the wall.

"Wings," he said, "use that AK to cover our ass. All right, people, let's launch!"

So saying, Michael Stone slammed the base of the aluminum tube and a rocket fired directly into the plastic bag containing the mixture of ammonium nitrate and fuel oil. The shock of the impact and flare bursting detonated the low-order explosive, and it exploded with a characteristic deep bass WHOOOM!

Inside the laboratory, everyone was rocked by the long, heavy overpressure wave of a low-order explosive, confused by the swirling green signal smoke and then, looking down at themselves, shocked into the momentary belief that they were about to die as they beheld themselves covered with blood and guts they had every reason to believe was their own, not that of the recently slaughtered and disemboweled laboratory animals packed in the plastic bags in front of the explosive.

Frozen in horror, Letzger and his men did not see momentarily the danger as Stone, Saye, Bitt, and Rosen rushed into the chaotic room and, with machinelike discipline, pivoting like mechanical men in a penny arcade, fired two shots each directly into the heads of the dreaded, white-coated monkey handlers. Some died before they could even distinguish between the explosive blast and the impact of the heavy bullets crashing into their skulls.

Sara Rosen put her hands to her face and screamed as to the blood and entrails already on her was added the blood and brains of the burst-open heads of the two assistants who had but a moment before been trying to force her into the Lexan chamber with Eddie Berg.

Dr. Letzger recovered from the shock first. He was standing next to the door to the room containing the acid vat. Hearing the first shots and taking advantage of the thick green swirl of signal smoke, he drew a Walther P-5 9 mm double-action semiautomatic pistol from under his white coat and, to the accompaniment of Sara's screams and the insistent whining of smoke alarms set off by the green haze from the signal rocket, ducked into the adjoining vat room.

Saul Rosen ran to his sister and knocked her to the ground, covering her with his body. He did it instinctively, although there was no longer any need to, the surgical shooting over almost as soon as it began. Michael Stone spotted Letzger's move and went after him. He kicked the door farther open from a position to its side, drawing 9 mm fire from Letzger, who was trying to get around the vat to escape through another door on the opposite side of the vat from the laboratory.

As Stone moved to return fire, he saw no target. Letzger was nowhere to be seen. Stone's eyes narrowed as he noted that the opposite door had not been opened. There were no windows. He concluded that Letzger had hoped to trick him into believing he had made good his escape but was, in fact, down behind the far side of the vat, perhaps even moving around it to take Stone from the flank. Stone dropped down himself, crawling beneath the gurney that fed the seething vat, coming to rest squatting with his back to the rim so he could bring his .45 auto to bear in either direction.

A sound to his right caused Stone to swing his pistol, held in both hands, arms outstretched, toward it, bending his head to clear the top of the gurney above him. Before he could get his sights all the way around, Letzger appeared, inching his way around the rim of the vat in a duck walk, right hand holding his pistol out in front of him, left hand sliding along the side of the vat. Seeing Stone under the gurney, the startled Letzger snapped off a shot that went wild, then sprung upward to hurdle the gurney and make his escape before Stone could get out from under it. As Letzger was in midair above the gurney, the squatting Stone tucked his chin down against his chest and, thrusting upward with his powerful legs, caught the bottom of the gurney squarely with his shoulders and propelled it sharply upward and backward on its hinges.

The gurney slammed into the airborne Letzger and knocked him backward over the rim. He hung there for what seemed to him an eternity as Stone, stepping to the side and turning to avoid the gurney now on its way back down, faced him. In that instant, the two men's eyes locked, Letzger's pleading. From somewhere he thought he had abandoned within himself, Stone found among the icy cold of a clicked-on operational SEAL a flicker of compassion. As Letzger descended, screaming, toward the fuming, roiling acid, Stone fired the heavy Colt. A big blue hole appeared in Letzger's forehead, and the back blew out of his head. He stopped screaming before the boiling acid reacted violently as it claimed him, as it had his victims so many times before.

Stone's eyes widened as he witnessed the destruction of Letzger. He thought back to the incident in the railway-receiving hangar. Jesus! he thought to himself. So *that*'s what's been going on here . . . *human* experimentation! No wonder they were trying to keep the lid on!

When the overpressure and *WharruummP!* from the low-order blast six floors below him awakened Helmar Metz, his first inclination was to dismiss it as the sonic boom from a military jet—a common annoyance in Germany, where U.S. Air Force fighters exceed the speed of sound regularly in practice. Then he remembered where he was. At that moment, the telephone rang. Fully alert now, he scooped it up. "Yes!"

"Mr. Metz, sir, Foley with uniformed security. Plant entrance. We got a multiple smoke-detector report on the twelfth floor, plus I felt something, like something blew up in the plant. I was gonna call the fire department, only in the standing orders here it says for anything on the twelfth floor, you gotta be advised first and authorize it."

"Correct," said Metz. "Well done. Call no one. I handle it."

"Yes, sir."

Metz hung up. He had slept in his shirt and trousers. Now he fastened his belt and put on his shoes and tied them with the speed that can come only from years in the military, removed a Walther P-5 from under his pillow and pocketed it, then moved quickly to the conference room where his men were sleeping to rouse them.

"Twelfth floor!" he commanded. "Come with me."

An eager aide rushed toward the elevator to summon a car.

"Nein!" Metz snarled. "If there is fire, the lift could stop at any time. We use the fire stairs."

"Mike! Mike!" Saul Rosen shouted through the door. "Come here; you won't believe what they've been doing here. Look!" He pointed toward the Lexan cabinet from which Eddie Berg had been released and was being held by Sara.

"I know, I know," said Stone, "human experimentation." He waved his hand at the laboratory equipment. "Look at the *scale* of this stuff. It's all designed for *humans.* That's why they were so hot to get those Polaroids back from Sara even though the things were empty. They were afraid someone might compare them with the size of the walls and ceiling and all and catch on that the stuff was human-scale. I mean, Jesus! Look at the size of that drum. I can't believe I didn't tumble to it."

"No, no, Mike. I mean, yes, you're right. But that's not what I mean. Look over here in that chamber they were putting Sara in—where we found Eddie and the others, the Mexicans." He pointed to two small cylinders, about the size of lunch-bucket thermos bottles, sitting outside the rear of the Lexan plastic chamber. From the top of each, woven metal tubing ran to a valve, then the two pieces of tubing joined each other, and the single tube ran into the chamber through a tight seal and ended, open. Each small bottle bore a label: GB(L)1 and GB(L)2.

Stone looked at the bottles and the chamber, taking in the tight sealing all around its joints and the door. "Dirty motherfuckers!" Stone said, his face growing dark. "They were gonna gas them all and then dissolve them in that acid back there." He waved his hand back toward the room holding the vat.

"No, damn it!" Saul said, exasperated. "Look at the gas bottles. See what it says on them?"

Stone's face was blank, uncomprehending.

"GB! Goddamn it, Mike, GB! Don't you know what that is? Don't you remember your training, for Christ's sake? I'll give you a hint. Remember all that stuff about these guys talking about Sara before she ever got here? Remember you grilling me about it because of what Ira Levin said? They weren't talking about Sara, Mike. GB means

Sarin, the deadliest nerve gas there is. But that's not all. There're *two* bottles, see? And an 'L' in parentheses! Now look at this." Saul held out a bloodstained notebook, but before he could go on, they were interrupted by the sound none of them would ever forget from Vietnam—a burst of fire from an AK-47.

Michael Stone used his command voice: "Later! Give me a sitrep!"

Saul Rosen's military training snapped in. "Eddie Berg's blind in one eye but otherwise okay. We got a totally blind Mexican who speaks no English. Sara's okay. We got another Mexican strapped to a frame over there with a hole in his middle and a picture window in it. I dunno; if we move him, it could kill him."

"We don't, he could end up taking an acid bath," said Stone.

"Our people?"

"Okay."

"Wings is engaging some guys tryin' to get on the floor from the fire stairs," Arno Bitt offered.

"Anyone speak Spanish?" asked Stone.

"I can." It was Eddie Berg, with a torn piece of Sara's dress around his eyes. It was an attempt at a bandage but looked more like a blindfold. "I think I know these guys."

"Tell 'em to do exactly as you say. We're gonna try to get them out of here, or at least get them some help."

"Okay," said Eddie. He lifted the cloth up from his remaining eye, squinted and blinked a few times to clear his vision in it, winced, and started to speak to the two men in rapid-fire border Spanish.

Stone moved rapidly beside Wings Harper, who touched off a two-shot burst as he arrived. "I've got one dead for sure. The others are not too eager to get their heads blown off. They've gotta be planning an alternative attack if they haven't figured one out already and started maneuvering."

"Yeah," said Stone. "Only we're not staying around to find out. When I give you the signal, move back to the elevator."

"Gotcha covered," said Wings. He kept his eyes on the sights of the AK as he spoke, and as he returned to the laboratory, Stone heard another two-shot burst and Wings's voice calling out, "Make that two dead!"

Stone led the way out of the laboratory. Sara Rosen was immediately behind him, followed by her brother, then Eddie Berg and the blind Mexican behind him, holding on to his belt for guidance. Bringing up the rear were Pappy Saye and Arno Bitt, rolling the Cermak table between them with the Mexican with the window in his abdomen still strapped to it for his own safety. Both Mexicans trailed dangling sensor wires still taped to their torsos. The group proceeded rapidly to the elevator bank under cover of a burst of automatic fire from Wings Harper's AK-47 to keep the enemy's heads behind the door, where they couldn't see what was going on. "Everybody know what to do?" Stone asked.

There was no answer to indicate to the contrary, so Stone hit the button to summon the far elevator. Mechanical noise soon confirmed that it was operating. As soon as the door opened, Stone checked the interior and, finding it empty, called out, "Wings!" Then he slipped inside and punched the button marked L, for lobby. The car descended, Stone following its progress by watching the floor numbers click off on the panel over the door. As the car approached the lobby, Stone moved to the front. He positioned his finger on the Door Open button, then turned around and faced the rear, the button panel at his back, so that with the door open, anyone looking into the car could not see him.

The elevator car slowed to a stop. A moment later, the doors opened, and Stone depressed the Door Open button and held it there. Outside, in the lobby, Foley, the uniformed security guard who had reported the sound of the explosion to Metz, heard the elevator's electronic tone announcing the arrival of the car and turned from his position at the television-screens monitoring desk in curiosity to see who would be coming down to the lobby at that early hour. Then it occurred to him that it might be Metz himself, and he hastened to greet him.

Before Foley could get out from behind his desk, straighten up his uniform, and get all the way over to the elevator bank, the door to the car opened and stayed open. There was no one visible inside. Puzzled, Foley moved to investigate, cautiously sticking his head inside the car. It was the last thing he remembered as Michael Stone slammed the heavy slide of the Colt .45 directly into the point of Foley's jaw, knocking him senseless.

Upstairs, on the twelfth floor, the other elevator car had been called by Saul Rosen as soon as Stone's car could be seen to leave. Under cover of the suppression fire of Wings Harper, who had joined them at Stone's signal, the Cermak table with its Mexican victim still strapped on had been carried to the rear by Pappy Saye and Arno Bitt, then the rest crowded in, and Saul held the Door Open button down, keeping the way clear for Wings to join them when Stone signaled that it was safe to descend.

With the sound of the electronic annunciator tone for the car Stone had taken came his signal. It arrived back, and its door opened, to reveal the unconscious Foley. Wings Harper slammed his boot heel down on the open half of a spent 7.62 mm AK cartridge casing and quickly jammed it under the door of Foley's elevator car to hold it open. Then, with a final burst of fire into the fire-stairs doorway, he jumped into the car with the others, Saul removed his finger from the Door Open button, slammed L, and the doors closed. For a moment that seemed a lifetime, nothing happened. Then, to the massive relief of all, the car descended.

When the car door opened at the lobby, Wings Harper had the AK at the ready, backed up by the handguns of Saul Rosen and the others, taking no chances on any change in situation for Stone. It was unnecessary. Stone was there to greet them with the prone body of the outside guard shackled hand and foot with his own handcuffs and those of the unconscious Foley, now twelve floors above. The guard's shoes were off and his socks, rolled neatly enough to win the approval of Aunt May, were stuffed into his mouth as a gag.

"Did you explain it to him, Eddie?" Stone asked with a nod toward the Mexican on the Cermak table.

"Yeah. He wanted to be let loose, but I told him if he got up, it might kill him."

"Okay," said Stone. "Out." All but the strapped-down Mexican were clear of the car within seconds. Stone leaned back into it and said, "Adios, señor," and pushed the button for the second-level basement, then ducked back out as the door closed and the elevator descended.

Arno Bitt glanced up at the floor annunciator of the first elevator. "Uh-oh," he said, "we're gonna have company in about a minute."

"No, we're not," said Stone. He darted to the right of the elevator bank and smashed the glass of the fire alarm with the butt of his Colt, then yanked the lever. Immediately a clangorous bell sounded, and the elevator stopped descending. "Y'know those signs in hotels say 'In case of fire, do not use elevator, use stairs'? Latest thing. They program the elevator to stop operating as soon as the alarm goes off. Saves lives."

"Yeah," said Pappy Saye, "ours."

"For Christ's sake," said Eddie Berg, now shaking from shock and holding his hand to his dressing-packed eye socket, "let's get out of here." The anesthetic was wearing off and his wound was throbbing. He turned away, using his good eye to look at the television-security monitors behind the desk, feigning interest in them to conceal his distress from the others.

"All right," said Stone, "let's launch. Saul, get the Mustang and take Eddie and our Mexican friend here to the hospital. Drop 'em off at the emergency room and don't wait around to explain. Get back to the house as fast as you can. I'll take Sara and the boys home in the van."

"No!" said Sara. "I go with Eddie!"

At that moment, Eddie Berg saw in a monitor a man holding a pistol ease his way out of a fire-stair door. It was a wide-angle shot and on the other side of the hallway shown was an open elevator door. With a shock, Eddie realized the monitor covered that part of the entrance hall outside the view of the monitoring desk. The man was only feet away from appearing from behind them with a drawn gun. As Eddie shouted, "Look out!" the man came around the corner, pistol in front of him. Eddie Berg leapt at him, trying to knock the pistol away. With only one eye to use, his depth perception was off, and he missed. The gunman didn't. Eddie took a 9 mm in the left shoulder and went down. Sara screamed. Michael Stone shot the man between the eyes with his .45 Colt, rushed to Eddie Berg, and helped him to his feet, asking, "Can you make it to the van, kid?"

Eddie just nodded. Saul took him from Stone and Sara ripped her dress again to make a compress that she pressed into the hole in Eddie's shoulder to stanch the flow of blood.

"All right, Saul, take the van with Eddie and Sara. We'll take the Mustang." Sirens sounded in the distance. "Go!" Stone commanded.

18

● HELMAR METZ STOOD IN FRONT OF THE ELEVATOR and observed with disgust Foley, who was seated on the car floor gingerly testing his jaw to see whether it was broken. "Describe your attacker," he said impatiently.

"Sorry, sir. I never saw him. Put my head into the empty—well, it *looked* empty—car and *wham!* the lights went out."

Metz reached down and freed the car door by removing the half-crushed 7.62 cartridge casing wedged under it, but because of the alarm interlock, the door stayed open. He threw the casing down on the floor and said, "Find the nearest telephone. Call the fire department and cancel the alarm. Then use the fire stairs and get down to the alarm control and turn it off. *Schnell!* I want the elevators back in operation."

Foley, who didn't speak German, had seen enough old war movies to know what *Schnell* meant, and he struggled to his feet and lurched off toward the fire stairs, several times almost falling down as his feet slipped on the rolling cartridge casings that littered the hall floor. Metz walked over to the door of the laboratory. One of his men was posted at the door. "Is it clear?" he asked.

Assured that no enemies lurked in the laboratory, Metz entered and surveyed the carnage. He moved about without speaking, stepping carefully to avoid the more obvious clumps of entrails and puddles of blood, and observed the dead. Each corpse had two closely spaced bullet holes in the head. Some of the cartridge casings were 9 mm. Others were the big American military 11.25 mm, or .45-caliber as they called it. His men who had caught a glimpse of the AK-47 gunner had described him as having dark clothing, a painted face, and a bandanna. Coupling that with the precision marksmanship, the British Special Air Service trick of mixing animal entrails with the breaching explosive, and the skill with a knife displayed previously by the intruder convinced Metz he was dealing with professional Special Warfare types. SAS veteran mercenaries perhaps? His men, who had managed to hear a word or two spoken by the AK gunner, were not sufficiently familiar with English to be able to distinguish a British from an American accent. Or could it be Al Rajul's people? If so, why the attack to free the American prisoners—and before the ship had sailed with what he had wanted so badly that he had kidnapped Hoess's son? Nothing was making sense and that disturbed Metz most of all.

Metz continued his inspection. Then, suddenly, it hit him. Where was Letzger? His body wasn't to be found. Metz went into the acid-vat room and walked all around the vat. The exhaust hood hummed as it sucked off the toxic fumes. All appeared in order. Well, Letzger was a clever fellow; perhaps he had managed to escape. If so, he'd show up shortly.

The telephone on the wall rang. Metz answered it. One of his men reported the death at the plant entrance of another of his men. "Bring the body here and clean things up immediately," he said, and hung up.

The telephone call snapped Metz out of his reverie and he barked a series of commands: "All corpses into the acid. The same with any other organic matter. Get all of these spent casings up. I don't want a single one found later under a piece of furniture. Then clean it up so we can get the carpenters and painters in without their wondering what happened here. Remove the door to the fire stairs and get a new one sent up. Putty up all bullet holes out there and paint over them. *Schnell,* or we'll have some extra bodies for the acid!" He turned and made his way back to the elevator bank and cursed to see that the door was still open, indicating that, although the alarm had been silenced, Foley had not yet figured out how to reset the elevator interlock. He was about to check his watch when Foley huffed and puffed his way through the remnants of the fire-stairs door after climbing the twelve flights back up. "Out of condition at your age?" Metz snapped as the breathless guard approached him. Foley was too tired to respond to the gibe.

"I got the alarm off, sir, but I couldn't reset the interlock on the elevators. It'll take an elevator mechanic. And the fire department's coming. They said they were already on their way and have to make a report."

Metz frowned. He was tempted to stand up to the firemen himself but concluded that things would look more normal if a uniformed guard handled it. "Tell them when they arrive it was a false alarm and that the company takes responsibility. Thank them for being so prompt and so on. And straighten yourself up. Look presentable."

"Yes, sir. I got a description for you, sir. Whittle, the outside guard? They had him all handcuffed up and gagged, but he got a good look at them. Big, tough guys. Very professional. Dark clothing. Bandannas. Camo paint on their faces. Handguns, mostly. Very cool. Christ knows how they got up there. They sure as shit didn't go through the front entrance."

"I see," said Metz. "Very well. Now get going and keep those firemen out of here."

Metz didn't wait for a reply. He turned on his heel and made for the fire stairs, taking the six floors up to the eighteenth floor with ease. When he arrived, he went straight to his accommodations in Kramer's office, walked over to the scrambler telephone, then hesitated. On the one hand, he was obligated professionally to keep his employer fully informed of important developments. On the other hand, he lacked the information to respond to Hoess's questions as to who was behind the attack. Lastly, Hoess had already given him his ultimate priority: See to it that the ship sailed as scheduled with its precious cargo so as not to endanger Hoess's son. Metz glanced at his watch: 0539. He must assume a worst-case situation . . . that the mission of the ship was known and an attempt would be made to stop it from sailing, the presence of the gas betrayed and a failure to deliver responsible for the death of Hoess's boy. His opposition was clearly professional, no matter who they were or for whom they were working. The best thing to do was to put himself in his opponent's place. How would he, Metz, ensure that the ship did not sail? To a veteran *Kampfschwimmer,* the answer was obvious: Disable the vessel. The opposition had already proven it had access to explosives. Limpet mine? Perhaps. But if they were really sophisticated, they would go for the propeller-shaft support.

His decision taken, Metz turned away from the telephone. His next report to Hoess would be to signal success. If he failed, it would be up to others to convey it. He went to the equipment he had sent over from Germany. He knew exactly where to look because he had packed it himself. Within moments, he retrieved a Draeger rebreather unit. Worn on the chest instead of the back as is normal scuba gear, the Draeger unit would allow him to breathe underwater without leaving any telltale bubble trail. When whoever they were came to disable the ship, Metz would be ready for them, lying in wait, with nothing to betray his presence, no matter how professional they were. Metz smiled a mirthless smile to himself. It wasn't all that long ago that he was the best frogman in the German navy. Once in the water, he'd show them what it meant to be a professional!

"Where's Sara?" Stone looked past Saul Rosen out the door to his home to see whether she was trailing behind for some reason.

"She's at the emergency room with Eddie Berg. Wouldn't leave until she's sure he's gonna be okay." He stepped into the front hall just as the grandfather clock intoned the three-quarter hour at 5:45 A.M.

"Goddamn it!" Michael Stone fumed. "They're sure to question her about how he was injured. The Mexican, too, for that matter. Just what I wanted to avoid."

"I know, Mike, but she's operating on feelings right now, not intellect. There was no use arguing. I told her to say she found them wandering around outside of Riegar, the blind leading the blind. That she was there getting ready for today's protest. Then to take a cab to her place when she left, not here."

"Why didn't you stay and bring her back yourself?"

"Because of this, Mike, remember?" Saul held up the bloody notebook. Pappy Saye and Arno wandered in from the kitchen, drinking coffee. "Wings is making pancakes, Mike. When do we debrief for the after-action report?"

"Please, Mike," Saul said urgently, "listen to me first. This is a scientific notebook of a guy named Letzger, back there in the lab. First, it confirms what I told you about what the GB on the bottles of gas meant. Look. . . ." Saul had the blood-splattered notebook open to an early page. At the top it read: *Monographie Nr. 62 zu Angewandte Chemie und Chemi-Ingenieur-Technik (Verlag Chemie 1951) Schrader, G. Die Entwicklung neurer Insektizide auf Grundlage organischer Fluor- und Phosphor-Vervindungen.*

Michael Stone furrowed his brow. "I can't read this stuff, Saul. Hey, Arno. Take a look at this."

Arno Bitt took the notebook, saying, "I speak German pretty good, but I'm not so hot at readin' it. Anyway, looks like this guy is starting out with a known. What's in a monograph, number 62, by a chemical and technical engineer named Schrader, written in 1951, about a new insecticide made by combining phosphorus and fluorine."

"Insecticide," said Pappy Saye. "Isn't that what the Nazis used to kill all them Jews in the gas chambers?"

"You're right," said Saul. "Zyklon B. It was formulated originally as a commercial insecticide. Proved so toxic, they decided to use it on the Jews. But that stuff's nothing to this stuff. Here, I told you, Mike, I'm in the technology-gathering business. Here's something I *can* read." He pointed down the page toward where appeared:

$$(CH_3)_2\ CHO-\overset{\displaystyle F}{\underset{\displaystyle CH_3}{P}}=O$$

"That," said Saul heatedly, "is isopropyl methylphosphonoflouridate, the chemical formula for Sarin. Military symbol, GB. The deadliest nerve gas in the world. One two-hundred-fifty-millionth of an ounce is enough to kill you. You don't even have to breathe it in, just let that microscopic amount get on your skin and you die, your muscles twitching, vomiting and shitting at the same time, drooling, in convulsions, coma and death from respiratory failure. Nice, huh?"

"Jesus!" said Pappy. "That shit was in that lab where we was at?"

"No," said Saul.

"But you just said . . ." Pappy protested.

"Lemme lay it out for you," Saul said. "First of all, that German study Arno read out for us was made way back in 1951. Sarin is nothing new. The United States has eight stockpiles of quarter-ton bombs and artillery shells full of the stuff. They're mostly in the South and West. The closest to us is in Aberdeen, Maryland."

"Man, how do you know that shit?" asked Pappy.

"It's my job to know. Mike'll explain later. At any rate, the United States is getting rid of it. It's just too damn dangerous. One leak, and you wipe out a major city, if there's one around. It's just not politically feasible in this day and age to keep something like that around in this country anymore. You've gotta have poison gas that's environmentally safe. How's that for an oxymoron?"

"Man," said Pappy, "any kinda moron would know better'n to have that shit around."

"Right," said Saul. "The solution was binary gases. Like the atom bomb. You take two subcritical mass–sized pieces of uranium two thirty-five. So long as they're apart, nothing. Slam 'em together and *wham!* Mushroom city. Same thing in the new gas technology approach. You have two chemicals, harmless when apart. Mix 'em up and it's all over. So both superpowers have it. Shit, even Iraq claims to have it now."

"So, what's the big deal?" asked Wings.

"Sarin has one limitation. It disperses very quickly. It's so deadly so fast that's usually not a problem. But an attacker can't deny an area for any time at all with it, unless the weather is very cold. That's the only condition under which it'll linger. So, naturally, both superpowers have been working on an all-weather lingering Sarin. Only, guess what, friends and neighbors? Riegar just won the race. And it's binary. Remember those two bottles in the lab with the tubing from each leading into one tube where it could mix? Remember the markings on the bottles? The L in parentheses after the GB? Well, look here in the notebook." Saul held his finger under a word in German.

"Man!" Pappy exclaimed in exasperation. "What's it say?"

"Langwierig," Saul answered.

"Lingering," Arno Bitt translated. "Jesus H. Christ!"

"To forty-five degrees Celsius. That's one hundred and thirteen degrees Fahrenheit."

There was a stunned silence. Saul Rosen let the full impact sink in on the others, then continued: "And now we jump to the back of the book, where, in the midst of the German, we suddenly find some Japanese: *Aka Maru.* Every Japanese ship I ever heard of was the *somebody* Maru. Want to take a crack at it, Arno?"

Arno Bitt held the book as if the notebook itself might be a deadly poison. He read for a minute, then said, "Holy shit. They loaded two fifty-kilogram cylinders—one of GB (L) One and one of GB (L) Two—last night on a ship named the *Aka Maru.* That's a hundred and ten pounds each. Deduct the weight of cylinders strong enough to hold that much liquid under inert gas pressure and you'd still have almost a hundred pounds of liquid, lingering Sarin when combined!"

"Lethal," Saul emphasized, "at a dose of one two-hundred-fifty-millionth of an ounce per person. I don't want to have to do the arithmetic, and I don't know where that ship in the Riegar dock is supposed to be going, but anyone wanna bet its name *isn't Aka Maru,* or speculate on what might happen if that stuff ever gets into the hands of Qaddafi?"

"Or Iran?" offered Arno.

"Or Iraq?" Pappy submitted.

"That fuckin' ship's going nowhere," said Stone. The grandfather clock boomed out the hour of 6:00 A.M. "Jesus," he said, "where's the morning paper?"

Wings Harper strolled in from the kitchen to announce flapjacks were ready, ignorant of the conversation that had taken place. The others glared at him. "Okay, okay!" he said. "I'll go bring in the paper. Little postop nerves, huh?"

The paper had been left on the steps outside the door. Michael Stone grabbed it, turned the pages rapidly, stopped at the weather, then hit it with his hand in frustration. "Damn! Tide's an hour from now. No way we'll get anybody to listen to our story in time."

"Does this," said Wings Harper, "mean we don't get to have breakfast?"

"How much longer," said Stephanie Hannigan, "to this mystery restaurant of yours?"

Brian Sullivan looked over at her from behind the wheel of his rental sedan and smiled mischievously. "Restaurant? And who said anythin' about a restaurant?" He negotiated a turn down a street still deserted at 6:00 A.M. along the river industrial district.

Stephanie's face clouded over, Naomi's reservations leaping to mind. "You said you had this terrific place to have breakfast with a great view of the river, and if you've got something dumb in mind like your apartment or something, you can just let me out right here. A morning walk will do me good."

"For heaven's *sake,* lass. Why of a sudden do y'take me for a fool or a rake?"

"Because when you ask someone to breakfast, they assume you're going to take them to a restaurant, especially when you build it up the way you did, and my friend Naomi Fine suspects your intentions, and here we are in the worst part of town, and you *admit* there's no restaurant, and—"

Sullivan cut her off. "Do I know yer fine friend, no pun intended? Does she know me?"

"No, but—"

"Have I ever done or said anythin' to you was untoward?"

"No, but—"

"Then can y'not spare me just a little trust? We're almost there and . . . hello, what's all this?"

They were on the street that would take them past the Riegar plant, but the way was blocked by fire apparatus and police. An ambulance was directly outside the entrance, and the flashing lights of all three types of emergency vehicles added to the garishness of the early-morning hubbub. Brian Sullivan pulled over. "Excuse me fer just a moment, please," he said to Stephanie, "me reportorial duties come before all." Before Stephanie could reply, he was out of the car and on his way over to a police officer whose face bore the map of Ireland. Sullivan displayed his Reuters press credentials and asked, " 'Marnin', Officer. Could you be assistin' me in makin' me honest livin' and tell me what it is is goin' on here?"

The police officer's face lit up at the lilt of Sullivan's accent. "It's from Derry, y'are, is it?"

"Originally, it is so."

"Well, then, if y'won't let on to the black prods it was O'Shea who told ya, we've got a bit of a mystery goin' on. The fire alarm was pulled in the lobby, yet when the firemen got here, the rent-a-cops denied all. Only there was a telephone call ta the police sayin' there was a man with a hole in him stuck in an elevator in the basement, an' sure enough, there was. Had a regular winda in him, he did. They're in there tryin' ta figger out how to move 'im now."

"Glory be ta God!" said Sullivan. "I'd better be gettin' that out right away. God bless ya!" He walked rapidly back to his car and got back in. The worried expression on his face drew a "What is it? What's going on?" from Stephanie Hannigan.

Sullivan didn't answer her. He backed the car a bit too fast for Stephanie's comfort and headed to bypass the Riegar plant, then tried to regain his composure. His cheer sounded forced as he said, "Fire at the plant. No need to interrupt our plans fer breakfast." He turned down a heavily timbered wooden ramp to the dock and parked in the lee of the *Aka Maru.* "An' here we are!" he said.

"Here?" said Stephanie, remaining in her seat. "We're going to have breakfast here?"

Sullivan got out, took a briefcase from the backseat, and opened Stephanie's door. "Y'can't see it from inside there, lass."

Reluctantly, Stephanie got out of the car. Sullivan pointed up in the air, and Stephanie followed his finger up to the bridge of the *Aka Maru,* towering above them. The ship was moored fore and aft to the dock, with her stern directly opposite Sullivan's automobile. With the exception of two loading cranes, her entire superstructure was aft.

"There?" Stephanie asked. "That's where we're having breakfast?"

"Well, not on the bridge, although we'll visit there." Sullivan walked Stephanie toward the stairs erected to lead up the gangplank to the weather deck. "I'll introduce you to the captain, then I have to interview some scientists ab'ard, then we have breakfast with the captain and the other officers. As you can imagine, from that height the view downriver is glorious."

"We have to climb all the way up there?"

"That we do."

"Oh, God," said Stephanie, "I've got absolutely the wrong shoes!" She reached back and slipped her heels off one at a time and carried them with her purse. "Men," she said with a vehemence that startled Brian Sullivan, "know absolutely nothing!"

Jan van Loon, the third mate, was waiting for them as they stepped aboard off the gangplank. He saluted casually and logged them in, then walked them around to what he called the main ladder off the weather deck, to the fore and center of the superstructure, then apologized for not being able to accompany them farther, as he had to return to his post.

"Ladder?" said Stephanie in exasperation. "I'm wearing a skirt. I'm not going up any ladder!"

Van Loon laughed. "It's just a nautical expression, ma'am. It's really a stairway, and you'll be quite comfortable. We do have real ladders throughout the ship, but the main ladder is something you'll find familiar. Bit of a hike, though, it's five flights up to the bridge deck."

"Hence the view," Sullivan offered cheerfully.

"How's the food on this boat?" Stephanie asked.

"Ship, ma'am," van Loon corrected. "The rule of thumb is, if it's small enough to be taken aboard another vessel, it's a boat. If not, it's a ship."

"You still haven't answered my question," said Stephanie in her best lawyerlike tone. "The food, remember?"

Van Loon smiled and in his British accent said, "The only American aboard besides the pilot is the cook, ma'am. The coffee's an acceptable substitute for a triple bypass, and you can't go wrong on the bacon and eggs."

"Fine," said Stephanie as she started up the stairs, "I can spend the day listening to my caffeine-fueled heart trying to slam blood through my cholesterol-plugged arteries."

Five flights later, flushed and breathless, Stephanie was introduced to Isu Horoko, captain of the *Aka Maru*. The captain bowed, and Stephanie wasn't sure what to do in response, curtsy? Bow? She settled for putting out her right hand and, to her relief, as the captain straightened up, he took it and gave it a polite shake. She was then introduced to Arthur Cole, the first mate, whose unmistakable Australian accent explained his breezy personality. Sullivan excused himself to confer with Captain Horoko, who instructed Cole to show Stephanie around the bridge. She moved immediately to the great glass windows, which, she had to admit to herself, did indeed give a magnificent view south, down the Hudson River.

"It's beautiful," Stephanie said finally, turning away from the view and toward Cole.

"It is," said Cole. Then, pointing with a sweeping gesture to an array of radar repeaters, loran controls, annunciators, binnacle, and telephones, he said, "I don't know how much interest you have in all this, but I can take you through it one at a time, if you like."

Brian Sullivan, Stephanie saw from the corner of her eye, was gesturing with a nod of his head toward the Riegar plant in his conversation with the ship's captain. He started back toward them, and Stephanie said, "No, no, I think we're going to have breakfast soon."

Sullivan corrected her, "In a few minutes, we'll join the officers in the wardroom, but I'm off first to interview the scientists. Won't be long. Hold my place at the table." He turned away without waiting for a reply and went back down the main ladder. Stephanie returned to the broad glass and the view.

One of the most impressive sights, Stephanie thought, was not of the river but the broad weather deck of the vessel that spread out beneath her gaze, five decks below, like a football field viewed from a skybox high up above the end zone. It was broad and flat. Its plane was interrupted only by two huge cargo-loading cranes, now quiet. She looked straight down and saw four men emerge from the area near the main ladder and move to a watertight door. Two by two, they appeared to be having difficulty carrying two metal cylinders through the door and downward. She turned to Cole. "Could you tell me what those men are doing?" she asked.

Cole looked downward in the direction Stephanie pointed and said,

"It appears our scientist passengers are moving some of their equipment—scuba gear, I think—down the ladder into area 1-Alpha starboard. That's the first three cargo bays forward of the superstructure on the right side of the ship. I caught a glimpse of them once when they were collecting their meals. Strange lot." He paused. "Speaking of meals, I'm to have the honor of escorting you into the wardroom for breakfast. Unfortunately, the seat next to you is reserved for your friend the reporter."

Stephanie smiled at Cole. "Well, there's always the seat on the other side of me."

"Alas," said Cole as they moved through the passageway, "that one's reserved for the captain."

Stephanie giggled lightheartedly. She was enjoying the unaccustomed attention of a number of attractive males at the same time.

"What's so funny?" Cole asked her.

"Oh, it just came to me. That huge flat deck. Take away the cranes, and it could be an aircraft carrier in an old black and white war movie. I can just hear Captain Horoko saying, 'Ah, so, Yankee pirot. You terr us where Amelican pranes com flom.'"

"I beg your pardon?"

"Forget it," said Stephanie, "you hadda see the picture."

At 0606 Michael Stone slid the Mustang up to the superunleaded pump at Buckley's Texaco, pushed the button for Cash, lifted the lever, and inserted the nozzle into his filler pipe. He set the trigger for slow delivery and, knowing the gasoline delivery would shut off automatically, went to the trunk and pulled out a two-tank scuba backpack. He carried it into the garage area, found the proprietor, and said, "Buck, can you spare some acetylene and oxygen?"

"Everything in the joint's for sale except the missus," said Buckley. "You want me to put it into *that* thing?"

"Yeah, and I'm going to need a torch head and some hose clamps."

"How 'bout some weldin' rods."

"Won't need them."

"Uh-huh. How much gas you want in them tanks? What'll they hold?"

"Just fill them until the pressure gauges are against the stops."

Michael Stone watched as Buckley filled the scuba tanks from large, heavy tanks he kept in his garage for welding and cutting metal.

"So, how's it going?" Stone asked to forestall any more questions about his curious request.

"Gettin' harder all the time," said Buckley. "I'm about the only real mechanic's garage left in town, and still the company wants to turn this place into a gas 'n' go joint like all the rest. I make my real living as a mechanic, not on the gas. As it is, I gotta be here six A.M. every day. With a gas 'n' go, have to man the place twenty-four hours. It's a bitch."

Stone watched carefully as the left tank gauge went to the stop from the acetylene tank. He picked up a piece of chalk that Buckley used to mark tire perforations with and used it to write C_2H_2 on it. Buckley unhooked the tank of acetylene and attached the tank of oxygen to the other scuba tank and filled it. Stone marked it O_2 with the chalk.

"How many clamps you need?" Buckley asked.

"Give me four and throw in a two-into-one hose splitter."

The two men walked back to the Mustang, where Stone put the scuba tanks back in the trunk and paid his bill, then drove the short distance back to Garden Street.

"Get the tanks filled?" asked Pappy.

"Yep," Stone answered.

"What's the plan?" Wings asked.

"I'm going for the fairwater," said Stone. "She won't get far with that gone."

"What's a fairwater?" Saul asked.

"Propeller-shaft support," Wings answered for Stone. "With that gone, when the screw starts to turn, the shaft'll bend. She'll tear herself up."

"You'll need HE for that," said Arno. "Don't tell me you've got some C-Four and detonators out in that damn garden shed of yours."

Stone laughed. "No, that's the problem. I've got no more explosive, high or low, and no detonators. I'm going to cut through it with an oxyacetylene torch." He turned over the scuba tanks and went to work, using narrow-gauge plastic garden hose, pruning shears, the splitter, and the hose clamps. "See," he said, "I can breathe pure oxygen for the time it'll take for this op. The splitter lets me bleed off as much oh-two as I need to feed the torch head here. The acetylene in the other tank feeds the torch directly."

"How you gonna light her off?" asked Pappy.

"I'll have to surface and use a waterproof match from my camping kit. It's light out now, and I'll only be on the surface for a moment, in the shadow of the hull. She's not that big a vessel. I'll cut through that son of a bitch in about fifteen minutes and haul ass."

"You want us for backup?"

"Thanks, Pappy, but this is the only scuba gear I've got. You guys all stay here until I get back and can figure how to get the authorities involved without getting us all twenty-five to life. If Aunt May comes down, tell her I'm off swimming." Stone completed his jury-rigging of the scuba tanks and took out a waterproof match. He turned the valves on the two tanks, lit a match, then touched off the torch. The flame was long and yellow. Stone adjusted the oxygen valve until the flame grew short and blue, then diamond small and white. Satisfied, he backed off until the flame was a bit larger and blue again for ease of relighting. "Take care of this for me, will you?" Stone said to Arno Bitt, and handed him his .45 Colt. He checked to see that his Gerber was still secure, picked up his wet suit, tanks, mask, and flippers, then said, "Saul, we'll be less conspicuous in the van. You drive. Bring the Browning, just in case."

Minutes later, Saul turned the van onto the ramp over the railroad tracks along the river and headed toward the Riegar dock. "Stop here," Stone said, surveying the scene through the windshield. He estimated the distance to the pier, then from there to the stern of Aka Maru, and did some mental arithmetic. One of the most important things he had learned in his training as a SEAL was the distance underwater each kick of his legs would propel him, and how to count those kicks to know when he had arrived at a predetermined place, guided by a compass-equipped navigation board. Stone had no board with him and, because of the daylight and relatively short distances involved, didn't need one.

"Park over there," Stone said, "in between those trucks. You'll blend right in. Keep your nose out a bit so you can see the area. That'll also give me a place behind you masked from all sides but the river. I'll go in from there and meet you back here."

As Saul backed the van into place, Stone donned his wet suit, flippers, and tanks, then belted on his Gerber and taped it securely. He picked up his mask and left by the rear door of the van. Saul waved to him and gave him the old intelligence-community sendoff line: "Have a good trip."

Minutes later, Michael Stone was kicking his way steadily six feet underwater and counting. Just where he expected to see it, the end of the Riegar pier appeared, first as a dark shadow, then, as he closed in on it, the individual timbers. He paused, then, using the pier end as a bearing, moved deeper under the water and started to count his kicks as he headed for the stern of the *Aka Maru*. There, above the water in the forest of timber supports of the dock, concealed in the gloom, Helmar Metz, black wet-suited and finned, black Draeger unit belted to him, waited like a moray eel in a coral hole for his prey.

Because of his low angle, Metz didn't spot Stone's telltale bubble trail until it was closing on the stern of the ship. Silently, he slipped under the dirty water to intercept it, his path free of any bubbles because of the Draeger rebreather unit that absorbed waste his lungs exhaled and fed him purified air through chemical action.

Stone slowed as he approached the dark mass of *Aka Maru*'s hull, then followed its receding swell toward the huge, looming propeller, projecting out from the stern hull on its shaft. He looked upward and, outlined in the light filtering from above, could see the fairwater, at the far outboard end of the propeller shaft, where it met at a right angle and rose vertically to join the hull.

Helmar Metz, lower down in the water, used the same filtered daylight to spot Stone. As an experienced frogman, he knew his enemy would seek to cripple the ship by attacking the propeller-shaft support. It was a standard procedure. A modest amount of high-explosive plastique—Semtex, for example—attached with any one of a number of different time-delayed detonators, and *poof!* the job was done. His course of attack was obvious. He would stay beneath his enemy's depth so he could see him but not vice versa. At the moment the enemy frogman arrived at the underwater intersection of the propeller shaft and its support, he would pause to let him begin to get busy with his explosive. Using that distraction, Metz would come up from beneath him unbetrayed by any bubbles, and, with his knife, disembowel his opponent and leave him to the fish.

Michael Stone arrived at the intersection of the fairwater and propeller shaft and paused to untape his torch head and retrieve a waterproof match. Seeing Stone engaged with what he believed to be his explosive in the dirty water, Metz launched himself forward and upward, knife out before him, for the kill. At that moment, the unsuspecting Michael Stone propelled himself to the surface to light his torch. By a factor of seconds and several feet, Metz's knife missed its target, and his body passed under Stone. Stone saw its shadow beneath him, dropped the torch head, which stayed hanging on its hoses, and drew the Gerber. At the same time, he executed a racing flip turn off the side of the hull of the *Aka Maru* and came up to Metz just as the German was turning himself. For a moment, both men sized each other up, Metz noting the torch head hanging from its hoses, a vulnerability in combat. Stone recognized the Draeger unit and recalled its own danger to a user.

Metz feinted with his empty hand as if to grasp the torch head. Stone counterfeinted as if he was going to block the move, and Metz, drawn in, struck forward with his knife. Stone moved his body slightly aside and trapped Metz's knife arm under his own. The powerful German flipped them both upside down in the swirling water but was unable to free his arm from under Stone's. They spun again, like two alligators fighting over a carcass. Then both men got the same idea at the same time and went for each other's air hoses. Both were successful in ripping the hose from the other's mouth. However, now Stone had a deadly advantage. Metz tried desperately to get his air hose back in place in his mouth before it could take in any water. To go for the surface was to open himself to death from Stone's knife. If he could continue to use the rebreather, he might be able to kill his opponent while the man was trying to get his own mouthpiece back in. He gambled.

Metz got his mouthpiece back in place before Stone replaced his, but some water had gotten into the Draeger unit. It turned what was sent back for Metz to breathe from life-giving air to a deadly caustic cocktail. As Metz clutched at his throat and kicked for the surface, Stone put him out of his agony by plunging the blade of the Gerber upward in the hollow underneath Metz's chin. The long, slender blade went through the base of the tongue, then upward through the soft palate and directly into the brain. When Stone felt the resistance of the blade striking the inside of the top of Metz's skull, he wiggled it around as would a biology student a needle in the brain of a frog.

Stone towed Metz's body underwater back under the dock and wedged it between two timbers. As he was doing so, he was shoved forcefully into the timbers himself by a massive pulse of water. As he recovered, he was hit by another, then another. The waves were coming with increasing frequency but with diminishing force.

Stone knew the cause immediately. It was the propeller of the *Aka Maru*. She was under way!

19

"WHAT'S HAPPENING? WHAT'S GOING ON?" STEPHA-
nie Hannigan asked van Loon as the deck beneath her feet started to
tremble from the vibration of the powerful, railroad-car-sized diesel
engine buried seven flights beneath her in the bowels of the *Aka Maru*.

"Ship's engine, ma'am," van Loon answered. "One gets used to it
after a while. Hard to sleep without it."

Stephanie checked her watch: 6:49. She ran to the great glass expanse
of the bridge deck. The horizon was swinging left. "We're moving!"
she cried. "We're going! What's going on? Where's Mr. Sullivan?"

Van Loon, now preoccupied with watching instruments, nodded
toward a door in the bulkhead behind him and said, "Radio room,
ma'am, last I saw."

Stephanie marched herself uneasily across the moving deck to the
door indicated by van Loon, struggled for a moment with the latch, and
entered. To her left, at a desk in front of an L-shaped bank of electronics,
sat a seaman holding one earphone of a headset against his left ear while
writing with his right in a log on the desk before him. To the right, on
the other side of the desk, sat Brian Sullivan. His briefcase was open to

his right and in front of him sat a jet-black GRiD 1450 sx laptop computer. A telephone connecting wire ran from it to a receptacle on the bulkhead. The screen was up and lit, and Sullivan was so lost in concentration on it, he failed to notice Stephanie until she was upon him. "Mr. Sullivan," she said, "we're moving! You invited me here for breakfast, to be finished by seven so I could get to work on time. It's ten of, I've had *nothing* to eat, and this damn boat is sailing down the river. So what are you running here? Some kind of white-slave operation? I'm kidnapped, right? Next stop Saudi Arabia?"

The radio operator looked up, wide-eyed. There was no failing to notice Stephanie Hannigan now. Brian Sullivan looked distinctly annoyed at the interruption. Stephanie noticed that the screen of the computer was covered by some kind of shorthand. Abruptly, the screen went dead, and Sullivan said, "Glory be to God, woman! Y'gave me a start! White slavery is it? Jesus, Mary, and Joseph, y'get a fine head of steam up when y'er hungry, a regular lioness she is when her stomach's empty. How many minutes ago was it we were talkin' about trust?"

Stephanie wasn't buying any. "Don't you add blasphemy to your sins, Brian Sullivan. I'm as Irish as you are, and I know blarney when I hear it. Trust is it? Then why'd you turn your computer off the minute I lay eyes on it?"

Sullivan's face darkened with anger. "Now, just a moment there, Miss High and Mighty. Number one, the screen went dark because it's programmed to if I don't use it for a short period. 'Tis automatic to save the battery. It's on battery because, as you so noisily noted, we've left the pier and I don't trust the ship's voltage not to crash my work. And I'm just as annoyed as you are to be sailin' away like this. That telephone wire's to the computer modem and I was in the middle of transmitting the results of my interview with the scientists aboard when the connection was broken as we left port—which we did, I'm informed, because of the commotion you saw as well as I did at the Riegar plant. Seems the animal protesters thought we had a load of beasts aboard and threatened to assault the ship to free them. With high tide only minutes away, the captain, very wisely in my opinion, decided to avoid trouble and leave immediately. You'll get the breakfast I promised, and a nice trip downriver, into the bargain. We'll get off with the pilot and return by train. I regret the inconvenience but certainly not the story: SHIP FORCED OUT TO SEA BY ANIMAL PROTESTERS. White slavery, indeed. 'Tis a high value y'put on yer feminine pulchritude, woman!"

"Okay, so I get a bit cantankerous before breakfast. But what do I do about work? I'm supposed to be in court this morning."

"Crawford," Sullivan said, addressing the radio operator, "would you mind patching Miss Hannigan through on the ship-to-shore phone to whatever number she gives you? I'd be much obliged."

"A pleasure," said Crawford, always ready to do a favor for a beautiful woman. "Number?"

Stephanie thought for a moment. At 7:00 A.M., it was possible that no one had arrived yet at the public defender's office. She gave Crawford Naomi Fine's home number. In moments, Crawford handed her the handset.

"Naomi? . . . Stephanie. You were right. I've been kidnapped."

"What!"

Stephanie laughed. "Relax, it's an inside joke. Do me a favor?"

"Sure."

"Call my office in a little bit and tell them I can't make it in until late today."

"Do I get to tell them why?"

"Remember that mysterious breakfast I told you I was going to?"

"Yeah."

"Well, it was aboard a freighter, down at the Riegar dock. Only there was a fire there last night and some commotion, something about the protesters rushing the ship. Anyway, we're on our way out to sea! Downriver, anyway. Mr. Sullivan and I get off outside New York harbor with the pilot. I'll take the first train back, but God knows when I'll get there. Be a love, huh?"

"Didn't I tell you, Neffie? Didn't I? What happens when you clear the harbor and they don't let you off? Jump off and swim? Are you sure you're all right? Is somebody making you say this? Are you being held against your will?"

"Oh, Naomi!" Stephanie laughed. "Don't I wish. You're such an incurable romantic."

"What's the name of the boat?"

"Wait." Stephanie held her hand over the mouthpiece and said, "What's the name of this tub again?"

"Aka Maru," said Crawford before Sullivan could respond. *"A-K-A M-A-R-U."*

Stephanie removed her hand from the mouthpiece. *"Aka Maru,"* she said.

"What?"

Stephanie spelled it out for her.

"What kind of name for a boat is that?"

"Japanese, I think. At least the captain is."

"Oh, my God!"

"Naomi. Please. Just make the call, okay?"

"All right. But you tell those people if you're not back this evening, I'll have the coast guard on them!"

"Thanks, Naomi. I love you, too."

Stephanie handed the phone back to Crawford and turned to Brian Sullivan. "So," she said, "who do you have to know to get some chow on this bucket?"

Sullivan switched off the GRiD and rose. With a mock bow, he said, "Right this way, m'lady."

Michael Stone, for all his urgency, did not forget his training. He surfaced back at his entry point slowly, then waited, motionless, long enough to check for danger. Finding none, he climbed out of the water and walked easily to the van, knowing that to run would attract the attention of anyone in the area. Casually, he reentered the van through the rear door. Leaving on his scuba gear, he said to Saul Rosen, "Home, James."

Saul followed instructions. As he pulled out he asked, "What happened?"

Stone's annoyance with himself and the failure of his mission was evident in his voice as he answered: "Damn near got myself ambushed by another frogman. Guy was good, too. I was lucky. By the time it was over, the ship got away."

"That'll teach ya not to have me point for you. You never could sniff out an ambush."

"Yeah." Stone growled in acknowledgment. "C'mon, let's get out of here. We've gotta get that ship intercepted before she makes it into someone else's territorial waters."

As the van made its way back to Garden Street at speed under Saul's deft driving, Stone rocked around in the rear getting out of his scuba gear. "Hey, Mike!" Saul called back over his shoulder.

"Yeah."

"Hope you're not still pissed about what happened up there outside the lab. I appreciate your straightening me out—and not doing it in front of anyone else."

"Forget it," said Stone. "Never would've happened if your sister hadn't been involved. That's why doctors don't want to operate on close relatives. My fault for exposing you to it."

"Anyway," said Saul, "soon as we get back, I've got another video-tape to show you. While you were off having a good time in the water, I got some work done. Tried to pick up the latest on the Riegar computers to see what the reaction was."

"What'd you come up with?"

"Zip. Not close enough, down there by the ship. But I got a nice sharp intercept, anyway. So sharp it had to be emanating from the ship."

"What'd it say?"

"Don't know. Couldn't read it. Some Middle Eastern language, I think."

"Arabic?"

"Uh-uh. My Arabic's as good as my Hebrew. More likely Farsi. Here we are," Saul continued as he turned into Stone's driveway. "Take a look at it inside."

"What good'll that do?" Stone asked as they both got out and went up the steps. "I wouldn't know Farsi from shorthand." At the word *shorthand,* Stone's memory triggered. The paper he'd taken from the dying Ira Levin was still in his wallet upstairs. "Okay," he said to Saul as they went through the door, "put it on. I'm going to change and be right back down. I want to show you something."

Pappy Saye heard them and came out of the kitchen. "Mike, you gotta come look at the television. CNN's up here, live, covering it from the plant, the P.D., and the hospital. There's a riot down the plant gate—Eddie Berg and the Mexican guy are giving interviews from the hospital. The cops found the dude with the hole in him at Riegar, and they're grillin' Sara down the station. So far, nothin' about us, but the shit could hit the fan any minute if that Berg kid gives us up as the ones sprung him. So far, though, he's just screamin' about human experimentation. But I dunno, man, things are gettin' out of control."

"SHIT!" said Michael Stone. "That's all we fucking need! I've gotta get someone down there to cover Sara while I try to get that ship stopped." He went to the telephone and dialed Stephanie Hannigan's office. "Yes. Good morning. Michael Stone for Ms. Hannigan, please?" Stone listened, consternation growing on his face. "Are you absolutely sure of this? No. No message. Thank you."

Stone hung up. *"GOD* DAMN!" he exploded. All turned to look at him, questioningly.

The outburst was all Stone allowed himself. Calmly he said, "A friend of mine, Stephanie Hannigan, an assistant public defender I was trying to get to go cover Sara for me, is aboard *Aka Maru* with that Reuters guy, Sullivan. Seems they got caught when the ship sailed ahead of schedule to avoid the mob. They'll be getting off with the pilot. Saul, figuring that ship's speed and how soon she'll be in international waters, we've got a small window. Nobody in Washington is even going to take my call, much less listen to me. Get on the phone, burn all the favors you've got, and see if you can get that ship stopped before she clears the territorial limit."

Stone didn't wait for Saul's answer. He started to bolt up the stairs, only to nearly knock down Aunt May, who was starting to hobble her way down. "Here, young man!" she reprimanded him. "There's nothing so urgent that you have to knock an old lady down the stairs of her own home! What's all the goings-on I hear downstairs, anyway?"

"You're right, Mazie, and I apologize. Lots of excitement in town. All sorts of things happening. The boys have it on television down in the kitchen." He kissed her. "Now, if you'll excuse me, I'll just get out of these wet things and be down in a minute."

Stone changed into slacks and a rugby shirt, took Levin's paper out of his wallet, then slipped the billfold into his hip pocket and went down to his office. Saul was there, just hanging up the telephone.

"Well?" asked Stone.

"Naval Attaché at the embassy's gonna do everything he can, but he says there's gonna be all kinds of questions he's in no position to answer. We'll see."

"All you can do is all you can do," said Stone to his friend. "Thanks."

Stone handed the paper he took from Ira Levin to Saul. "What do you make of that?"

Saul studied it. "It's Arabic," he said, frowning. He read the note slowly, as if puzzled: " 'Al rajul min al jazira al khadra.' " Suddenly his eyes widened. "Al Rajul!" he said excitedly. "Where did you get this?"

"I took it from Ira Levin after he died."

"Son of a bitch," Saul said, letting out his breath slowly. "The Mossad got it."

"Got what? Goddamn it!"

"Al Rajul. The Man. Remember, I told you it wasn't a proper name, that there was more?"

"Yeah, yeah. So what is it?"

" 'Al Rajul,' " Saul read. "The Man. 'Min al jazira al khadra': From the green island."

"From the green island," Stone repeated. "What the fuck does that— Holy shit!"

"Sullivan," Saul said. "He's probably the guy who shot Levin."

"Been right under our noses all the time," Stone agreed, "just waiting to get his hands on that lingering Sarin."

"What a beautiful double-cross," Saul said. "No matter what lunatic it was supposed to go to—Qaddafi, the PLO, Saddam Hussein, Rafsanjani—they've all supported Al Rajul at one time or another. . . . He's ripped them off."

"Maybe," said Stone, "maybe not. He could have been here ramrodding the whole program, or keeping an eye on it until it was ready for delivery. At any rate, Sullivan's got it now."

"If his name's Sullivan," said Saul Rosen, "mine's Goebbels."

"Whatever," said Stone. "It'll do for now. The question is, what's he up to? Where's that intercept you think came from the ship?"

"Right here." Saul held up a videocassette.

"You pretty sure it's Farsi?"

"Not sure, no. But it's not Hebrew, and it's not Arabic. I'd say Farsi was a good bet, but I couldn't swear to it."

Stone picked up his telephone and consulted his desk pad, then dialed. He held his hand over the speaker and said to Saul, "Roll one of the televisions in here you guys were using earlier—one hooked up to a VCR. Then load that tape in it, okay?"

"Sure," said Saul, and left the room.

"Hudson Cab," said the voice on the other end of the telephone.

"Yeah, listen," said Stone. "This is Michael Stone. I'm at 182 Garden Street in the city, and I'd like a cab sent over right away. If possible, I'd like a driver I've used before. I've got an elderly aunt with a bad leg, and this guy was good with her. She likes him."

"Yessir. What's his name? I'll see if he's available."

"That's my problem. I can't remember. He was a foreign guy. I think just recently in this country, still speaks with quite an accent. Try a few names on me. I'll try to pick him out."

"Well, there's Thomas, he's a Jamaican . . ."

"No, this was a white guy."

"Hispanic?"

"No. Keep going."

"Singh? He's from India."

"No."

"How 'bout Montazeri?"

"He's not Italian, is he?"

"No, no. Iran. But he's been here awhile. Since the Shah left."

"Yeah. That's the guy. Have him come in the house so he can help me get my aunt out to the cab."

"Ah . . . okay. He's available. Be right over."

Saul Rosen opened the door and wheeled in a television on a cart. A VCR was on the bottom shelf. He busied himself connecting cables and plugging the set in, then loaded the videocassette and pushed the

Start button. There was a hash of lines for a few moments, then a picture held. At that moment, the front door chimed like the grandfather clock. "I'll get it," said Stone, and left the room.

"Mr. Stone?" asked a very thin, worn-looking man in a shirt and slacks.

"Yes," said Stone. "Come in."

"I wasn't sure. They said I was here before for old lady, but I have no memory."

"Don't worry," said Stone, escorting the man into his office. "You're at the right address and about to make the quickest twenty dollars you ever made."

"Yes?" The driver's eyes brightened with interest.

Stone pointed to the television screen. "Can you read that?"

The driver moved closer and into a position directly in front of the screen to avoid a reflection from the window on the glass.

"Yes," he said. "Is Farsi. I speak."

Stone picked up a pad from his desk and took one of the pens from its holder, poised to write. "What does it say?"

The driver squinted at the screen, then said, "Look, mister. Whoever you are. I'm just a cabdriver. I happy to be in this country. I want no trouble. . . ."

Stone took out two twenty-dollar bills from his wallet. He did it slowly, the driver's eyes following the move every inch of the way. Sweating, he turned back to the screen and said, his voice trembling, "Say to . . . ah, no, no. My English is not so good, you know? Ah, *Instruct,* that is it. 'Instruct the soldiers of God . . .' " The driver paused and looked nervously over his shoulder at Stone. Stone waved the two bills and said, "Go on."

The man took a cloth handkerchief out of his pocket and mopped his face. He turned back to the screen and said, " 'Instruct the soldiers of God . . .' ah, 'what follows,' or, 'the following: For the glory of God and revenge upon the Satanic infidels . . .' " The driver's mouth worked, but for a moment no sound came out. Then he said, " 'Revenge . . . infidels, you are to be given the . . . the . . .' How do you say it? Ah, *privilege,* that is it, 'privilege of martyrdom and . . . immediate entrance . . . or, admittance . . .' ah, 'admission into paradise by . . . by . . . *releasing* that which has been given . . .' no . . . *'entrusted* to you, upon the . . . towers that are his pride'?" I am sorry. It does not make sense, but that is what it says."

"You're sure?" asked Stone.

"As best my English, yes."

"Continue."

"What?"

"Keep going."

The thin man wiped his mouth nervously with his hand: " 'Give God's soldiers . . . the soldiers of God . . .' ah, 'the holy writings, and they shall obey your every instruction . . .' no . . . *'command.'* Like orders, no?"

"Any more?"

"No, that is all." The man was shaking as Stone handed him the forty dollars and said, "You just forget all about this, okay?"

The terrified man was halfway out the door already, saying, "Is already forgotten, mister. Thank you. And please, you call me no more!"

Stone closed the front door, returned to his office, and read the translation back to Saul Rosen without interruption.

> Instruct the soldiers of God as
> follows: For the Glory of God and
> revenge upon the Satanic infidels,
> you are to be given the privilege of
> martyrdom and immediate
> admission into paradise, by releasing
> that which has been entrusted to
> you, upon the towers that are his
> pride. Give the soldiers of God the
> holy writings, and they shall obey
> your every command.

Saul Rosen looked stunned. "Are you thinking what I'm thinking?" he asked.

Stone nodded soberly. "It's a triple-cross. Sullivan, or Al Rajul, or whoever the fuck he is has got some suicidal fanatics, most probably Iranian, who're gonna release that gas as the ship passes Manhattan.

They've got a good hundred pounds of lingering binary Sarin under pressure. At one two hundred-fifty-millionths of an ounce per death, JESUS! And who knows when it will disperse! Call your attaché friend. Tell him what the stakes are now."

"I don't know," said Saul, his face contorted with concern. "Before, we were talking about stopping the ship before she got out of international waters. *Now* she's gotta be stopped before she reaches Manhattan! What with the bureaucratic bullshit . . . I don't know, Mike. I just don't know."

"Well, we can't just throw up our hands, for Christ's sake! Look, you stay here and work the phone. I'll take Wings, Pappy, and Arno and see what we can do."

"I *would* put Metz on if I could find him, sir. Unfortunately, he and most of his men are not to be found." Georg Kramer's voice was anxious and defensive as he spoke on the LPC-10 telephone Metz had brought with him from Germany. "I've spoken to two uniformed guards, and they were most forthcoming. What few of Metz's men remain are not. They keep telling me to talk to him. Not only that, I can't find Letzger. All I know is that Metz and Letzger were holding that woman who took the photographs originally and the leader of the animal-protest mob. They had them in the primate lab. There was a rescue attempt by what appears to have been mercenaries. It was successful. The twelfth floor was shot up, and there was an explosion. The fire department was called and told that a severely injured man was trapped on the B-2 level in an elevator. They insisted on entry and found an experimental subject. We denied knowledge and asserted it was a plant by the protesters who got in and sent a false alarm. But the others are talking to police and—"

"Did the ship sail?" Hoess asked. Even over the scrambler, Kramer could detect the anxiety in his voice.

"Yes, sir."

"Are you certain?"

"Sir, I can see the dock from my window. The ship is gone."

Hoess sighed with relief. "Very good, Kramer. Find Metz and Letzger. I want to speak to them both. Call our law firm in New York.

Get someone up there right away and fill him in. Then have him call me also." Hoess hung up. No matter what the degree of trouble at the American plant, he had kept his bargain with Al Rajul. He waited by his regular telephone for the call that would instruct him as to how to retrieve his son.

In the wardroom of *Aka Maru,* Stephanie Hannigan took a piece of whole-wheat toast and, wiping from her gleaming white plate a last bit of yellow from eggs "fried, over easy," popped it daintily into her mouth.

"And was breakfast to yer complete satisfaction, Miss Hannigan?" Brian Sullivan asked.

"Yempf," said Stephanie, her mouth still full, "it wampf."

"Well, then," said Sullivan, rising, "if you'll excuse me, I have a bit more business to attend to. Why don't you return to the bridge and enjoy the glorious view, and I'll rejoin you shortly."

"Can I take my coffee?"

"Certainly, miss," said van Loon. He poured more hot coffee into Stephanie's mug as Sullivan left. "And you might find a bit of old sailor's lore helpful. Even though we're not at sea yet and there's no true roll to her, we're steering to follow the channel and there are the currents. But even in a heaving sea, if you carry your mug before you *without looking at it,* you'll find you won't spill a drop."

"Why is that?"

"Hanged if I know, miss, but it's been passed down from sailor to sailor for generations. And it works."

Stephanie smiled her thanks, rose, and, not looking at her mug, made her way from the wardroom to the bridge. There, the bright June sun streamed through the glass and illuminated the verdant hills on either side of the sparkling surface of the Hudson. Stephanie basked in the radiant warmth of the sun, drank in the beauty, and turned to the pilot: "Where are we now?"

"Be coming up on the Beacon-Newburgh bridge soon. Then there's Storm King Mountain . . . the Palisades . . . it's gorgeous."

"It certainly is," Stephanie agreed. "It's a great day to be alive."

At that moment, Brian Sullivan, briefcase in hand, was climbing down the ladder from the weather-deck access to the second deck area 1-Alpha. He stopped at the watertight door to the first of three cargo bays on the starboard forward and, using a spoon he'd pocketed in the wardroom, rapped on the heavy metal of the door. It opened a few inches and, in passable Farsi, Sullivan said, "I bear a message."

The door opened enough to admit him, and Sullivan entered the gloomy confines of the bare, single bulb-lit cargo bay. An unkempt-looking Iranian man said, "The message?"

"You have the machine?" Sullivan countered.

"It is ready."

"Summon the others."

The Iranian disappeared into the second cargo bay and returned with three companions. They were all young males, scraggly-bearded, in soiled Western-style trousers and shirts. The throbbing of the great diesel engine filled the room. Brian Sullivan opened his briefcase and withdrew a can of white spray paint. He looked about in the gloom, spotted an 8 mm projector set on a box, then moved to the bulkhead opposite it, and, spraying steadily and evenly, painted a large white rectangle on it.

As the four men watched him intently, Sullivan moved back under the light, picked up a small reel of motion-picture film from his briefcase, and threaded it into the projector. That done, he picked up the projector wire by the plug and led it over to the light. The briefcase yielded a screw-in electrical receptacle that he put into his pocket. Then he gingerly unscrewed the hot light bulb, put it into his briefcase, and replaced the bulb with the electrical receptacle. By feel in the total darkness, Sullivan inserted the plug of the projector into the receptacle, then followed the wire back to the machine, and, after fumbling a moment, turned it on.

The film was black and white and without sound. It jumped from time to time because it had been played often and the sprocket holes were worn. The focus was good, however, and the image projected was crisp against the still-wet white paint. There was a sharp intake of breath from the four men, followed by a murmur of reverent approval when they saw the image of the late Ayatollah Khomeini waving his hand in blessing at a crowd underneath his window. As the

Imam backed through the window, the camera followed him as he
went to a desk. There an aide placed before him a small pile of papers
bearing printing in Farsi. Slowly and deliberately, the aged leader was
shown signing the documents, one after another.

The camera, obviously hand-held because of its jiggle, moved
around and to the rear of Khomeini, zooming in slowly upon the
documents and the Ayatollah's hand holding a pen. It held close on
the document long enough for even the barely literate to read it:

> By my signature, I certify that the
> bearer has died the holy death of a
> martyr in the course of striking the
> severest of blows against the Great
> Satan, and I implore Allah personally
> to grant him immediate entry to
> Paradise.

The leader of the four men read it aloud to the other three, who
were illiterate. As soon as they understood what they were watching,
excited conversation broke out among them. It was a bit fast and
colloquial for Sullivan, but he caught the gist: While it was a tenet
of Islamic faith that anyone who died in a jihad would, as a martyr,
earn admission to Paradise, to die in possession of one of the documents
they had just seen subscribed by the sainted Imam himself, now seated
with Muhammad at the throne of God, would *guarantee* it. Such a
treasure would be worth any sacrifice.

Sullivan snapped off the projector after the brief film ended, followed the wire back to the plug, and replaced the light bulb.

"You have such a document?" asked the leader, awe in his voice.

From his briefcase, Sullivan produced four pieces of paper. He held
one under the light. The men crowded around, trying to touch it.

"Look only," Sullivan said. "Satisfy yourselves as to what they are."

The four men studied the paper intently, then three of them looked
expectantly at the fourth. "Is it true?" one asked him. "You can read.
Is it the same as we saw?"

"It is the writing of the Holy One," the fourth man assured the
others. Then, to Sullivan, he said, "Your orders?"

"You have something for me?"

The man pointed to a dark corner of the bay. Sullivan went there and found a canvas container. He opened it and inspected the contents carefully. It was a chemical-warfare suit, Soviet-made, the latest model. Satisfied, Sullivan returned the suit to its container and addressed the man who appeared to be the leader of the Iranians. "When we reach the north end of the island of Manhattan, I shall return to give you the Imam's writings, one for each of you. You are prepared to do as I instruct you?"

"Anything, sir."

"Your current instructions are to guard the cylinders with your lives until you can deliver them off Tripoli, correct?"

"Correct."

"There is a change of plan. The message is as follows: 'For the Glory of God and revenge upon the Satanic infidels, you are to be given the privilege of martyrdom and immediate admission into Paradise, by releasing that which has been entrusted to you, upon the towers that are his pride.' At my signal, you will carry the gas cylinders through the passageways to the aft steering compartment. From there, make your way through the storage cubbyholes and passageways to the emergency ladder that leads upward, between the inner framework and the outer skin of the hull, to the port side of the fantail. There you shall release the gas against the Great Satan's greatest city and—"

"Go to Paradise!" came the ecstatic interruption.

"To Paradise," said Sullivan, "you will surely go. The middle of the channel is but seven hundred feet from the Manhattan shore at the northern end of the island where the great bridge, named for the father of their country, crosses the river. When we pass under it, I will give you the signal. By the time you are ready, the ship will be in position next to the heart of the city. The prevailing winds are onshore. The blow you strike at the pride of the Great Satan will go down in history."

"Yes!" the men agreed excitedly. "Yes! Yes! May we see the Holy Writings again?"

"Later," said Sullivan. "When I return, you shall possess them for eternity."

* * *

"This thing amphibious or what?" asked Wings Harper as Michael Stone eased the low-slung Mustang over the bumpy railroad tracks north of the Riegar plant and east to the very edge of the Hudson River.

"Wish it was," grumbled Stone. "It'd solve a lot of problems." He drew up to where two huge barges were tied to the wharf and each other. They had contained sand and gravel that had been unloaded into piles ashore for sale to construction companies, and were awaiting a tug to take them back for another trip. Stone checked the line being used. As he had estimated, it was two-inch nylon hawser—a lot of it. With two passes of the serrated blade of the Gerber, Stone sliced through the rope, then called to Arno Bitt: "You still got my uncle's Zippo?"

"Right here, Mike," Arno answered, tossing the lighter to him. Stone caught it in one hand, flipped the top back and thumbed the spark wheel. The lighter blazed on the first try, and Stone used the flame to melt together the severed end of the nylon rope to keep it from unraveling. Then he lifted the far end of it, a spliced loop securing the line to a heavy iron cleat on the far barge, and, with the aid of Wings, rapidly coiled its approximate hundred-foot length into the back of the trunk. When they were finished, the coil was too high to close the trunk lid.

"Fuck it!" said Stone. "Lean forward, guys."

Pappy Saye and Arno Bitt dutifully leaned forward in the backseat and Stone wrenched the seat's back from the Mustang and threw it aside on the gravel. He and Wings reached down and shoved the rope into the newly freed space and were able to close the trunk lid.

"Thanks," said Arno, leaning back against the hard rope, "that's much more comfortable."

Stone and Wings jumped in the car and Stone drove it beside the railroad tracks south toward the plant. As he came abreast of the maintenance shack, he stopped, slid a tire iron out from under the front seat, and motioned to the others. "Crowd around me, guys, gimme some cover here." The others got out and, as Stone stood in front of the padlocked shed door, blocked him from view as he slipped the tire iron into the hasp, wrenched it loose, and entered.

Through the light of the open door, Stone could see that he had guessed correctly. Among the tools were welding equipment—including hoods, aprons, gloves, and an assortment of rods—torch heads, and several tanks of oxygen and acetylene. Stone grabbed four pair of gloves, hopped back in the car, and said to the others, "Well, come on. We've got an op going here!"

"Goddamn!" Pappy Saye said five minutes later. "Look at this traffic. Just what we need—rush hour!" Stone flicked the wheel of the Mustang and used the acceleration to be found only in lower gears, massive torque, and sticky tires to bolt ahead of yet another commuter on the South Road. Pappy Saye, who now sat to his right, muttered uncomplimentary things about the mothers of most of the drivers on the road. Arno Bitt and Wings Harper were jammed into what passes for a rear seat in a Mustang, knees practically under their chins, backs against coils of hawser. Their weapons were on the floor for concealment, and, for insurance, the top was up, making everyone even more uncomfortable.

Wings Harper rubbed his eyes. "Man," he said, "I could use some shut-eye."

"Gettin' old," Arno accused. "We all went a week without sleep in BUD/S."

"There!" Stone exclaimed. He shot right at Wappingers Falls and cut over to the old road, above the river. It was two-lane, and thus shunned by commuters. He turned south again and the five-liter V-8 howled as the little coupe rocketed ahead under fourth gear, then dropped a note as he shifted into fifth. He took a hand off the steering wheel long enough to turn the gain all the way up on the alarm on his radar detector, moved into the left lane long enough to blow past a pickup truck, and back over again to avoid a head-on collision with a startled woman in an ancient Dodge coming the other way.

The Hudson River stretched ahead and below them. "Pappy," said Stone, "there's a pair of compact ten-power binoculars in the glove compartment. See if you can spot that ship up ahead."

"I can see to the next curve in the river, Mike. Nothing." Nevertheless, Pappy dutifully took out the glasses and peered through them. Stone shot under the approach to the Beacon-Newburgh bridge, the red convertible raising rage in local drivers who were frightened by the fact that he was past them before they noticed him behind them. "We're okay on this Route Nine-D. With luck, we'll catch her at the Bear Mountain Bridge. The river's crooked as a ram's horn there—near West Point. The main thing's to get ahead of them."

Stone slowed to get through the little town of Cold Spring, then speeded up again and roared down to Garrison. As he slowed to get through town, he said, "Okay, Pappy. That's West Point across the river. Bear Mountain Bridge coming up. Start scanning."

A commuter train buzzed along the old New York Central tracks to their right. Stone pulled rapidly ahead of the train, then blew past an IROC Z-28 Camaro driven by an androgynous-looking youth who was so startled, he dropped the cigarette from between his lips onto his lap. Infuriated, the driver of the Camaro took off after Stone as he streaked downhill toward the right-hand turnoff to the bridge.

"Nothing," said Pappy. "At least the next bend's a short distance, could be just around it."

"That ship must be cookin'," Arno offered.

"So's the asshole behind me," said Stone as the Camaro, having swung wide to try to pass, was forced back into line by a delivery van coming the other way.

"He's gonna try to beat you to the bridge turnoff," said Wings. "Once he gets ahead of you on that two-lane bridge, he's on the Palisades Parkway, and he figures it's bye-bye."

"But I'm not going across the bridge!"

"Yeah, but he don't know that, Mike. Most people do."

"Well, then," said Stone, "let's just make him sure." Stone put on his right-hand turn signal and accelerated. The Camaro stayed with him, confident he could dart around the Mustang when Stone braked for the turn. Only Stone, who intended to go straight and up the hill in front of him, didn't brake. Too late, the Camaro driver realized he'd been suckered. He braked hard and tried to turn onto the bridge, spun out, and crashed, rear end first, into the steel of the bridge superstructure. His gas tank ruptured, gasolene hit the hot exhaust pipe, and the car burst into flame. "That," observed Stone, "ought to draw what few police are around off speed patrol for a while."

The river swung sharply southeast, and Stone had to slow up for

Peekskill, then, south, Buchanan. "See anything?" he asked any of them urgently.

"Nope."

"Negative."

"Nada."

"Damn!" said Stone. "We're not gonna be able to see the river for a bit, and it'll be slow going." At Montrose, he picked up a limited access highway and more speed. The river came into view again, then disappeared, reappeared at Ossining, and then, farther south, the road moved inland too far to see the river.

"Well, the hell with it," Stone said. "Better to get ahead than fiddle-fuck along like this." He moved along, blind to the river, as best he could, jumping lights when the other three agreed the way was clear and no police were in sight. At North Tarrytown, he gambled, giving up time for another view of the river, and cut over west on Beekman Avenue. "There she is!" Pappy Saye sang out, looking through the binoculars. "Way over. She's getting ready to go under a bridge with a long overwater approach."

"That's the Tappan Zee," said Stone. "You're sure?"

"Her stern's near right at me," said Pappy. *"Aka Maru."*

"All right!" Stone exclaimed. He wheeled the Mustang southeast onto Main Street until he got to Tarrytown, then took Route 9 south a short distance to below the bridge and joined the New York State Thruway. At exit 7-A, he got off and took the Sawmill River Parkway south, weaving rapidly through traffic, alternately infuriating and terrifying other, less skilled drivers in much less powerful vehicles.

The Sawmill River Parkway is known for its police traffic surveillance, so it was with relief that Stone turned off onto Route 9-A outside of Riverdale to get back over to the river. He gunned it through Van Cortland Park and, just before the bridge separating the Bronx from the island of Manhattan, they were high enough to get a good view back to the river. *Aka Maru* was coming!

Stone spun rubber out of the toll booth and onto the Henry Hudson Parkway south toward the George Washington Bridge. As he went by the Cloisters, his luck ran out as a New York City patrol car stared in disbelief at someone going ninety miles an hour in the city. Lights flashing and siren screaming, the patrol car floored it after Stone's Mustang. "Well," said Stone, "I guess I'm gonna need a lawyer for this one." He pulled right and wound the V-8 as tight as he could. The engine screamed as 240 horsepower hurled them forward. The police car moved over to follow, falling behind.

As the two cars neared the wide-swinging turnoff for Riverside Drive, just underneath the bridge, Stone signaled right, then used all the stopping power of his brakes and the adhesion of his "Gatorback" tires to swing left and onto the Riverside Drive exit. The police car's driver, seeing that he could not possibly duplicate the feat in his patrol car, didn't try. He braked, stayed on the parkway, slowed to normal speed, and got on the radio for assistance.

Stone got the Mustang down slow enough that he could make a hard left at Riverside Drive, then another as, finally at non-attention-attracting normal speed, he fed himself into the spaghettilike maze of the approaches to the George Washington Bridge, following the signs to the lower level.

The traffic in the left-hand lanes, coming into the city from New Jersey, was still heavy. The right-hand lanes, from New York to New Jersey, less so as Stone moved the Mustang out onto the bridge proper. Because they were in the right-hand lane of the Jersey traffic, they could see the river north easily. *Aka Maru,* running with the outgoing tide, was moving toward the bridge rapidly, hugging the New York side of the river, where the channel was. Her high superstructure was clear. Stone decided he couldn't implement his plan from the right-hand lane, too much chance of being spotted from the bridge, and, like all SEAL operations, Stone's plan depended upon complete surprise.

Stone moved to the curbside lane and, slowing, lowered the top using the switch on the dash. The top was down by the time the car came to a stop about seven hundred feet out onto the bridge. The four men bailed out without bothering to open the doors. Stone popped the trunk and took the keys. Arno and Pappy Saye took the rope. Stone grabbed the four pairs of welder's gloves. Cars piled up behind them, blowing their horns. Calmly, the SEALs ignored everyone else and armed themselves. As Wings Harper brought out the AK-47, the fat man in the Cadillac immediately behind them stopped blowing his horn, said, "Oh, Jesus Christ!" and struggled to get down under the dash.

"South side!" Stone shouted over the noise as sirens could be heard in the background. Wings Harper leveled the AK, and all traffic in adjoining lanes screeched to a halt in a series of rear-end crashes. The four men ran to the middle of the bridge, where a low fence defined the westbound lanes, and vaulted over it onto a wire netlike grid through which the Hudson could be seen clearly far below them. The net-grid sagged under the weight of the four men as they traversed it quickly, vaulted over the other side, and stood against the low fence as the traffic ripped by at forty-five miles per hour.

Again, Wings did his AK-47 intimidation number, with the same accordion-effect, crash-provoking result, and the men ran to the south side of the bridge and vaulted another railing onto an expanded metal walkway, through which the water was also visible. Stone leaned over the last of the protective railings. There, about another half foot out, ran the slightly rusted aluminum-painted massive outer girders of the bridge.

Stone studied the understructure. Four men could perch on the outer box girder, but it would have to be in line. That wouldn't do for what he had in mind. He looked further. From every other riveted plate where the box girders were joined, there ran a wind gusset, another girder that ran at an angle from the outside of the bridge framework in to join the middle of the horizontal roadway support beams at their center. "There!" Stone shouted over the traffic noise, and he led his men over the railing out onto the foot-wide box girder, along which they walked precariously in the gusting winds, high above the river, up to the wind-gusset connection. Using that triangle of steel as their perch, they squatted. Stone took the melted end of the nylon hawser, played out some line, then swung it down hard against the wind-gusset steel. As the end hit the bottom edge and curled back upward, Pappy Saye hung on to Stone's belt to hold him as he reached down and caught it. He took the spliced loop end from Arno and fed the single end through it. Then the men, shutting their peril from their minds, pulled the hundred feet of rope all the way through the loop and coiled it up.

As Stone and his men were coiling the rope, the backup of rush-hour traffic behind the abandoned Mustang and rear-ended cars was already attracting the attention of a local radio news traffic reporting helicopter.

"We've got a real mess going on on the west-bound lower level of the George Washington Bridge, Tony. There's a car abandoned in its lane and a series of rear-enders. The backup has clogged the on ramp from the West Side Highway. People waiting to turn off are already stopped dead, and that's having an effect on the rest of the south-bound traffic as they try to crawl around them. Take an alternate route, folks. There's *thousands* of people down there already with nothing to do but take in the scenery along the river 'cause they're not going *any* where and . . . hold it! Stay with me, Tony! There's something going on down there on the south side of the bridge. I can see one, two, three, *four* men out on the girders, right over the water. I dunno what we've got here, but they're in perfect position for a mass suicide!"

The bow of *Aka Maru* was just nosing under the north side of the bridge as Stone and his men completed their task and Stone handed out the welder's gloves. All four donned them, then Stone and Pappy held out the big coil of hawser, ready to drop it.

Stone gauged the speed of the ship and the distance carefully, aware that if he dropped the line too soon, it could be seen from the high bridge of the stern-mounted superstructure of *Aka Maru,* and that too late a drop meant a complete miss. Despite the stakes, he was calculating coldly, like a machine. "Now!" he said, and dropped the line.

The heavy line dropped fast, its weight helping prevent sway from the gusts. It hung out, full length, just feet above and ahead of *Aka Maru*'s bridge deck overhead. "Go!" Stone commanded, and he dived onto the rope, 212 feet above the water, grasping it only in his two gloved hands. As prearranged, Wings dived next, followed by Pappy Saye and Arno Bitt, only a foot between them.

"They jumped!" the helicopter reporter shouted into his microphone. "Good God, all four of them! There's a ship coming under the bridge. They're gonna hit it! Oh, Lord, Tony, with this wind, we can't get too close to the bridge. . . ."

The four former SEALs hung on to the rope literally for their lives, but they didn't think of it that way. For them, it was a means of insertion, nothing more, no matter how incredibly dangerous. As they gripped the rope and slid at a speed almost that of a free-fall, they were conscious only of the terrible heat building up on the insides of their hands. They had no second pair of gloves inside the welder's, as SEALs do as insulation when they perform a fast rope insertion. The ship passed beneath them looming larger and larger as they fell toward it. The terrible pain building up in their hands made the maneuver seem to be in slow motion, as if it would never end. Yet in just four seconds, all four men were on the overhead of the bridge deck of *Aka Maru,* whirling in agony to hurl the searingly hot welder's gloves from their scorched hands.

Stone and Arno ran to the opposite sides of the bridge and dropped first to the deck, threw open the doors, and entered, .45-caliber semiautomatics pointed at the stunned crew members. A second later, they were joined by Wings Harper and his AK-47, and Pappy Saye, .357 Magnum revolver at the ready. Stephanie, who had been admiring the Manhattan skyline, spun around at the noise and reacted with an incredulous "Oh . . . my . . . GOD!"

Stone put his pistol to the head of van Loon. "Sullivan!" he barked.

"Left . . . the bridge . . . a few minutes ago. What the bloody hell . . ." He left the question unfinished as Stone pushed the muzzle of his pistol hard into him.

"The Iranians!" Stone snapped. Still shocked, no one answered.

"It's a suicide team!" Stone said. "You've got minutes before those fanatics let loose a nerve-gas attack!"

Stephanie recovered first. She remembered what Cole had told her when she asked where the "scientists" were going. "Area one-Alpha starboard!" she said abruptly, then added, "That means the right side of the boat!"

"Wings," Stone ordered, "take over aft steering. Pappy, you and Arno seal the watertight doors on one-Alpha starboard. Jam 'em!" The men were on their way as he said to van Loon, "Take me to the fire-control panel—now!" Cole, seeing that Stone was now alone, made a move toward him. Stone shoved van Loon and snapped a shot at Cole's foot, about an inch from his toe. The blast of the big

Colt thundered in the confines of the bridge. Stephanie screamed. Cole froze. Van Loon pointed to the panel. "All right, everyone but the pilot and Ms. Hannigan, hit the deck, facedown!" Stone ordered. "Steady as she goes, pilot. Touch a microphone and you're a dead man."

The traffic helicopter had fallen in behind *Aka Maru* after she had passed under the bridge. "No sign of any of 'em now, Tony. They had a rope! Dropped right onto the roof of the ship's bridge! You'd never believe it! This could be a terrorist takeover. I was too far away to see if they were armed, but I'd assume they were. Let's get the police on this, Tony, and stay with me. Traffic's at an absolute standstill down there now, all along the river. Our reporting may be partially responsible," he continued, starting to get carried away, "as people listening to us on their car radios, already bumper-to-bumper, stop to watch this Hudson River drama play itself out right in front of them. Stay with me!"

Down below, Arno Bitt returned to the bridge deck of *Aka Maru.* "There were two watertight doors," he announced. "One leading from the weather-deck ladder passageway, another into the third bay. They're jammed."

Stone turned to the fire-control panel while Arno kept the crew covered. He checked the fire code displayed on it to determine the proper switch, then threw the one that flooded cargo area 1-Alpha starboard on the second deck with carbon-dioxide gas. "All right, pilot," he said, "beach this vessel on the Jersey side."

"What!"

"You heard me. Stick her in the mud. This ship's going nowhere."

The pilot, two guns on him, shrugged and spun the wheel to starboard.

"Michael—" Stephanie began.

"Later," Stone said crossly. "I'm busy now. And I know starboard means right, for Chrissake. I was in the navy, remember?"

Pappy Saye came back to the deck. "C'mon, Pappy," Stone said to him, "let's go hunt us an Irishman. Arno, hold the bridge."

"Aye, aye," said Arno as Stone and Pappy headed for the weather deck.

"Where you wanna start, Mike?" Pappy asked.

"Let's see if we did any good in one-Alpha starboard first. If it's empty, we're after five guys instead of one, and that gas could get us all any minute."

The two men went down the hatch in the weather deck to the ladder that led to the three cargo bays that made up 1-Alpha starboard. Stone looked at his watch. "It's been enough time," he said. "Let's do it."

Pappy cleared the jam on the watertight door and threw it open, staying behind it out of habit. Stone was flat against the bulkhead on the other side of the door. "Wait," he said, "until enough air can get in there." They waited until Stone judged it was safe to enter, then did so in the classic one-covering-the-other fashion. Lungs sucking for air, they found the four Iranians slumped over their gas cylinders. One still clutched a piece of paper with writing on it that Stone now recognized as Farsi. "Well," he said to Pappy, choking on the remaining CO_2, "I don't envy them their chances for paradise."

"Come again?" said Pappy.

Stone shook his head. He was about to answer when his eyes, now accustomed to the gloom, spotted what looked like a pile of canvas over in a corner. He went over to it. It was Brian Sullivan, dressed completely in his state-of-the-art Soviet chemical-warfare protective suit. Stone opened it and felt for a pulse. There was none.

"What's that outfit?" Pappy asked.

"Latest Soviet chemical-warfare outfit. So good it'll protect even against Sarin."

"Well," said Pappy, "if it's so fuckin' good, how come it didn't protect him from plain ol' C-oh-two?"

Stone smiled grimly. "That suit protects by being able to filter the smallest microscopic particles of gas out of the air."

"But, when there ain't no air—"

"You smother like anybody else," said Stone. "Suit or no suit."

The two men walked away, past the other four bodies and toward the watertight door. Pappy looked down at the Iranians and said, "Hey, Mike, what was you gonna say about not envyin' those Iranians?"

"Well, Pappy," said Stone, "how'd you like to be them right now, giving an after-action report to the Ayatollah himself . . and telling him you fucked up?"

Pappy Saye grinned. "Yeah," he said as he ducked through the door. "Paradise, my ass!"

20

● WHEN THE TELEPHONE RANG IN HIS STUDY AT home, Walter Hoess started, even though he was expecting the call. "Herr Hoess?" the caller asked. Hoess recognized the sound of the voice. Frantically, he said, "I kept my part of the bargain! The ship sailed as scheduled with what you asked for aboard!"

"Calm yourself, Herr Hoess. We know you kept your part of the bargain, and we are prepared to keep ours. Pay attention. What I say will not be repeated. It is now oh-two hundred hours. At precisely oh-two forty-five, you are to be at the public telephone on the southwest corner of the Bahnhofplatz. Alone. When it rings, pick it up and you will receive further instructions. Tell no one or the boy dies. We watch and listen."

"But there's barely enough time to—" The telephone went dead in Hoess's hand. He rushed through the still house to the interior of the garage, picked a set of keys from the keyboard, and entered the 500 SL Mercedes convertible that lurked like a black panther among the more placid sedans.

Hoess pressed the remote switch for the garage door and started the

Mercedes. It seemed to him an hour was consumed by the door sliding slowly up and back against the ceiling. Before it was fully open, Hoess shot through it and into the chill June German night.

A lone truck lumbered across the Bahnhofplatz as Hoess turned onto it. He circled until he came to the public telephone and, leaving the engine of the Mercedes running, he got out and ran over to the telephone booth. There, by light of the tiny booth dome light, he checked his watch. He prayed that it was correct. If so, he had three minutes to spare. They were the longest three minutes of his life.

Precisely at 0245, the telephone rang. Eagerly, Hoess snatched the receiver from its cradle. Freed from the weight of the receiver, the cradle rose, activated a mercury switch, and the ensuing blast of Semtex plastique vaporized the booth, Hoess, four feet of the earth beneath them, and much of the Mercedes.

The echo of the explosion had barely stopped resounding throughout the Bahnhofplatz when a worn Audi sedan rolled up to the northeast corner, opposite the site of the blast. A rear door opened and a blindfolded teenage boy was thrust out onto the sidewalk. From inside the car, a voice the boy's father would have recognized said, "You see, boy, we keep our word."

The attractiveness of the twenty-two-year-old female yeoman first class sitting behind the gray steel desk in the outer office of the commanding officer of the Brooklyn Navy Yard was marred by the look of disapproval on her face as she surveyed the four men who had just entered the room. Three of them were in uniform, hastily purchased whites, bedecked on the left breast by stacks of "fruit salad"—decorations from several nations—all topped by the infamous "Budweiser" insignia of those dreadful sailors answerable only to the SEAL admiral. The black sailor's stack of medals was almost ridiculous. It ran all the way up from the top of his pocket to almost his shoulder seam—like some foreign field marshal or something, she thought. Well, much good it would do him. The man in her boss's office today was *not* the commanding officer of the Navy Yard. These three were going to do a carpet dance before the SEAL two-star admiral from the Pentagon himself. She had no idea what the civilian was doing

there. Perhaps he was the complaining witness to what she was sure
was their misconduct. Her voice was icy as she called the roll. "Master
Chief Petty Officer Virgil R. Saye, retired?"

"Here."

"Chief Petty Officer Herman S. Harper, retired?"

"Yo."

"Chief Petty Officer Arno H. Bitt, retired?"

"Present."

"And Mr. Michael C. Stone."

"Correct."

"You may go in. The admiral is expecting you."

Stone led the way to the inner door. It bore the stenciled words
COMMANDING OFFICER. He gave a single knock and, at the prompt
"Come in," opened it and held it for the other three. They entered and
marched into a line abreast in front of the big walnut desk behind
which sat Rear Admiral Joseph Lee Dietz, USN. On the left breast of
his whites were about half the decorations of Wings Harper and Arno
Bitt and a third of those of Pappy Saye. Atop them sat the big golden
Trident, the "Budweiser" emblem of a SEAL. Starting with Pappy
Saye, the three retired noncommissioned officers barked their rank and
names as they saluted smartly, each following his identification with
the words *Reporting as ordered, sir.* Michael Stone quietly closed the
door, walked up to join the other three in line, and said, "Michael
Stone, sir."

"Yes," Dietz acknowledged, returning the uniformed men's salute,
"at ease." He didn't ask them to sit down. On the desk before him,
at his left hand, lay a pile of documents. Dietz proceeded to pick up
each in turn, identify it, then put it down to his right. His tone of voice
was annoyed at first, but as he read off the titles of each succeeding
document, it got increasingly irritated and he put the papers back down
on the desk with more and more force. "Memorandum of Inquiry
from the Secretary of Defense to the Chief of Naval Operations, with
enclosures. Buck slip, immediate attention, deadline reply from CNO
to commanding officer, Naval Special Warfare Command—that's me,
in case any of you have forgotten. Attachments: Tab A, Letter of
Inquiry from Director of Central Intelligence to SECDEF, with en-

closures as follows: letterhead memorandum report of preliminary investigation with inquiry to the DCI from Director, FBI. SIGINT intercept report and code word TEMPEST classified inquiry to DCI from Director, National Security Agency. Memorandum of Inquiry from Director, Defense Intelligence Agency to DCI, enclosing Letter of Inquiry from Defense Advanced Research Projects Agency. Preliminary report of incident and request for instructions to SECDEF from the Executive Secretary, National Security Council. Letter of *Protest,* no less, from SECSTATE to SECDEF, enclosing copies of correspondence with the embassy of Israel. Request for Guidance to SECDEF from the Press Secretary of the President. *Demand for Explanation* to SECDEF from the White House Chief of Staff, enclosing copies of newspaper stories from all over the country and the world, not to mention assorted rations of shit from the police department of the city of Rhinekill, the police department of the city of New York, the Mohawk County Sheriff's office, the fire department of the city of Rhinekill, and the police department of the Port Authority of New York and New Jersey, *plus"*— here Admiral Dietz held up a thick file, which he slammed down on top of all the others—"a copy of all of the above accompanying a request to the CNO for instructions from the goddamn Naval Investigations Service! *DO YOU PEOPLE HAVE ANY IDEA WHAT YOU'VE DONE?"*

Wings Harper and Arno Bitt were white. Pappy Saye was biting down hard on the inside of his right cheek to keep from smiling. In the most calming voice he could muster, Michael Stone said quietly, "Well, sir, we did manage to save the city of New York."

The SEAL Admiral slumped back in his chair, all the anger in him dissipated. "Yes." He sighed. "You did. You exposed the smuggling into the United States of foreign nationals held prisoner by agents of a foreign drug conglomerate for purposes of gruesome human medical experimentation; the development of a lingering version of the world's deadliest nerve gas and an attempt to smuggle it out of the country in violation of the export laws; the technical intelligence-gathering activities inside this country by an agency of a friendly government; and the freeing of a woman undoubtedly lured aboard the vessel to be used as a hostage if necessary. And, as you said, you saved the city of New York from a terrorist nerve-gas attack. And that, of course, is the problem."

"The problem?" Stone was nonplussed.

"Exactly," said Dietz. "To whom do the American people look to protect them from things like that?"

"The government?" blurted Wings Harper.

"Precisely. Their government. Or, more correctly, their governments, plural, from the local to county, to state to federal, depending on the problem. Now, what do you think it would do to the confidence of the American people were they to learn that all of that was going on and all their different levels of government hadn't a clue? That they were saved from all of that by four self-appointed cowboys and a foreign intelligence agent?" Dietz's question was rhetorical, and he answered it himself. "They'll put all the rest of us in the same class as Congress, for Christ's sake!"

"But, sir," Pappy Saye protested, "nobody knows yet it was us who done it, and CNN's even sayin' that, based on the tactics, it hadda be a SEAL op!"

"You're right, Pappy," said Dietz. "They are." He lounged back in his chair and looked at the ceiling, as if inspecting it for fly specks. "Now, men," he said, "let's look at our options for a minute."

"All that other stuff was the windup," Stone muttered under his breath. "Here comes the curveball." Dietz heard it but let it go. "On the one hand," he said, "you have broken virtually every municipal ordinance and state and federal penal law on the books. You'll be heroes, of course, so I think it reasonable to assume that all your sentences will be suspended. You three," he said, waving at Arno, Pappy, and Wings, "will lose your pensions, of course, and Mr. Stone his license to practice law. But, as I say, you'll have the comfort, in your poverty, of being heroes—that is, until something else occurs to occupy the popular imagination and bump you off the front pages."

"And on the other hand . . ." Stone said sarcastically.

"On the other hand," said Dietz, without missing a beat, "if the assault on the ship, which had the effect of physically preventing the release of the poison gas, its coming under government control, and the killing of the terrorists, was, essentially if unofficially, a SEAL operation . . . Now, just suppose it could be converted from an *un*official to an *official* operation. What then would be the result?"

Again, Dietz's question was rhetorical. Again, he answered it himself. "There's enough here to be spread around to keep everybody happy, I'd say. I'm sure the CIA's been on to this Al Rajul fellow for some time, and duly turned him over to the FBI when he entered the United States. The NSA intercept alerted us to the compromise of the TEMPEST program, and they discovered the new wrinkle of using a computer modem and graphics card to transmit digitalized instructions in a field-expedient situation. The Coast Guard was of inestimable help in tracking the *Aka Maru* once she entered U.S. territorial waters. The Immigration and Naturalization Service and Customs have smashed yet another vicious exploitation of undocumented Mexicans, one of whom was rescued by the brave men and women of the city of Rhinekill's fire department, at the very same time that the Rhinekill police discovered and broke up a hideous episode of human medical experimentation."

"That leaves out the Mohawk County Sheriff's office," Stone said dryly.

"Who did excellent work in recovering a stolen Cessna aircraft," Dietz replied cheerfully.

Pappy Saye could control himself no longer. Laughing out loud, he said, "What about the DIA?"

"Letter of commendation from SECDEF himself for brilliant liaison work."

They were all laughing now. "And the NIS?" asked Arno.

Dietz picked up the thick request for instructions. "Good job. Case closed."

"How's this gonna work?" asked Wings.

"You three will be happy to know," Dietz said, "that since one June you have been back on active duty on special assignment. You've each got another decoration coming—although I don't know where you're going to find room to put yours, Pappy—and, of course, back pay. You will remain on base here at the Navy Yard for immediate debriefing by NAVSPECWAR personnel standing by to do so. Following that, you will assist in the preparation of an after-action report. Upon completion, you will retire from service with the thanks of your country and never—repeat, *never* discuss this top-secret episode with anyone unless ordered to the contrary by competent authority. Now I'll have a word with Mr. Stone alone. Dismissed."

Pappy, Wings, and Arno saluted smartly, did a snappy about-face, and left the room. Admiral Dietz regarded Stone warily, then said, "Sit down, Mr. Stone, sit down."

When Stone had seated himself on the sofa across the room from the desk, Dietz said, "Your situation presents a problem the others' do not, Mr. Stone. You are not a reservist. Unlike Pappy, I never had a chance to operate with you—a bit after my time—but by all accounts in the teams and your record, you were a respected and able officer. It would not be inconceivable for the Department of Defense to have contracted with you temporarily as a consultant for ninety days, starting, say, first of last April. In that capacity, you accompanied active-duty personnel on a classified op for which you were very well paid in accordance with the danger, a condition of said employment being that you discuss it with no one. What do you say?"

Stone's voice was quiet and polite but determined as he said, "No, thank you, sir."

"What! Young man, you're making a serious mistake."

"No, sir. I made a serious mistake when I resigned my commission instead of fighting that bullshit medical all the way up to Bethesda."

"Well, you're about to make another. This time, you'll lose the right to practice law."

"I've thought about that. I've decided I don't want to practice law anymore, anyway. I'm not all that good at it, and I want to spend my life doing something I'm damn good at."

"And what might that be?"

"A SEAL officer. An *operating* SEAL officer."

"Oh, for heaven's sake, man! You can't turn back the clock. That's quite impossible."

"As you say, sir." Stone rose. "Well, good day, sir."

Dietz jumped up. "Wait a moment! Where are you going?"

"Well, as you said, sir, I'm going to lose my license to practice law, so I'm going to have to earn some money another way. Right now,

I'm on my way to see a news-magazine editor who thinks I'm a lawyer with an extraordinarily newsworthy story to tell, not a naval officer not permitted to speak about a recent classified operation."

"That's blackmail!"

"No, sir," Stone answered politely, "it's extortion." He turned to leave.

"Wait!" Admiral Dietz was sweating. If he didn't control this situation after suggesting to the CNO that he could . . . Dietz didn't even want to think about it. He sat back down, defeated. "All right," he said, "what do you want?"

"My commission back. Lieutenant Commander. Regular navy, my medical record corrected to show fit for operations as a SEAL and so assigned. Retroactive to one June. That should do it."

Dietz was making a note. He looked up, his voice tired. "Report for duty here at oh-eight-thirty, in uniform, to sign your paperwork, debrief, and work on the after-action report."

Stone struggled to control his elation and sound hard as he said, "There's one more thing, sir."

"What!" The fight came back in Admiral Dietz. "Now, you listen to me—" Stone, for the first time in his life, interrupted an admiral.

"It's Pappy Saye's reactivation. Make that until he puts in his papers again, this time voluntarily. And fix his medical, too, so he can operate again."

"My God, Stone. Be reasonable! Do you know that man's age?"

"I know his condition, sir. As for his age, with all due respect, sir, he's a lot younger than you are, sir."

"All right! You've got it! *Dismissed!*"

As Stone disappeared through the door to be greeted by his men, Admiral Dietz dissolved in laughter. By God, he'd done it! He'd brought it off. And gotten two top SEAL operators back in the teams where they belonged, too. He chuckled to himself. That Stone was a hell of a good officer, but he'd never make admiral. Just not slick enough.

"For heaven's sake, Michael Stone, where are you going all dressed up like that?" Aunt May had rarely seen her nephew so resplendent. For a man who'd just reentered the navy, spending that amount of money on civilian attire just didn't make sense.

Stone grasped his aunt by the shoulders, squeezed them gently, and looked into her eyes with a devilish expression. "Ah, Mazie," he said. "I'm off to see a beautiful woman about getting her pregnant."

Aunt May froze. "How . . . how *dare* you say such a thing! Oh! Here I was just sorry about you having to leave again . . ." Tears welled in Aunt May's eyes. "But if you're going to turn out to be that kind of person, it's just as well. I couldn't—"

"Mazie, for Pete's sake, what's wrong with getting a woman pregnant when you're married to her?"

Aunt May raised both her arms in the air with a strength that surprised her nephew. "You mean you're . . ."

Stone grinned. "Well," he said, "if she's crazy enough to have me."

Aunt May really started crying then.

EDGE-OF-THE-SEAT
ESPIONAGE
AS ONLY ST. MARTIN'S CAN PROVIDE!